COUNTING SOULS

A NOVEL

Donald R. Buchanan

For more information about the book or author, visit buchanan.us2.authorhomepage.com.

Cover and title page images: *Two Men before a Waterfall at Sunset* (detail) by Johan Christian Dahl. The Metropolitan Museum of Art, New York, Gift of Christen Sveaas, in celebration of the Museum's 150th Anniversary, 2019.

ISBN (hardcover): 978-1-7370349-1-9
ISBN (paperback): 978-1-7370349-2-6
ISBN (e-book): 978-1-7370349-0-2

I dedicate this book to Stephanie,
my best friend and wife of forty years,
and to my family: those who have come before,
those with me today—Shelby, Connor, Laine, and Dylan—
and those who will follow.

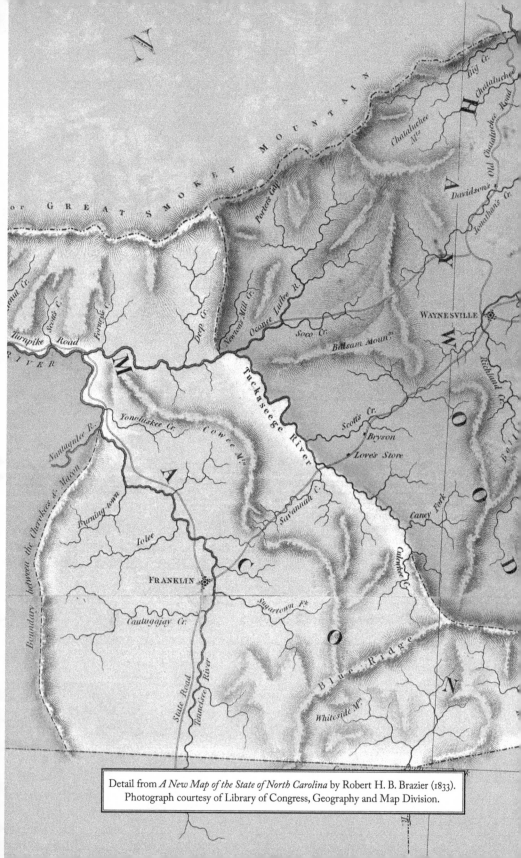

Detail from *A New Map of the State of North Carolina* by Robert H. B. Brazier (1833). Photograph courtesy of Library of Congress, Geography and Map Division.

Part One

It weighs upon the heart, that we must think
What uproar and what strife may now be stirring
This way or that way o'er these silent hills.

Samuel Taylor Coleridge, "Fears in Solitude" (1798)

CHAPTER 1

May 1, 1829—Raleigh, North Carolina

IT WAS LATE afternoon, a beautiful spring day, and shafts of brilliant sunlight streamed through the tall windows of the wood-paneled office. The shutters formed alternating bands of light and shadow, and motes of dust floated aimlessly, appearing, disappearing, then reappearing, as they sailed through the ribbons of light. They sparkled as they twirled in the sunbeams. Soon, their dance was disturbed by swirling clouds of thick tobacco smoke. Wafted upwards in little eddies, they vanished in the dark recesses of the high ceiling.

Colonel Robert Love leaned back in his chair and blew a long, fresh cloud of cigar smoke, sending more of the dust motes spinning through the office. In his right hand he held a fat cigar and a snifter of whisky, its amber contents glistening. His left hand stroked his trimmed gray beard as he watched the plume of smoke and dust ascend. Love was sixty-nine years old, a veteran of the Revolution, the War of 1812, and a North Carolina state senator. He carried himself with stiff military bearing, even when no one was watching. He was tall and slender, and he still had a thick head of gray hair that he gave full rein. His tailored blue swallowtail suit coat with knee breeches, silver buckles and dove-gray stockings had not been in fashion for thirty years, and his imported silk top hat adorned the corner of the desk. He was one of the wealthiest and most powerful men in western North Carolina.

"Beverly, this is damn fine whisky. Where'd you come by it?" His voice was jagged with a lifetime of drinking, smoking, and shouting, softened only by the lilt of his southern drawl and the vestiges of the Scots brogue he inherited from his father.

Beverly Daniel was the US marshal for the District of North Carolina, an office he had occupied since the spring of 1808. A bachelor at fifty-three, he loved horses, hunting, and his position, especially the power that came with it. Like Love, he was thin, but stood a few inches shorter. His hair was just graying around the temples and was receding, which he attempted to camouflage with a subtle part and swooping comb-over. He pulled it off with a minimal loss of dignity. His clean-shaven face was florid and weathered from the Carolina sun, with wrinkles around his eyes that softened an otherwise hawklike visage. He sat behind his imposing desk, his feet up and crossed, his polished boots the color of weathered oak. He held his cigar and whisky in a mirror image of the grip employed by Love, who sat across from him.

"It's Bowmore Scotch, twelve years old. Seems a criminal venture was attemptin' to smuggle in a load without payin' the proper duties over in Wilmington, and my old friend Jim Watson confiscated a couple of cases. He knowin' my weakness for good aqua vitae, and owin' me a favor for settlin' a ruckus they had over there last year, was good enough to ship me a case. I'll give ya a bottle before you leave, if you don't lemme forget it." His deep voice and long drawl hung in the air like the smoke and dust.

Love was in Raleigh completing the annual legislative session. In response to an abolitionist pamphlet published by a free Black man, David Walker of Virginia, the legislature had passed a series of laws to tighten control over enslaved people. They outlawed publication of the pamphlet, required owners to keep their slaves on their property after dark, and provided for roving patrols to enforce the curfew. They prepared legislation for the next session to consider making it illegal to teach Negroes to read and write. The two men discussed the rising threat they feared.

"I'm tellin' you, Beverly, folks are nervous there's going to be some kind of insurrection. We gotta nip this thing in the bud right now. I saw the rantin's of that pamphlet, and if that tripe gets out they's no tellin' what trouble'll be stirred up with the darkies."

"You're right, people are fearful. You had any problems on your place?"

"No, I don't put up with any bullshit. I just added four from an auction up in Virginia, as a matter of fact. They was selling some slaves off of Thomas Jefferson's plantation to cover the old man's debts. Hard to believe I now own property that once belonged to the great Jefferson and got 'em at a good price too. Speakin' of presidents, what do you hear from Washington City these days?"

"The good news is Old Hickory ain't shot or stabbed nobody, but it's early yet." Daniel shook his head, chuckled, and took another sip of whisky.

"He has a thin skin and an exaggerated sense of what constitutes his 'honor.'"

"That he does. You never know when he's gonna go off. I heard you got sideways with him back in Tennessee a ways back over some horse business?"

"My Lord, that's been forty years ago. I was at my farm in Greasy Cove and Jackson was staying at the Taylors', down the road from my place. I owned a beautiful horse, Victor of All. God, Beverly, you should have seen that animal; sixteen hands, black as midnight with a white star on his forehead. He couldn't be touched. I still see him in my mind like it was yesterday, runnin' through the fields, mane and tail flyin'. I swear that horse knew he was a champion, he was so damn haughty." Love looked out the window, lost for a moment in the memory before continuing. "Anyway, Jackson had a couple of fine horses with him, and Andy bein' Andy, he suggested we set up a race. Half the county set up camp on my farm, the wagers growin' and the whisky flowin'. Somehow Jackson's Nigra jockey got hold of a bottle. Mornin' comes and he cain't stand up, much less sit a horse. Jackson accuses me of gittin' him drunk. That was bullshit and I told him so. I offered to postpone the race, but he'd have none of it; said he would 'by God sit his own horse.' He spent the whole race lookin' at my horse's hindquarters and lost by three lengths. He comes flyin' up afterwards and near run me over. Jumped off and started hollerin' I'd fixed the race. I called him a damn liar and a sore loser. We stood nose to nose for some minutes, cussin' and spittin' until some fellers pulled us apart. I still cain't believe he didn't pull a knife on me on the spot."

"You didn't part that way?"

"No, no. Jackson's got the shortest damn fuse I ever saw, but his tempers pass like clouds over the sun. Next thing I know he's knockin' at my door with a bottle and two glasses, and we spent the evening rockin' on my front porch like nothin' ever happened. Never did apologize though, and I figured it best not to press it. I think he later spread the rumor I challenged him to a duel, and he declined. I think that was when he was tryin' to clean up his reputation to enter politics. He's not a man you want for an enemy though, and I ain't never publicly called him the liar he is."

"But you were an elector for him in '24 and '28?"

"Well, it weren't like I was gonna vote for that fop Quincy Adams. Despite everything, you know Jackson's one of us. He's a mean son of a bitch, though."

Daniel shifted in his chair, took another draw from his cigar and blew the smoke up into the dancing dust, sending it swirling in all new directions.

"That he is. You know he's pushin' some new legislation on the Injun issue? He won't rest until every red Injun east of the Mississippi's been shipped west."

"He spent his life fightin' 'em and ain't never had no tolerance. They don't seem like much of a threat anymore to me though . . . all whipped out."

"Yeah, but he's got a fire in his belly for 'em and won't let go of it."

Daniel took a swig of whisky and Love followed suit. Outside, a pair of mockingbirds fussed in the limbs of a massive magnolia, its big leaves shining in the fading sun. The birds squawked and raised and lowered their wings as mockingbirds do when declaring their territory. Their argument continued for a time, filling the temporary lapse in conversation, until they removed their disagreement to a respectable distance and quiet returned to the yard.

"You think the Cherokee'll put up much resistance out your way?" asked Daniel.

"They love them mountains and they're backed into a corner. That last treaty was pressed hard. I'm sure they thought they'd bought 'em selves some peace with all the land they give up. Most of 'em have took up farmin' and got religion, built houses, and some even bought Negroes. So, yeah, there'll be resistance, though what form it'll take's hard to say. They're still savages, and I don't reckon they'll ever be civilized. Some of 'em took the oath and supposedly now they're 'citizens.'" Love sneered. "Damn travesty. Old Hickory's got the right idea."

"If Jackson has his way, that's gonna open up a lot of land. You surveyed all that area back in '20, I guess you know the whole of it better'n anybody."

"I headed up the effort and laid off my sections, but there was a sizable team. Rugged country . . . beautiful. The time I spent roaming them hollers was some of the best of my life. Don't get me wrong, it was hard work, and I spent many a cold, wet night shiverin' my ass off. I actually had an ass back then. Wish I'd enjoyed it more."

"Hindsight."

"Gittin' old requires you to hone your powers of discernment when it comes to assessin' your recollections, a skill few of us ever master." Love studied his cigar before continuing. "Well, we've philosophized and enjoyed some good tobacco and fine whisky. But I'm guessin' you got some business you wanted to attend to on this fine afternoon?" Love said with a wry smile, lifting his glass a half an inch, and tilting his head by the same proportion.

"In fact, I need your help. Federal census got to be collected next year. I'm responsible for gittin' it done and need to add some assistant marshals to handle it. I was hopin' you could help me with Macon County."

"I'm old to be traipsin' off to the mountains again." Love laughed.

"And I couldn't afford you! But I was hopin' you could recommend somebody to handle it. Gonna be a tough job: new county, rugged country, poor roads, a vast area to cover, and Indians who might be in a foul mood. The pay'll be decent, but they'll have to post a bond that'd be forfeit if they don't produce the reports on time."

"That sounds like a tall order." Love stared into his whisky glass for a long time before looking up. "I think I may have just the man for you. My nephew Thomas Love would just fit the bill. He lives in Macon, outside of Franklin. He's a smart feller, got some education, went to Chapel Hill for a spell, got a good head on his shoulders, knows the country 'bout as well as anybody."

"Is that the General's son?" Daniel asked, with a slight tilt of his head.

Love flushed a bit and cleared his throat. "Yeah, he's Tom's boy, although you could hardly find two more different men. My brother's brash and boisterous, Young Tom is quiet and thoughtful. They have not always seen eye to eye."

"His namesake?"

"Yeah, but I like to think young Thomas was named for his grandfather and my father-in-law, General Thomas Dillard. Both my brothers and I married the three Dillard sisters."

"That must make for some interesting family gatherings!"

Robert grunted in response.

"Well, if you say Thomas is the right man for the job, that's good enough for me." Daniel took his feet down from the desk and leaned forward, facing Love. "Will he be agreeable to takin' this on?"

"This'd be a splendid opportunity for him. I'm sure I can convince him."

"Excellent. There is one more thing. Between you and me, Robert, I missed out when the Cherokee lands first opened up. I'll be lookin' to retire in a few years, and I'd like to make sure I git in the game this time round. We don't count Indians in the census, unless they pay taxes, but I'd like your nephew to do a little scoutin' and point out the prime parcels as he's out that way. You think that'll be a problem?"

"Naw, I don't see that being an issue at all. I'd like that information myself."

"Good. You talk to him and let me know if he's agreeable. We'll be havin' a meetin' this fall with all the deputies to discuss the new forms, get 'em deputized, post the bonds, housekeepin'. I look forward to meetin' him."

"I appreciate this, Beverly."

"What do you say we adjourn this meetin' and grab supper down at Hunter's Tavern, unless you have other plans?"

"Be happy to, although I'm sure the whisky won't be as good down there!"

They touched glasses and finished off the Bowmore, two men, acknowledged paragons of their society, discussing the buying and selling of one group of human beings and the extermination of another, over a dram of whisky and a good cigar.

Outside, the mockingbirds had returned and resumed their disagreement under the magnolia. As the two men stood and shook hands, they sent a storm of new dust motes swirling through the shafts of the fading daylight. They sent the fates of a handful of people swirling as well.

CHAPTER 2

May 21, 1829—Outside Franklin, North Carolina

THOMAS LOVE SAT on a pile of boulders near the foot of Cullasaja Falls, watching the water cascade down the slick black rocks. He didn't remember the steps that led him to this spot, and he had lost track of how long he had been sitting there. He stared into the torrent, watching the water change every second but somehow never change. The steady roar filled his ears and vibrated through his body. The overhanging branches of a massive, ancient chestnut shaded him, and the sunlight danced around him as its leaves fluttered in the soft breeze, painting the rocks and the water in a moving tapestry. Trilliums grew in profusion along the banks, and their white flowers seemed to explode when shafts of sunlight would find their way through the canopy to settle on the blossoms. The air was fresh and warm, and the rich, earthy smell of last fall's decaying leaf litter wafted through the forest. It was a perfect spring day in the mountains, a delight for the senses, but it was all lost on Tom.

He was far from this idyllic spot and didn't see the sun or the flowers or hear the water or smell the lush forest. Instead, he was trapped in a dark room on a cold winter day, where voices spoke in hushed tones and muffled sobs echoed off the walls. The minutes crawled by like hours. Shadows moved through the room in slow motion. He sat by a bed and looked down at the face of a young girl, her eyes half-closed, her dark hair, damp with fevered sweat, wrapped around the pale skin of her face. Her breathing was labored and shallow and made a sound like dried leaves blowing across the porch. She opened her eyes and found her father. "Daddy, I'm afraid," she whispered. He squeezed her hand and put his face against hers. His throat so tight it felt like he was being strangled. Straining to control his voice he said, "Oh, my darling, don't be afraid. You're gonna get well, and when spring is here again you and me are goin' to the falls to that spot you love and pick wildflowers. I'll read your favorite poems and we'll take a picnic and stick our feet in the water." But she closed her eyes and drew her last small breath and left him crying into his hands, begging God to give her back, begging for forgiveness for whatever sins he had committed that caused her to be taken, begging to trade his life for hers. But there was no answer, only silence, his pleas ignored, and she was gone.

Today would have been Rebecca Love's ninth birthday, the first birthday Tom had spent without her since she had died that cold December day. He realized he had come here to this glen, her favorite spot in the world, because he wanted to be close to her again, and thought he might feel some piece of her here, some part of her essence, some of the joy that she had radiated, that was now missing from his world. For months he had mourned, a drowning man grasping at flotsam after his boat has gone down in stormy seas. Some days he raged, other days he spent blank eyed and lost. He lost weight, eating without appetite. He went through the motions of life, doing what he had to do, day after day, his heart broken and his soul in tatters.

Rebecca's death was the latest and most dramatic in a string of failures. He had quit the university in Chapel Hill before his senior year when he found out his wife, Sarah, was expecting Rebecca. His father, a hard man, had turned his back on him and they rarely spoke. He took the bit of legal studies he had at school and tried to start a law practice, but what work he found paid little. He had taken loans from his brothers and cousins to keep his family fed in the leanest years, and he was not sure if or when he could repay them. His Uncle Robert had sold him the farm for a pittance, but despite his best efforts, the elements had conspired against him, and most of last year's crops had rotted in the field from too much rain in the spring and not enough in the summer.

Now the only thing keeping him afloat was drifting away from him. Every day he looked into Sarah's eyes and saw the hurt and frustration building, the distance between them growing. What to say or do to bridge the growing gulf eluded him. He couldn't save their child, he couldn't save their marriage, and he couldn't save himself. An old flintlock pistol rested in his lap. The fine-grained wood glowed in the light and emitted its own warmth, a stark contrast to the cold blue barrel. His hand moved towards the weapon, seemingly of its own volition, but a shock, like static discharge, caused him to freeze. Or had he imagined it? His arm dropped back to his side, his head reclined against the rock, and he looked up again at the falls.

It had been two days since he had eaten. Tired and weak, he stared into the cascade. His chest rose and fell with each breath, but his body felt detached. Transfixed, the falling water filled his senses and overwhelmed the noise inside his head. He floated, weightless. The water tumbling over the rocks slowed and individual drops caught the rays of sunlight and reflected them like stars, glittering, brighter and brighter, more and more of them, until his entire field of vision sparkled. He could hear the individual drops fall against the rocks, shattering like small pieces of glass. The sounds grew and merged, becoming a steady hum, a vibration more a feeling than a sound. Together, the light and the sound became indistinguishable, enveloping Tom, absorbing him, replacing him. How long the spell lasted, he couldn't tell, but it faded away and he found himself once again faced with reality.

The weight of the pistol was now obtrusive, its presence, malevolent. He couldn't leave Sarah alone with the children, a farm to manage and debts owed. No matter how hard the alternative would be, he couldn't take the easy way out. He stood up from the riverbank and trudged to his horse, the pistol heavy in his hand. As he mounted, he looked back one last time at the falls and thought again of his daughter before setting off down the trail towards home.

The horse and buggy pulled up in front of the house to a cacophony of barking dogs. Sarah Love opened the front door and peeked out until she recognized the driver, her husband's uncle. "Uncle Robert!" she cried, and rushed out to greet him, followed by two young children. "What is this?" she asked as she looked at the ornate buggy.

"Sarah, my dear! Come here and give your Uncle Robert a hug." After a heartfelt embrace, he waved at the buggy. "I've grown too old to sit a horse

for an extended period and am reduced to gettin' around in this contraption."
He scratched his horse behind the ear and wrapped the reins around a front
porch post, looking around the yard as he did. "Where's Tom?"

Sarah twisted her head without answering. "Julia, git some oats from
the barn for the horse. James, git a bucket of water from the spring for it
to drink." After the children scampered off, Sarah turned again to Robert.
"Tom's off in the woods, I reckon, Uncle Robert." A cloud seemed to have
passed over her face.

"Everything alright, Sarah?"

"No, Uncle Robert, ain't nothin' right. I'm worried about Tom. I fear he's
losin' his mind." She turned her face from him again.

"Come now, honey, it cain't be that bad. Let's go inside and tell me what's
goin' on."

Sarah gathered herself, straightening her hair. "I'm sorry; I didn't mean
to tell you that. I just ain't had nobody to talk to." He followed as she turned
and made her way into the house.

The house was a pair of log cabins connected by a breezeway. One cabin
contained the kitchen, with a sizable fireplace where the cooking took place,
and a large roughhewn table and chairs where the family took their meals.
From the open rafters above hung the last few strings of a variety of dried
fruits and vegetables. Late spring was a lean time for families in the mountains. The grains and other vegetables gathered from last year's harvest were
almost gone, and they could expect no new produce for several weeks until
the garden they planted in April started to bear. The smokehouse was also
nearly empty, with only the least desirable cuts of the salted pork from the
hogs they killed last November remaining. The kitchen walls were whitewashed to make the space seem brighter, since there was only one window.
Windows were expensive and rare on the frontier and drafty when the cold
winter winds were blowing.

In the other wing of the cabin was the family's living room and sleeping
quarters, whitewashed like the kitchen. A thick "crown" window provided
a modicum of light. The crown, a byproduct of the manufacturing process,
made images appear distorted like a reflection in a shiny doorknob. They
furnished the living room with an assortment of handmade chairs and side
tables, including a rocker by the hearth. Next to the rocker was a small

harp Sarah had inherited from her mother. On one wall hung a landscape painting, a wedding gift from Tom's family, with two men admiring the view of a mountain waterfall. Beneath the picture was a sturdy bookshelf with perhaps two dozen books, Tom's modest library. In the middle of the room, against the back wall, a set of steep stairs led to the loft where the bedding was located. Tom and Sarah slept on one side and the children on the other.

Sarah led Robert into the kitchen and had him take a seat at the table. "You must be hongry. How 'bout I fry you up some eggs and bacon? I got some biscuits and sorghum too."

"That sounds fine. You and the young'uns eat yet?"

"Yeah, we et a while ago. Rest your legs while I get started." With that, she was out the door. She passed her son struggling with a large bucket of water for the waiting horse, walking through a flock of chickens and their scurrying chicks as they scratched the ground for food. "James, aifter you get the horse his water, pull a handful of green onions from the garden and bring 'em to me." James nodded and Sarah ducked into the springhouse. The structure was made of fieldstone and covered with a slate roof. The stone kept the interior cool year round, allowing the family to keep milk, butter, cheese, eggs, and some meats from going bad. Inside, Tom had lined the spring opening with stacked stone and created a small pool with river rocks, surrounded by a series of ledges. Several earthenware jars sat half-immersed in the cool, clear water. A basket made from twisted branches and lined with raw wool sat on one ledge, filled with a dozen big brown eggs. Sarah picked up one of the small jugs and sat it on the ledge. She pulled the ends of her apron to form a ready-made basket, in which she placed four eggs and a small slab of bacon from another ledge and, with the jar, made her way out of the dark recess and into the bright May sunlight, blinking as her eyes readjusted. She crossed the yard, making a mental note of which of the chickens she would have to kill to prepare their uncle a proper meal if he was going to stay any length of time.

Back inside the kitchen, she laid out her larder and pulled a large frying pan from a hook on the wall. Robert stood in front of the fireplace, stoking the embers and positioning a fresh hickory log on the grate. "You still had a few hot coals, so we should be good in a bit," he said over his shoulder.

"Now tell me about what's goin' on with Tom while we wait for the fire to ketch up." He turned to face her.

Sarah continued to work, cutting the slab of bacon into thick slices as she spoke, looking at the bacon instead of him. "Tom'll be mad I told you this, but I'm worried about him. He ain't got over losin' Rebecca."

"I know how much he loved the child."

"When she passed, right aifter Christmas, I never see'd a man so troubled. I tried my best to console him, but I was grievin' myself, and had to take care of the house and James and Julia. That was a dark time. The cold was awful, and the snow was piled up and kept comin'. We didn't know what to do with her pore little body." Sarah wiped her eyes with her sleeve and struggled to keep from choking on her own voice. "Tom took her to the barn and stayed there with her whilst he tried to make a coffin out of boards from one of the stall doors he took down. I went out to check on him and take him some food and found him sobbin' on the floor, the tears froze in his beard. I was afeared he was gonna freeze to death, and begged him to come in the house but he wouldn't leave her by herself, said he was afraid wolves or somethin' would hurt her, though they ain't been no sign of wolves in all the years we've lived here."

"I cain't imagine what it was like for you both."

"He said he had to finish her coffin. I told him he had to come in soon or we'd lose him too and I couldn't make it by myself. That seemed to stir him some, and he got up and started nailing the pieces together. Hour or so I went back to check on him. He'd finished the coffin and laid her in it. Standin' over her, a-talkin' to her, he didn't notice I'd come in. He was tellin' her he was sorry and askin' her to forgive him."

"Why was he apologizin' to her? She died of the lung fever, didn't she? That's what my brother told me."

"Yes, Tom took her to church in Franklin the Sunday afore Christmas. They was goin' to have a Christmas play and Rebecca begged Tom to go see it. They set off afore light to get there in time. During the day the weather changed. It turned off cold, and they got caught out in it. It started sleetin' on 'em on their way back and by the time they got home at dark, they was both chilled to the bone. Rebecca seemed fine the next day, but the day after she started runnin' a fever and coughin'. We couldn't get her cooled down. She just kept gettin' weaker and weaker. Tom blamed himself for takin' her to church, for not keepin' her warm and dry, for not bein' able to get her to a doctor. He blamed himself for movin' us so fur away from town. I tried to reason with him. You know Tom is a good father and husband. But nothin' I said got through to him."

"Grief's hard on people."

"James went out and begged him to come inside. He started cryin', standin' there shiverin' and that seemed to affect Tom. He put the lid on the coffin and come in the house. We buried her the last day of the year up on that little rise looking out over the river. Tom ain't been hisself since. God knows nobody misses that child more'n me. I give birth to her. I mourned as well, and I'll never forget her as long as I live, but at some point you've got to git on with livin'. I fear Tom's given up on livin' and I don't know what to do."

The shadows were crawling across the valley floor as the sun edged towards the long blue ridgeline of the western mountains. Robert sat in a rocking chair on the front porch of his nephew's house, looking across the fields flanking the river. The corn and their companion pole beans, along with a section of potatoes and sorghum, were growing in the rich, dark soil of the bottomlands. Off to one side of the house was a decent vegetable garden with okra, squash, pumpkin, watermelon, peppers, lettuce, and cabbage and a variety of herbs. A small grove of apple and peach trees flanked the vegetable garden. If the rains fell regularly, and there was no blight or insect infestation or flood or hail storms, Tom and Sarah could feed their family and animals through another year. Robert could see how hard they had worked. The Cherokee had cleared and farmed this tract for countless generations and it had been part of Robert's acquisitions after the last treaty. He had been glad to part with it to help Tom get started.

Robert's gaze drifted off to the small rise where he could see the rough headstone that marked little Rebecca's resting place. He thought again of Sarah's story of that cold, dark time and what they had been through. He had lost a child once himself, long ago now. Though it had died an infant, the pain was still sharp. He couldn't imagine what Tom had been going through. He remembered visiting a few years back, when Rebecca was maybe seven years old. She had sung an old Scottish song, "Blue Eye'd Mary," with Sarah playing the harp. He could still hear her sweet girlish voice blending with the gentle pluck of the strings:

> Can I go along with you fair maid she answer me genteelly
> Just as you like kind sir, replied the charming blue eyed Mary
> As we walked o'er yon meadows braes the flowers they were
> springing
> As we sat down on yon mossy bank the skylark she was
> singing.

No skylark singing now, but quail at opposite ends of the fields were echoing back and forth their plaintive cry of "bob-bob-white." In a burst, the covey nearest the river flushed and Robert looked to see what had disturbed them. A man leading a dark horse emerged from the edge of the forest, coming towards the house. Robert stood as two hounds bounded off the porch and charged across the fields. "Sarah, Tom's home," he called, and threw up his hand.

Tom stepped out of the woods on the ancient river trail, worn smooth by countless Cherokee moccasins. Looking up the long hill towards his farmstead, it took Tom a moment to recognize the old man on his porch as his Uncle Robert. His first reaction was fear as he thought something might have happened to Sarah and the children. Then he saw Sarah step out on the porch and wave and that fear dissolved, replaced by another: What had Sarah told Robert and what did his uncle want?

Tom ate like the famished man he was. Sarah had fried the chicken she had targeted, and she served it along with beans and potatoes, fresh lettuce from the garden and salt-rising bread with fresh-churned sweet butter and buttermilk. She had saved the fried liver for Tom, knowing it was his favorite. She sat and watched him eat, relieved by his return and confused by his changed demeanor. When he made eye contact with her, he crinkled his eyes at the corners as she had seen him do a million times before, as though the past several months had never occurred. She wondered what

Uncle Robert thought, given the Tom she had described earlier today and the one sharing supper with them now. The children sensed the change as well and chattered away like the blue jays that owned the maple tree out front.

"Can I get ya'll seconds?" Sarah asked, as Robert and Tom wiped their mouths.

"I cain't eat another bite. That was delicious, Sarah," said Robert.

"Just what the doctor ordered." Tom reached out and patted her hand. Tom's drawl was not as pronounced as his uncle's or most of the men in the county. He had been self-conscious at Chapel Hill after classmates mocked his accent, and he labored while there to soften his twang. His father mocked him for it when he returned home. Tom developed the ability to drift into the vernacular depending on the audience. In his head, though, he never heard his accent.

"Then ya'll head out on the porch. I know you gotta lot to catch up on."

"I brought a couple of good cigars, Tom."

Tom and Robert pushed their chairs back and made their way onto the porch. It was twilight now, and the first lightning bugs of the evening were flashing across the yard, looking for mates. The bob whites had settled in for the evening, replaced by a couple of whip-poor-wills whose calls resounded across the valley. Settled into the rocking chairs, the men lit their cigars, their fire glowing in the evening shadows.

"I never tire of hearin' whip-poor-wills," Robert said. "Don't hear 'em as often as you used to. All the people moving in around Waynesville are runnin' 'em off."

A tree frog nearby added its voice to the evening chorus.

"Have you ever noticed that sometimes the lightnin' bugs seem to flash in unison? They'll be goin' off at different times and then for a minute or two, they'll all light up at the same time. I've always wondered if it's intentional." Tom grunted in reply.

For a time they sat smoking their cigars, looking for order in the chaos. Finally their patience paid off, as the fireworks show fell into sync and the night seemed to pulse as all the beetles flashed together for a handful of moments, then returned to the unordered chaos. They both grinned at their fortune.

Robert took a deep breath and then said to Tom, "Sarah told me about Rebecca. I'm so very sorry, Tom. How are you doin'?"

Tom responded with a long breath of his own. "I don't know that I'll ever get over it, Uncle Robert, but I spent some time alone in the woods the last couple of days and I reckon I'm gonna be alright. I have to be for Sarah and the children."

"That's good to hear. Sarah's worried about you."

"Reckon I have a lot to make up to her. I ain't been able to give her the life she deserves."

"You've had some rough luck these past few years. That's why I've come to see you. I got a means for you to get your way clear."

"What is it?"

"I had a meetin' with Beverly Daniel in Raleigh a couple a weeks back. He's in charge of collectin' the census next year, asked me for a recommendation for someone to handle Macon County. I told him you'd be just the man."

Tom stopped rocking for a moment and looked at his uncle. "What would that involve?"

"Well, you'll visit every house in the county, count the number of people livin' in the house with their ages, and record 'em on sheets you turn in to Daniel."

"Every house in the county? How long would that take?"

"Not sure, but Daniel figured it'd be about six months startin' the first of June. They're still messin' around with the forms in Washington City."

"Uncle Robert, I got the farm to take care of, and the road buildin' juries down this way, and I'm tryin' to grow my law practice in Franklin. How could I take on such a responsibility? I feel like I'm over my head already."

"Let me tell you why I think this is a splendid opportunity for you. First is the money. You could make a few hundred dollars doin' this. Think what that'd mean for you and Sarah. They pay a fee on the number of people you count. Since Macon's such a big territory, they'll pay a bonus. Second, you'll get to meet every man in the county. We've talked in the past about you maybe runnin' for office someday. Think of the advantage you'd have, if you meet every voter in the county and get paid for it to boot!"

"We talked about it, but I don't know that I'm cut out for public office."

"Don't underestimate yourself. They ain't nobody in this county I've met with a better head on their shoulders. Andy Jackson is looking to run the Cherokees out of the rest of this area. Daniel wants to know how things look in the Nation. That wouldn't be part of the official job, but he'd be beholden to the person who provided that intelligence. Once that land comes available, you and me'd have the inside track on the best parcels to go after."

"They gave up so much land with that last treaty and them that's left have settled down. A family joined the Baptist church in Franklin last year. Seekeekee and John Walker opened that trading post over near Beaverdam and been tradin' with the settlers. Where would all those people go?"

"I helped Seekeekee set that trading post up, but they ain't nothin' you or me can do to dissuade Jackson. So we can either fume about it or put ourselves first in line to benefit from it. If we don't, somebody else will."

Tom nodded his head in reply.

"It'd be an adventure! You remember when we did the survey back in '20? You'll get to explore all that beautiful country again. I know what happened to Rebecca has hit you hard. You need somethin' to take your mind off it while you heal. Plannin' and preparin' for this and then carryin' it out would be a balm to your heart. Think about it. This is a once-in-a-lifetime opportunity, and it's yours for the takin'."

Tom leaned back in the chair and tried to take in everything his uncle had just dropped on him. "Uncle Robert, I hear what you're sayin', but how could I leave Sarah to run the farm by herself while I'm off countin' folks?"

"I thought of that too. A while back, I bought four darkies at auction up in Virginia. They was owned by none other than Thomas Jefferson and sold off to settle the debt left by the old man. One of the males is your age, and they trained him on a number of trades at Monticello. He worked the fields, did some blacksmithin', made nails, did some carpentry work; you name it, he did it. The female worked in the house gardens and kept house as well. You can buy 'em from me."

Tom was unsure how to answer or proceed. This was not a discussion he had expected. He was bone tired from his time in the woods. He stared into the gathering darkness, looking at the flashing lights of the growing legion of lightning bugs, as if they could provide illumination for his quandary.

"Uncle Robert, I cain't afford to buy people from you."

"You can pay me out of the money from the census work. Since this whole thing'll benefit us both, I'll give you a great deal on 'em, two hundred for the male and fifty for the gal. You'll clear two hundred and fifty dollars. When they start droppin' younguns, your investment'll grow. You'll get more out of the farm, maybe add a cash crop like tobacco. Then we'll add some prime Indian lands to our holdings. The family'll be set to prosper for generations."

"I don't know what to say, Uncle Robert. You've been so good to me and Sarah. I often ask myself, 'What have I done to deserve this?' Every time I stumble it seems you or Sarah or someone else is there to pick me up. If you think this is best for us, how can I turn you down?"

"It is and you cain't," Robert replied and looked away into the dark.

"What are their names?"

"Isaiah and Ellen."

One of the whip-poor-wills was closer now. Tom tried to place where it was hiding: maybe under that old cedar. No, it was up near the hill where Rebecca was buried. The two men sat smoking their cigars, watching the lightning bugs, and listening to the mountain symphony, each lost in his own thoughts.

CHAPTER 3

May 22, 1829

AFTER BREAKFAST THE next morning, Tom spoke to Robert as he harnessed his horse and prepared his carriage for the trip back to Waynesville.

"How is this gonna work, Uncle Robert?"

"When I get back home, I'll send one of my men here with the servants. I'm also gonna send you some maps I have from when we did the survey. Over the next few months, study up and start plannin' how to break the territory into manageable chunks. If you got six months to complete the work, break the county up into six districts, and do one a month, say."

"I was thinkin' along the same lines. Most of the people live near Franklin, so there'd be more work there but less travel. Away from town it's sparsely settled, but there'll be a lot of travel gettin' there and findin''em all. Some of the new settlers are way back in the hollers."

"Right. I know you're worried about bein' away from the farm and your family, but if you plan it all out, you can break it up into manageable chunks that'll limit your time away. And with the help of the slaves, the farm work won't suffer."

"I'm worried about that. You got your overseer to handle your people. I won't have anyone. Sarah cain't be expected to manage that while I'm gone."

"Of course, you're right. I'd think you'd take the male with you, and Sarah and the female'd stay here and help take care of things. He could manage your livery, make camp, fix meals and such, allowin' you to focus on gettin' the counting done. You'll be more efficient and reduce the time away."

"That's a good idea."

"You should also start gatherin' as much information as you can from the county administrators. Sheriff Bell should have information about how people are spread out."

"Yeah, and John Dobson is a friend of mine. He's the county registrar. Jacob Siler is the surveyor. He may have some useful information."

"Make do with the resources available."

"You talked to Daddy about this?"

Robert looked over Tom's shoulder. "No, I ain't, not yet. If you agreed, I was plannin' on stoppin' by his place on my way back home. I ain't seen him in a spell. How's he gettin' along?"

"You know him as well as me. He's on the road a lot 'tween his properties. I fear he drinks too much. I'm not sure how Momma's put up with him this long."

"God has seen fit to provide our womenfolk with uncommon wisdom and patience, your mother in particular. I hope to find her in good health and spirits. I'm back in Raleigh the middle of next month, and I'll let Beverly Daniel know you're on board. He's plannin' a meetin' this fall in Raleigh or Morganton for all the deputies to take their oaths, post their bonds, and receive their instructions. I'll let you know the exact date so you can make preparations."

"Post a bond?"

"Yeah, I forgot to mention that. They'll deputize you as an assistant US marshal, and we'll have to post a bond to guarantee you'll submit the final reports on time. If Daniel don't make the deadline to submit the completed documents to the secretary of state, he has to forfeit his bond, which is sizable. But don't worry; I'll post your bond."

Tom looked dazed. "Is it too late to back out? I'm already so beholden to you for everything you've done for me and my family. If I was to fail in this and you forfeit a bond, I don't know how I would live with myself."

"Tom, I've got full confidence in you or I wouldn't have put your name up and asked you to do this. This is gonna be great for you. Now go tell Sarah and the children to come and kiss their old Uncle Robert goodbye."

As they watched the carriage roll away down the rutted red clay path, Tom put his arm around Sarah and pulled her close. Sarah wrapped her arms around him and buried her head in his chest. She took a deep breath and let her husband's scent wash over her. She felt his muscular arms squeeze her and his lips kiss her hair. "We need to talk, darlin'," Tom said.

"Just let me stand here a minute."

Tom put his hand under her chin and lifted her face to his, looking into her green eyes. "I'm sorry, Sarah."

"Sorry for what?"

"Sorry for everything. I feel like such a failure. You deserve so much more. But mostly I'm sorry for losing Rebecca."

"I know how it hurt you. You was so close to her, and she worshipped you. It weren't yore fault."

"When I went out in the woods, I wasn't sure what I was lookin' for." The picture of the pistol lying in his lap flashed through his mind. "I went up to the falls that she loved. I had an experience I don't know how to describe, but I felt like Rebecca was with me there."

"She'll always be with us, and we'll see her again in heaven someday."

Tom kissed her and then released his embrace. He told her about his conversation with Robert, about the census, about the land and the slaves. She pulled away from him and looked at him in astonishment. "You agreed to all of this without even talkin' to me?"

"You were already in bed by the time we come in. I did what I thought was best for us, for our family. Uncle Robert has done so much for us. We wouldn't have this place, our home, if it wasn't for him. He believes this is a great opportunity for me, for us. How could I turn him down?"

"But slaves, Tom? We built this place and farmed it ourselves for years now. We've ain't never needed slaves. Two people we don't know livin' here on our farm? Where will they sleep? How will we feed two more mouths? We can barely feed ourselves most of the time. What if they're mean? How you know they won't kill us and the children and run off?"

"Uncle Robert wouldn't send people like that here. They were owned by Thomas Jefferson, for God's sake. He says they are well behaved and would cause us no problems. I trust Uncle Robert, don't you?"

"Of course, but this is just . . . I love our life here the way it is. It's hard, but we get through, you and me and the children. I don't want our life to change, and this is so drastic."

Tom stood silent for a long time before answering in a low voice, almost a whisper. "We'll make this work. Can you tell me it wouldn't be good to have more help around here? We could clear more land, add more crops. We could grow and sell tobacco, pay off what we owe our family, maybe put away some cash to cover us through hard times. Washington, Jefferson, Madison, they all owned slaves. Uncle Robert, father, your brother, they own 'em too, and they're all prosperous while we scratch out a livin' here. I cain't see no other way to get ourselves clear. Please trust me on this."

"Sometimes good men do evil, Tom, but call it by another name. I'm your wife, not your slave. I don't like this and I'm tellin' you so. But you've made this commitment and I'll support you as best I can. I just pray this ain't somethin' we regret the rest of our lives." She pulled away from him and walked back to the house with her shoulders set.

Tom stood staring into the distance, praying the same thing.

CHAPTER 4

May 23, 1829—Waynesville, North Carolina

ISAIAH LAY IN the rope cot staring at the ceiling of the small cabin as the long night gave way to the gray light of the coming day. He had been awake for some unknown time, listening to the breathing and snoring of the four other men with whom he shared this small stinking cabin. He would start this day as he did every day, and finish it as he finished every day: remembering Monticello and those few short years of relative happiness he had shared with his wife, Anne, and their little daughter Susan, and worrying about what had become of them. Where were they now? Were they safe? Were they together? Did they have enough to eat? Were they being abused? Would he ever touch Anne's sweet face again, taste her sweet lips on his, feel her arms around him as they made love? Would he ever hear Susan's voice again as she erupted in squeals of laughter as he lifted her high over his head? The work at Monticello had been backbreaking and the reprisals from the overseer for even minor infractions had been brutal, but at least he had been able to lay his head down at night with his girls nearby. Waiting for the sun to rise and another day of work to begin, he remembered his life then and how it led him to this place and time.

It was the spring of 1826, and Thomas Jefferson was dying. He had been in failing health for some time, but he clung to what remained of his life with the dogged determination that had characterized his every endeavor. As the days passed, the emotions of the slave families on Mulberry Row seesawed between fear and anticipation as rumors swept through the quarters like small wildfires. First, Monticello and its Black inhabitants would be sold to a new owner. Then, the president would free all the slaves in his will and give each of them a plot of land to repay them for their service. Word spread from someone in the Hemings family that indeed each of the slaves would be freed after his death, but the plantation would stay in the family intact and they would each be on their own. Everyone trusted the Hemingses would know the truth because of the special relationship they held with Jefferson. If they said the slaves were to be freed, it must be true! As spring turned to summer, anticipation reached fever pitch. The Fourth of July was approaching, and no one was sure if the old president would make it for the fiftieth anniversary of the signing of the declaration. As the day approached, the significance was not lost on the inhabitants of this small island that was Monticello. With his passing, the author of the founding document could bring the words to life for those who had labored for him for so long.

Isaiah was lying in bed with Anne in their sweltering cabin on the night of July 3. He was bone tired and covered with sweat and grime from a hard day in the fields. They would not have to work tomorrow on the anniversary of American independence. In years past it had been a day of celebration, but the death watch for the president had cast a pall over the plantation. Uncertainty was buffered by hope, and that emotion consumed Isaiah. For the first time in his life, the idea of freedom seemed tangible, possible. He had often dreamed of running away and making his way north, but with a wife and child, he knew the odds against successful flight would be insurmountable. But now, the idea of being emancipated with his family filled him with a joy and excitement he had never known. Unable to sleep, he thought of what his life could be. He dreamed of taking Anne and Susan west to the new states where there was no slavery, standing on his own homestead, plowing his own land, sitting on his own porch, sleeping under his own roof. He thought of the children he and Anne would have, each of them born free, never knowing shackles or whips or unending toil without reward. His children, playing on his farm, going to school and getting an education and being allowed to go into the world and pursue their own dreams. He pictured himself an old man, with grandchildren on his knee. Everything he and Anne had been through, and their parents and grandparents as well, their suffering and their despair, could be infused with meaning by each of the days he would live in freedom with his family around him. It was almost too wonderful to imagine. Elation gave way to fatigue and Isaiah drifted off, his waking dreams dissolving into those of sleep.

Jefferson died on the fiftieth anniversary of the Declaration of Independence, as did his old friend, accomplice, and sometime nemesis John Adams. The atmosphere at Monticello was manic, divided between the genuine sorrow felt at the death of Jefferson, even among the slaves, and the anticipation that freedom was near. The great man was buried at five o'clock on July 5 on a gray, rainy day in the simple ceremony he had requested. For the next few days the overseers enforced only labor necessary to keep the population of Monticello fed and cared for, which only fueled the expectation in the quarters that their deliverance was at hand. Early on the following Monday, the overseers turned out all the slaves. There was a hush over the crowd as the chief overseer, a man named Ralston, stood on the old oak stump where announcements and assignments were made. In one hand he held a cane he used as a club when the mood struck him.

"The period of mournin' for President Jefferson is now over. It's time to resume your labors. I have your assignments for today." His voice was rough and tinged with foreboding. A murmur went through the crowd as the slaves looked from one to another, whispering questions and expressing their shock.

"Quiet!" Ralston shouted. The foremen behind him edged forward, at least two of them with guns held in their folded arms, the others with clubs or whips held at their sides. "I know about the rumors what's been circlin' through the quarters. They are false. The executor of the president's estate has reviewed his last will and testament, which provided that the following individuals are to be released: Joseph Fossett, Burwell Colbert, Madison Hemings, John Hemings, and Eston Hemings. Everyone else shall remain the property of this estate and the president's heirs. I've been assured by the president's grandson ya'll will continue to be treated right so long as there's order and discipline and everybody does their job."

For what seemed a long time, the only sound was the gentle breeze rustling the leaves high above in the tall oaks. Isaiah dropped his head and looked at the ground. He saw an ant scurrying through the dust with some crumb it had scavenged, and he thought, "This is my life. I'll never be free. I ain't nothin' but an ant carryin' a heavy load for the rest of my days, and it ain't even my load. And when I cain't carry the load no more I'll die like this ant in the dust and no one'll ever know I lived," and he stomped the ant into oblivion. As he did, he clenched his fists, and from somewhere deep down in his soul came a primal shout, one word—"NO!"—that shattered the still morning air. His shout was followed first by a low moan, and then his one word repeated from a hundred throats as each of his fellow slaves realized that their dreams of emancipation had been dashed: "NO!" Women were sobbing and grown men wept. Isaiah saw his father Jeremiah fall to his knees, his hands covering his face. At the same time he felt his arms grabbed by powerful hands and then everything went bright as he felt the air knocked out of him. A foreman had punched him in the gut with the end of his club, and like his father, he was now on his knees in the dust, gasping for breath. A gunshot shattered the air and then echoed over the crowd.

"Silence!" shouted Ralston, and a tense hush fell over the crowd again as they wiped their eyes. "This is not order and discipline!" His face was red with anger as he pointed at Isaiah with his cane. "Forty lashes for that man for that outburst, and twenty for any of you who follow his example!"

Isaiah was dragged to the whipping post that stood in the center of the Row and chained with the shackles that hung there. They ripped away his shirt, and a foreman took a short whip and beat Isaiah's bare back until the blood flowed. Isaiah did not cry out until the ninth lash, when the pain overwhelmed him. He passed out sometime around the twentieth lash. They left him to hang unconscious while they gave the rest of the slaves their assignments and escorted them off to their day's labor.

The next two weeks were an unrelenting blur of pain for Isaiah. He slipped in and out of consciousness and alternated between intense chills and burning fever during the times he was awake. He could only lie on his stomach and had to be helped to the slop pail to relieve himself. Anne tended his wounds as best she could at night after her work. During the day two of the older women would come by and check on him and try to get him to eat and drink. Flies hovered in swarms around him during the day, and mosquitoes plagued him all night. When he slept, he had nightmares about the whipping and when he was conscious, his lost dream of freedom haunted him. Anne worried he was dying and was afraid to let little Susan see him. Isaiah too thought he was going to die and there were times he wished he would. He had a dream one night that he was crossing a raging black river and his boat overturned in swirling rapids. Washed over the side, he felt himself going under. Unable to swim, he struggled to get to the surface, his heart pounding as he held his breath. Just as he was about to surrender and breathe in the dark water, someone grabbed his arm and pulled him above the water where he gulped air. He awoke gasping for breath, covered in sweat. His fever had broken, and he lay shivering in the pre-dawn hours, remembering the nightmare.

As morning broke, Isaiah struggled to sit up. He called out for Anne, but there was no answer. He sat on the side of the bed, his head in his hands as he waited for the nausea and dizziness to subside. The door to the cabin opened and Ralston stood glaring into the shadows.

"God, it stinks in here," he said. "I trust you learned your lesson, and there'll be no more outbursts?"

Isaiah made a croaking sound from his parched throat in reply.

"I'll take that as a yes. Take one more day to get your feet back under you. Tomorrow is the Sabbath. Monday I expect you back at work. You can work a few days in the nail shop until you're ready to go back to the fields." Teenage boys worked in the nail shop, hammering out the nails that the plantation sold in the markets in Charlottesville and Richmond. Isaiah had spent several years as a youth in the shop. It was hot, hard work, but at least it would be out of the sun and the backbreaking work in the fields while he recovered. "One more thing. I assigned your woman to work down at Shadwell. If you keep your nose clean, I'll move her back up here in a while. I'll let her visit on Sundays. Any more trouble out of you though, and I'll send her down to Poplar Forest"—Ralston paused for a long time before finishing—"or by God I'll sell her ass south."

Shadwell was part of the Monticello plantation across the Rivanna River. Jefferson was born there and inherited the property from his father. Poplar Forest was a plantation Jefferson and his wife, Martha, inherited from her parents. It was near Lynchburg, about seventy miles from Monticello, and might as well have been in a different country as far as slaves separated by the distance were concerned.

"No sir, please," Isaiah begged. "I will cause no trouble. Please don't take Anne and Susan from me."

"Then we have an understanding. I'll send Jenny over with some food and clean clothes. Get yourself cleaned up and be ready for work first thing Monday."

For the next few months Isaiah regained his strength and worked every task assigned to him without complaint. As the scars healed across his back, they drew the skin taut so that just standing up straight was a painful exercise. He developed a slight stoop to his posture that he would carry the rest of his days. Each of those days was the same, working from sunup until sundown, falling asleep in the cabin he now shared with other men, and starting all over again with the rooster crow the next day. He lived for one thing alone: the arrival each Saturday night of Anne and Susan. They made the trek up the mountain with other separated families. Isaiah's roommates found other cabins to spend the night in so the family could be alone. Tearful embraces initiated each reunion as Isaiah held his beloved girls. They would catch up on their activities of the week over a sparse supper, both of them minimizing the drudgery of their lives while highlighting some minor bright spot to save the other worry, each trying to lift the other up. Some nights they would join other slaves around a campfire to share stories or songs, but usually they spent the precious time alone together, savoring each moment. They would wait for Susan to fall asleep, and when they heard her soft snoring, they would quietly make love, and for a few fleeting moments they were just two lovers alone in the darkness with nothing separating them, instead of two weary prisoners seeking the one solace of their existence. Then Monday morning would come and they would end their short time together as they had begun it, with tearful embraces and brave farewells as Anne and Susan made their way back down the mountain and Isaiah went back to work. Once he had passed the hours of labor dreaming of a future of freedom. Now, his daydreams were limited to Saturday night and counting the hours until he would be together with his girls again.

Winter came, and as the days shortened and the fields lay fallow, the hours of labor diminished. At Christmas, Anne and Susan were allowed to spend the entire week with Isaiah. Isaiah asked Ralston on more than one occasion when they could live together again, but each time he was told it would be soon. Time passed and Isaiah could only seethe to himself. His greatest fear was still that they would ship the girls to Poplar Forest, so he bit his tongue and trudged on. He gave Anne a necklace he made from small pieces of copper scavenged from the blacksmith shop. He had beaten and polished and strung them together, and putting it around Anne's neck was the happiest moment he'd had since Susan's birth. Anne cried and said it was the nicest present she ever received, and then she corrected herself and said it was the only present she had ever received, and that brought fresh tears from both of them. Isaiah gave Susan a small stuffed toy he had made. Jenny had given him some scraps of indigo-dyed linen she had scrounged, and he had carefully cut, sewn, and stuffed it with rough wool into what passed for a rabbit, identifiable by two long ears that flopped over as Susan hugged it and squealed. They shared Christmas dinner with members of their extended families, attended a church service on the grounds, and sang carols around an enormous bonfire. Isaiah was as happy as he had been in a long time. The week passed too quickly and after New Year's he told them goodbye again. The time together made the parting all the more painful. He stood hugging them until an overseer prodded him and told him they had to go. He told them he loved them and that he would see them again Saturday, and he kissed Anne one last time on the forehead. They turned and started down the mountain to Shadwell under leaden skies as Isaiah stood in anguish. It was the last time he had seen them.

Three days later, the inhabitants of Mulberry Row were brought together again on the common ground. Ralston took his place with his cane, flanked as usual by the foremen. It was a cold, windy day, and the slaves huddled together for warmth as best they could.

"Master Randolph has some gentlemen coming in today to appraise the value of the plantation. They'll be looking at the land, the buildings, and you. I expect each one of you to be on your best behavior and to assist the appraisers in any manner they request. I will address any disturbance in the most forceful manner. Am I understood?" Ralston glared around at the shivering slaves as they nodded their assent.

The appraisers arrived at ten in the morning and began their tour of the property. Around two o'clock, foremen began taking individual slaves into the barn. About an hour later Isaiah was led inside and directed to stand in front of a table. Two middle-aged White men were comparing notes, a pile of papers spread out on the table before them. Two younger White men stepped up beside him.

"What's your name?"

"Isaiah."

The foreman who had escorted him in struck him on the back of the legs with his cane. "You say 'Sir,' boy."

"Isaiah, sir."

"How old are you, Isaiah?" the other asked.

"I turned twenty-eight on New Year's Eve past. I was born December 31, 1800."

"What are your duties here?"

"I done many things: made nails when I was a boy, been a carder, worked the smithy, reroofed this very barn, worked the gardens and the fields."

"You sired any children?"

Isaiah hesitated for a moment. "Yes sir, got a little girl name of Susan."

"Very good." He nodded to a man standing nearby, who moved towards Isaiah. "Git yer clothes off so Mr. McNabb can examine you."

"Sir?"

Ralston stepped up behind him and prodded Isaiah with his cane. "Get yer clothes off, Isaiah, and be quick about it. We got a lot of people to see."

Isaiah stiffened his back as best he could and felt his blood rise hot under his skin. He delayed a moment too long, and Ralston struck his buttocks with the cane. "Don't make this unpleasant, Isaiah."

"You mean more unpleasant than standing nekked in this cold barn in front of a bunch of strangers?"

Ralston turned his head and nodded, and two foremen grabbed Isaiah by the arms and put manacles on his wrists. One of them then grabbed his collar and ripped his shirt off. The other jerked the thin rope that served as

Isaiah's belt and his pants fell to the floor. McNabb stepped forward and told Isaiah to open his mouth. Isaiah stood silent, unmoving. Ralston struck his bare hips again with the cane. One foreman grabbed him in a headlock while the other one held the manacles. McNabb pulled his lips back and examined his teeth.

"Teeth look good," he said to the men at the desk.

"Turn him around."

At the sight of Isaiah's scarred back, the two men at the desk looked at one another and then at Ralston.

"As you can tell, Isaiah can be stubborn. We had an incident a couple of years back after President Jefferson died. We had to make an example of Isaiah here to maintain order. He never attempted escape though and we ain't had a problem since, right Isaiah?" Isaiah stood silent.

"Well, unfortunately this looks like unruliness and has a negative impact on valuation. Otherwise he appears healthy enough. Let's have the next one please."

The men at the table compared notes again and made an entry in one of their ledgers. Isaiah was half dragged out of the barn. On Ralston's orders they forced him to sleep in the manacles that night without food.

A few weeks later, the slaves of Monticello were all shackled and led out to the common ground again. It was warm for a winter day, with clouds scurrying across the sky. There would be rain later. Besides the overseers and foremen, several strangers milled about. They separated the slaves into two groups, the men in one and the women and children in the other. They were lined up in several rows and the strangers walked among them, stopping to look at individuals, asking the overseers to assist them in more intrusive inspections. This continued for over an hour, with the slaves looking at one another or standing immobile as they endured the humiliation of being poked and prodded like farm animals. The man in charge whispered to Ralston and the slaves were led to the barn, followed by the strangers.

For the next several hours they stood or sat in the barnyard until pulled from the group and led into the barn. Those left waiting whispered to one another, trying to remain inconspicuous. Isaiah's brother, Jerry, sat next to him. Leaning close, he asked Isaiah what was happening.

"We are bein' sold," Isaiah responded and dropped his head.

Isaiah and Jerry, their parents and other siblings, and most of the slaves gathered there had been born and lived their entire lives at Monticello. They had always belonged to the Jefferson family. A hard and frequently cruel existence, Monticello had been their home and their universe. They heard the rumors about financial troubles plaguing the estate, and the visit from the appraisers a few weeks back had fueled the anxiety and speculation swirling around the mountaintop.

"You mean the whole plantation is bein' sold or just us?" Jerry asked.

"Hard to say. I don't think they would take us one at a time if the whole plantation was bein' sold." Then he thought of Anne and Susan.

"Quiet over there!" a foreman shouted, and Isaiah and his brother were left to mull the ominous possibilities in silence. Isaiah wondered if the slaves down at Shadwell were going through this same ordeal. He hadn't heard from them since they started down the mountain after the holiday. He was choking, his heart pounded, and he struggled to breathe. Then he heard his name called and felt hands on his arms, pulling him up. They led him into the dark barn, the only light a series of lanterns. He was stripped again and stood like a statue, staring over the faceless heads into some distant place, seething.

"Gentlemen, I present Negro number forty-eight, a fine specimen, strong, with many skills. Twenty-eight years old. Let's start the bidding at two hundred and fifty. Who would like to begin?" said the auctioneer, standing close to Isaiah.

"Have him turn around," came a voice from the shadows.

Isaiah felt hands on his arms, turning him around. Between the shackles and his pants around his ankles, he almost lost his balance. A murmur went through the group as they saw the scars on his back.

"Is he a runner?" asked one.

"No sir!" replied the auctioneer. "I'm told he caused a commotion one day in the yard after President Jefferson's death. He was made to be an example, but there has been no problem since. He never run."

"That was some example!" said one man, and the others in the group laughed.

"I'll bid a hundred and fifty," said one.

"A hundred and seventy-five!" shouted another.

"Gentlemen, this is a strong Negro in the prime of life. He was disciplined, yes, but he learned his lesson. Let's have bids that properly reflect this outstanding value, please."

"You say he learned his lesson, but them scars don't lie. Two hundred."

"Do I hear two fifty?"

"Two twenty-five."

"I'll go two fifty."

"Excellent! Do I hear two seventy-five?" There were only murmurs from the group. Further pleadings fell on deaf ears. "Going once, twice . . . sold to Mr. Branscomb."

"I have a wife and child!" Isaiah shouted, and the strangers all turned to look up at him.

"There's no mention of a wife in the appraisal papers," said Branscomb.

"There is no wife," replied the auctioneer.

"I do have a wife, and a child! Anne is my wife and Susan my child. They're at Shadwell!"

"Nonsense. The Jefferson's maintained extensive records and there's no mention of this Negro being married. They may have coupled and had a child, but that's not uncommon. It don't make no difference, anyway."

"We were married! We said our pleas and troth on top of this very mountain four years ago May!"

"There's no record of it?" said Branscomb.

"None at all, and they been separated over a year," replied the auctioneer.

"We were only separated because Ralston wanted to punish me. We were just together over Christmas."

"Is the female and the child for sale?" Branscomb looked first at Isaiah and then at the auctioneer.

"A dealer from Georgia bought the lot of thirty from Shadwell last week. They were shipped south three days ago. Does your bid stand?"

"Yes, I suppose so."

Isaiah trembled now with rage. "You sold my wife and child south away from me! Anne! Anne!" he shouted and fell to his knees, supported by the two men who had escorted him in.

"Take him out!" said the auctioneer, and Isaiah was dragged from the barn as he struggled and screamed his wife's name.

"Next! Number forty-nine . . ."

Isaiah and three other Monticello slaves, two men and a woman, had been bought by Branscomb, the agent for Colonel Robert Love. They were transported to Waynesville in the back of a wagon, shackled together in irons. Isaiah remembered little of the journey south from Charlottesville. He sat despondent in the back of the wagon, his heart aching with misery and his head frantically trying to devise some plan to get his girls back. Escape was impossible, and even if he escaped, how could he track down Anne and Susan? The auctioneer had said a dealer from Georgia bought them. They could be anywhere, and who would help a runaway slave searching for his family? He decided his best option was to plead with his new owner to help him find them, but he had no idea what kind of person his new owner would be, or what he could offer to gain help. His mind turned to the family he had left behind in Monticello. His mother had died a few years back, but his father was still alive, as were his two brothers and two sisters. What had become of them? He realized he might never see them again, and his misery intensified. He was alone in the world, separated from his family, torn from the only home he had ever known, on his way to a strange place to toil for the rest of his life without hope. What kind of god would allow one of his children to suffer such a fate?

"What have I done to deserve this," he asked himself. He had prayed so many times to be reunited with his wife and child, to be free, and this was how those prayers were answered. He clenched his fists and cursed God.

They arrived at the Love farm late in the afternoon a few days later. Isaiah looked around as he and the other slaves climbed out of the wagon. This was no Monticello. The big house was two stories with a wide porch wrapping around three sides. There was a good-sized barn and several outbuildings. The slave quarters were down the hill from the house, alongside a small creek. There were eight small cabins and a larger cabin with two chimneys. Isaiah and the others were led to the creek and allowed to wash the dust from the road from their faces and arms. Then they were led to separate cabins, given a fresh set of clothes, and ordered to change. They met back out in front of the large cabin where they were faced by a tall White man with a barrel chest and a thick black beard. He stood for a few minutes looking over the group. Four young Black children appeared from behind one of the cabins and stood gawking at Isaiah and the others.

"My name is Johnston. I'm the head overseer here. I work for Colonel Robert Love, your new owner. He's a fair man and a good Christian. As long as you do your work, mind me and the foremen, and cause no disturbance, you'll be treated fairly. If, however, you cause me any trouble, your life here will be hard and unpleasant. Supper's in the main cabin. Go ahead and eat before the rest of the crews come in from the fields. Get your fill and rest up because you have a hard day ahead of you tomorrow. I'll come around and talk to each of you to find out how you can best be put to use."

After supper, Johnston came over to Isaiah, who was sitting on a log looking out over the fields in the fading light.

"You must be Isaiah."

"Yes sir."

"I understand from Mr. Branscomb that you have several skills. What did you do at the other plantation?"

Isaiah told him about the various jobs he held at Monticello.

"That's good to know. I think we will have some work for you in the smithy. In the meantime, we're clearin' a new field down on the creek bottom tryin' to get it ready for spring planting. You'll be workin' on that tomorrow."

"Yes sir. Mr. Johnston, can I ask you somethin'?"

Johnston looked at him before responding. "Go ahead."

"When Mr. Branscomb bought me at Monticello, I told him and the other gentlemen that I was married and got a little girl child. They said they didn't have any record of it, but I swear me and my wife, Anne, took our vows right there at Monticello. We knew each other since we was little children, grew up together. She was workin' a different part of the plantation when we was sold. They told me they had been sold to a man from Georgia. I would do anything, give anything, to be reunited with them. I would work harder than ten men if I could just have them here with me. Can you please help me?"

"Branscomb told me there was some trouble with this. I don't know if we can help you or not, but I'll talk to Colonel Love about it. He's a powerful man and may have some ideas. In the meantime, you give me your best efforts and we'll see what we can do."

"Thank you, sir. I will." For the first time in days, Isaiah felt a semblance of hope.

For almost three months, Isaiah was as good as his word. He had worked without complaint, clearing, plowing, and planting fields. He had worked in the blacksmith shop and had helped repair farm equipment. Every Saturday he would ask Johnston if he had received any word, and every Saturday Johnston would tell him Colonel Love was working on it. Isaiah didn't know if this was true, but he had to believe. As Isaiah lay in the rope cot thinking back on his journey and worrying about his girls, his life was about to take another turn.

Robert Love returned home late in the evening. The trip had gone well and he could see his plan unfolding. He was up early and after a spare breakfast went to talk to Johnston.

"Mr. Johnston, I sold two people to my nephew over in Macon County. Prepare Isaiah and Ellen for the journey and have Wright take 'em over as soon as possible. He's been there before and should know the way."

"Yes sir. Colonel Love, if I may, you might recall Isaiah claims he has a wife and child sold apart from him. You were gonna look into it?"

"Yes, I had Branscomb send a letter to the lawyers who handled the Jefferson estate. They said their records didn't show any marriage. They identified the dealer who bought the group in question, a Mr. Hemby, out of Augusta. My staff in Raleigh did some checkin' and it appears this Hemby is a seedy character. We're tryin' to track 'em down, but nothin' so far. I'll have my secretary follow up."

"Thank you, sir. I'll let him know. We'll miss his talents here, sir. He's a hard worker and learned a lot on Mr. Jefferson's plantation. He has been on his best behavior hopin' to get your help with his family situation."

"Tell him we'll pass along any further information we get through my nephew, although between you and me, I don't hold out much hope that they can be located at this point. He'll have to make do with the gal."

Johnston went to Amos Wright and told him he would transport two of the slaves to Tom Love's farm outside Franklin. Then he went to tell Isaiah the news. He found him in the blacksmith shop repairing a wagon wheel.

"Isaiah, I got some news for you."

"Yes sir?"

"I just spoke to Colonel Love. He got word that a man out of Augusta, Georgia, bought your woman and the child. He sent a letter to him to inquire as to their situation."

Isaiah stood motionless, a knot forming in his throat. "Georgia?" was all he could manage.

"Yeah, the man who bought them's from Augusta, but we won't know if that's where they are until we hear back from him."

"How far is Augusta from here, sir?"

"A couple hundred miles, about half as far as from here to Charlottesville."

"Yes sir. Thank you, sir. This is the first good news I've had in a very long time."

"Now the second piece of news. Colonel Love has arranged for you and Ellen to go work for his nephew, Thomas Love, on his farm over near Franklin, about forty miles from here. The Colonel has promised to follow up on your family and send word to you by way of his nephew."

"Is Colonel Love not happy with my work?"

"On the contrary. He's very close to his nephew and would only send him someone he had confidence in. I worked with Thomas Love before. We helped him with his barn raisin' years back. He's a good man and won't mistreat you if you behave as you have here, and the Colonel'll keep working on finding your family."

"How many Negroes does Mr. Thomas own?"

"None to my knowledge; I believe you'll be the first. Now finish up here and get your things together. I want to get ya'll on the road before the day gets away."

Isaiah returned to the wheel with his mind racing. He had word of Anne and Susan, although they were hundreds of miles away from him. He knew nothing about Augusta, but his whole life overseers had threatened him and the other slaves with being "sold south," so the knowledge that they were somewhere in Georgia, maybe on one of the big cotton plantations, filled him with dread. And now he was being moved yet again, to a place he had never heard of, to work for a new master under unknown conditions.

They set out early in the afternoon in a wagon loaded with a few supplies and the human cargo. Isaiah and Ellen sat across from one another, chained to side rails, as the wagon bounced along the often-rutted road. Twenty years old, a shy, pretty girl who talked little, Ellen had come south with Isaiah and the other two men from Monticello. She was the youngest child of Rachael, a friend of Isaiah's mother, Mary, and Isaiah had known her since she was a toddler. The two had rarely spoken over the years, given the difference in their ages, though they had grown closer since they had gotten to the Love farm. She sat now, looking over Isaiah's shoulder into the passing forest, her mind lost in her own thoughts. Isaiah attempted to speak to her a couple of times, but Wright, the wagon driver, told him to keep quiet, so they all spent the time in silence. Ten miles outside Franklin, the wagon hit a deep rut in the red clay road and lurched to one side, almost throwing Ellen off backwards. Wright stopped to assess the situation, found they had damaged the right front wheel, and let fly an avalanche of profanity.

"Get down here, Isaiah!" he yelled as he unlocked the chain releasing him from the wagon. "Don't get any damn ideas either. Take a look at this and tell me if you think we can fix it."

Isaiah studied the wheel and made his determination. "Look like the lynchpin is bent or broke. I'll need to get the wheel off to see if I can fix it.

Gonna be a job either way. We need to ease it down this slope here where we can get it flat enough to get somethin' under the axle, a log maybe."

As the afternoon shadows lengthened, they worked to get the wagon to a flat part of the road. They used a wooden box and the side slats from the wagon to get the wheel off, and Isaiah began repairing it. Wright had Ellen start a fire and prepare a supper from the supplies they had on hand. As darkness approached, Isaiah informed them he was finished, but he wasn't sure how long it would last, and that he didn't recommend trying to go on in the dark. Wright let loose with another string of cuss words and set about making camp for the night. After they had eaten, Wright chained Isaiah to a tree and Ellen to the back of the wagon and told them to get to sleep and that they would be off at first light.

Isaiah lay on the cold, hard ground and marveled yet again at the depth and magnitude of his circumstances. As the fire died down, he drifted off to sleep. He woke with a start sometime later, disoriented, stiff, and cold. The fire was out now and the darkness was impenetrable. Some sharp sound had awoken him, some animal taken by a predator in the forest, a rabbit perhaps. He lay still and tried to see into the darkness, shivering from the cold, damp dew. He heard it again and tried to pinpoint its location. It sounded twenty or thirty yards away, on the other side of the wagon from him. Had Wright and Ellen heard it? He debated whether he should call to them when he heard it a third time, followed quickly by the unmistakable sound of a sharp slap and a woman's cry. "Ellen?" he called and pulled at his chains to no avail. "Isaiah!" came the response, followed by another slap and the muffled sound of struggle. "Ellen?" No response but the jingle of chains. Isaiah pulled at his own chains until he felt them cut into his hands and warm blood flow down his arms. "Ellen!" No response but a whimper. Isaiah was crying now, the tears flowing down his cheeks, his muscles taut with contorted rage. "Anne!"

After a few minutes, the sounds had stopped altogether. Isaiah lay motionless at the base of the tree, wondering if Ellen was dead. He heard footsteps approaching him, and a moment later he felt a blinding pain and the air rush out of him as he was kicked in the gut. He curled into a ball, trying to protect his head and ribs from the blows he expected. Instead, as he struggled to get his breath, he felt Wright looming over him. "Shut your mouth or I'll kick your goddam teeth in. If you know what's good for you, you'll go back to sleep and pretend you had a bad dream. One word of this from you and you'll regret you were ever born." Isaiah felt him move away, and he lay there thinking, "I already regret ever being born."

CHAPTER 5

May 24, 1829

Tom was on his back with Sarah beside him, her head on his shoulder and her leg draped over his. Her long blond hair fanned across his chest and shoulders and tickled his nose, and he breathed in the smell that always reminded him of freshly cut hay. They had made love quietly in the gray light as the sun was just coming up, careful not to wake the children snoring on the other side of the loft. Tom traced meaningless patterns across her back with his finger, touching her ever so lightly, tickling her the way she liked. Outside, a rooster shattered the early morning peace, announcing the new day.

"I'd better get breakfast started," Sarah whispered, as she heard the children rustle.

"Just a few more minutes," Tom replied and lifted her chin to kiss her on the forehead.

"If I must," Sarah said and snuggled in tighter. "I'll stay here all day if you ain't careful."

"That'd be nice, wouldn't it? What would we tell the kids though?"

"I'll think of somethin'," she said, and she laughed with the little giggle that sounded like bells tinkling. "This is the first time we've made love since . . ." Her voice trailed off too late as she realized she had broken the spell. The incessant rooster held forth again.

"That cain't be, can it?" Tom's mind raced through the last few months in a single moment. "I'm sorry, Sarah."

Sarah propped herself on her elbow and looked into Tom's eyes. "Nothin' to be sorry for. Just never leave me again, even in your mind."

"I promise," he said, and he kissed her forehead and then her lips as the rooster crowed a third time. "Up and at 'em, I guess. I hope we get some rain today."

Tom was standing in the vegetable garden in the morning sun, leaning on the end of the hoe handle and stretching his back as the sweat ran down his brow, when he saw the wagon emerge from the woods headed up the drive towards the house. He walked down the row he had been working, stopping to attack a protruding shoot of poke salad he had missed on the way. He arrived in front of the house at the same time as the wagon and recognized one of his Uncle Robert's hired men driving. Racking his brain, he finally came up with the surname. "Mr. Wright, good day to you."

"And good day to you, Mr. Love," Wright responded and stepped down from the driver's seat. As he did so Tom for the first time noticed the two people seated in the back of the wagon, opposite one another, their heads bowed, and Tom realized who they were. "Colonel Love sends his regards. Here's the two Negroes I believe you was expectin', 'long with some stores the Colonel thought you might need. I intended to be here yesterday evening, but had some trouble with the wagon wheel and had to stop for the night to make repairs. The Colonel wanted you to have the loan of the wagon as well for the duration of the job you're undertakin'. I'm to leave one mule and return to Waynesville on the other. The Colonel also asked me to give you this letter. Where you want me to put the stores?"

"In the barn over yonder for now," Tom said, taking the letter.

"Isaiah, Ellen, out of the wagon!" Wright shouted. "Start unloading the stores into the barn there. Master Tom'll show you where to put 'em?"

"Yes, yes . . . the first stall on the right I use for storage. Put 'em in there."

Isaiah and Ellen climbed out and lifted the first of the several boxes from the wagon, their chains rattling with their efforts. As they started towards the barn, Tom moved closer to Wright and asked in a whisper, "Are the chains necessary?"

"Yes sir, I'd keep 'em secured for the time bein'."

"My uncle said they were submissive."

"I'm sure that'll prove to be the case, sir, but it's been my experience that until you have shown 'em who's boss, there's always the risk of an . . . unforeseen situation. I'd take no chances until you have taken their full measure. It's hard to tell how they'll react to changed circumstances."

Tom felt the hair on the back of his neck stand up. "Yes, of course."

"Well, Mr. Love, I hate to run, but I need to get back to Waynesville as soon as possible. The Colonel'll be expectin' me." He began unharnessing the mules.

"Of course. Before you go, have they eaten yet this morning?"

"We ate a quick breakfast while breaking camp."

Tom nodded and looked up as Isaiah returned to the wagon for the next box of supplies and made eye contact with him for the first time. They looked at each other until Isaiah lifted the box and turned back towards the barn. Ellen was right behind him and the exchange repeated with her. Tom stood leaning on his hoe, as the three people completed their tasks, his mind whirling as he tried to grasp the magnitude of what was transpiring. As he stood there, he felt himself being observed, and he turned to see Sarah staring out the front door, watching the scene unfold. Their eyes locked and a multitude of thoughts, questions, and concerns flashed between them as they read each other's mind across the yard. Sarah finally pushed the door closed. Tom turned his gaze back to the wagon and realized both Isaiah and Ellen had caught the exchange with Sarah. Tom flushed and turned to look at Wright, who was leading the mule. "There's cool water in the springhouse over yonder. Help yourselves," he said, as Wright stopped in front of him. When Isaiah and Ellen were out of earshot, Wright spoke.

"Mr. Love, when we stopped last night, things got a little out of hand. It was just me with the two of 'em broke down on the road. I thought the girl was tryin' to run off at one point and tackled her. Turns out she was just getting away from the wagon to relieve herself. The male got agitated and hurt his hands on the manacles. I don't know if they'll say anything, but I wanted you to hear it from me. Negroes like to tell tall tales sometimes." He diverted his gaze to follow Isaiah and Ellen as they made their way down the little path. "Here's the key to the manacles."

"Thank you for informing me, Mr. Wright. Please pass along my regards to my uncle."

"I will, sir, and best of luck to you," With that he mounted the mule and started back down the drive. Tom watched him go and wondered about the story he had been told.

Isaiah and Ellen knelt in the shadows of the springhouse and washed their hands and faces in the cool, clear water. They had not spoken since the horror of the past night and had ridden in silence the last few miles of their journey, Ellen refusing to look at Isaiah the entire way.

"I'm so sorry, Ellen. I wanted to help you but couldn't. Are you alright?" He put his hand on her shoulder. She jerked away at his touch and he realized she was crying.

"No, I'm not alright!" she hissed. "I miss my momma and daddy and my sisters and friends. I don't know where they are or where I am! I'm alone in this wilderness and I cain't defend myself against monsters like that man. I wanna go home. I'm scared! I want to see my momma!" She lay down on the damp stones and sobbed.

Isaiah tried to comfort her. "Shh, child, you gotta git holt of yourself. We don't know what these people are like or what Wright told him. I ain't your family, but I'm all you got for now. We'll have to hold one another up till we figure out how things stand. I'll protect you as best I can, but we have to put on a brave face till we get the lay of the land here. Can you do that, Ellen?"

She pushed herself up and nodded to him in the shadows, wiping away tears. He handed her a gourd with some water and told her to drink, which she did. He patted her shoulder as she drank and caught her breath from the sobbing. "Are your hands alright?" she asked.

Isaiah looked down at his raw wrists, the abrasions clear now that the dried blood and dust were washed off. He said, "I'm fine. This ain't nothin'," and he recalled the weeks of agony after the whipping at Monticello.

"You two alright in there?" came a voice from outside, echoing off the stone interior.

"Yes sir, we comin' out now." Isaiah helped Ellen up, and they bent over as they stepped out of the darkness into the bright light.

Tom stood there holding his hoe like a staff and looked them over. "My name's Thomas Love. This is my farm. My wife Sarah and I have worked this place by ourselves for years. We have three . . . two children, James and Julia." Tom paused, before continuing. "I've never had servants before, so this'll take some gettin' used to. There's a lot of work to do here, and I expect you'll pull your weight. Do that and follow my instructions, I can promise you'll not be mistreated. Any questions?"

Isaiah bowed his head and shook it almost imperceptibly.

"Was there somethin' you wanted to say, Isaiah?" Tom dipped his own head, trying to make eye contact with Isaiah. Isaiah lifted his chin in a show of defiance and glared at Tom.

"Well sir, every master, every overseer I ever known has give the same speech: if we just mind and work everything'll be okay, and we'll be treated well."

"You been mistreated?"

"Well sir, I been worked like a barnyard animal since I was a boy old enough to walk. I been hit, kicked, and whooped worse than any dog ever was. Been fed slop, denied water when I was thirsty, forced to sleep in quarters no better'n a outhouse, froze in winter, burnt up in hot summer, separated from my ma and pa and now from my wife and child. Yes sir, I'd say I been mistreated."

They stood there for a long time, neither of them speaking, looking into one another's eyes, searching for something, neither of them willing to be the first to break their gaze, to show anything that could be misconstrued as weakness. Finally, Ellen broke the spell. "Where we gonna stay?"

Tom twisted the hoe in his hands and paused a minute before looking away from Isaiah and turning his attention to Ellen. "Well, that's an issue. We'll get to work on a cabin soon as possible. Until then, you'll stay in the barn."

"With the other livestock, sir?" said Isaiah, and Tom turned to look at him again.

"Just one cabin, sir?" Ellen interrupted once more.

"You two cain't share a cabin?"

"That won't be proper, sir. Me and Ellen ain't married, and I got a wife and child."

"You mentioned that. Where are they?"

"Colonel Robert was helping to find 'em for me. We was separated at Monticello and sold to different people. Before we was brought here, Colonel Robert said he had tracked 'em to Augusta, Georgia, and promised to keep looking for 'em till he finds 'em. Only thing I ask in this life is to be with 'em again. If they's anything you can do to help me, I'd be grateful."

"This is all news to me. My uncle didn't mention any of this. I assumed that you and Ellen were together. Give me some time on this. In the meantime, we'll get you somethin' to eat. You'll have to make the best of the arrangements in the barn until we can get cabins up."

"Yes sir. What about these?" Isaiah lifted his hands in front of him, and the chains made a clanking sound that seemed to echo off the springhouse stones. Tom stared at them, remembering what Wright had said.

"Of course we shall remove them." Sarah stood there, her face soft, her blue calico homespun dress covered in part by a white apron. The May sunlight on her blond hair gave it the color of golden wheat. "I'm Sarah. We're glad to have you here. Tom, why don't you show . . . Isaiah, is it?"

"Yes ma'am."

"Show Isaiah around the farm. You're Ellen?"

"Yes ma'am," Ellen responded with a slight dip of her chin.

"Ellen, come with me and we'll get dinner together. Tom, get those chains off. Let's go, daylight's wastin'." She turned and started for the house.

Tom took the key from his pocket and unlocked Ellen's chains first. She hurried to catch Sarah, who was halfway across the yard. He then turned to Isaiah and looked at him again as he unlocked the manacles. "Don't make me regret this."

"I won't, Mr. Love. What good it do me to run? Where would I go? I don't even know where I am. Like I said, most important thing in the world is gittin' my family back, and I'm hopin' that 'tween you and Colonel Love, ya'll will help me."

Ellen followed Sarah into the cabin, where two children sat at a table, stringing and breaking shell beans.

"Hello," Ellen said in a soft voice. The children stared wide eyed and mumbled in response.

Sarah brought a bowl of potatoes and a small knife and placed them on the table in front of Ellen. "You worked in a kitchen before, Ellen?"

"Oh, yes ma'am. I worked in the kitchen back at Monticello some, and at Colonel Love's farm too."

"Good, then you peel and slice these taters for us. Don't slice 'em too thick."

"Yes ma'am, I mean, no ma'am," Ellen said, and she sat down at the table and picked up the knife and started peeling. Sarah moved around the cabin, getting the rest of the meal together. James and Julia stared furtively at Ellen as she tried her best not to acknowledge their gaze. Julia broke the awkward silence. "Why's yore skin so dark?"

"Julia!" Sarah turned to her, and Julia looked back and forth between her and Ellen.

"It's alright, ma'am. That's the way the good Lord made me, same as he gave you those pretty blue eyes," she said to Julia, who blushed at the compliment and squirmed.

"Your eyes are pretty too," she said, and then: "Can I touch your arm?"

"Julia!" Sarah exclaimed again.

"Of course you can, if I can touch yores." And she reached her arm across the table to the little girl, who stroked the top of Ellen's forearm.

"Now my turn." Ellen stroked the girl's arm with the back of her hand. "Well?"

"It's soft, it feels like Momma's."

"Can I feel too?" said James, who had been watching the exchange with amazement.

"Same deal?" she replied and placed her arm in front of the boy, who copied his sister's cautious touch.

Sarah stood at the end of the table watching the exchange. "You seem to be good with children, Ellen," she said at last.

"Yes ma'am. I was the oldest chile, so I was always watchin' my brothers and sisters while my momma workin'," she said as she pulled her arm back across the table.

A dozen questions raced across Sarah's mind. She was not one to beat around the bush. She still shocked Tom from time to time with how direct she could be, but she decided it best to go slowly and not push Ellen. She couldn't imagine what it must be like for the girl in this situation. "Well I could sure use help with these two," she said and turned back to her task, adding over her shoulder, "those beans and taters will not fix themselves." As she stood slicing green tomatoes, she whispered to herself, "Oh, Tom Love, what have you got us into?"

"This is a purty place you got," Isaiah said to Tom as they walked down the hill towards the bottomland, the rows of corn rippling like waves breaking towards the river below. "You clear and plant all this yoreself?"

"Most of the land was cleared by the Cherokee, who knows how long ago. There was a small village downriver where they set up fishin' weirs. Ruins are still there. I had some help from my uncle and some folks in town with the barn raisin'. Some neighbors helped with the cabins, but I built the spring-house, the corncrib, and the hog pens, stood up the little blacksmith shop over yonder." He pointed to a small building away from the house. "I make most of my tools there. Just the basics, mind you, hoes and claw hammers, and the like. I been making hinges, although that's a work in progress. I understand from my uncle that you've done some smithin'?"

"Yes sir. They put me to makin' nails at Monticello when I was just a boy. When I got a little older, they moved me to the big smithy. We made a lot of tools: wagons, barrels, plows. I learned a lot there."

"I've heard about Monticello since I was a boy. What was the president like?"

"He seemed a smart man. As he got older he got out less, spent more time in the big house with his books and drawin's and such. They was always people comin' and goin', visitin' him."

"Was he a kind man?"

They had reached the river and stood silently for a moment, watching the water flow. It had been a wet spring, and the river filled its banks and ran swiftly past them. A red-winged blackbird gripped the side of a long cattail on the far bank and greeted them with its loud trill, swaying in the breeze. Isaiah responded but chose his words carefully.

"I didn't have many direct dealin's with the president, to judge him that way. If he found fault with somethin' we was doin', he'd pull the overseer aside and talk real low to him. After he left, the overseer would let us know the president was unhappy, if you understand my meanin'?"

"Yeah, I do."

"He was more kind to some of his servants than others." Isaiah remembered James Hemings and Peter Fossett, and the privileges they enjoyed. "He weren't no mean man, from what I could tell. He'd smile and speak sometimes as he was making his rounds, ask you how you was doing. We learnt early not to complain to him if he asked, cause as soon as he gone, the overseer make it hard on you. Hard to say if the president was aware how they treated us. They was a lot of space between Mulberry Row, where we lived, and the big house."

"I've read that the president planted a variety of crops?"

"Oh, yes sir. He always plantin' new things, tryin' to see how they'd grow on the mountain. He's be out walkin' among the gardens and fields, inspectin' the plants, takin' measurements, writin' in his little books. I'll tell you though, man named Wormley Hughes was the one what made everything work. I swear ole Wormley could grow a stalk a corn out of a rock." Isaiah smiled at the memory of his friend and mentor. "President relied on him for just about everything at Monticello. Ole Wormley dug the president's grave when he passed. Wouldn't let nobody help him."

"He was a colored man?"

"Yes sir. We was sure the president would set ole Wormley free after all he done for him. Last I see'd Wormley he was watchin' his wife and youngun's sold off to different owners. Same day they sold me to Master Robert."

"Can we use any of what he did here?" Tom asked, changing the subject.

"I reckon so. We had fruit trees. Take cuttin's off one kind of tree and tie it up on another tree, *graftin'* my daddy heard it called. There was grapevines, but they didn't do well. President liked his wine, but could never make his own to his satisfaction. He had this idea about mixin' the crops in different fields each season. My daddy was told planting the same crop in the field every year wore out the soil, so we'd mix it up and let some fields rest for a season or two."

"Do you miss Monticello?"

"Only life I ever knew. They was hard times, and it was always hard work, sunup to sundown. But I was with my family and friends. We leaned on each other and lifted each other up when it got so you wanted to just give up and lay down, no matter what happened to you. More than anything I miss my wife and daughter."

"How did ya'll get separated?"

"They was punishin' me. All us slaves expected President Jefferson to free us when he died. Some house folks said they heard him talk about it with his family. I'd lay in bed after workin' in the fields all day and dream about what it'd be like when we was free. I dreamt about havin' a place like this, some place to call my own." Isaiah paused and looked around the farm with the green pastures and fields and the mountains towering in the distance. A breeze came down the valley, making little whitecaps on the river. It carried the sweet scent of sourwood trees blooming on the edge of the tree line. Over the next few minutes he related the story of his time at Monticello and how he came to be separated from his family.

"Daddy!" James stood at the top of the rise, shouting between cupped hands. "Momma says it's dinnertime and for ya'll to come and wash up to eat!" Tom waved, and James went back inside.

They started up the hill towards the house and a hot meal. As they walked, Isaiah surveyed the farm and the fields. He had learned much during his years at Monticello. What would he do if this was his farm? He noticed a small mound of red dirt and a flat stone beneath a copse of trees. "Somebody pass?"

Tom followed Isaiah's gaze to Rebecca's grave. "My oldest girl, Rebecca, died at Christmastime. She was nine years old."

"I'm sorry."

Tom looked at him and nodded without replying.

The letter from his uncle sat in Tom's lap, as he considered its implications. He picked it up and read it for the third time.

Dear Thomas,

Greetings and I trust this letter finds you, Sarah, and the children in good health and spirits.

I have sent the two servants Isaiah and Ellen to your care. I trust you will find them to be able workers. Isaiah seems to possess above average intelligence for a Negro and has mechanical skills he displayed on my farm. He may express agitation to you regarding a woman and child he claims are his family, who were sold to another owner around the time I acquired him. He has pressed the issue repeatedly, and I told him I would do what I could to locate them. After some investigation, I found that a slave broker from Augusta, Georgia, purchased them. I sent correspondence to his attention but have received no reply to date. I will advise you if I should gain additional information. However, I'm not sure there is much we can do even if we are able to locate them. It is never my intention to separate families if avoidable, and while it is not my responsibility to affect a reunion, as a Christian I will make some effort to restore them if it is economically feasible.

I expect to call on Beverly Daniel in a few weeks in Raleigh, and I'll let him know you agreed to serve on the census. Any details I can gather as to the planned meeting he mentioned holding this autumn, I will pass along. I dropped in on your parents on my way home. They send their love.

In addition to the servants, I took the liberty of sending provisions to help you through the next few weeks. I also instructed Wright to leave the wagon and one of the mules for your use. In one of the boxes you will find a fiddle a friend recently gave me as a gift. Unfortunately, my fiddle-playing days are past, but I hoped you might take it up. I realize some of the music has gone out of your life with the loss of our poor dear Rebecca. No instrument can ever replace the pure, sweet strains of her beautiful voice, but hopefully when we're together again, your home will be filled with music, with you playing the fiddle and Sarah on her harp.

Until then, I am, your loving uncle, Robert.

Tom dropped his hands with the letter to his lap and looked out towards the river, not focusing on anything in particular, his mind wrestling with his uncle's words. He felt a hand on his shoulder and jerked out of his reverie to find Sarah standing beside him.

"You gotta stop sneakin' up on me!"

"Don't take much sneakin', you're so distracted these days. What's that you're readin'?"

She took the chair beside him and he summarized the contents of the letter. He watched her expression tighten and then soften. She laid her head back against the rocker, and let her gaze dissolve on the horizon. She sat like that for a long time, as he waited for her reaction. He wasn't sure what to expect. Without looking at him, she spoke.

"Tom, we're now responsible for two people we didn't know from Adam and Eve yesterday. Isaiah must be heartbroken if this is true about his wife and child, and Ellen is hurtin' too, and scared. God knows I would be."

"I know. I cain't imagine bein' separated from you and James and Julia."

She turned to look at him now. "You cain't make them sleep in the barn, Tom. It smells like manure and the flies are terrible. James claims there was a black racer on the back side when he was fetching water yesterday."

"What am I supposed to do?"

"I'll make up pallets for 'em in the kitchen."

"Sarah, don't be ridiculous. We cain't have 'em sleeping in the house!"

"Listen to me, Tom Love. You made this decision and I'm tryin' to live with it. They ain't animals, and if they're gonna stay on this farm, they're gonna be treated like humans or you can turn 'em loose right now."

"I'll treat them as best as I can, but they ain't sleeping in the kitchen where we eat! The corncrib is empty and we'll make 'em pallets out there, or they can sleep here on the porch. I'll start on the cabins tomorrow."

Sarah glared at him before storming into the house, slamming the door behind her. Tom propped his foot up on the porch rail and leaned the rocker back, closing his eyes. He heard a humming and opened his eyes to see a hummingbird hovering in front of the red bee balm Sarah had planted at the corner of the porch. He watched it flit from blossom to blossom until it must have had its fill and zoomed off towards the fields.

Isaiah and Ellen stood in the vegetable garden, hoeing weeds as Tom had directed them after their meal.

"What did Mr. Love say to you when ya'll was lookin' around?"

"He asked 'bout President Jefferson and Monticello. We talked farmin'. I told him 'bout Anne and Susan. They had a little girl die a while back. That's her grave yonder."

"You didn't tell about that man Wright and what happened, did you?"

"No, course not. What did you and the missus talk about?"

"We didn't talk much. She seemed nice enough. The children seem well behaved."

"They got a nice place here."

"The mountains are purty and it ain't too awful hot. They don't seem likely to whoop us much, you reckon?"

"Too early to tell. You never can tell what'll set a White man off, but he don't seem too harsh. Does she seem like a hard mistress?"

"I'm like you, too early. She's a strong woman though, and I don't want to cross her if I don't have to."

They hoed for a while in silence, making their way down the long row. Ellen was the first to speak again. "They seemed to think we was a pair, Isaiah."

"I set it straight."

Ellen stopped her work and looked at Isaiah. "You love and miss Anne. I hope to God you and her and Susan are reunited soon. But you a man and men got needs. I don't care what the Loves think or what you think, but I don't want no man, do you hear?"

"Ellen, I ain't . . ."

"Just listen. It ain't about you. Wright weren't the first man to force hisself on me. They was men at Monticello mistreated me too. The main thing is I don't want to have no children. I cain't bear to bring another soul into this world to be a slave and go through what I been through and then have 'em taken from me. I cain't do that." And she bowed her head on the hoe handle.

Isaiah put his hand on her shoulder and waited until she composed herself. "I know, Ellen. I'd never take advantage of you that way. We'll just be friends, and when Anne gits here, we'll all be better for it. All we got for now is each other."

CHAPTER 6

May 25, 1829

EARLY THE NEXT day, Tom and Isaiah started working on building the cabins. Tom had cut timber the previous year, clearing the land for future fields and firewood. He laid aside a good quantity of white oak logs he planned to either sell or use for other building projects. They were sufficiently dry to be usable now, and the two men set about sorting the best ones.

"You cut all this yourself, Mr. Tom?" Isaiah asked after they worked up a good sweat.

"Yep, over several weeks. It was winter and early spring though, so I didn't get as hot as we will today."

Tom and Isaiah both stood just under six feet tall, and both of them were lean and strong from years of hard work. They talked little as the morning progressed, rolling and lifting the heavy oak logs into piles, sorting them by length and circumference. By the time they counted out enough for two small cabins, they were both lathered in sweat. After a brief rest, Tom picked up a two-man crosscut saw and asked Isaiah if he ever used one. Isaiah laughed and said too many times to count. With that, they began cutting the logs into uniform lengths.

Hour after hour they sawed the hard oak, each push and pull of the blade a separate contest. As they worked, the two men took measure of one another. Tom had worked with many men over the years: other settlers as they joined their labor to carve out a piece of the wilderness, his neighbors as they cut roads through the mountains of the new county. Few men ever outworked him. As Isaiah bent his back to the task, Tom watched the muscles ripple in his arms and recognized that Isaiah's strength matched his own. Isaiah too had worked with many men, but never a White man. He was accustomed to the master sauntering across the fields inspecting the progress of the slave's work, and to the overseer breathing down his neck, ready with the whip if he deemed his efforts insufficient. But like Tom, he now recognized the strength of the man across from him. And so they labored, neither wanting to be the first to slow down or exhibit fatigue, their pace quickening rather than slowing with their exertions. They didn't stop until they cut the last log. They stood panting, their hands blistered, their arms and backs aching. The sun was now straight overhead and the late May heat baked them. Isaiah stepped into the shade of an ancient elm tree and took off his shirt to cool down. When he turned to get some water, Tom inhaled sharply through clenched teeth at the sight of his scarred back, making a hissing noise that drew Isaiah's attention.

"Does it look that bad? I cain't see it."

"They did that to you just for hollerin'?" Tom asked, incredulous.

"Yes sir. However bad it looks, it hurt worse. I nigh on died, they told me. It still hurts when I stretch."

"You pulled that crosscut alright. Is it bothering you now?"

"No sir, not bad."

"Sarah's got some balm she makes out of onions and honey. Smells like hell but seems to work. We'll get you some after dinner. Let's get to notching the logs."

The sound of axes echoed across the valley as they notched the stout oak logs. As Tom rolled a log from the pile, he saw Isaiah raise his axe over his head and move towards him. Tom raised his arm, turned his head and closed his eyes in reflex, his heart stopping. A rush of air brushed his cheek as the axe whistled past his head and the ground thumped beside him. He opened his eyes, a brown shape writhing on the ground a yard from his feet, the axe anchored in the ground, bisecting the thrashing form.

"Copperhead, Mr. Tom! 'Bout gotcha!"

Tom stepped back and put his hands on his knees, letting out a long breath. He watched the copperhead continue to coil and uncoil in its paroxysm of death. It was over three feet long, with a thick body.

"Sarah always says, 'If it was a snake it would've bit ya.' Thank you, Isaiah."

"Did you think I was about to hit you with the axe?"

Tom stood full up and took another breath before answering. "It was just reflexes."

"We best be careful. They's liable to be a nest of 'em."

Tom picked up the back half of the now-still snake and let it hang straight before throwing it off away from their work area.

"Watch the head. They say they can still bite fer a spell after they're struck."

"I've heard the same." Tom took his axe and struck the head one good time before flinging it away.

They continued to notch the logs as the sun slid behind the mountains. Tom replayed the image of Isaiah coming towards him with the axe over and over, while he maneuvered the logs, expecting another copperhead to appear any moment.

As summer approached, the inhabitants of the farm in the mountains grew more accustomed to one another. The men alternated their labor between raising the cabins and clearing the new fields, which included cutting firewood from the downed trees for winter. Tom calculated the amount of wood needed to get them through the cold months and how much to cut and split each day to build the reserve. The women spent their days tending the garden, gathering and preserving food, and preparing meals for the family. The children fed and watered the livestock, gathered eggs, and churned the milk into butter. Everyone spent a couple of hours in the fields hoeing weeds and "cultivating" the rows. Isaiah and Ellen expected their labors to last from sunup to sundown, as they had their entire lives, and they were surprised that after supper, their toils were generally over for the day.

The Loves spent most evenings on the porch, reading to their children while the light lasted, watching the lightning bugs come out as the shadows lengthened, listening to the sounds of the mountain evening. Crickets provided the chorus, accompanied by tree frogs and eventually the big croaking bullfrogs down by the river. The red-winged blackbirds kept up a steady trill as they jockeyed back and forth among the cattails. A squadron of barn swallows, which nested in the barn, came out every evening and provided an aerial show as they performed acrobatics a few feet above the ground, catching mosquitoes and gnats. There was usually a covey of quail calling and answering across the fields, and they were invariably joined by a whip-poor-will as dusk approached. This summer a mating pair of barred owls made a nest on the other side of the river, and the family listened intently as they called to one another. James spied the male one evening in the top of a dead poplar at the pasture edge. They stared at one another, neither of them moving, until the owl grew bored, spread his mighty wings, and disappeared into the woods.

Some evenings the Loves would make their own music. Sarah would pull on the harp and sing old songs her mother taught her. Tom tried to master the fiddle his uncle had given him. He hadn't played in years, but it came back to him in fits and starts. The children begged for their favorites and sang along as best they could. James asked his mother to play "Blue Eye'd Mary." She exchanged glances with Tom and then started the sweet, sad song Rebecca sang so many times. She made it through most of the first verse, but her voice failed her as her throat tightened and she trailed off quietly.

For the first few weeks, Isaiah and Ellen spent their evenings alone together. They walked and talked about their childhoods and their families and tried to focus on the pleasant memories of Monticello. One evening Sarah asked them to join the family on the porch. Everyone was uncomfortable until the music began. Sarah asked Ellen if she knew any good songs. She tried to beg off, but Isaiah spoke up: "Sing 'In that Great Gettin' Up Morning,' Ellen. I heard you sing that back at Monticello." The Loves all chimed in, encouraging her. Finally she relented, but on the condition that Isaiah sing the "Fare ye well" response, to which he agreed.

She took a moment to compose herself, and then, in a voice that was clear and strong, Ellen sang the opening of the old spiritual: "Well, in that great gettin' up morning!"

Isaiah responded in a deep baritone, "Fare ye well, Fare ye well," and for the next several minutes the pair performed as many verses of the song as they could remember. It had been longer than either of them could remember since they last sang, and they poured their hearts into it. The Loves sat mesmerized listening to them perform until Julia joined Isaiah in the response. Tom picked her up from the porch floor and sat her in his lap, holding her close, and then he too joined Isaiah in the next chorus. Sarah and James followed, until it sounded like a camp-meeting choir, their voices carrying and echoing across the valley. When Ellen could recall no more of the verses, she dropped her voice to a near whisper, signaling Isaiah to bring the song to an end. When the last "fare ye well" was sung, the group sat quietly. The birds and insects seemed to have stopped their own songs to listen, and the farm was quiet. A rooster behind the house crowed, shattering the stillness. "Let's sing it again!" Julia said.

"I'm sorry, I cain't sing that song no more." Ellen dropped her head and examined the detail of the calico dress Sarah had given her. Julia dropped her head as well, unsure what she said to put a damper on the evening's festivities.

The Love farm was not a plantation. It didn't have an impressive name like Jefferson's Monticello or Jackson's Hermitage. There was no stately drive arriving at a columned mansion, no overseer or Mulberry Row, no whipping post. A rutted lane through a primeval forest led to a clearing, sheltering a modest farm with hand-built cabins and outbuildings. Four people, living and working side by side, struggled each day to make sure there was food to eat, roofs over their heads, and a warm fire when the winter winds blew cold. Neither Isaiah nor Ellen labored under any misconception, however. They were not partners in this enterprise. Tom and Sarah were not cruel masters, but they were masters nevertheless. That four people, isolated in their wilderness enclave, might be humane to one another, and manufacture moments of pleasure from a harsh existence, did not diminish the unrelenting trauma endured by Isaiah and Ellen. Separated from their loved ones and facing a future of hard labor for someone else's benefit, they knew that their situation was tenuous, and their lives could be uprooted again without warning.

By the end of June, Tom and Isaiah had finished the two cabins, faster than either of them would have thought possible. They were small but well built, each with its own short porch, two windows for ventilation, and a fireplace. Isaiah built rope beds and a table and two chairs for each cabin, impressing Tom with his carpentry skills. As the two captives lay in their separate cabins the first night, they both realized how alone they were, and sleep took a long time coming.

The next morning Ellen woke up sick to her stomach and went outside to throw up. Weak all day, she thought she was going to pass out tending the garden in the midsummer sun. Sarah sent her into the kitchen cabin to cool off and start getting supper ready. She felt better by mealtime but only picked at her food. She woke the next day and was sick again. On her way to start breakfast, she met Sarah coming from the outhouse. She was pale and her brow glistened with sweat. "I think you gimme your illness," she said to Ellen as they drew close.

"I'm sorry, ma'am. I ain't never had nothin' like this. Do you think it's some kind of fever? I ain't hot or got any shivers, just sick at my stomach."

Sarah stopped and turned to look at Ellen, who stopped as well. "When was your time of the month?"

"I . . . I don't remember. Ain't thought about it with everything going on. Guess it must have been around the middle of May." Then she realized: the terrible night on the road to the farm; the beast holding her down on the hard ground, his stinking breath in her face. "It cain't be!" And she put her hands to her throat in horror.

Sarah put her arm around her and they walked back to her cabin in the early morning light. They sat at the small table and Ellen told her the whole lurid story between half-muffled sobs. Sarah listened patiently, patting her hand, trying to soothe her. "Missus Love, I don't want this baby. I don't want no baby but I shore don't want that monster's baby inside me! I would rather die myself than have it! What can I do?"

"I understand, and I'd feel the same way. But they ain't nothin' to do but bear it. God'll help you find a way. I'm pregnant too. We got morning sickness, and it's liable to stick around for a spell." She remembered the night Tom made love to her after so many months, how happy and content she had been lying in his arms afterwards. Now she would have another child, and the realization gave her a rush of joy. She put her hand on her stomach, then looked at Ellen and her emotions plunged from joy to guilt and sorrow. She would welcome a new life into the world, the product of her love for her husband, while this poor child, barely a woman, would be forced to bring a life into the world from the most horrific circumstances, with no husband to share the load or lean on. "I'm sorry, Ellen. If you hadn't been brought here, you wouldn't have been at the mercy of that vile man and be in this condition."

"I don't blame you, Missus Love; you and Mr. Tom been kind to me and Isaiah since we come here. It ain't you personal, it's this whole thing. That man weren't the first White man to force hisself on me. As long as we property to be used, this be our lot. That's why I want no babies. I never wanted to bring another poor soul into this condition."

Sarah sat stunned. "You're right, but you must listen to me. You cain't be talkin' that way in front of any White people. It's dangerous. I don't know by what power our lives have come to be crossed this way, but as much as it's in my power, I mean to see no further harm comes to you, or to the baby you bring into the world, understand?"

"Yes ma'am."

"Now let's get cleaned up and get food on the table. We're gonna have to work hard while we can to get ready for two new mouths to feed around here."

Sarah and Tom argued for the better part of the evening. His elation about the news of another child turned to frustration and anger when he learned of Ellen's plight.

"Sarah, I'm sorry that happened to her, but it doesn't change anything."

"My God, Tom, I never imagined us being in such a predicament! Why did you ever agree to this?"

Tom hesitated a long time before responding. "I don't know, Sarah. I've thought about it every day since they got here. It was one thing when Uncle Robert proposed it. It's been something else since we've been with them every day for two months. Isaiah's worked as hard as I have. I would be bitter as hell, and maybe he is down deep, but he doesn't show it. Same's true for Ellen. Maybe there is something at work here we cain't see yet."

Summer rolled slowly through the mountains, and life for the inhabitants of the Love farm fell into rhythm: up with the sun every day, each attending to their separate chores in the cool of the morning. They worked the fields until the midday heat drove them out, when they would share dinner under the shade of one of the enormous maple trees, and tell stories or laugh about the day's events. The adults would tease the children about their fear of the honeybees droning in the tassels of the tall corn while they cowered below picking pole beans. Isaiah taught James to catch June bugs and tie string around their back legs, then watch as they flew in circles around his head at the end of their tether. Julia would try to join in, but she couldn't stand the scratching of the insects' barbed legs as they struggled to escape, and would always let them go before they could be harnessed. Tom would fashion small dolls out of corn husks tied together in knots and give them to Julia to pacify her, and she would entertain herself with elaborately imagined tea parties.

Nature bestowed her blessings in profusion that summer in their valley. The rains were regular, and the crops flourished. Every outbuilding was bulging with drying vegetables and grains, and the final harvest was still to come in. The livestock were fat and bred prolifically. They would have several hogs to slaughter in the autumn, as well as one of the cattle. At Isaiah's suggestion, Tom bartered one of his Hereford bulls for several sheep from one of his neighbors, and after the initial shearing, they spent days washing and working the raw wool. Both Isaiah and Ellen had worked with wool at Monticello, and they walked the Loves through carding and combing the fibers to prepare for spinning and weaving. Sarah reckoned they would have enough to make warm winter clothes with enough left over to barter or sell in Franklin. Isaiah's proficiency in the blacksmith shop was impressive, and he turned out new tools for use around the farm and some destined for the market. They repaired and upgraded the farming equipment, including the wagons and plows. With each passing day Tom came to depend more and more on Isaiah, wondering how he ever managed the farm by himself.

Every day Isaiah worked as though it were his farm. Every night he lay down alone in his silent cabin and thought of Anne and Susan. The ache in his heart never subsided. With each passing day, Sarah and Ellen watched their bellies grow with the new lives inside them. Sarah, knowing what to expect, tried to encourage Ellen, but Ellen could only think of the violence of the rape and fear the ordeal of delivery so far from her mother and sisters. She witnessed childbirth at Monticello and heard the screams and knew women to die in its throes, and the fear haunted her dreams. She worked as hard as Isaiah all day, and when she lay down alone at night, she prayed she would lose the child in the darkness or that she would awake and find it had all been a nightmare.

CHAPTER 7

October 11, 1829

AUTUMN HAD ARRIVED, the days were shorter and cooler, and the mountains exploded in a blaze of color with the turning of the leaves. Tom sat on the porch on a clear, crisp Sunday morning gazing across the river, shimmering in the early sunlight, to the mountains in the distance. Red maples were in full color and they formed a tapestry of reds, oranges, and golds. The tulip poplars had already lost most of their dull yellow leaves, and the oaks had just started turning russet. Sumac lining part of the far riverbank was bright scarlet, with the red-winged blackbirds that had spent the summer on the cattails perched on their swaying branches. A flock of mallards floated down the river, bobbing and diving for food, until something startled them. With a burst of honking, a spray of water, and a flash of wings, they rose from the river surface as one and flew downstream just above water level. Just then Tom saw what had flushed them: a red-tailed hawk launched itself from the limb of an old loblolly pine and took off after them, disappearing around the bend of the river.

Tom held a cup of coffee in one hand, the beans purchased at the market in Franklin with proceeds from his successful trading the previous week, and a letter in the other. His Uncle Robert had written him, as promised, although the correspondence had taken several days to make the journey from Waynesville to Franklin. Such was the frontier postal system. Tom had read it multiple times now and was absorbing its contents while he enjoyed the coffee and the beautiful morning.

Dear Thomas,

I hope this correspondence finds you and yours in good health and spirits. All are well here and send their regards. The harvest this year was plentiful and Providence continues to spread its blessings on us, as I hope it has on your family as well.

Beverly Daniel has confirmed to me that he is holding meetings starting the first week of November to deputize the deputy marshals and provide instruction and materials necessary for the administration of the census next year. He selected the time assuming the harvests would be in and hog killing would not have started. He has decided to hold meetings in different towns around the state because of the distances involved. The meeting for the western counties will be in Morganton on November 3rd. I would be happy to accompany you and make the initial introduction and assist you in posting the bond. Unless I hear otherwise, I shall expect you here on or about November 1st. That should allow us adequate time to get to Morganton for the meeting.

In addition, I have finally received a reply from the slave dealer in Augusta regarding the family of your man Isaiah. He has indicated that the woman and child were sold with several others to a plantation in Anderson, SC to a Mr. Benjamin Jordan. There were no other details. I have sent a letter to this gentleman confirming his possession of the people and am awaiting his response. Perhaps some arrangement can be made that is satisfactory. I will advise when and if I receive a reply.

Very warmest regards, Robert

He played out the various issues in his head. What would he need for the trip, what would Sarah think about him going away for days, and what should he tell Isaiah about his family? He folded the letter and placed it in his pocket and held the warm cup between both hands. He thought about what a difference a year could make. Last October his life had seemed so simple. Now Rebecca was gone, Sarah was carrying a new child, he had two slaves living on his farm, and he was about to travel to Morganton to take on a responsibility he could only imagine.

"What will my life look like this time next year?" He realized he said this out loud.

The coffee cup was empty now, and he could put off the responsibilities of the day no longer, but the rocking chair held him in its grasp as the minutes ticked away. He did not want to leave this spot, didn't want to face the responsibilities just yet. The red-tailed hawk had reappeared, circling above the river, riding the rising columns of air ever higher, its pursuit of the mallards having apparently failed. He was jealous of the hawk, envied its freedom, and wondered what the world looked like from up there in the clear blue sky.

Isaiah was watching the hawk as well. He worried about the chickens scratching around in the yard between the cabins. They seemed oblivious to the threat the raptor posed as they focused all their attention on the grain Isaiah threw out to them. "Good morning, Mr. Tom," he said as Tom made his way across the yard, scattering the chickens as he waded through them.

"Good mornin', Isaiah. I hope you rested well?"

"Yes sir, tolerable well, and you?"

"Fine, thank you, just enjoyin' this beautiful mornin'," Tom responded, pausing before breaking the news. "I got a letter from my uncle yesterday, Isaiah. He believes he has located your wife and daughter."

Isaiah stood motionless, his mouth open, the revelation exploding in his mind. "Oh my God! Where are they?"

"They were delivered to a man in Anderson, South Carolina. My uncle sent him a letter to confirm it. He's waitin' for a reply. I think we're close, Isaiah."

"Where is Anderson?"

"About halfway between here and Columbia."

"How far from here?"

"A long way, Isaiah . . . over a hundred miles."

"What's the man's name what has 'em?"

"My uncle didn't say," Tom lied. "I'm going to meet him on my way to a meeting in a few days, and I'll find out. Hopefully he'll have a reply to his letter by then. We just need to be patient until we get all the information."

"Patient, Mr. Tom? I ain't seen my wife and child for nigh on a year. How patient you be if it was Miss Sarah and James and Julia?"

"I'm tryin' to understand how you feel, and I'm doing my best to remedy the situation. We're getting closer, believe me."

"What are we gonna do if the man in South Carolina has 'em?"

"We're goin' to offer to buy 'em from him, my uncle and me."

"What if he don't want to sell?"

"We'll have to cross that bridge if we come to it. There's no point in speculatin' about worst cases right now."

Isaiah's expression was one of incredulity. "You'll excuse me, sir, but I've been livin' worst cases my whole life. If he won't sell 'em, you must sell me to him. We'll be back together that way."

"Isaiah, we may be talkin' about one of those big cotton plantations. You don't want to go there."

An image of Anne working in a big cotton field, sweat rolling down her face, mixed with tears, an overseer standing over her with a whip in his hand, flashed in front of Isaiah, and he almost lost control. "Don't wanna go there?!" he said between clenched teeth. "My wife and little girl are there! Would you sit here if Miss Sarah was being worked like a dog hundreds of miles from here, cause you didn't want to be there? Hell no, you wouldn't!"

Tom stepped forward, his face mere inches away from Isaiah's. "Be careful, Isaiah, you forget yourself. I'm tryin' to help you, but you won't talk to me that way, you hear me? I know you're angry and frustrated. I would be, in your shoes, but forgettin' yourself and lashin' out at me will not make matters better for you, do you understand?"

Isaiah stood looking into Tom's eyes, his pulse throbbing in his temple. "Yes sir," he said, his jaws still locked. "But know this: I cain't wait forever. Some way, somehow, I'll be with my family again, or die in the attempt." With that, he turned from Tom and walked off. Tom watched him walk away. A shadow floated over the ground and he looked up to see the hawk circling overhead. The chickens saw it as well and went scurrying for the cover of the coop.

CHAPTER 8

November 1, 1829

THICK CLOUDS ROLLED in all day from the northwest, accompanied by a stiffening breeze, heralding the first serious cold snap of the fall. The trip from Franklin was uneventful, and Tom spent the hours swaying in the saddle, lost in thought, bundled up in the big coat Sarah had made for him last winter. He made the trip on Shadow, the big gray mare whose temperament and endurance he knew he could rely upon, with Jed the pack mule carrying his supplies. Around noon he stopped in Cullowhee to bait the animals, let them rest, and stretch his legs. The little settlement had grown since he had last been there. A man named Shook, who owned the tavern and livery, told him the new inhabitants were second-generation Germans who made their way down the Appalachians from Pennsylvania. He was pleasantly surprised to see the settlers had started a school. The town was a Cherokee village until the Treaty of Washington in 1819, and there were still Indian families living in the valley, although their children weren't allowed to attend the new school.

From Cullowhee he had made his way around Balsam Mountain and into Waynesville, arriving at his uncle's farm. Approaching the main house he stopped, peering through gathering shadows at a knot of men in a clearing near the slave cabins. He slid from his horse, stiff and sore from the long trip, as the group turned his way. He spotted his uncle, a grim look on his face. Robert gave some instructions and made his way to Tom. As the group separated, Tom saw a Black man, his back to Tom, his arms chained to a whipping post, his back covered in blood and gaping welts. Standing a few feet away was Amos Wright, the man who had delivered Isaiah and Ellen to Tom's farm, a bullwhip in his hand.

"Hello, Tom, we've had some trouble today, a runaway, just recovered and being disciplined."

"Is he dead?"

"No, of course not. Twenty lashes are all. He'll be fine in a few days and I daresay he won't be runnin' again. Come, let's get your animals taken care of and we'll clean up for supper. You're tired and hungry from your trip, no doubt. Mary Ann cain't wait to see you. Johnston, have someone take care of my nephew's animals."

Tom looked over his shoulder as he followed his uncle towards the house and saw them release the bleeding slave from the pole, falling in a heap on the bloodstained ground. He felt bile rise in his throat.

"Uncle Robert, that seems harsh."

Robert stopped as they reached the steps leading up to the front porch. "You don't understand, Tom. I got several thousand dollars invested in those people. The one that run cost me over three hundred dollars alone. What am I to do? If I don't discipline him, the others'll think they can attempt escape with impunity. Am I to watch as my life savings disappears down the road?"

"Why did he run?"

"Who knows why they run? I'm a lenient master, probably too lenient. They have roofs over their heads and I am generous with food and drink. Their workloads are reasonable. I give half a day Saturday and all day Sunday as rest. I try to keep families intact, unlike the big planters down in Georgia. Speakin' of which, I received a response from Benjamin Jordan, the man I mentioned in my letter, about the woman and child your man Isaiah made such a fuss over." Robert appeared glad to redirect the conversation.

"What've you found out?"

"He says he believes they are in his possession, at least they answer to the names we provided. He says he's willin' to part with the pair for five hundred dollars, a ridiculous sum."

"That is an insurmountable sum for me."

"He thinks since we've tracked 'em down we must set some special store by 'em. He's just negotiating. I made him a low counteroffer, and we'll see how he responds. I gotta tell you though, there's a chance he's not motivated to move much. You may have to tell your man it's a lost cause."

"It's his wife and child. He'd have me sell him if that's what it takes for them to be together again."

"Well, that might be the outcome. We'd have to play poker to get his full value, though."

Tom stared at his uncle. "I don't think I could bear to see Isaiah delivered to some big cotton plantation."

"Couldn't bear?" Robert stared as if confused. "Tom, I cain't tell you how important it is that you not become attached to your servants. They're your property, not your friends, not your family. You'll have to make decisions to protect your investment and your judgment cain't be clouded by emotion."

"I don't know. It's hard when you work side by side. He and Ellen have played with my children. In fact, Ellen is going to have a child, and so is Sarah."

"Congratulations, that's good news! See, your man has already started another family. This whole thing may blow over."

"Isaiah ain't the father. Your foreman, Wright, raped her on the way to my farm."

Robert's face darkened for a moment. "How do you know this?"

"Ellen told Sarah, and Isaiah confirmed it to me. He raped her on the side of the road while Isaiah was chained to a tree."

"They could've contrived the story to hide their own infidelity. Or perhaps the woman seduced him and now regrets her actions. Wright is a rough man, but I would not expect a report such as this."

"Uncle, I don't think you believe either of those two alternatives. A slave would take a terrible risk accusing a White man of such an act if they were lying. I believe 'em."

Robert stood thinking, before releasing a long sigh. "Yeah, you're right. I just hate the thought of losin' Wright. He's an effective foreman, but I don't guess I can put up with that behavior."

"Shouldn't he be charged with the crime?"

Robert laughed. "Based on what, a Black man's word? They cain't testify in court or file charges against a White man, and I wouldn't allow it nohow. It'd set a terrible precedent. I'll dismiss him and send him on his way, and that'll be the last we hear of it. Now let's get inside. My old bones don't bear the cold so well anymore."

As they climbed the stairs, Tom took one last look across the yard at the whipping post in the fading light. Wright stood nearby, flicking the whip. He turned to look at Tom and the two men exchanged a cold, hard stare. The distance was too great for Wright to have overheard the conversation, but Tom knew he had made an enemy of a hard man.

CHAPTER 9

November 3, 1829—Morganton, NC

ROBERT INTRODUCED TOM to Beverly Daniel. The three men stood in the lobby of the Catawba Hotel, the newest and largest hotel in Morganton, the county seat of Burke County. Morganton served as a court center for most of western North Carolina, with enough traffic to justify a couple of decent-sized hotels. As the western terminus of the Great Wagon Road, the town had been the jumping-off point for settlement of the western part of the state for German and Scots-Irish settlers who made the long trek down the spine of the Appalachians from Pennsylvania.

"Let's get a table and have dinner. Get to know one another." They picked a table in the corner away from the bar and sat down. The dining room was filling up and the steady drone of dozens of conversations guaranteed a certain amount of privacy.

"Your uncle tells me you went to school at Chapel Hill?"

"Yes sir. I studied there for almost three years." Tom was nervous. His uncle seemed more formal than usual. This dinner had the feel of an audition, and Tom was determined to make a strong impression.

"Was Denison Olmsted teaching there during your term?"

"Why yes, sir! Professor Olmsted was one of my favorite teachers. He taught geology and chemistry. He was a brilliant man and shared his knowledge in the most infectious manner. How is it you know Mr. Olmsted?"

"I met the professor in Raleigh when he presented the results of his geological survey of the state to a legislative committee. Everyone was quite impressed, though not enough to appropriate him any funds. We had dinner afterwards and discussed natural philosophy and a wide range of topics."

"He's a true renaissance man. I understand he left the university a few years ago?"

"Yes, he accepted a professorship at Yale and returned to his home state. I don't believe he could reconcile himself to accept our 'peculiar institution.'"

"No, he was uncomfortable with it. It caused much consternation around the campus. He got into a few debates with some students. Doctor Caldwell, the president of the university, was also from the North. He didn't express his opinion on the matter, as did Professor Olmsted, but neither did he rebuke him."

Robert gave Tom a sidelong glance and attempted to change the subject. "Tom is excited about the census."

"I am, sir, and thank you for the opportunity."

"Of course. I'm curious, though. With a university education, what made you decide to settle on the frontier? You could have made a career in Raleigh."

"I fell in love with the mountains when I did the land survey with my uncle, and later with Dr. Olmsted on his explorations, talking and reading, Wordsworth, Keats, Byron. I met my wife Sarah there. She loves the mountains even more than I do. She wouldn't last a fortnight livin' in a big town."

Daniel nodded as he appraised Tom. "I've been as far west as Asheville, and I can appreciate your enthusiasm . . . beautiful country. I'm sure your uncle has told you about the census duties. You'll learn a lot more when we meet with the other deputies tomorrow. I have a special mission for you, though. Robert, you told him about the intelligence we would like to gather on the Cherokee?"

"Yeah, but you may want to expand on it."

"Well, it's not too complicated. Old Hickory wants to open up the rest of the region to White settlers. Military effort might be required to make that happen. I need to ascertain what resistance might be encountered. Since the census'll require you to cover the entire region, I'd like you to assess the situation and report to me what you see. Can you do that?"

"Yes sir, I know the Cherokee. My farm sits near one of the old Middle villages. They don't seem like much of a threat anymore, to be honest."

"I understand. Your uncle and I had a similar discussion. I'm just an old soldier followin' orders. If you are uncomfortable with this request . . ."

"No sir, I just know how attached they are to the mountains. They've given up so much land already."

"Maybe nothin'll come of it. Hopefully we can take what you find out and communicate that up to the people advising Jackson and he'll leave well enough alone. You might be able to help 'em. But it's important we know the facts: numbers, where they're clustered, their frame of mind, who their leaders are . . . Can you do that?"

"Yes sir, if you think it might help."

Tom lay awake staring through the dim light at the smoke-stained ceiling of the hotel room, while his uncle snored loudly in the other bed. Although tired from the long trip and stuffed from the enormous meal they shared with Beverly Daniel, he couldn't sleep. He missed his bed back home and wished he was there now with Sarah. The scene he witnessed at his uncle's farm kept replaying in his mind, and the mission Daniel had outlined worried him. He eventually recalled the discussion about his days at Chapel Hill and Professor Olmsted.

It had been a long time since he thought of his teacher and friend. He was the smartest man Tom had ever known. There were few subjects you could broach that he didn't know something about, and in most he was well versed and highly opinionated. He was foremost a scientist, but he also loved literature and poetry, and somehow melded those two visions into one harmonious worldview. He was demanding and pushed his students with zeal, but for those who embraced his ardor, he was generous with his time and knowledge. Tom had fallen into that camp and spent many hours outside class debating his mentor. The professor delighted in sharing his books and his ideas, and Tom never left his office without at least one new reading assignment. When Olmsted asked Tom to assist him in surveying the western mountains as part of his geologic analysis of the state, he jumped at the chance.

They spent an entire summer exploring the mountains. The memory of that summer came flooding back to him. Climbing mountains with

Cherokee names, they stood on the balds marveling at the blue waves of peaks stretching off into the distance. They hiked through old-growth forests of fir, chestnut, and oak, and examined rocks and their strange formations. Tom listened as the professor mused about the causes of the folds and fissures. Olmsted explained the debates going on in science and shared his opinions. He believed the mountains to be millions of years old, formed by violent upheavals and eroded over time to reflect their current appearance. Tom remembered standing near the foot of one mountain, his hand touching a granite outcropping, trying to imagine millions of years.

In the afternoons, they made camp and read book passages in the waning light. They spent several days reading Thomas Paine's *The Age of Reason*, exposing Tom to ideas he had been afraid to explore himself. Olmsted also introduced Tom to the poetry of Wordsworth. One pleasant evening, as they rested beside a little pond, he read "Lines Composed a Few Miles above Tintern Abbey." From the opening lines, it enthralled Tom. The middle of the poem touched him as nothing he had ever heard, and he could still recite it word for word, lying there in the hotel in Morganton.

> And I have felt a presence that disturbs me with the joy
> Of elevated thoughts; a sense sublime of something far more
>   deeply interfused,
> Whose dwelling is the light of setting suns, and the
>   round ocean
> And the living air, and the blue sky, and in the minds of man:
> A motion and a spirit, that impels all thinking things, all
>   objects
> Of all thought, and rolls through all things.
> Therefore am I still a lover of the meadows and the woods,
> And the mountains; and of all that we behold from this
>   green earth . . .

Rebecca loved the poem, and they read it more times than he could remember. Thinking of her now, he could see her sweet face and bright eyes. What a difference Olmsted made in his life, changing his view of the world. He remembered a discussion they had about slavery. Olmsted was born in Connecticut and had gone to Yale. His hero was Thomas Paine. He hadn't witnessed slavery firsthand until he came to Chapel Hill. He told Tom there was no way to reconcile slavery with an enlightened view of the world. Tom put up a defense of the institution, the usual arguments he heard from his father and uncle and other people in his young sphere, but as the words left his mouth, he saw the disappointment on his mentor's face. He flushed even now at the memory of it. What would Olmsted say to him now? Sleep came, but it was a restless sleep.

CHAPTER 10

November 4, 1829

Tom walked into the hotel's dining room and saw his uncle talking to Beverly Daniel. There were maybe a dozen other men in the room, some standing in conversation, others sitting having breakfast. A fire crackled in the stone fireplace that took up most of one wall, a black bear hide hung above the wooden mantel. Tom made his way across the room.

"Good morning, Tom. Did my snoring keep you up last night?"

"No, it wasn't that bad," Tom lied. "I just couldn't turn my mind off. How 'bout you?"

"Had to get up and piss three times, but that's the price of living this long, I guess. Me and Beverly took care of the bond. I got business over at the courthouse, so I'll catch up with you gentlemen this evening after your meetings," Robert said, leaving the room.

"Tom, let me introduce you to someone." Daniel took him by the elbow and walked over to a short man with salt-and-pepper hair and spectacles, furiously attacking a large piece of ham with his fork and knife.

"John Phillips, I would like to introduce you to Thomas Love. Thomas here is going to be handling Macon County for us. John completed the '20 census for Haywood County and is going to be helping organize the effort and compile the results from all the western counties next year."

Phillips stood, and the men shook hands. Tom took the chair adjacent to him as Daniel excused himself to greet another man across the room.

"So, you're going to be handling Macon for us next year?"

"Looks that way."

"I handled part of that territory ten years ago, when it was still part of Haywood. I cain't believe ten years have passed. Time flies. I expect things have changed out that way with the Indian lands opened up and settlers pourin' in?"

"Yes, it has. Roads goin' in, land bein' cleared, but it's still fairly wild."

"When I made the rounds ten years ago, I could ride a couple of days between some farms. Of course, the roads were mere trails in many places. Where do you live?"

"Just outside Franklin, off River Road. How about you?"

"Asheville, in town. I own a little bookstore, do some bookkeeping. What do you do?"

"Farming, do a little lawyerin' on the side, mostly wills and real estate transactions. Not much volume out our way though, and runnin' the farm takes most of my time."

"How'd you get roped into the census?"

"My uncle, Robert Love, is friends with Mr. Daniel. He put us together. Seemed like a good way to make some extra money."

"Ah, I didn't put that together when we were introduced. I saw Colonel Love speakin' to Beverly earlier and said hello. I remembered him from the last census. He's a famous figure in these parts."

"What words of wisdom do you have about the census, seein's how you've done it before?"

"Well, like most things, it's a mixed bag. First, it's hard work, because of all the travel. It'll be especially true for you, given Macon is so large, sparsely populated, and rugged. The cities and more populous counties are difficult in a different way. They don't have to travel as much, but they have a lot more households to visit and more records, of course. It's interesting to meet all the different people, hear their stories."

"How do most of them respond?"

"A lot of 'em are suspicious, Scots-Irish mostly, and they come with a healthy dose of mistrust of government from the old country. Most are second generation, and they grew up hearing their grandparents' tales of the clearances. Are you familiar with the clearances?"

"We're Scots ourselves, so I grew up on stories of our people being thrown off their land to make room for sheep and being shipped to Ulster Plantation as a bulwark against the Catholic Irish."

"Good, then you'll know where they're comin' from. Bear in mind, some of them are just plain mean. They moved to the frontier to be left alone, and you won't always be welcome. I guess you know most of this, though. These people are your neighbors. Many of 'em will be downright overjoyed to have company. Take a few newspapers to share, and you'll be amazed at the welcome you get. They'll ask you about the news of the day, what's going on in Franklin, and about their neighbors when they find out you been door to door. Play that up, and you'll have few problems. Some of them will talk your ear off though, and you have a schedule to keep."

"I can see that. I'm sure as the day goes on I'll think of other things to ask you."

"Gentlemen, we'll get started in about fifteen minutes, so finish up whatever you're doing." Beverly Daniel was standing at the front of the room with a pair of boxes on a table beside him.

"Beverly runs a tight ship. Good to meet you, Thomas."

"I'll let each of you introduce yourselves. If you could stand and give your name and the county you'll canvas," Daniel said. Tom watched as the other men in the room spoke.

James Hill of Iredell County; Peregrine Roberts of Lincoln; Richard Allen of Wilkes; John Galloway of Ashe; Butler Gray of Burke; Walter Dillard of Rutherford; John Clayton of Buncombe; Finian Edmondstone of Haywood County. Tom was the last to stand.

"Thank you all. Let me introduce John Phillips, my adjutant, who will coordinate the western counties and roll up the results." John stood and Tom smiled and nodded to him.

"All of you have posted your bonds. Each of you should have also received a copy of the federal legislation that authorizes collection of the census. Show that to anyone who challenges your authority. The pay schedule is included as well. There's a provision related to a premium for jurisdictions greater than forty square miles, for which all of you qualify. As marshal, there are penalties associated with my office receiving payments or other remuneration from you as deputies for filling these positions. For the record, as witnessed by those gathered here, have any of you made any payment or promise of payment to any person for the privilege of serving as a census taker?"

The room was silent as Daniel looked around the room. "Very well. Now, if you will all stand, I'll administer the oath."

Each of the men stood and raised his hand and repeated the oath Daniel recited.

"Alright gentlemen, you are now officially assistants to the United States marshal for the District of North Carolina. I know each of you will act accordingly. I'm passing out copies of the forms we'll be using for this census. This'll be the first time every census taker in the country is using the same standard form . . . enormous improvement. In previous years, every marshal provided their own paper formatted with their own design. There were also additional schedules for industrial statistics Congress wanted collected. You can imagine that this made collection difficult. With standard forms and no schedules, this should make your job, and Mr. Phillip's, easier. Take a few minutes to familiarize yourself with the layout, and then we'll discuss some specifics and answer questions. I also included the instruction all the marshals received, which may answer some of your questions."

Tom and the others browsed the sixteen-by-eighteen-and-a-half-inch sheets in front of them, as the room hummed with side conversations. Tom read the instructions that reeked of bureaucracy and thought to himself, "Only lawyers or politicians could make something this convoluted."

Daniel cleared his throat after a while and continued. "The form should be self-explanatory. The official enumeration date is June first of next year. You have six months, until December first, to complete your surveys. When conducting your survey, you'll inquire as to the inhabitants who occupied the household as of the first of June and prepare two copies for delivery to my office. I file one set with the clerk of the superior court and send the other set, with the total enumeration for the state, to the secretary of state's office in Washington.

"There are spaces for twenty-eight families per page. List the name of the head of household, and then in the boxes provided, the number of persons in the household as they fall in each age range. On the second page, there are columns for slaves and freed colored persons, and people who are deaf and dumb or blind, and unnaturalized aliens. Only Indians who are taxed are to be included. That'll be especially important for Macon County, Tom. Questions, gentlemen?"

"How do we handle people living in boardinghouses?"

"First verify they don't have households elsewhere. If they don't, list them as heads of household."

"How do we know if the Indians pay taxes?" Tom asked.

"You should start with the tax rolls in your county courthouse. I would think the number is small. If they're living on a farm, and not in one of the villages, you'll have to inquire if they are paying taxes. Just so you all are quite clear, any miscegenated persons, whether part Indian or part Black who ain't slaves are to be counted as free Blacks on the rolls."

Someone asked about the best writing instruments and Phillips responded, "I have found that the new metal nibs are very effective, though not inexpensive. I'm a traditionalist though, and still like my quills. The best ink is made by Maynard and Noyes. They produce a very stable iron gall ink that is smooth and durable. That brings me to another point. We cannot stress enough the importance of neat, legible entries on the documents. You'll be recording the entries in some unusual places and circumstances. Smeared entries, fading ink, or liquid stains are unacceptable. These documents are the essential element in a convention required by the Constitution. They'll be retained by the federal government, perhaps in perpetuity. Historians may someday peruse these documents, and your name will be on them. Let that knowledge guide your efforts."

They spent the next few hours discussing logistics, supplies, and strategies. Six months sounded like a long time to complete the work, but as the men thought about their own counties, and their own personal obligations, the enormity of the undertaking dawned on them. Besides Phillips, two of the other men had worked on the 1820 census. Between them, they shared stories about their adventures and challenges, and things they learned to make the endeavor less daunting. That was part of the reason Daniel had convened this meeting so far before the start of the survey. The men would have until June to research their counties, study maps, talk to county officials, and make their plans to canvass the territory in the most efficient manner. Daniel knew he risked changes coming from Washington, but that was to be expected. It was Washington, after all. But the additional time the men could use for planning should more than offset any adjustments they would have to make on the fly. Tom had already been doing some planning of his own, based on the conversations he had with his uncle and the maps he had received.

The afternoon was also filled with a lot of laughter. All the veterans had stories of knocking on doors and being met by men and women in various stages of undress. There had also been propositions by some womenfolk, and there was much joking and ribald humor about which of the men had accepted those propositions. They all had at least one story of being challenged at gunpoint by some woodsman who questioned their motives or was sure the census was some government plot to enforce a new tax, shut down their distillery, or appropriate some or all of their land. In every instance, the census taker had talked the offended frontiersman down.

"Don't let that lull you into a false sense of security," Daniel advised. "We've been fortunate here in North Carolina, but there have been instances of census takers being assaulted and, in some cases, wounded." The men glanced at each other as they absorbed this information.

"Are we permitted to carry firearms ourselves?"

"Of course you can travel with your arms," Phillips replied. "Most of you will travel through the woods, and you are of course allowed to protect yourself and hunt. Discretion is the key here. How do you feel when a man shows up at your door with a musket over his shoulder, unless you know his intentions? You'll have to use your best judgment."

"We don't want to alarm you," Daniel interjected as he sensed the disquiet spreading among the men. "In the vast majority of cases you'll be welcomed as a neighbor, or at the least as a welcome diversion from their daily labors. If you make it clear right up front that the census is used for determining representation, and that it's not for assessing taxes most people are more than willing to cooperate. It's been my experience that the hardest thing is gettin' out the door after you've gathered your information. However much time you allot per household, add twenty-five percent for making your farewells and a graceful exit."

When the men had covered every topic, Daniel addressed the group. "Gentlemen, I think we've done all the damage we can do for now. I'm sure you'll think of other questions over the next few weeks. Please direct them to Mr. Phillips in Asheville. We, in turn, will correspond with you in the coming months if there's additional direction. Let me close by saying that your country appreciates the hard work you all will do next year. Enjoy what I hope will be a rewarding experience."

CHAPTER 11

November 5, 1829

THE NEXT MORNING, after another restless night, Tom and Robert set out on the return trip to Waynesville. The sky was clear, and it was pleasant for early November. Sunshine felt warm on their backs as they bounced along in the carriage headed west. Ahead of them the mountain peaks were obscured in early morning fog, wisps curling up into the blue expanse like smoke from a campfire. Tom shared the results of the census meeting, and together they plotted the broad outline of a strategy to tackle the undertaking.

"I thought about having the Franklin paper run an article about the census a few weeks before I start. Get it out there that I'll be coming round. They can provide some background, talk about the purpose, and maybe save me some time repeating the script at every house."

"Good idea. Maybe print and hang a few posters around town. You can also let the preachers know. They can spread the word."

"I'll do that. I'm also planning on meeting with the sheriff and some other functionaries. They'll have a meeting after the first of the year, and I can talk to them all at once."

They spent the rest of the ride discussing politics and horses, farming methods and days gone by. As the carriage pulled into the drive leading up to Robert's house, the sun had disappeared behind the mountains and evening was fast approaching.

Johnston, the head overseer, met them as they pulled up in front of the barn, followed by two teenage slave boys.

"Welcome home, gentlemen. I trust your trip was pleasant?"

"Very productive, but glad to be home, as always."

"We'll take care of the horse and carriage, Mr. Love," Johnston said as he nodded to the boys, one of whom took the horse by the bridle as the other removed the bags from the carriage.

Johnston followed Robert and Tom as they started towards the house, and he cleared his throat as they reached the front steps. "Mr. Love, I took care of the matter with Wright while you were away, as you asked."

"How did it go?"

"It was unpleasant. Wright's a rough man, and he did not take it well. I thought we might come to blows before it was all said and done. I gave him his severance as you directed, and he went down the road in a foul mood."

"That is unfortunate. Thank you for your attention to the matter, Johnston."

"Certainly, sir. One additional issue: he was especially angry with you, Mr. Tom. I won't repeat the foul oaths he uttered, but I'd advise you to exercise caution as you make your way home. He blames you for his dismissal."

Tom glanced at his uncle and then back at Johnston. "Thank you, Mr. Johnston. I'll stay alert." His concern was not for himself, but for his family back at the farm.

As they mounted the steps, Robert took Tom's arm and spoke in a low voice. "I was afraid Wright would prove difficult. He's a hard man, Tom. You should give him a wide berth."

"I wouldn't go looking for trouble, uncle, but if Mr. Wright threatens me or my family, he will get more than he bargains for. Maybe I should head home tonight?"

"In the dark? Good God no. Get a good night's rest and head out first light," he said as he opened the front door.

Mary Ann Love met them in the foyer and kissed them both on the cheek. "Welcome home, you two. How was your meetin's?"

"Everything went very well. Beverly Daniel asked that I give you his warmest regards. I smell supper. Is that fried chicken?"

"Yes, it is. Your sense of smell has always been better than your hearing!" She helped Robert with his coat. "You two relax and we'll have supper on the table shortly. There's a letter for you on your desk, Robert. It came yesterday."

The men stepped into Robert Love's study. It smelled of old leather, whiskey, and cigar smoke. A fire burned in the fireplace and candles had been lit, giving the room a warm glow. Tom went and stood at a bookcase on one side of the big mantel and perused the titles in his uncle's collection. Robert sat down at his desk and opened the letter with a long silver opener he had been given by one of his children for his sixtieth birthday.

"Well, I'll be damned," he exclaimed.

Tom turned and faced the desk as a log collapsed in the fireplace, sending sparks flying up the flue and the shadows dancing in the room. "What is it?"

"It seems Mr. Jordan has accepted our offer. He's willing to part with the slave woman and her child for the price I proposed."

"That's excellent news!"

"Yes, I'm sure." Robert paused. "Odd, though. I expected a counteroffer and some back-and-forth negotiation. Either my price was too high or there's something we ain't seeing here."

"Maybe he's just tryin' to be a decent human being and reunite a separated family."

Robert looked up from the letter and studied Tom for a long moment before speaking. "I've always admired that about you, Tom, your willingness to see the best in people, even someone you've never met. I guess I've lived too long and met too many sons of bitches to expect anything other than ulterior motives. You may be right, but I wouldn't bet on it. Nevertheless, we'll see about getting this done. How do you want to proceed?"

"What do I do about the money? I'm already more in debt to you than I can ever repay."

"Let's just deal with the logistical issues for now. I'll arrange for a letter of credit with the bank. We don't want anyone carrying that amount of cash through the wilds of South Carolina. I hear the place is full of brigands." He sighed. "Do you want me to send Johnston to bring 'em back?"

Tom thought for a minute, and the picture of Wright raping Ellen on the side of the road intruded into his mind. He knew his uncle trusted Johnston, but he had also trusted Wright. "I'll go and get 'em."

"That's a long trip, Tom, are you sure?"

"Yes sir, I am. I'll go home tomorrow and let Sarah and Isaiah know, and then make preparations to leave within the next fortnight. Will I need to take anything with me for the bank?"

"I'll take care of that. I hope this works out, Tom, but you must be prepared to walk away if this man's playing games."

CHAPTER 12

November 6, 1829

Tom was up before the dawn and after wolfing down his breakfast was on the road as the sun came up, excited about seeing Sarah and the children and telling Isaiah about his family. He could imagine the look on their faces when he told them and also imagine Sarah's response when she realized he would be gone again. In the back of his mind he was also thinking of Wright, and as he made his way down the road, he kept an eye peeled ahead for anything out of place. His uncle had insisted on giving him one of his pistols to supplement the musket he carried, and more than once he touched the handle as it sat tucked in his belt. He made good time and midmorning encountered a wagon loaded with barrels pulled by a pair of mules and driven by an old man with a gray beard stained with tobacco juice.

"Mornin', sir," Tom said as he approached them.

The old man pulled the reins, called on the mules to a halt, and spit over the side of the wagon, wiping his mouth with his sleeve. "And to you as well. Where you headed, young man?"

"Franklin. I have a farm just south of there. You?"

"Carryin' a load of sorghum to Waynesville to sell. How's the road ahead?"

"Clear and smooth. I left my uncle's farm at dawn and made it this far in good time. How's your journey been?"

"Same here. Left my place north of Cullowhee first light. All clear the whole way."

"Did you happen to pass anyone on the way?"

"Nope, you're the first person I've seen. You lookin' for somebody?"

"No one in particular. I just saw some tracks and thought there might be someone ahead of me to share the road with. They're probably a few days old though," Tom lied, not caring to share more information with the stranger.

"You have it to yourself, unless they's somebody behind me. It was busy in Cullowhee, though. Patrollers caught a runaway yesterday afternoon, and they got him trussed up trying to find out who he belongs to. Don't take much to get a little place like Cullowhee stirred. Well, I got to get going if I'm going to get this sorghum to market."

They parted and Tom continued his journey. He felt some measure of relief that the farmer had not passed Wright lying in wait along the road, at least not in plain sight. He continued his good pace and expected to be in Cullowhee at midday. Food and some water for him and the animals and he could be home by dusk.

Tom descended the last stretch of elevation and saw the Tuckasegee River shimmering in the midday sun, with the town of Cullowhee on the other side in the little valley it occupied. He crossed the bridge and made his way to the center of the town, past the new cabins. As he approached the crossroads, he saw a group of men standing around talking. Drawing closer, he saw they surrounded a Black man with his hands chained to a post, his head resting in the crook of one of his uplifted arms. The men turned around to look at Tom as he approached, and the Black man lifted his face as well.

It was Isaiah, his left eye swollen shut and a trickle of blood running from his mouth. Their eyes locked for a moment, and then Isaiah dropped his head again onto his arm.

Tom took a deep breath and tried to calm his mind. He needed to be careful until he figured out what was happening, but he felt his face flush with heat. As he dismounted, he looked over the faces of the White men standing in the knot. There among them he saw Amos Wright glowering at him. Tom almost stopped in the middle of dismounting, but forced himself to finish the motion. As he planted both feet on the ground, he felt the pistol in his belt and touched the handle. "Good day, gentlemen. Who's in charge here?" he said in what he hoped was an even voice.

The men looked around at each other before a tall man with a trim black beard and a brown slouch hat said, "I guess I am, Robert Hawkins," and stepped forward. "I know you, Mr. Love. We worked together on a road jury a few years ago. Cut a stretch of road twixt here and Franklin. I'm in charge of the patrol this month. We picked this Negro up on the road yesterday with no papers. Trying to sort this out and get him back to his rightful owner. This feller here says he owns him"—he nodded towards Wright—"but the Negro denies it, says he belongs to a gentleman in South Carolina, named Jordan."

Tom swallowed hard at the mention of the slave owner from South Carolina. How was that information known? "Mr. Hawkins, I remember you as well. That was some labor we put in that summer; a tough stretch of road. Both of these fellers are liars. This man belongs to me. His name is Isaiah, purchased from my uncle, Robert Love, earlier this year. I was in Morganton this week, sworn in as a deputy US marshal for next year's census. I left this man on my farm, thinking I could trust him to attend to his duties. It appears I misplaced my trust."

As Tom finished, Isaiah raised his head and looked at him as the other men watched. Tom expected to see some contrition on Isaiah's face, but Isaiah once again dropped his head onto his arm.

"I see," said Hawkins. "Well, what are we to make of this man's claim of ownership?" He nodded again at Wright.

"My uncle recently employed this man. His name is Amos Wright, and he was discharged for a variety of offenses. He is, among other things, a liar and a blackguard."

"You goddam son of a bitch!" Wright lunged at Tom, taking a wild swing. Tom saw it coming and sidestepped, tripping his attacker as he did. Wright fell facedown in the mud. Before he could recover, Tom drew the pistol from his belt and stuck the barrel in Wright's face. Wright froze, as did the other men standing there.

"You ever try to strike me again and you won't live to repeat your mistake. Mr. Hawkins, are you deputized as magistrate in your duties as captain of the patrol?"

"I reckon so. Sheriff Bell deputized me. I assumed my authority was limited to apprehendin' runaways."

"I'm pressin' charges against this man for assault and attempted theft of a slave. Ya'll witnessed his attack and false claim of ownership." Tom looked around at the group of men who all nodded in unison, glancing at one another. "I'll take possession of my property. Thank you for catchin' him. I'd like you to take charge of Wright here and remand him over to Sheriff Bell in Franklin. You can tell him what happened and swear out your testimony. Tell him I'll come by his office as soon as I can to swear out my complaint."

Tom dictated these instructions with such an air of authority that neither Hawkins nor any of the other men thought to do other than follow them. Hawkins told two of his men to secure Wright and the others to get their horses.

"Mr. Love, what of the Negro's claim that he's owned by a man in South Carolina? You got any proof that you're his rightful owner?"

"Unfortunately, I don't carry that kind of evidence around with me. I wasn't expectin' to encounter this situation, as I'm sure you'll appreciate. His wife and child are owned by a planter down in South Carolina. We been trying to purchase 'em. I assume he was plannin' on marchin' there to join 'em. Is that right, Isaiah?"

Isaiah once more raised his swollen face from his arm and spoke in a hoarse rasp. "Yes, I mean to be with my family."

"And Mr. Love is your rightful owner?"

"Yes."

"I suppose that's sufficient." Hawkins nodded to the two men who stood ready to release Isaiah from the post. Isaiah slumped to the ground with a moan and lay there in the road.

"How'd he come by his injuries?" Tom asked Hawkins.

"He resisted. He's strong, took all four of my men to wrastle him to the ground. I was about ready to shoot him. He ain't hurt too bad, though. You should adopt tighter measures to keep him in place when you're away. Next time we might not be here to capture and return him to you. If you hadn't come along, I was about ready to turn him over to this man. He had a good argument, and the Negro knew him." Hawkins's other two men had bound Wright and were leading him away to the horses. He turned and looked over his shoulder at Tom as he went.

"Wright delivered my slaves this spring. That's how he knew him."

"He sure don't like you."

"No, I was responsible for his gettin' sacked. I had my hand on my pistol the entire way from Waynesville, thinkin' he might ambush me."

"We'll see him safe to Franklin. You want to ride along with us?"

"No, I'm gonna get somethin' to eat and let the horse rest a bit before we push on. You saved me a great deal today. I'm indebted to you."

Tom shook Hawkins's hand and in a few minutes he and his men were saddled up and riding down the road he and Tom had cut those years ago. When they were out of sight, Tom looked at Isaiah, still lying in the road, his eyes closed. Tom took a waterskin off his saddle and knelt beside him.

"Can you sit? Drink some water." Isaiah pushed himself up, leaned against the post and grimaced in pain. Tom held the pouch to his lips, and he drank in several large gulps before choking and coughing. "What the hell were you thinking?"

"I was goin' to find my family."

"Well, you were going the wrong damn direction. You left my wife and children and Ellen by themselves and them with child?"

"You told Miss Sarah when you was 'spectin' to be back, and I waited 'til the last minute so they wouldn't be alone for long."

"It don't take long for an accident or something serious to happen. If anything has happened to them, it's going to be hard on you. How did you find out about Jordan?"

"I found the letter from your uncle in the house. You lied to me. You said you didn't know who bought my girls. You said I should trust you. Why you lie to me?"

Tom stared at Isaiah a long time, his brow furrowed as his mind wrestled with what he had just heard. "How did you know what the letter said?"

Isaiah turned his head away from Tom. "I learnt to read at Monticello. Peter Fossett was a friend of my daddy's. He learned from James Hemings, and ole Peter taught me a little every evenin' after supper while they was still light. I picked it up right quick. He would sneak little books out of the big house; said they was so many they wouldn't miss 'em."

"Why didn't you tell me you could read?"

Isaiah turned back to look at him. "You know Black folk ain't allowed to read, Mr. Love. Get caught with a book at Monticello was twenty lashes, no matter how old you was. For all I know you'll have me whipped now that you know."

"I ain't decided how to punish you, but if the women and children are in any trouble, it's gonna be hard on you. I told you I was working on gettin' your family."

"Why you lie to me you didn't know who bought 'em?"

"Because I figured you'd run off and try to get to 'em, and I was right."

"I tole you I'd be with 'em, or die tryin'."

"You should have trusted me anyway. My uncle made an offer for 'em, and this Jordan accepted. I was on my way home to tell you. I'm going to go get 'em soon as I can make the arrangements."

"Dear Lord. Is it true?"

"Yes, with any luck I can have 'em back 'fore Christmastime. How bad are you hurt?"

"They busted my ribs. Hurts something awful to take a deep breath. My head's hurt pretty bad too; been seeing double off and on. I ache all over but I don't think nothing else is broke."

"Can you stand?"

"I don't know. I'll try."

Tom helped him to his feet and pulled one arm over his shoulder to support him. He led him to the stables at the corner of the road and lowered him onto a box. The owner of the establishment, Jacob Shook, had stood watching the commotion in the road from his porch, and he made his way to meet them. He had known Tom and his father for years and had last spoken to Tom on his way to Waynesville.

"We rarely have this much excitement in Cullowhee. Good to see you again, Tom. Can I be of help?" Jacob said.

"Thank you, Jacob. Yes, I could use some oats and water for the horses. Do you have some old cloth? I'm gonna try to wrap his ribs tight until we can get back home."

Tom brought the horses over to the stable and let them eat the oats from the bucket Shook set in front of them. "Can you sit a horse back to the farm?"

"I think so, if we don't do no gallopin'."

"We'll take it easy. Jacob, do you have a horse you could sell me or that I could rent from you to get home?"

"I have a good mare I could let go for sixty dollars, or give you the loan of her for say two bits a day."

"I'm not sure how quick I can get back here, so I guess it would make more sense to buy her. I could use another horse, anyway. Let's take a look."

After some negotiation, Shook agreed to part with the big black mare for fifty dollars, and threw in an old saddle. He accepted a letter from Tom for the debt until he could get back with the cash. An hour later Tom helped Isaiah up onto the horse and they started down the Franklin Road, Isaiah swaying in the saddle, struggling to remain conscious.

By this time of year the oak trees were the only ones still holding their leaves, glowing russet brown in the afternoon sun. The tulip poplars dominated September. By early October they shed their leaves and the maples, burning orange and red, lit up the forest like a blaze. The mighty chestnuts and hickories turned the canopy yellow again by the end of October. But with November, having patiently waited their turn, the oaks reigned and gave the landscape the softer, warmer hues that signaled that autumn was coming to an end. On the ground, the leaves retained some of their vibrant color, creating a carpet of many hues. In the coming weeks their color would fade as they dried and turned the mottled gray and brown of the forest floor in winter. But for now they were still bright and moist and they delivered up that glorious earthy scent of fall as they lay silently under the blue sky and the autumn sun.

Tom and Isaiah emerged from the woods as the last rays of daylight faded in the gloaming. They stopped and looked across the open fields at the little farmhouse. Wisps of smoke rose from the chimney. The dark river curled around the bottoms like a giant snake. His cattle stood feeding in the pasture, rushing to get their fill before they huddled for the night to chew their cuds; twenty head of fat Herefords, their red bodies bright against the emerald grass. Interspersed with the cattle were four white-tailed deer, less visible in the twilight. The deer snapped to attention as the men and horses came into sight, followed a half second later by the cattle, turning their white faces up the hill in unison. The deer bounded away, their tails flashing as they leaped across the fields. Tom swelled with pride at what he and his family had built, before nudging his horse towards home. He passed Rebecca's little grave as they ascended the hill, about the same time one of the barred owls' calls echoed through the dusk.

Ellen put supper on the table as Sarah crouched next to Isaiah and in the firelight examined the cuts and bruises that covered his face. The children sat transfixed, watching their mother and listening as their father described the series of events that had unfolded over the last few days. Ellen froze in her steps when Tom mentioned Amos Wright and placed a hand on her swelling abdomen. Sarah was none too gentle as she removed the wrapping from around Isaiah's ribs, revealing the large, ugly bruise that covered his rib cage. Isaiah took a deep breath as she touched it and he released it with a long hiss.

"It's a wonder you didn't git yourself kilt, and Tom as well. It was bad enough leavin' me and Ellen here alone with the children, but to not even tell us you was a-leavin'. We were worried half to death! I gave you credit for havin' more sense. Did you really think you could go traipsin' off across the Carolinas and not get picked up by the patrol or worse, picked up by some slave trader and sold south? What good would that have done your family?"

"I guess I didn't give it enough thought," Isaiah said through clenched teeth, his voice little more than a hoarse whisper.

"Where does it hurt?"

Isaiah motioned to a place about the middle of his rib cage.

"That's the best we can hope for. Leastways it's not one of your short ribs. You coughed up any blood?"

"Most of the blood was from my mouth. They knocked one of my teeth loose."

"You best hope Tom don't have to pull it. He's a worse dentist than he is a doctor."

"I thought I bound him up pretty well, considering the circumstances," Tom said.

"Can you eat, Isaiah?"

"If I chew on my right side."

"After supper I'll get a fire goin' in his cabin," Tom said.

"We shouldn't leave him alone, especially if his head's hurt."

"I'll stay in his cabin with him," Ellen volunteered.

"Will I need to use the manacles, Isaiah?" Tom said, and Sarah looked at him.

"No sir. I don't believe I'll be doin' any travelin' for the time bein'."

"That's good to hear."

"But I'll need to be better soon to accompany you to fetch my girls."

Tom had not relayed that part of the story to Sarah yet, and she gave him another sharp look.

"Uncle Robert made arrangements for the purchase of Isaiah's wife and daughter with the planter in South Carolina. I plan on leavin' within a fortnight to get 'em. I figure four days to get there and four days back. Isaiah, you're not in any shape to travel, and I wouldn't allow it anyway. You gotta stay here and take care of the farm and animals."

"You're leavin' agin?" Sarah said with a pained expression.

"I don't see any choice. Who else'd do it? I don't trust any of Uncle Robert's men, and gettin' 'em here ain't part of the deal with the planter, not that we'd trust him either. It's got to be me, and Isaiah's gotta stay here to help you, assuming there's no more disobedience on his part."

"How will you know my girls? What if they's trying to trick you?"

"You'll have to describe 'em to me and tell me somethin' only they'd know."

"I can go with you, Daddy," James volunteered from a corner of the room.

Tom looked at his son and smiled. "Thank you, James, but you're too little for such a trip, and your momma'll need you here."

"He should go with you," Sarah said. "I'd feel better knowin' you two were together."

"Sarah, it's a long trip and who knows what the weather'll be." He pictured the ride back from Franklin with Rebecca shivering in the sleet storm.

Sarah read his mind. "We'll talk about it later."

Chapter 13

November 7, 1829

AFTER BREAKFAST Tom mounted his horse and rode into Franklin. He found Sheriff Bynum Bell there in his office in the newly constructed courthouse.

"Howdy, Tom, figured I'd see you today. You wanna tell me what this is all about?"

Tom took him through the whole sordid affair, including what Isaiah had told him about the original trip from his uncle's farm. When he finished, Bell, who sat reclining in his chair listening to the story, leaned forward and put both arms on the desk, looking at Tom.

"Tom, you must know I cain't issue no warrant based on the testimony of a Negro."

"My uncle told me the same thing. I told you so you'd have the background. I assume Hawkins and his men told you about him attackin' me and making false statements to try to steal my slave?"

"Yeah, they told me when they brought him in. I took their oaths. What you want out of this, Tom?"

"The man's a menace. I don't doubt that given the chance, he'll try to harm me, my family, or my slaves. He needs to be tried and punished."

"I understand your position, but you know the law as well as I do. We don't have a penitentiary in this state. I can hold him here in jail until the circuit judge and prosecutor come round again, probably after the first of the year. I'll present 'em with the evidence, but my guess is he's not gonna want to go to the trouble of a trial, 'specially if all this business with the slaves'll come up. Odds are he'll try to get him to plead guilty to assault and recommend to the judge that he be fined or whooped, with time served here in jail as his punishment. You've seen 'em in action. Don't you reckon that'll be the split?"

Tom looked out the window at the rough little town so recently carved from the wilderness, thinking about what the sheriff had told him. After awhile, he looked at him again. "No, you're right. That's probably the best we can hope for. I gotta make a trip to South Carolina on some business here in the next week or so. You gotta promise me you'll hold him here at least 'til I get back. I cain't be away from home if he's loose."

"I'll take a few days to let the circuit judge know we're holdin' him. It's usually a month or more afore he can put us on his rotation. That's why I said it would be after the first of the year."

"That'll have to do. I expect to be back well before the middle of December if everything goes accordin' to plan. Try not to make his stay too pleasant."

"I couldn't if'n I tried. That's a cold little cell we have. Take care of yourself on your travels and we'll see where things stand when you get back."

CHAPTER 14

November 27, 1829

TOM WAS CHOPPING wood when the latest letter arrived from his Uncle Robert. The arrangements with Benjamin Jordan had been finalized and accepted. Jordan was told to expect Tom or his representative the first week of December. The letter of credit was established with the bank, and the documents were enclosed. He offered one more time to have his men pick the woman and child up and transport them back to his farm, but he understood Tom's position and wished him safe travels.

Isaiah, still recovering from his broken rib, appeared close to tears when Tom told him. He pleaded again to accompany Tom on the trip, but Tom still refused. Sitting on the bed in his cabin, Isaiah grabbed Tom's right hand between both of his and held it, looking up at him.

"Mr. Tom, I can never thank you enough for this."

"Just promise me you will take care of things here so I can do this."

"I promise, sir."

Tom had planned to give Isaiah lashes for running away, but Sarah had talked him out of it, convincing him that his injuries were sufficient punishment.

"You deserved a whippin' for runnin' away before. If you hadn't been so beat up, I would've done it. Any other owner would've."

"I know, I been beat for less."

CHAPTER 15

November 30, 1829

T OM LAY WATCHING Sarah sleep as first light broke outside. She could only sleep on her back now, when she could sleep, as the baby revolted any time she tried to rest on her side. Her blond hair fanned out around her head, and in this light, Tom thought it looked like the halo around an angel's head he had seen in a painting at the university many years ago.

He had fallen in love with her the first time he ever laid eyes on her. He had been with the survey team heading into the wilderness in the spring of 1820 when they stopped at the Brittain and Silers trading post for supplies. The outpost stood at the confluence of Muskrat Creek and Wayah Creek, and had as many Cherokee customers as White ones. Tom had accompanied his uncle inside the establishment to pick up sundries when he saw Sarah Brittain behind the counter. She was a vision: sixteen years old, with flaxen hair and green eyes that sparkled like emeralds against her rosy cheeks and lips. He was dumbstruck.

"Can I help you?" Her voice lilted, harp strings to Tom's ears.

Robert looked at his nephew standing there with his mouth half-open and his head tilted to one side, making not a sound, until he nudged him in the ribs. "I believe the young lady asked you a question, Thomas."

Tom blushed and began stuttering something about hominy grits and bacon. Sarah laughed and blushed as well. They were married the next year. In all the time he had known her, he had never heard her utter a mean word. Angry sometimes, but never mean. She was kind and loving, patient and gentle, honest and loyal. Tom had told her many times that she was his North Star. Whenever he was conflicted about something, she would set him straight, and she was never wrong in matters of the heart.

She opened her eyes and looked at him, stretched and yawned. "How long you been starin' at me?"

"Just a little while. I like watchin' you sleep."

"Feel the baby! It must be awake too. Kept me awake half the night."

Tom put his hand on her belly and felt the powerful movements. "That never ceases to amaze me."

"You should feel it from the inside! I don't know, Tom. This is a big baby, and so busy. I don't remember any of the other children bein' this busy this soon."

"Another boy, I'll wager!"

"No doubt. Hurry back to me, my love. It's not the same when you're not here."

"I'll get there and back as fast as humanly possible. I need to get up and get going as a matter of fact," he said, and he kissed her first on the lips then on the forehead.

Sarah had won the argument. James would accompany his father on the trip. The boy needed to spend time with his father, and James's presence would make Anne and Susan more comfortable. Tom couldn't argue with her. They had eaten a hearty breakfast and then loaded the wagon with supplies to last them for the journey. Sarah had included a couple of her and Rebecca's old dresses and coats for Anne and Susan. Ellen had told her they might have nothing but the clothes on their backs. They loaded the wagon and said their farewells, and Tom and James set out down the road.

He took the new turnpike that followed the Tennessee River headed south. The road was in good shape, and they made steady progress. The first few miles they rode in silence, enjoying the new scenery. They passed a few wagons headed north, but mostly they had the road to themselves.

"Daddy, how do you know which way to go?"

"Well, I looked at maps I have and planned the best route. There are only a few roads to pick from, so it ain't too hard. We're goin' south now. See the sun on our left? That's east. It'll pass overhead at noon and then start settin' in the west, on our right. We'll get into Georgia in the afternoon. With luck we'll make it to the Chatuga River crossin' afore dark and spend the night. In the mornin' we'll head east towards Pickens, South Carolina. We'll turn south again until we get to Anderson. I brought a map with me. I'll show you how to use it after supper. Learn how to read a map and tell directions and you'll rarely get lost."

James seemed lost in thought, as if he was imagining himself trekking through the wilderness with his map. His reverie ended, and he was off on a new tangent. "What if we get there and Isaiah's wife don't wanna come with us?" he asked.

Tom looked down at his son and pondered his response. "Well, son, I have not thought about that prospect. I'm sure they miss Isaiah. I know he misses them."

"Are we gonna own them like we own Isaiah and Ellen?"

After another long pause, Tom replied, "Yes, son, we're gonna buy 'em from this feller and they'll work on the farm with Isaiah and Ellen."

"I don't think Isaiah and Ellen like workin' on the farm."

"Why do you say that?"

"I heard 'em talking one night when they didn't know I was around. Ellen said she misses her momma something awful, and she told Isaiah she didn't want to have no baby. She's scared."

Tom recalled Sarah's first pregnancy and how scared she had been. The delivery had been an ordeal that lasted hours, but Rebecca arrived and Sarah was beaming and he had never been happier.

"I know she's scared, but everything'll be alright, and Isaiah'll be happy once he's back with his family."

"He told Ellen that one day he wants his own farm and don't want to work for nobody but hisself. Can Negroes own farms?"

"Yes, they can, if they're free and can afford to buy the property, but it's rare."

"How do they get free?"

"If their owner wants to free 'em, he can. Sometimes they let their slaves work side jobs to raise money to buy their freedom, like blacksmithin'."

"Isaiah's a good blacksmith. Are you going to let him work to buy his freedom?"

"I ain't plannin' on that. We got a lot tied up in him workin' for us. Let's see how things play out once he gets his family back with him. Maybe he'll be happier with things."

"Maybe so. I'd hate to see Isaiah leave."

They rode along in silence until James spoke up again. "Daddy, could somebody make me a slave?"

"No, son, White people ain't slaves. Back in colonial days, White people comin' to America from Europe were indentured, but not slaves."

"What's that?"

"They were poor and couldn't afford to pay for passage on ships coming to America. Wealthy people here would pay their passage, and they'd have to work for them until they paid them back. When their time was up, they'd be free and could do as they pleased. Some of our ancestors were indentured."

"Why ain't the Negroes indentured?"

Tom sighed. "Jamie boy, you ask good questions. I don't have all the answers. I guess it cost less money to buy a slave than to pay for indentured servants or free workers. Some folks think it's just natural for Negroes to work for White folks."

"Will I have to own slaves when I'm grown up?"

"No, son, you make up your own mind about it. That's a good many years off, though. Who knows how things will be then."

Tom looked at his son and envied his innocence. Could he have ever been that innocent? He tried to remember being a child, seeing the world through a child's eyes, before trials and tribulations harden perceptions and expose the world for what it is. Or, he wondered, does experience cloud our vision? Maybe things are simpler than we make them out to be. In that moment, he recalled the purpose of his trip and decided that nothing was simple.

The conversation turned to less weighty matters and the morning to afternoon. They arrived at the river crossing before dark and arranged for the night's stay. The proprietor suggested they visit the falls before dinner, telling them it was worth the hike. They made the trek up the narrow trail and stood in amazement at the torrent of water cascading into the canyon below. James's eyes were wide with awe, and Tom saw how much he resembled Rebecca, remembering how she had loved their waterfall. He was thankful Sarah had insisted he bring his son on this trip. He realized he had taken his son for granted this last year, time lost he couldn't make up. Sarah knew the long hours on the road and moments like this would force her two boys to restore their bond. "Sarah always knows," he thought. The late autumn sun was setting, and the temperature dropped, so Tom and James made their way back to the tavern with the waiting fire and a hot supper of fried trout.

CHAPTER 16

December 1, 1829

A THICK FOG ROLLED in overnight and spread a damp gray blanket over the mountains. Tom and James stepped onto the porch of the tavern and heard nothing but the dull roar of the river in the distance. They harnessed the horses to their wagon and set off for the ferry, barely able to see the road in front of them, guided more by the sound of the rushing waters than their vision. Frightened by the fog and the noise, the horses grew restive, nickering to one another and twitching their ears and noses in alarm. Out of the vapor a deep voice boomed, "Whoa there!"

Tom jerked hard on the reins, and one of the horses, now terrified, reared up in the traces.

"I didn't mean to skeer ya, but if you ain't careful you'll get mired up in this mud down here and we'll play hell gittin' you out."

A giant of a man stepped out of the mists and approached the side of the wagon. Tom felt James wedge himself under his arm, getting as close as he could to his father. The man wore a wide-brimmed leather hat with one small crow feather sticking out of the band. His face was swarthy with a full black beard and mustache. Long, unkempt hair fell from under his hat and lay fanned across his shoulders. He wore a long black coat and tall leather boots.

"Mornin'. Name's Simpson and I run the ferry. I take it you're lookin' to cross?"

"Yes, my son and I are headed to Pickens. Thanks for keeping us out of the mire. We've let the horses navigate to here. I don't know that I've ever seen fog this thick."

"Yeah, it's pea soup. Been like this all week. It burns off once the sun gets up, but early mornin's have been rough."

"Can we cross in it?"

"Oh sure, don't affect us much at all, so long as we can get you on and off without miring up. Best if you hop down though and lead your horses. They'll respond better to you than me."

Tom jumped down and helped James, who still cowered at the sight of the big man. He handed Simpson three bits for the fare and Simpson guided him down to the ferry, avoiding the quagmire. The horses were skittish about transitioning from dry land to the rickety raft, and after seeing it through the mist, Tom shared their concern. After some cajoling the horses, wagon, and passengers were safely aboard. Tom examined the two stout ropes that were connected to the ferry. The guide rope passed overhead through a metal eye, anchored by a six-foot cable to the middle of the boat. The heave rope ran through a pair of metal eyes connected to the railing just above water level. Both ropes were strapped to a big poplar tree on the near shore, and disappeared into the fog on their way to the far shore.

"Pole or pull on the rope?" Simpson asked.

"I'll man the pole if you don't mind."

"Makes no never mind to me. Stand on the downriver side if you please. River's fairly flat and wide here, but she's movin'. I need you to lean into it and pole into the current as well as across. All right. Here we go. Heave, Mr. Love!"

Tom had poled many boats across the Tennessee, and now he planted his legs and, with a grunt, put his back and strong shoulders into pushing the boat from the shore as Simpson pulled hard on the heave rope. The raft lurched and Tom could feel the current pushing them downstream. The rope began straining at the overhead eye and Simpson redoubled his efforts.

"Lean into it, Mr. Love, or we'll be letting you out at the bottom of Tallulah Gorge!"

Tom pushed with a fresh urgency and soon sweat was breaking on his brow, despite the cool temperature. His arm muscles, taut from years of cutting wood and working the farm, fell into rhythm as he pushed and angled the long pole. He glanced once at James, who stood beside the wagon trying to make himself as small as possible. Tom winked at him to reassure him.

"How we doin', Mr. Simpson?"

"Halfway there! You'd make a fine ferryman, Mr. Love."

Suddenly there was a loud thump, and the raft shuddered. Tom almost dropped the pole, and he saw James stumble to his hands and knees. The horses rolled their eyes wildly and trembled in their traces. Tom looked at Simpson, who was peering over the left side of the raft. The rope was straining and now the boat tilted to that side.

"Downed tree in the water has struck us amidships! We have to free ourselves now, Mr. Love!"

Tom grabbed the pole and scampered over the wagon. "Hold on, James!" he yelled as his son's panicked eyes looked up at him. The small tree was wedged against the side, the water churning up over it and across the floor of the boat. He picked a spot along the trunk of the tree and aimed his pole at it. With every ounce of his strength he pushed against the tree, trying to force it back towards the shore they had departed. It didn't budge. He pulled the pole back and picked another spot farther down the base of the trunk. Simpson was on his backside, his feet against the front edge, pulling on the rope with all his might. The boat was tilting farther now, and Tom realized that if he didn't free the jam immediately, they were going to capsize midstream, dumping them all in the river, or the rope was going to break, sending them careening downstream. He jammed the pole down and back and the tree cartwheeled away. The current caught it and spun it from the floundering boat, which lurched back to level. The sudden shift caught the passengers unawares. Tom fell back against the wagon, and the horses stumbled keeping their footing. Simpson was still on his backside, pulling again on the rope. Tom balanced a moment to catch his breath and then remembered James.

"James!" he shouted as he lunged back over the wagon.

"Here, Daddy!" came the response. "Help!"

Tom scrambled to the side of the boat and found James in the water, holding tightly to one of the wagon trace lines he had grasped during the melee. Tom grabbed the line and pulled James to him. When he was within reach, he took him by the coat and dragged him aboard.

"Are you alright, son?"

"Yes, just cold," he said as a shiver went through him.

"Best to get him to the far shore as quick as we can, and we need you on the pole to get us there, Mr. Love," Simpson said through gritted teeth as he continued to strain at the rope.

Tom grabbed the pole and pushed with all his remaining strength, looking down at his son with each lunge. After a few minutes of combined exertion, the ferry at last bumped onto the far shore. Simpson jumped out and began securing the boat to the moorings. Tom laid the pole on the deck and lifted the shivering boy to his chest, wrapping his arms around him and rubbing his back through the sodden coat. He carried him onto the riverbank and spotted the little shed Simpson used as his shelter on this side of the river. He took James inside and rushed to remove the dripping clothes and then wrapped James in his own coat. Simpson eased the door open.

"Is the little fella alright?"

"Yes, just frozen to the bone. Can you get your stove fired up there?"

"Will do. I have your team and wagon off the boat and secured. That was a close call. You saved us and the boat too. I'm in your debt."

"I just did what had to be done. You ever have that happen before?"

"Never, not in all the years I've been ferryin'. I've had all kinds of debris strike the boat, but never anything that big and never anything get hung up like that. I'm glad this mishap didn't kill us all." He huddled over the small stove, striking his flint against his fire steel until he had the dry tinder burning and then added kindling.

"How you doin', son?" Tom asked.

"I'm alright. Your coat is warm."

"I'm glad you had hold of the traces, otherwise we'd be chasin' you downstream. You scared me to death." He hugged him again, imagining what had almost been.

After an hour James was warm and dry, wearing fresh clothes. Simpson gave him an old quilt to wrap in and told him he could give it back on the return trip. He tried to give the passage money back, but Tom refused. With

James loaded into the wagon, they set off down the road as the fog lifted. After a while, the sun came out and warmed them both.

"Daddy, what happens when we die?"

Tom looked at his son, the quilt wrapping around him like a cocoon, nothing but his face visible. He remembered first seeing that little face, red and screaming at his birth. Now he had a little row of freckles sprinkled across cheeks and nose. How quickly the years had passed since he had first arrived. He tried to remember the first time he himself had contemplated death as a child, but could not recollect a specific instance.

"Did you hear me, Daddy?"

"I'm sorry, son. I don't know how to best answer you. That may be the hardest question there is. We have to wrestle with it our entire lives. The truth is I don't know, and I don't think anybody knows."

"When I fell out of the boat, I knew I was going to die sure and it scared me bad."

"That's only natural, son. But they's a difference in being afraid of dying and being afraid of death. When we're in danger, we react with fear and we fight to stay alive. Death happens after we die, and that fear is of the unknown. Last year when Rebecca died, I asked myself the same question you're asking."

"Momma told us you was very sad and that we shouldn't bother you."

"Your momma watches out for all of us. When Rebecca passed, I went up in the woods and sat by that waterfall we all like. You remember it? I was hurtin' inside worse than I ever hurt. As I sat watching the water tumble over the rocks, somethin' came to me."

"What was it?"

"It came to me, if God is everywhere, all across the universe, all the time, we must be part of Him. I sat there next to the falls, and I figured we're all part of Him, you and Momma and Julia and Rebecca, and not just us but everything. Every rock, every hawk flying up in the sky, all the stars at night, everything. Does that make sense?"

"I think so."

"That's all we can do, son. So it seemed to me, if we're all part of God, when we die, whatever makes us . . . us, is still there: our thoughts and our memories and our love, they're still part of God and they never go away."

"Is that heaven? Momma says Rebecca is in heaven."

Tom looked out at the road ahead of them before answering. "I reckon so, but I don't know that heaven is some separate place. If God is everywhere, then heaven must be everywhere too. The problem is we cain't see it or touch it. Remember we were talking about the difference between the fear of dying and the fear of death?"

"Yes sir."

"The way we experience the world every day is kind of like the fear of dying. We have to see the world in the regular way to get by. We have to work and feed and clothe ourselves and our families, so we have to be about the business of living, and that takes most of our time and energy. But now and then, if we let our mind be still, we can know that we're part of everything. Sometimes I feel it when I'm looking up at the stars at night. There's so many of 'em and they're so far away, but it seems like you could reach out and grab one of 'em. Or sometimes when I'm in the woods, I'll be sitting real still waiting for a deer to show, and when I'm perfectly still and quiet, it's like I'm part of the woods, the trees all around me, the earth under me, the breeze in my face."

"Does everyone get that feelin'?"

"It don't seem like it, son. Most people are so busy just living and so afraid of dying, they never feel part of everything. Some people are mean, separate and alone, and that keeps them from feelin' it. But there are people who spend a lot of their time studyin' on it and writing about it, poets mostly, it seems like." Tom smiled.

"Could I feel it?"

"Of course you can. You've always been a thoughtful child, your mind turning all the time. It's funny, cause it occurs to me your mind has to be prepared to experience what we're talkin' about. You have to study how the world works and how things connect. You have to be sharp and not let people convince you of silly ideas that keep you from getting' at the truth of things. It's kinda like farmin'. You know how we prepare the fields in the springtime, turnin' the soil and breakin' it up, mixing in the manure to make it rich? Then we plant the seeds and tend 'em all summer, keepin' the weeds out. In the fall we gather in the harvest. Our minds are like the fields. We have to prepare 'em by getting a good education and learnin' how the world works. We have to tend 'em by not letting ignorant people influence us with superstitious ideas, like the weeds in the fields. If we do all that, maybe we can know the true nature of things." Tom smiled again, pleased with his analogy.

"I can do that, Daddy."

"I know you can, son, and I'll be right here to help you if I can." He clicked his tongue and popped the reins to spur the horses on. They were behind schedule with many miles to go.

Sarah knocked at the cabin door and waited for Isaiah to appear.

"Hello, Miss Sarah," he said, surprised to find her at his door.

"Ellen's feelin' poorly, the mornin' sickness and all, and with your head and ribs busted up, I figured I ought to check on you."

"Thank you, ma'am. I reckon I'll live. Head still hummin', and it hurts to breathe deep, but I'll be alright. Just straightenin' up a bit in here. Don't want my girls comin' into a pig sty, though they ain't much to straighten," he said, turning to look around the little cabin. "Been meanin' to thank you for doctorin' me and for talkin' Mr. Tom out of whoopin' me."

"He told you that?"

"No ma'am, I just figured."

They looked at each other until Sarah spoke. "It would've made no difference. I was mad myself, you runnin' off, but I got to thinkin' what I might venture if one of my youngun's was off sommers away from me."

"Yes ma'am. I guess your heart takes over and your head just gotta go along." He paused. "It ain't right taking a man's family away from him. You can bear bein' worked and even whooped, but drive a man near crazy to split him off from his family."

"That is cruel." Sarah looked away and ran her hands down the front of her apron. "We'll all be glad to have you reunited. Otherwise, are you happy here so far?"

Isaiah hesitated. He wasn't sure what she expected, and he didn't want to cause offense. "It's pretty country. You and Mr. Tom have not been unkind to us." His voice trailed off and he looked away.

Sarah was tired, having hardly slept the night before. The baby moved constantly. She had battled for months to keep her emotions in check, as they roiled just below the surface like magma, magnified now by the chaos of pregnancy-fueled hormones. She had lost her daughter, had feared that she was losing her husband, had grappled with the arrival of Isaiah and Ellen and the horror of their treatment. Now it all came rushing to the surface.

"I cain't say I know what you're going through, Isaiah. I can tell you sometimes I feel like a prisoner here myself." Her face reddened as the words spilled from her mouth. "Tom don't make me feel that way!" she said, trying to recover. "It's just bein' a woman out here by myself so much. I love my family and this farm and these mountains. It's just, my life stretches out before me sometimes and they ain't nothin' but cookin' and cleanin' and changin' shitty diapers and tryin' to make sure they's food on the table, and sometimes they's a wagon wheel layin' on my chest and I cain't lift it offen me, and I'm smotherin'."

Her voice cracked as her throat tightened and her eyes burned. She wiped them with her sleeve and felt a strange combination of embarrassment and relief as she had articulated her anguish for the first time out loud to another human being. She stood there looking at Isaiah, not sure how she expected him to respond.

Isaiah stood mute in response, uncertain what to say or do. If this were Susan, or Ellen even, he would take them in his arms and comfort them, but he did not know what to do with a White woman carrying on like this. He just stood mute, watching her until she turned her back and walked away without another word.

As he watched her go, he was sorry for her, but only for a moment. He knew her life was hard, and he could tell she was troubled, but whatever her circumstances, she had had control in deciding them. He assumed she had married the man she loved of her own free will, had moved with him to this land they owned together, and raised a family that would share in their prosperity. If they were unhappy here, they could sell their land and move somewhere else, to a town where she wouldn't be so alone. She was free to do what she wanted to an extent he could only imagine. If she had expected pity, she would have to look elsewhere.

CHAPTER 17

December 3, 1829

IT WAS EARLY morning when Tom turned the team into the drive of the Jordan plantation. They had spent the previous night in Anderson after arriving late in the afternoon. The rest of their trip had been uneventful, and they had made good time under dry skies. James had shown no ill effects from his time in the icy river, much to Tom's relief. The innkeeper gave him directions to the Jordan plantation, and they found it with no trouble.

The main house was large, but not overly impressive from Tom's perspective. He had built it up in his mind on the long trip, and it didn't live up to his expectations. It had two stories and a porch that wrapped around the front and the east side, giving it a rather lopsided appearance. The top of the porch appeared to be a balcony rather than a roof, with a railing surrounding it and double doors that opened off the second-floor rooms. The house was white and well maintained. There were several outbuildings, including a barn he envied. He figured it must have a dozen stalls. Several handsome horses stood grazing in a paddock, and they all raised their heads as they spotted the wagon. Tom's horses perked up their ears in response, and one of them whinnied, setting off a riot as a pack of bird dogs that had been lounging under the porch came bounding towards the wagon, baying as though on a hunt. Tom could see a double row of small cabins lining a dirt path behind the barn, maybe two dozen in total. An old Black lady with a white head rag sat on the steps of one cabin watching half a dozen small children, three or four years old, playing in the path with sticks and a ball of unknown material.

"Good morning, sir. How can I help you?"

Tom turned to see a middle-aged White man wearing a slouch hat and leather work gloves and apron approaching the wagon from the barn. "Good morning. I'm here to see Mr. Jordan. I believe he is expecting me. My name is Thomas Love."

"I'm Benjamin Jordan. Good to meet you. I apologize, I was working on one of my horse's hooves. He has a crack, and I was making sure it's nothing serious." He removed his gloves and shook Tom's hand. "And who is this young man?"

"This is my son, James." James accepted Jordan's handshake timidly.

"You're up and at early. Have you had breakfast? Can I get you anything?"

"No, thank you. We spent the night and had breakfast in Anderson. It didn't take long to reach your plantation. Nice place you have. The barn is impressive."

"Don't let my wife hear you. She says I spent more time and money on the barn than the house, but thank you for the compliment."

"I trust my uncle's correspondence provided everything you need?"

Jordan dropped his head and sighed and then looked at Tom for a moment before replying. "Yes, Mr. Love, it was very thorough. I'm afraid I have bad news, though."

Tom swallowed and set his jaw. His uncle had warned him there might be last minute haggling to increase the price. "What's the problem, Mr. Jordan? I assumed everything was settled between you and my uncle regarding the terms."

"I wish it were the terms. The Negro woman you come for died last week."

Tom felt like someone had punched him in the gut. Isaiah's face flashed before him. "What happened?"

"Don't know. She was fine one day and the next she was pukin' and running a high fever. She couldn't stand for anyone to touch her belly. That went on for a day or two, and then she died. Must've been some kind of blood poisoning. I sent word to your uncle, but the letter probably passed you somewhere on the road. I'm sorry you've come all this way for nothing."

Tom stroked his chin and bit his lip as he struggled to think of what to say. What was he going to tell Isaiah? Suddenly he remembered the little girl. "What about her daughter, Susan?"

"One of the women that come in that group took her under wing. She says she was the woman's cousin. She's down in the quarter with the other youngun's."

"Will you let me buy her? It's gonna go hard on my servant when he finds out his wife's dead. Havin' his girl might relieve some of the pain."

"You shore put a lot of value on your slave's feelin's, Mr. Love. You should be on guard for that. Look, I try to be a good Christian. It's unfortunate they got separated, but it happens all the time. They git over it purty quick. I'd give you the girl, but I already lost money on the mother. Gimme a hundred dollars for my troubles and you can have her. How's that sound?"

Tom was about to propose a counteroffer when he realized what was at stake. "I'll accept your price. I'll need to complete the paperwork for the letter of credit. Can I see the girl?"

"Of course. Andrew?" Jordan shouted towards the barn.

"Yes sir!" came the reply from a young man with straw-colored hair, stepping out of one of the stalls.

"This is my son, Andrew. Son, go down to the quarter and have the foreman send that little gal that lost her mam up here."

A few minutes later Andrew returned, followed by a young Black woman holding the hand of a small girl, her hair in pig-tails.

"Jenny wanted to come with her, Pa."

"That's fine, son. This here is Mr. Love from North Carolina. He just bought young Susan here and is gonna take her back to his farm."

The little girl recoiled and buried her face in the folds of Jenny's dress, as Jenny tried to calm her.

"She a li'l thing and just lost her momma. Please, sir, don't take her away from us." Tears appeared on her cheek as she pulled Susan closer, as if they could not be separated if they held each other tight enough.

"Your name is Jenny?" Tom stepped towards her and knelt so that he was at eye level with Susan.

"Yes sir."

"Are you kin to Susan?"

"Yes sir, our momma's was sisters. When she was dying, she made me promise to watch after her Susan."

"Were you with her at Monticello?"

Jenny looked surprised at the mention of the Jefferson plantation. "Yes sir, that's where I was born and lived until I come to be here." She glanced nervously at Benjamin Jordan, who stood to one side observing the interrogation.

"Did you know Susan's father?"

"Yes sir, her father was Isaiah. He a good man. They separated him and Anne after President Jefferson passed. We ain't never heard from him since."

"Isaiah works on my farm. I came here to buy Anne and Susan from Mr. Jordan and take 'em back to be with Isaiah. I didn't know Anne had passed. It's gonna be hard on Isaiah when he hears what's happened. If I can take Susan back to be with him, I hope it'll make it easier on him. Do you understand?"

Jenny could only nod. She knelt as well and held Susan by the shoulders, looking into her eyes, which were also filled with tears. "Susie, this gentleman gonna take you to your daddy. You remember yore daddy, don't you?"

"No, I want to stay with you, Jenny! Please don't let 'em take me away, please!"

Jenny pulled her to her chest and stroked the back of her hair as the child sobbed. "Oh darlin', it's gonna be alright. Your daddy's a good man and wants to be with his little girl. I remember how he used to ride you around on his big ole shoulders when you could barely walk. You know I want to stay with you, but we got no say in this chile. Jesus'll watch out for you and keep you safe and you'll be back with your daddy. It's for the best."

She stood up now and faced Tom, with Susan still grasping her. "Mister, please promise this little child won't be mistreated. She cain't stay and I cain't go, though my heart breakin' in two. I got two little children of my own that I gotta care for. I promised her dyin' momma I'd protect her and here I am, her poor body barely cold, breakin' my promise."

"No harm'll come to her. I got two children of my own. This is James, my son. I come all this way to get Isaiah's family and take 'em back to him. I wouldn't let her be mistreated."

"Thank you, sir. When you see Isaiah again, tell him Anne's last thoughts was of him and this little girl. She pine'd over being separated from Isaiah ever since we left Monticello. She loved him dear. Here, take her. I cain't stand this no more!" Jenny pulled the crying child from her and pushed her into Tom's grasp. "Goodbye, child! God be with you." She turned and ran down the path back to the cluster of cabins, disappearing into one of them. Susan strained to follow her, calling her name, still reaching for her as Jenny disappeared. Tom held her as tightly as he could without hurting her and succeeded in turning her to face him.

"Susan, listen to me. It's gonna be alright. I know you're scared, but they ain't nothin' to fear. I'm gonna take you to your daddy, and I know he'll be very happy to see you. Come here and sit in the wagon while Mr. Jordan and I conclude our business. James, show her some things we brought for her." Tom picked her up and placed her in the wagon's bed as James scampered up and started going through the basket Sarah had prepared for this moment. Susan sat crying against the side rails, her shoulders heaving as she sobbed. Tom saw Jenny running back up the path, stopping when she reached the wagon, breathless.

"This necklace was the only thing Anne owned other than the clothes on her back. She told me to save it for Susan till she was old enough to take care of it. Isaiah made it for her. He made this little dolly for Susan too." She handed the necklace to Tom and the doll to Susan and turned and ran down the path again. Tom studied the necklace and put it in his vest pocket.

Jordan escorted Tom onto the porch and the two men took seats at a small table. Tom signed the drafts for the revised amount and Jordan wrote out a bill of sale. It was all done in a matter of minutes and they stood and shook hands. "Thank you, Mr. Jordan."

"Certainly, sir, my pleasure. Could I give you some advice though, albeit unsolicited? If you intend to be a planter, you need to harden up. Your Negroes are just property. You cain't let emotions and sentimentality cloud your judgment. You're young and I can understand. It took me a while to learn the way of things. They ain't family, for God's sake."

"You're the second person to tell me that, Mr. Jordan. Every man has to decide how he handles his business. I don't have a big plantation with overseers handlin' the slaves, just a farm in the mountains. Me and my wife work side by side with our two servants. I try not to be sentimental, but I don't want to be callous either. Thank you for the advice, though. I'd better get on the road now. Good day to you."

Tom climbed into the wagon, looked back at James still fumbling through the basket and the little crying girl, and flicked the reins to start the horses back down the long drive.

James eventually found a coat and wrapped it around Susan's shoulders, after which both of the children fell asleep in the swaying wagon. Tom was thankful for the peace and passed the miles deep in thought. Foremost on his mind was how he was going to break it to Isaiah that his wife was gone. He kept replaying the scene of Susan and Jenny's separation in his mind, and he wondered if he had done the right thing. James had tried his best to comfort Susan, and Tom was touched by how patient and tender his son had been with the child. He was grateful to Sarah for suggesting he bring the boy along. Sarah would know what to do with this whole situation and help make it better. A few minutes ago he had dreaded the thought of arriving back at the farm. Now he could not wait, because Sarah was there and she would help him make it right.

CHAPTER 18

December 6, 1829

ISAIAH AWOKE TO the sound of the rooster crowing in the pen near his cabin. He had been dreaming of Monticello. He was a boy again, nine or ten years old. They had given the slaves the day off because President Jefferson was coming back to the plantation after his years in Washington City ended. They made preparations days before his expected arrival. Family and guests descended from miles around to welcome the great man home. A feast was prepared and a festival atmosphere permeated the plantation. In his dream Isaiah was cheering with the other boys, running alongside the president's carriage as it made its way up the drive to the big house. Everyone gathered on the front lawn, and a cheer rose from the assembled throng as Jefferson emerged. Isaiah found his way to his father's side in the crowd. Seeing his son craning to get a view, he lifted him to his shoulders, and Isaiah surveyed the proceedings from the lofty perch. It was springtime, and the dogwoods and azaleas were in bloom. The White guests were all dressed in their finest attire, the women in beautiful, colorful gowns. Cheer after cheer went up for the president. Isaiah sat atop his father's broad shoulders, the cheers sweeping over him in waves.

He lay there thinking back on that day. His memory of it so clear, so vivid. There are for most of us a handful of memories like that from childhood, some from momentous occasions, but others more mundane, marked only by how indelibly they are imprinted in our memory. They are so sharp, one can relive the moment, not just recall it, but be there again, seeing the sights, hearing the sounds, and the smells. Such was Isaiah's memory of that day, and he relished it now, until the rooster crowed again and roused him from his revelry. It seemed like someone else's life now. Here he was in a different place, alone in his cabin, the people who shared that day scattered to the four winds or gone entirely from the world. In a few weeks he would turn thirty years old. There had been few days in his life as happy as that day at Monticello, just a handful. Today will be another one, he thought. Today he would be reunited with his beloved wife and child. He didn't know what the future would hold, but as long as they were together again, he could bear anything.

The clouds had rolled in around midday, and the blue sky had given way to slate gray. The clouds were billowed like sand on the seashore after the tide has gone out. A soft wind was blowing from the southwest, and it was a warm day for December. Tom was thankful that he had enjoyed such fine weather for the duration of the trip. The pleasant day had no effect on the little girl riding in the back of the wagon. She had not spoken more than a handful of words the entire way, and every so often Tom would hear her muffled sobs. James had given up trying to comfort her and now rode up front with his father. Tom had told her at breakfast that she would be with her father today, hoping to cheer her up, but it had no effect. Tom wondered if she would even recognize Isaiah, since it had been a year since they had been together. As they got closer to home, a dark worry crept into his mind: What if Isaiah's grief turned to rage? If his cooperation over the last months was tied to achieving reunion, how would he behave now? Eager to get home, but dreading the inevitable conflagration, he covered the remaining miles to the farm, his mind as dark as the clouds above.

Isaiah had spent the day completing his chores and sprucing up his cabin. His ribs were still sore, but he ignored the pain and spent his nervous energy scampering around the farm and scanning the road every few minutes. It was late afternoon, and he was milking the cows when he heard Julia shouting and the barking of the dogs heralding his family's arrival. He stood too quickly, and a flash of pain cut through him like a knife. The blood rushed from his head, leaving him dizzy. He took a breath while the pain subsided and his vision cleared. How would it look to pass out in front of Anne and Susan? He stepped into the yard where Sarah and Ellen had joined Julia, watching the wagon roll up the drive. The two women were well into their pregnancies, and each stood with her hands on the small of her back. He remembered seeing Anne stand that way before she delivered Susan. He saw Tom and James on the front seat and craned his neck, but didn't see his girls. When he could no longer contain himself, he trotted towards the wagon, every step accompanied by a jolt of pain.

Tom watched Isaiah make his way towards him and brought the team to a stop. James jumped from the wagon and ran towards his mother, shouting. Tom climbed down just as Isaiah reached him. Isaiah was still trying to see into the wagon when Tom stepped in front of him and put his hand on his chest.

"Isaiah, wait a minute. I have to tell you something."

Sarah and Ellen had made their way to the wagon as well, and there was a tense moment of silence. Sarah and Tom exchanged a quick glance that expressed more than words, and Sarah dropped her head and put her arm around James. From the back of the wagon there was movement, and Isaiah saw Susan peek over the side rails. He pushed past Tom and rushed to the side of the wagon.

"Susan, my darlin'!" he said, and tears rolled down his cheeks. The little girl recoiled into the bed of the wagon in fear. As Isaiah leaned over the boards to reach her, he realized she was alone. He turned to Tom in confusion.

"I'm sorry, Isaiah. Anne passed away before we got there."

"You're lyin'!" Isaiah grabbed Tom by the lapels of his coat and stood with his face inches away from Tom's. "Where is she?" he demanded.

Tom reached into his pocket and retrieved the necklace Jenny had given him. He took Isaiah's hand, opened it, and placed the necklace into his open palm. Isaiah stood looking at the gift he had crafted for Anne in that other life so long ago, and then fell to his knees, his hands clasped around the necklace. His tears fell and his chest heaved with sobs. All his plans, all his dreams, all his hope disappeared like the tears falling into the dusty yard.

Susan was still crying in fear. Isaiah looked up and through cloudy eyes saw his daughter. He stood and approached the crying child, reaching out his hand and placing it on her shoulder, dropping the necklace to the ground in the act. Ellen retrieved it.

"It's alright my darlin', Daddy's here. Don't you remember me? I missed you so bad."

He lifted her from the back of the wagon, grimacing as his injured ribs protested. He put her on the ground and knelt beside her, putting his hand under her jerking chin, and lifted her face to look into her eyes. In that moment she recognized her father and buried her face in his chest, her small arms wrapping around him. Together they held each other and wept, rocking back and forth as Isaiah whispered to her.

Tom walked past the horses to Sarah and hugged her for a long time, kissing her forehead, pressing his cheek against hers. "We were too late," he whispered in her ear. "She died just the week before, some kind of stomach illness. I don't know what to tell Isaiah. I brought his daughter home to him, though she didn't want to leave the woman who cared for her, Anne's cousin. That was one of the hardest things I ever had to watch, but I couldn't come back without her, could I?"

"Of course not. You did the only thing you could do. Only time will heal the loss, but having his daughter can help soften the pain. I'm just glad to have you back home again. How did James do?"

"I don't know what I'd a done without him. I was so grateful he was along."

Ellen spoke up. "We should get 'em to go inside. I'll bet the little girl is hungry."

Sarah agreed, and they coaxed Isaiah and Susan to stand. Isaiah held the little girl in his arms as they made their way to his cabin, Ellen walking with them, her hand on Isaiah's shoulder. The Love family stood together, watching these people who shared their world now, walk down the hill in the lengthening shadows, the only sound muffled sobs.

CHAPTER 19

December 21, 1829

AUTUMN HAD SLIPPED away, the days growing shorter and the mountain nights colder and longer. The solstice arrived as it did every year, but this year it seemed bleaker than usual, as the light waged an epic struggle against a heavy, overcast sky. Midday looked like twilight, as though the sun had surrendered the contest. The day mirrored the mood that had pervaded the farm since Tom's return. Everyone went about their chores in a trancelike state. Even the children, sensing the pall that enveloped the adults, were subdued. Neither Tom nor Sarah knew what to say to ease the misery that Isaiah and Susan were enduring. Sarah thought it best to just give them time to grieve. Tom thought motion and activity were better balms, but he was not confident enough to disagree with Sarah. The days crawled along in silence, conversations carried in hushed tones.

A few days after their return, Tom had taken Isaiah aside and explained in greater detail what had happened in South Carolina. He told him what Jenny had said about Anne's last thoughts, thinking they would comfort him, but Isaiah just nodded and looked away towards the horizon, as though she might come walking over the hill after all. Susan was never far from Isaiah. She followed him around the farm like his shadow, as if she feared he would wander away and leave her alone in this strange place. James and Julia had attempted to engage the child, as their mother had suggested, but she would turn away and disappear behind her father, grasping his trouser legs in her small hands.

Ellen had been taking meals to Isaiah's cabin, and she had gradually gained Susan's confidence. The three of them would eat together at the little table Isaiah had made, with Susan sharing more and more of what she remembered about their trip south. She wouldn't talk about her mother's passing, and Isaiah would not push her. She was able to name the entire group that had made the trip from Monticello to the Jordan plantation, and Isaiah and Ellen would exchange nods and glances as they pictured the faces of the friends and family. Ellen had been childhood friends with Jenny and she smiled as Susan talked about how she had cared for her. After Susan would drift off to sleep, Ellen and Isaiah would sit in front of the fire and talk. They now knew where some Jefferson slaves had ended up, and they wondered where the rest had gone, and if any remained at Monticello. As different names would come up, they would reminisce about their memories of that friend or that cousin. Sometimes they would laugh as they recalled a funny incident or character quirk, but inevitably they would find themselves in tears as they remembered a particular loved one, knowing that they would never see them again or even know what had become of them.

CHAPTER 20

December 22, 1829

TOM WAS FEEDING the hogs when the rider emerged from the woods. As he drew closer he recognized Bynum Bell, the sheriff, and waved in greeting. Bell dismounted and shook Tom's hand.

"Good morning, Bynum. I'd ask what brings you out this way, but I figure it has to do with your prisoner. Would you like to come and sit a spell?"

"Good morning, Tom. Thanks, but I cain't stay long. The circuit judge and prosecutor came through Franklin a couple of days ago, earlier than I thought. I explained the charges to 'em. It played out just like I thought it would. I wanted to come fetch you, but the judge didn't want to git held up for a trial. I brought Wright before them and they offered him a deal: time served and twenty lashes. Told him if it went to trial it was gonna be hard on him if he was convicted and they promised him he would be. Wright hemmed and hawed fer a spell, but he saw the judge gittin' impatient and took the deal. Hezekiah Hicks laid on the lashes and did a fine job. You know what, though? Wright never made a sound. Twenty solid lashes from a stout man and he never even whimpered. That's a hard man you've made an enemy of, Tom."

"Looks that way. Couldn't be helped."

"No, I reckon not. Anyway, the judge warned him against any future offenses, told him to observe the peace, and suggested he leave Macon County if he had no property here. Wright told him he never wanted to smell Macon County or North Carolina again. He rode out this morning, riding west. I headed this way as soon as he was out of sight."

"I appreciate everything you've done, Bynum. You're a good friend."

"Just doing my job. Not sure I'd be sheriff if it hadn't been for the support of the Loves."

"I still need to come into town and sit with you about this census business. It's coming next year and I want to make sure I have all the groundwork laid."

"Of course. I brought it up at the last council meeting, so the ball is rollin'."

"Good, I'll plan on swingin' in next month. I hope you and your family have a nice Christmas."

They made their farewells and Bell mounted up and headed back into Franklin. Tom watched him ride away and caught himself looking over his shoulder. He made a mental note to keep his rifle at hand going forward, just in case.

CHAPTER 21

December 25, 1829

SARAH PREPARED CHRISTMAS dinner, with a fresh ham from the November hog killing as the centerpiece. Neither Isaiah nor Ellen had ever eaten ham. At Monticello they had given the slaves the leftover lesser cuts to prepare their holiday meals. Sarah had insisted that the slaves join the family for the dinner and, given everything that had happened, Tom did not resist. As he looked around his table, he recalled Benjamin Jordan's advice and wondered what he would have to say about this arrangement.

After the meal, Sarah distributed gifts. She had gloves for the children, a shirt for Tom, and coats for Isaiah and Ellen. Over the past few days, she had taken some clothes of Rebecca's that she had been saving for Julia and altered them to fit Susan. It was the first time Sarah had seen the little girl smile. Tom gave the girls dolls he had made and gave James a knife his father had given him when he was a boy. He gave Sarah a necklace he had purchased in Morganton. While Sarah and Ellen cleared the table from dinner and the children examined their gifts, Tom walked over to Isaiah and stood beside him.

"This has been a hard year for both of us, Isaiah. I lost my little girl this time last year. I know our losses are different, but I want you to know I understand some of what you're goin' through."

"Thank you for bringing my little girl back to me. If I'd lost both of 'em, I don't think I could go on. I just wish I could have been with my Anne when she left this world. Knowin' she died in a strange place, thinkin' of me, is almost more than I been able to bear. What bothers me near as bad is wonderin' if she's layin' in some unmarked grave with no one to mourn her or remember that she once lived and loved. I see you sometimes in the evenin' out by your little girl's grave, and my heart breaks thinkin' that they's no one to watch over my darlin' Anne."

Isaiah dropped his head and Tom stood silent, trying to think of something to say.

"I got somethin' for you. Since I found out you can read, I been holdin' on to this book. It's called *The Swiss Family Robinson* and it was one of my daughter's favorites. I think you'll enjoy it. But you must listen to me. You know the kind of trouble we'd see if anybody was to find out. Hide it in your cabin and only take it out when you can read safe, alright?"

"Yes sir, thank you. This is kind of you." Isaiah took the book and looked it over, flipping through the pages. "It's got pictures. I didn't know they made books with pictures."

"What books did you use to learn to read at Monticello?"

"The Bible mostly, little books that Peter could slip out of the house with no one noticin'. They was a book by Benjamin Franklin, *Poor Richard's Almanack*, that we read over and over. Peter told me that President Jefferson and Mr. Franklin was friends from the days of the Revolution. They was another book by a man named Paine."

"Thomas Paine?"

"Yes sir, that was his name. The book was *The Rights of Man*."

They were silent for a moment, their gaze locked, each remembering the contents of the book and the ramifications of a Black man absorbing its message. Tom broke the silence. "I remember the book well. It had a big impact on me back in school when I read it for the first time. I still have my copy." He glanced over at his bookshelf. "*The Swiss Family Robinson* is not as . . . advanced, but I wasn't sure how far along your readin' was."

"Been a long time since I had a chance to read. I know I'll enjoy it, Mr. Tom. Thank you."

"You're welcome, Isaiah. Merry Christmas to you and Susan."

CHAPTER 22

February 23, 1830

THE SNOW STARTED falling in the night, and as the dawn struggled to make its presence felt behind the heavy gray clouds, a blanket of white covered the ground several inches deep. Isaiah shattered the morning stillness, banging on the cabin door. Tom and Sarah stood blinking in the doorway half-awake as Isaiah informed them: "Ellen's water done broke and I think the baby's comin' quick!"

Together Tom, Sarah, and Isaiah made their way through the snow to Ellen's cabin, where they found her covered in a cold sweat and writhing in pain. Sarah bent over her and put a hand on her brow. "It's gonna be alright, Ellen. How long ago did your water break?"

"Might be going on an hour. I done lost track of time. It hurts so bad!"

"I know, but we're going to get you through this. You gotta try to relax and take slow, long breaths. Isaiah, get that fire built up, it's cold in here, and get a pot of water boilin'." As Isaiah jumped into motion, Ellen cried out, and then fell into a low moan as a contraction rolled through her.

Tom took Sarah by the arm and pulled her to the side. "Do you want me to ride to Franklin and fetch Martha Dickey?" Martha Dickey was a midwife who had helped deliver both James and Julia. She was in her sixties now, but was the only midwife within a day's ride of the farm.

"We ain't got time. You never know with first babies. I'd hate to try to deliver her myself if you're caught out in the snow."

"Maybe I could send Isaiah?"

"How would he find their place? I cain't see her gettin' out in a blizzard with somebody she don't know anyways."

"You're right."

"We can do this. Go to the house and get towels, my scissors, and twine." Tom stared at her with a quizzical look on his face, imagining the two of them delivering this woman's baby in the middle of a snowstorm. "Go!" she said, and he snapped out of his reverie and went back out into the snow.

"Isaiah, where is Susan?"

"I told her to stay in our cabin."

"She's probably scared half to death. Go git her and take her to the house and tell James he's to look after her and Julia today. Can you make 'em somethin' to eat and not burn down the house?"

"Yes ma'am. I can do that." He turned and followed Tom.

Sarah watched him go and through the open door noticed that the snow had picked up in intensity. "Lord, get us through this day," she prayed and turned her attention back to Ellen.

"I'm so scared, Miss Sarah!"

"Nothin' to be scared of Ellen, I'm right here with you. I've delivered three children of my own and helped the midwife with two others. We'll get through this. Just trust me and listen to what I tell you, alright?"

"Yes ma'am, I will."

"I'll get you some water. Have you ate since supper?"

"No ma'am, but I ain't hungry."

"I know. It's good that you haven't ate. We don't want you sick at your stomach." As she turned around to get the water pitcher off the table, Sarah felt a sudden pain that stopped her in her tracks. She grabbed her belly and held her breath until it passed.

"You alright, Miss Sarah?"

"Yes, Ellen. The baby just gave me a pretty hard kick is all. I'm fine." In the space of a heartbeat a thought crossed Sarah's mind, triggering a moment of panic: What if her baby comes today?

"I don't have time to think about that," she told herself.

The snow fell all day and by late afternoon everything was covered in a shroud of white. Tom shuttled back and forth between Ellen's cabin and their house, keeping the fires stoked in both and checking on the children. Between him and Isaiah, they were able to keep all the humans and the farm animals fed. Isaiah ducked out to milk the cows, and returned to sit with Ellen, allowing Sarah a break. She sat by Ellen hour after hour, mopping her brow, rubbing her back, and encouraging her as the contractions grew in duration and intensity. As dusk approached, she pulled Tom aside and whispered in his ear.

"It won't be much longer now. I need you to help me and pay close attention to what I do, alright?"

"Of course."

"Listen, Tom, I think our baby may be coming soon too. You may have to deliver it by yourself." Then she snapped, "Don't look at me that way!" as Tom took a step back and dropped his jaw. "There is no one else to do it, do you understand me? Ellen is going to be in no shape after she delivers, and I don't think you want Isaiah delivering your baby, do you?"

"No."

"That leaves you. You men always carry on about bein' so strong. Well, if I can have a baby you can help me deliver it, do you understand me, Thomas Love?"

"Yes, Sarah Love." He placed the palm of his rough hand against her cheek and kissed her forehead. He gave her a weak smile while he felt his gut clench. Sarah turned away as Ellen cried out again and shivered as she pictured herself in Ellen's position without another woman to help her.

It was two hours after dark when Ellen gave birth to a baby girl. She had labored for over twelve hours and now lay exhausted, her eyes closed. Sarah cleaned the baby and then quietly stepped beside Ellen. "Ellen," she whispered, "you have a daughter," and she presented the child to her, swaddled in a soft towel. Ellen opened her eyes and looked first at Sarah and then at the little bundle. Without a word, she turned her head and closed her eyes again. Sarah turned to look at Tom, who could only shrug.

"Can I hold her?" Isaiah asked from a darkened corner of the cabin.

"Of course." Sarah placed the child in Isaiah's stout arms, where he cradled her.

"She's a handsome little lady, Ellen. What you gonna name her?" Isaiah asked after peering down at the baby's face for a few moments.

"I don't care. Name her whatever you want," Ellen replied in a low, hoarse voice they could just hear.

"Don't worry. I'll talk to her," Isaiah told Sarah so that only she could hear. "She's just tuckered out. She'll feel different when she gets her strength back and sees this little face."

"Of course she will." Sarah turned to continue cleaning up and suddenly bent over and gasped. "Oh Lord, my water just broke." Tom jumped to her side and took her arm. "Get me to the house. Isaiah, stay here and take care of Ellen and the baby."

Tom led her to the cabin door and opened it to a blast of frigid air and a landscape that seemed to glow even in the darkness. The snow had stopped around sunset, and now stars were twinkling in the dark winter sky, appearing and then reappearing as the departing clouds scurried away towards the east. There was a foot of snow on the ground, and Tom walked in front of Sarah as he supported her and tried to clear a path to the house.

They opened the door to see the three children sitting in front of the fire. James sat in the middle of the two girls with a book on his lap. At the sound of the door they turned in unison, each of them with a look of fear as they saw Tom, with Sarah leaning heavily against him.

"It's alright. Momma's gonna have the baby tonight. Ellen has a little baby girl." Sarah struggled to sound calm, even as a contraction cut her short.

Tom helped her to a chair and then began surveying the room, trying to imagine how he was going to manage this situation. "Sarah, I don't believe you can make it up the stairs. I'll bring a mattress down here, alright?"

"Yes, that should work."

"Julia, get your momma some water. James, can you take Susan to Ellen's cabin? She can help her daddy with Ellen and the baby. And bring back the scissors and twine and any clean towels we left there." Tom looked at the three children standing with their eyes and their mouths wide open. "Now, please!" raising his voice, and the two girls responded by breaking into tears.

James took Susan by the arm, put on his coat and helped her don hers, and led her from the cabin. Julia ran to her mother's side.

"It's alright," Sarah said, half to Julia and half to Tom. "Go get the mattress and one of the old quilts. I'm alright for now."

Tom fled up the stairs as Sarah pacified Julia. He was back in a flash, dragging the lumpy mattress and an old checkered quilt behind him. He rearranged the few pieces of furniture to free up space and placed the mattress on the floor in front of the fireplace, adding a log to the fire, which sent up a spray of sparks and brightened the room with new flames. James returned, panting, placing the scissors, twine, and towels on a chair and presented himself to his father for his next assignment.

"Good boy. Now go put water in the kettle over the kitchen fire and get it hot, but don't burn the kitchen down, alright?"

Sarah now moaned with the onset of another contraction. "They're pretty close together, Tom."

CHAPTER 23

February 24, 1830

THE WIND PICKED up as the night deepened, howling and whistling around the doors and windows and moaning in the eaves. It was sometimes hard for Tom to distinguish between the sounds created by the cold northwest wind and those made by Sarah as she labored on the pallet on the cabin floor in the flickering light of the lamps and the fire. Tom couldn't figure where she got the strength. She had been up since dawn of the previous day, worked without cease to deliver Ellen's baby, and had now been suffering in labor for hours. He was exhausted himself, which only increased his amazement at her stamina. The clock on the mantel showed half past three in the morning. He had propped Sarah up on some pillows and was rubbing her lower back, where she said the pain was concentrated. She stared into the fire through half-open eyes. As Tom looked at the back of her head, her beautiful blond hair tousled and matted from her exertions, the glow of the fire surrounded her.

"Tom, I'm worried," she said after the last contraction had passed. "They don't seem to be coming any closer together. I wasn't in labor nearly this long with James or Julia. Rebecca took a long time coming, but she was the first, and they say the first always takes longer. I wish Rebecca was here now."

"I know, honey. It's because you're so tired. I don't know where you're gettin' the strength."

"I'd give anything to sleep. Listen to me, Tom. If I don't make it through this . . ."

"Stop! Don't say that. Don't even think about it. We're gonna come outta this, together." Fear swept through Tom's heart, like the icy wind that blew outside. He remembered the agony he had endured with Rebecca's passing and thought that pain would pale in comparison to losing Sarah. A world without her was not a world he wanted to live in. His life for hers, he tried to negotiate with God, a simple deal. Then it came rushing back to him, kneeling beside Rebecca's bed, pleading for her life, bargaining his life for hers. But she had gone, and he was still here.

"Promise me you'll take care of yourself. I know you'll take care of the children, but I worry about you. When Rebecca passed you went somewhere deep inside yourself, and I was afeared you couldn't come back. If I don't make it, you cain't go back there, cause I won't be here to help you find your way home. Promise me."

"Listen to me, Sarah Love: I ain't going nowhere and neither are you. We're gonna bring this baby into the world and we're gonna be together until we're both dodderin' old fools surrounded by a passel of grandkids, do you hear me?"

"Yes." And she shuddered with the force of another contraction. "I think it's coming, Tom," she said when she could again catch her breath.

Tom and Sarah Love delivered a boy into the world at four o'clock in the morning. He cut the cord and tied it off as Sarah had showed him with Ellen's child. He wrapped the baby in one of the few remaining clean towels and handed him to Sarah. She touched his cheek and kissed him on the forehead. "He favors Rebecca when she was born, don't he?"

"A little bit. What do you wanna name him?"

"My grandfather was named Jesse. Could we name him after him?"

"Are you sure you want three children whose names all start with *J*? But after what you've been through, how could I deny you anything? Jesse it is."

CHAPTER 24

February 27, 1830

THE SNOW WAS still on the ground and piled in drifts as Isaiah made his way to Ellen's cabin. He rapped on the door, and when there was no answer, he called through. "Ellen, can I come in? I brung you dinner." When there was still no answer, he lifted the wooden handle that served as a doorknob and peered into the dark cabin, lit only by the flickering flames that remained in the hearth.

"I ain't hungry, Isaiah. I just wanna sleep. The baby cried off and on all night. I ain't had two hours of sleep all put together," Ellen said in a hoarse whisper.

"You still gotta eat, and I'll get your fire goin' agin. It's cold in here. You and the baby don't need to be gittin' sick. I'll be real quiet so as not to wake her." He placed the food on the table and new logs on the coals, which he poked. The logs caught up and brought added light to the cabin, the shadows dancing away as the flames grew. The baby slept through it, nestled in the crib Isaiah had made. Ellen stirred from under the covers and took a chair at the table, examining the food Isaiah had brought.

"Have you thought of a name yet?"

"I told you to name her. I don't care."

"Name her Rachael."

Ellen looked up at him with a mixture of anger and sorrow, and then spoke in a voice choked with emotion. "That's my momma's name. You want me to give this child, the child of that . . . that . . . monster, my momma's name?"

"Ellen, listen to me. I know yore hurtin'. I cain't imagine what you been through. It was bad enough what was done to you, but to carry the child and go through that birthin', I cain't imagine. But I know how I've been grievin' since I found out 'bout Anne, and I think the pain we're both feelin' must be alike. It ain't right what's happened to us, and it makes my heart hurt and it fills me with a rage that I can barely choke down. I go by turns wantin' to die and wantin' to burn this world down. But then I look at Susan. I'm all in the world she's got. I gotta go on for her. That little child in the crib didn't ask to be brung into this cold world, much less through the pain you been put through. It mighta been better if she'd never been born, but she's here now and she's innocent of it all. She ain't responsible for what that man did to you. She's a victim like you. Her life's gonna be hard enough as it is without her momma raisin' her to carry that shame. I thought if'n you named her after your momma, you could think of her, and not how she come here."

Ellen put her face in her hands and sobbed. Isaiah patted her shoulder and sat with her while she cried. Finally she composed herself, looked over at the crib and said, "Rachael," in a voice Isaiah could barely hear.

"There's somethin' else I wanna ask you, Ellen." She looked up at him through her tear-filled eyes.

"That baby needs a father, and my Susan needs a mother. I know I ain't the man you might have picked for a husband, but we find ourselves here together on this farm in the wilderness, with no other of our people round I know of . . ."

"Yes," Ellen said and took Isaiah's hand between hers.

"I'll never let you regret it. And I promise you, some way, somehow, we gonna be free one day."

CHAPTER 25

April 4, 1830

SPRING CAME LATE to the mountains, making its eventual arrival all the more welcome. The trilliums were in bloom, along with the flame azaleas and the trout lilies. A brilliant sun shone in an azure sky, and the world seemed new. The fields were turned and plowed and ready for planting. A full moon on the eighth was auspicious, and if the weather held Tom planned to drop seed starting that day. It was the first Sunday in April, and all nine souls on the Love farm gathered in the little copse of trees overlooking the river for the wedding of Isaiah and Ellen.

They stood under a giant oak tree that must have been two hundred years old. Isaiah held Ellen's hand in his left and Susan's in his right. Ellen held Rachael cradled in her left arm as she cooed and squirmed. Tom stood before them as Sarah, holding Jesse, and James and Julia looked on. Tom had never performed a wedding, but he remembered his own well enough and walked them through the simple vows. After they said the words, Isaiah and Ellen jumped the broom she had made for the ceremony.

Isaiah thought back to the day he had married Anne. He hoped she would understand, if she was watching from somewhere unseen, and at that moment a gentle breeze wafted across the river and he knew she would.

After the ceremony, they all headed back up to the house for the afternoon meal. Isaiah and Tom followed behind, and Isaiah thanked him for performing the service.

"Mr. Tom, could I git a piece of paper sayin' me and Ellen is married? I didn't have one for me and Anne. I don't know if it'd made a difference, but pieces of paper seem to carry great weight with White folk."

"Of course, Isaiah, I'll draw it up after dinner. You're right about papers. Most of bein' a lawyer is arguin' over who has a paper and who doesn't. I hope you and Ellen have happiness together and you never have to show anyone else your papers." Tom hesitated for a minute before going on. "What name would you like me to use?" The only reply a quizzical look from Isaiah. "A family name, a surname, like Love or Jefferson."

"I see. I never give it no thought. Lemme think on it."

The two men continued up the hill in silence, thinking about the question from their own perspectives. Tom thought about his family history and how one of his ancestors had decided on the name *Love*. He imagined a burly Scot with a thick red beard and bright blue eyes standing on a windswept hill in the Highlands declaring that henceforth his descendants would be called the *Loves*. He smiled to himself, thinking how far removed the reality no doubt was from his imagination.

Isaiah wondered about his family history. Only a handful of enslaved families at Monticello had been given surnames, those with the closest relationships to the Jeffersons: the Hemings family, the Fossetts, and the Hubbards. The other slaves had only Christian names, given to them by their masters. Their parents couldn't name their own children. Like Tom, Isaiah wondered about his ancestors. His father had told him that his father's grandfather had first been brought to America as a slave. They had passed down almost nothing of life in Africa to Isaiah's generation. The horror of the Atlantic passage was the oldest family memory. Weeks trapped in the dark, stinking bowels of the slave ship left a scar each generation bore. The first thing they had taken from his ancestor, other than his freedom, was his name. Isaiah could only wonder what his original name had been, or what his family's home in Africa had been like. That knowledge was lost to him, never to be recovered. Now he must choose a name, a White name that his family and his descendants would carry. He frowned, thinking of the responsibility.

"I choose the name Paine," he said, startling both himself and Tom, who stopped and stared at him.

"That's a good name. I'll draw up a marriage certificate for Isaiah and Ellen Paine."

SCHEDULE of the whole number of Perso

Name of County, City, Ward, Town, Township, Parish, Precinct, Hundred, or District.	NAMES of HEADS OF FAMILIES.	FREE WHITE MALES.											
		Under five years of age.	Of five and under ten.	Of ten and under fifteen.	Of fifteen and under twenty.	Of twenty and under thirty.	Of thirty and under forty.	Of forty and under fifty.	Of fifty and under sixty.	Of sixty and under seventy.	Of seventy and under eighty.	Of eighty and under ninety.	Of eighty and under ninety.
		under 5	5 to 10	10 to 15	15 to 20	20 to 30	30 to 40	40 to 50	50 to 60	60 to 70	70 to 80	80 to 90	90
	Samuel Raynolds	1				1							
	John Ledford Senr		1	1	2					1			
	Hezekiah Burns	2	2	1			1						
	Anderson Russell					1							
	William Bersey		1										
	Joshua Ammons		2				1						
	John Ammons		1						1				
	Young Ammons		1			1							
	Samuel Robe	2							1				
	Samuel Hyde	1				1				1			
	Travis Allmon	1	2			1	1						
	Thomas Love Gen	1		1			1						
	David Rogers	2	1	1			1						
	Matthew Jones	1	2	1									
	Sarah McDaniel	1	1	1									
	John Griffen				1	1						1	
	Gilbert Halls		1										
	James Poted	2	1	1			1						
	Ebenezer Scroggs	1				1							
	William Bryson				2				1				
	Barsley Willson	1	1				1						
	Levy Lambert				2				1				
	William Hicks	1					1						
	Silas McDowell	1			2		1						
	Elizabeth McDowell												

A page from the *Fifth Census of the United States, 1830*, showing entries for Macon County, North Carolina. Photograph courtesy of Allen County Public Library Genealogy Center.

DUFF GREEN, PRINTER.

PART TWO

Have I not reason to lament
What man has made of man?

William Wordsworth, "Lines Written in Early Spring" (1798)

CHAPTER 26

May 1, 1830

TOM SAT AT the kitchen table gazing at a map of Macon County. There were several maps stacked underneath, which he had spent the last few weeks gathering and studying. It was one month until the census officially began, and he was still wrestling to come up with the most efficient strategy to canvass the sprawling territory. He had his uncle's map from the 1820 survey in the stack. It was ten years old, and the decade had seen a flood of new settlers moving into the Cherokee lands. Some settlers had bought land in the auctions at Franklin, only to find the property still inhabited by Cherokee under reservations they had made in the last treaty. New roads were being cut all over the county. Tom helped build some of them, and he saw a handful were missing from even the latest map. Also missing were the locations of some Cherokee villages. The major towns like Nowee, Burningtown, and Cowee were permanent, but other villages moved from time to time to take advantage of more fertile land, proximity to firewood, and better fishing. Tom leaned back in the chair and ran his hands through his hair.

"It's almost time for supper, Tom," Sarah advised as she passed behind him preparing the evening meal. "You've been starin' at them maps for hours now. Why're you havin' such a hard time?"

"I don't know. I keep thinkin' there's a perfect plan I should come up with, but there's just so many unknowns. There are more roads and new homesteads than any of these maps show. This thing's just bigger than I had imagined, and the closer it gets, the bigger it seems."

"They may not be a perfect plan. You might have to make it up as you go along."

"Kind of like life, huh?" He gave her a grin. "You're right, but with this much territory to cover and a deadline to meet, I cain't afford to waste time and energy."

"Where are you figurin' to start?"

"I have this map from the 1820 survey that Uncle Robert did. It broke the county up into eighteen districts, and each district into sections. If I do three sections a month, I should finish on time. The problem is just a few of the districts around Franklin have most of the people, so they'll take longer. The outer districts have fewer people, but more ground to cover, so I gotta account for more travel time."

"Start with Franklin and see how it goes; get a feel for how long each house takes and then figger out how much time to allow."

"That's what I was thinkin'. There are other things to consider, like the weather and what needs doin' for the farm. All the plantin's done. Everything has come up alright. There'll be weedin' and hoein' and all the usual chores. Then harvest and hog killin' will be around before you know it, and that happens just as I'm windin' up the census."

"We'll take care of the farm. You take care of what you gotta do."

"When I took this on, I didn't know we'd have two babies to contend with. How are you supposed to take care of the farm and the young'uns?"

"Ellen and me'll take turns watchin' the young'uns. Isaiah'll take care of all the big work."

In the past week Isaiah had finished building a two-wheeled carriage for Tom. Tom had explained to him he needed something to carry supplies, including the census documents, but he didn't want to take the wagon because it was needed on the farm and it was so large, it would overburden one horse on the mountain roads. Using spare parts from an old abandoned wagon and farm implements, Isaiah built a small, lightweight carriage. It had one seat for the driver atop a storage compartment, shaped uncomfortably like a small coffin, mounted between the two wheels. On top of the box, he attached a metal rod that passed through two eye bolts. Wrapped around the rod was an oilcloth tarp he had made by soaking a large piece of cotton cloth in boiled linseed oil and rust shavings. It could be unrolled to form a water-resistant lean-to shelter when Tom found himself forced to spend the night outdoors.

"One thing to remember," Isaiah said when showing how they worked. "You cain't get 'em near fire. I left one near the forge to dry when I was working on the carriage and nearly burnt down the shop."

Isaiah had also created several waterproof containers to hold rolls of census sheets. He had made tubes out of sections of leather, which he wrapped in oilcloth, with hammered pieces of tin to serve as end caps. The rolled-up census sheets fit into the tubes, safe from the threat of water damage. The ingenuity of Isaiah's creations astounded Tom. They solved the biggest logistical concerns that had been troubling him: transportation, shelter, and protecting the precious census documents from the elements. The carriage looked a little strange, but it was light enough for a single horse or mule, small enough to maneuver the narrow roads he would have to navigate, and sat tall enough to ford the many streams he would have to cross.

"I ain't worried 'bout Isaiah's ability to manage things around the farm. After he tried to run off though, I worry he might try it again if I ain't here."

"He was goin' to find his family, Tom. Would you 'a done any different if you were in his shoes?"

"Who knows, but it was still foolhardy."

"Things are different now. He married Ellen, and he's got her and the young'uns to think on. He wouldn't get far with 'em in tow and he wouldn't leave 'em behind."

"You're right, but I still got this unease about leavin'. I got regrets 'bout this whole undertakin'."

"Well, you're committed now. It'll do you no good to fret. Now clear the table so I can set supper."

May was wetter than usual, and the crops and the hayfields grew in profusion. So did the weeds, and when the residents of the farm weren't tackling the other chores, they were pulling or hoeing horse nettles, poke salad, and all the other weeds that plagued farmers in the mountains. When it was too wet to work the fields, Tom was poring over maps and a list of names he got from John Dobson, the county registrar, from deeds filed since they established the county, along with those transferred from Haywood County. As near as he could tell, there were over eight hundred households in the county, spread over hundreds of square miles of mountains and valleys. As the month passed and the start of the census loomed, Tom grew increasingly anxious about the task before him. There was also an undercurrent of excitement and adventure that buoyed him, as he thought about going back into the deep woods. He remembered the time spent with both his uncle's survey team and Professor Olmsted on the geological survey. Now, after many years, he was going to relive those experiences. He was going to spend the summer and fall riding through the most beautiful land on earth; virgin forests of ancient hemlocks and firs, rivers and waterfalls of crystal-clear water, hollers filled with mountain laurels and wildflowers of every description. Camping under the stars, he would fall asleep to the sounds of the forest at night, crickets and tree frogs and katydids, owls and whip-poor-wills. The more he thought about it, the more at peace he became. In the prime of his life, his farm thriving, and his family growing, he was getting paid to spend half the year on a once-in-a-lifetime adventure. No one on earth was better suited to complete this mission, he told himself. One day in the far-off future, when he was an old man and the wilderness had been tamed, he would look back at this across the sweep of years and remember the time he was the census taker.

CHAPTER 27

June 1, 1830

TOM WAS UP before the sun. He had been packing most of the last week and had double-checked his gear to be sure he had forgotten nothing. He stood doing a mental inventory after breakfast and declared he was ready to go.

"What about these?" Sarah asked with a coy smile as she pointed to the tubes containing the census documents. They were arranged in a box next to the door where Tom had put them.

He looked at her sheepishly. "I suppose I will be needin' them."

He packed the forms off to the carriage and rearranged his belongings to make room, chuckling that he had nearly driven off without them. One tube contained the last map he had made. He had created his own sections, using rivers and streams as borders. They were permanent and well-marked on the maps, and he would know he had completed a section when he reached water's edge. It had been such a simple solution, and it embarrassed him that he had taken so long to come up with it.

In the traces was Rufus, a big gray mule, five years old, indefatigable and imperturbable. Tom figured he would be perfect for the long days and the tough roads ahead. He considered taking a dog along for company, but when he thought of the ruckus that would ensue every time they approached houses with dogs, he decided against it.

He held little Jesse for a time, kissing him on the forehead before putting him back in his cradle. Next came Julia and then James, telling him to be the man of the house while he was gone. Then he took Sarah by the hand and led her outside beside the carriage to say his goodbye in private. He hugged her for a long time, smelling her hair and feeling her breath on his chest. He put his hand under her chin and lifted her face to look into her eyes.

"I'll be back in a week. I'll miss you every single minute we're apart."

"Please take care of yourself. I know how you are. You'll git busy and forget to eat until you're starvin'. And don't take no unnecessary chances. Promise me."

"I promise. I love you, Sarah."

"I know. I love you too, Tom. Now go so you can finish this thing."

He hugged her again and then kissed her on the lips and once on the forehead. He climbed up onto the awkward-looking carriage, took the reins and flapped them once.

"Let's go, Rufus!" He looked down at Sarah one last time. "One week."

"One week," she said, as she put up her hand and waved him away.

Rufus nickered, leaned into the harness and pulled the carriage into motion. The first step of the enterprise was officially underway.

The road to Franklin meandered through lush forest, with the early morning sun piercing the canopy where the trees were thin. The woods were alive with the trill of songbirds and buzzing insects. Cardinals and finches flitted from tree to tree, tracers of crimson and gold in their wake. Mountain laurel bloomed white and fuchsia by the little springs and creeks that occupied every fold in the hills. At various points the road would open to a meadow, the morning mist hovering over masses of violets, their purple flowers covering the meadow like a quilt. Swallowtails and sulphurs swarmed above the blossoms in profusion, their yellow wings in constant motion, as though the air itself was vibrating. Sometimes the road hewed close to the riverbank and the sounds of the forest gave way to the water churning over the dark rocks. Spiderwebs stretched between the trees, arching over the current, their architecture illuminated by bands of morning dew like strings of diamonds. A red fox sat atop a rocky outcrop on the far bank, a silent sentinel observing the passage of the strange contraption through its territory.

At one bend in the road, it startled Tom to see a Cherokee man standing across the river. He would have missed him if not for the sun reflected off his copper armband. A purple-and-gold turban covered his head. His sleeveless shirt was ivory, covered by a vest with the same purple and gold colors as his turban. Deerskin pants and knee-high moccasins completed his wardrobe. Ornate tattoos covered the copper skin of his arms and neck. A rifle leaned against the tree beside him, and a tomahawk hung from his waist. He looked to be about the same age as Tom. He raised his right hand in greeting and Tom responded in kind. Rufus's ears perked up as he caught sight of the motion. Tom knew many of the Cherokee who owned farms, but he didn't recognize this man. He assumed he was hunting, and since he appeared to be alone, saw no cause for concern.

Tom passed a handful of farms on his way to Franklin: Gilbert Falls's place, the Ammonses' farms, the Almans', the Hydes', and a few others. They were his closest neighbors, but he kept to his plan, bypassing them to start with the residents of Franklin. There was no traffic on the road this morning, and he enjoyed the sights and sounds in quiet solitude as he made his way north. He had made this trip many times, but the splendor of the scene seemed more pronounced to him today. "We wander through the world oblivious to the beauty all around us," he thought, "our minds focused on surviving. All the while, nature's wonders surround us, offering to share their blessings, while we soldier on, apart and aloof."

The sun was overhead as Tom approached the bustling outskirts of Franklin. Several acquaintances waved greetings and commented about his carriage. He made his way to the center of town and pulled Rufus to a halt in front of Jesse Siler's house. Tom had known the Siler family for years. The Siler clan owned a significant amount of land in the county. They were also successful merchants. The store they owned in partnership with Sarah's family, the Brittains, had been the first trading post in the territory.

Everyone assumed that Sarah would marry one of the Siler boys, and Tom often felt her family was disappointed when she chose him, although they seemed happy to have their family linked with the prominent Loves.

Tom took one of the cylinders containing the census sheets from the carriage, along with a box containing his pens and ink, and walked to the front door of the two-story house, which opened before he could knock.

Harriet Siler stood beaming in the doorway, her coal-black hair pulled back and wrapped in a tight bun. She wore a fashionable cotton dress dyed a pastel blue, befitting the wife of a successful merchant.

"Thomas Love! What a pleasant surprise!" she gushed. "Come in, come in!" She led him to the tastefully appointed drawing room just off the foyer and motioned for him to sit on the sofa, placing his materials on the low table in front of him. A moment later Jesse Siler appeared in the doorway. He was a few years older than Tom, with a sprinkling of gray hairs to show for it. He had a close-cropped beard and his teeth showed the effects of years of cigar smoking. His well-made, gray wool suit was snug, and he had put on weight since Tom had last seen him. They greeted each other and exchanged pleasantries as Tom explained the purpose of his visit.

"I'm conducting the census for the county, and yours'll be the first name on the roll."

"Bynum was telling me about that. How do I come to receive such an honor?"

"I would say it is because of your status in our community, but the truth is you are the first house on Main Street," Tom said with a chuckle.

Tom rolled the blank document out on the table and made room on the sofa for Jesse to join him. He explained the process, showing him the columns he would be completing.

"And you gotta do this for every family in the county?" Jesse asked.

"That's right, in person."

"That's quite the undertaking. How long you figurin' it'll take you?"

"I have until December first and I think it'll take all of that."

"And these records are going to Washington City?" Tom replied with a nod. "That's interestin', my name on some roll for future generations to see. And when they see Macon County, mine'll be the first one. Thank you for the honor, Tom."

Tom got the information he needed about the ages and genders of the Siler family members and recorded them on the roll.

"How many Negroes do you own?"

"Sixteen altogether: fourteen on the farm and two to help here with the housework and at the store." He gave Tom the breakdown of their ages: four boys under ten, four girls under ten, one male under twenty-five, one teenage girl, three adult males, and three adult females. Tom recorded their numbers on the second sheet of the census.

"So twenty-three people total in your household; is that everybody?"

"That covers it. You don't need no more'n that?"

"No, that's it. Did you have anything else in mind?"

"I figured they'd want to know where we was born, schoolin', that sort of thing. I couldn't recollect what they wanted back in '20. Seems they just want a count now."

"I was surprised myself, but I'm glad it's not as detailed as you're describin' or they'd have to pay me a lot more," Tom said, laughing. While they waited for the ink to dry, Tom and Jesse talked about business, the growth of the county, and the latest gossip from Harriet.

"Your family's done well, Jesse. You all should be very proud."

"We owe it all to my grandfather, Plikard Dederic Siler. He made all of this possible."

"That is an interesting name."

"He was German. He come to America during colonial times with nothin' but the shirt on his back. My daddy Weimer said he stowed away on a ship for the crossing to Philadelphia. Somehow he started a mercantile business, and when the Revolution commenced, he gambled on the Americans, supplyin' the soldiers with food and clothin'. After the war, he got a passel of land grants. I wonder sometimes where we'd be if he hadn't had the courage to come to a new world and side with the rebels. Took guts. They named Siler City over in Chatham County for him, where he's buried."

"We all owe a debt to that generation."

Tom gathered his materials, thanked the Silers and made his goodbyes. Outside, he placed his documents back in the storage box and climbed into the seat for the short drive to the next house. "One down and how many more to go?" he thought to himself.

The next house belonged to James Gray, a veteran of the War of 1812. Like the Silers, he was given land grants for his military service, and like them, he also owned a house in town and a farm outside town. He and his wife, Mary, were sitting down for the midday meal when Tom knocked at the door, and he accepted their invitation to join them. Mary and Sarah were childhood friends, and Tom gave her a complete update on the Love family. After dinner, Tom spread out his papers and collected the census information on the Gray family, consisting of James and Mary, a teenage son, a daughter under five, James's nephew in his twenties, and four slaves managed by a foreman working the farm.

"Does that cover it?" Tom asked.

The couple looked at one another before James answered. "There is another child, a boy four years old. He's colored but not a slave."

"He's free?"

"Yes." Neither of them added anything in the way of explanation. There was a long silence as Tom made the entry, and then he reviewed the numbers with them.

"Alright, I believe that does it. I can't thank you enough for dinner."

"You are most welcome, Tom. Please tell Sarah to come and see me when she's in town next, will you?" Mary asked.

"Of course," he said, and he made his way back to his carriage. As Rufus started towards the next house, Tom wondered to himself about the circumstances that would lead to the Gray's having a small free colored child living with them. The county was still small. It seemed to him if there was some associated scandal, he would have heard about it. He shrugged his shoulders and made a mental note to discuss it with Sarah.

He pulled up to a whitewashed frame house on the corner of Main Street, one of the larger houses in town. A Black woman wearing a black dress with a white apron and a turban opened the door for him. He introduced himself and was shown into the dining room. Tom set his papers on the table and waited. A few minutes later a tall, thin woman in her thirties appeared in the doorway. "Well howdy, Tom Love!" Elizabeth Alman said. Tom returned the greeting.

"John is down at the tannery. If this is about taxes or his business, I'm afraid you're gonna have to take it up with him."

John Alman operated a tannery on the outskirts of town that was the source of considerable consternation among the townsfolk. The smells and refuse from converting animal carcasses into hides and leather goods were considered a terrible nuisance by those households unfortunate enough to be downwind, although there was not a family or business that didn't depend on the products of the operation. Working under those conditions had to be trying, and it was reflected in John Alman's personality. He was coarse and acerbic, and between the smell that followed him and his caustic misdemeanor, most people tried to avoid him.

"Nothing like that, Mrs. Alman. I just need a count of the number and ages of people living here. I believe you can provide all that I need."

Alman had seven men living in the household in their twenties, including him, and three young men under twenty. He provided room and board for these nine men, who worked in the tannery. There was also his wife, their daughter, and the female slave who had shown him in. Tom wondered what the workload must be for Elizabeth Alman and the woman, cooking and cleaning for ten men. He finished his entries, thanked Mrs. Alman for her time, and headed to the next house.

Sheriff Bynum Bell was sitting on his porch, his feet up on the railing, leaning back in a straight chair reading a newspaper when Tom pulled up in front of his house.

"That's a helluva contraption, Tom."

"Thank you, Bynum. I see you are hard at work as usual."

Both men laughed as Tom climbed the stairs and shook hands. Bell offered him a seat, and they sat side by side looking out towards the western mountains.

"You hear Congress passed that Indian removal legislation?" Bell asked.

"No, when did that happen?"

"Couple a weeks ago. You know how slow news travels to these parts. They gonna offer 'em land out west for givin' up their land here and in Georgia and Tennessee. If they don't move voluntarily, they will make provisions to force 'em to go."

"Speaking of news traveling, could I get any old newspapers you don't want? John Phillips, who did the 1820 census for Haywood, told me that most of the people back in the woods don't get a lot of news and having an old paper'll sometimes open doors."

"I think I can scrounge up a few copies. Although they make the best ass wipes."

Tom laughed but knew it was true. "I'll bet Jackson and the folks in Raleigh are beside themselves at the prospect of kickin' the Indians out. You expectin' any trouble?"

"Who knows how it'll roll out. I'm guessin' there'll be a show of force."

Tom nodded. "I saw an Indian I didn't recognize today on the road comin' in. He was by hisself on the far side of the river down near the Fallses' place; looked to be huntin'."

"Hmm. I don't think word would've gotten to 'em yet. I just found out yesterday. Did he seem hostile?"

"No, not at all. We exchanged salutes, and I continued on."

"Well, I'll keep an eye out."

"What other news have I missed?"

"The folks up in Raleigh are in a lather about the Nigras. They found some freedmen with abolitionist pamphlets. They revoked their status and sold 'em south. Word is they're going to pass legislation outlawin' any abolitionist literature."

"Seems like that'd violate the first amendment, don't it?"

Bell looked sideways at Tom for a minute. "You sound like a lawyer, Tom. You think the big planters in the tidewater give two shits about the Constitution when they're worried about an uprising? They're also increasin' the penalties for coloreds readin' or Whites teachin' them. Speaking of Nigras, did I tell you I bought me one?"

Tom was still pondering the comment about Negroes reading, and the books he had given Isaiah. "No, you hadn't mentioned that."

"I bought a young gal, nine years old, figured Mary could use some help around here. She's young, but I got a good deal on her. Bought her from your cousin Dillard."

"Is that so? What about her parents?"

"Didn't cross my mind to ask."

"So it's you and Mary, the three boys, and the slave girl for six in your household?"

"That's right." Tom recorded the information. "There's one more thing you should know, Tom. Amos Wright was last spotted near Tellico a while back. A merchant here in town was up there tradin' with the Cherokee and saw him."

"I thought they ordered him out of the county."

"He was, but Tellico's right on the Tennessee border and in the middle of the Nation. There's not a lot I can do, but watch out just the same. You have to be up that way?"

Tom started to mention the instructions Beverly Daniel had given him for reconnoitering the Cherokee, but thought better of it. "They's a couple of homesteads up that way. I'll be watchful." He stood up and stretched. "I'd best be going, Bynum. I want to get a few more households before I find somewhere to light for the night."

"You're more than welcome to bunk here, Tom."

"Thanks, but I'll be out on the other edge of town if I don't get tied up, and I don't want to cover the same ground twice."

The afternoon was passing, and Tom tried to move the next few interviews along as quickly as he could. Most of the people living in town also owned some land for their farming requirements: a barn for the milk cows and horses, a chicken coop, a pig pen, and a garden. Some owned larger farms away from town. But the difference between the farmers in Franklin and the farmers out in the county was their professions. The families in town owned stores, ran small manufactories for household goods, or provided for the administrative operations of the town and county. They were shopkeepers, tanners, and cobblers. They ran the livery stable and the blacksmith shop. They made shoes and hats, clothes and coats. They taught school and buried the dead. Tom knew almost all of them. He had traded with them, and in his role as a lawyer and justice of the peace, he had represented them in preparing wills, deeds, and contracts.

By the end of the day, Tom was seven households into the census and already felt behind. He knew every stop would entail the required exchange of pleasantries. He also assumed different households would need varying levels of explanation about the purpose of the census. But he hadn't expected the levels of interaction he had experienced in just one afternoon. Everyone he interviewed also wanted to interview him. How was his family? What is the news from Raleigh; from Washington? Who's going to run in the fall elections? Tom patiently answered their questions.

The shadows were spreading across the streets as he came to Joshua Roberts' house, the first one built in Franklin. Roberts was a lawyer like Tom, but he had been practicing longer, and with his office in town, he got the lion's share of the work. Tom was comfortable with that, the farm taking most of his time and attention. The two men had been legal adversaries frequently, but it was never personal, and they were apt to reconvene in the saloon at the end of hostilities. Tom was again met by a Black servant and shown to the extensive, by frontier standards, library, which he envied. A few minutes later Roberts and his wife, Lucinda, appeared in the doorway. He was five years older than Tom and already had a few streaks of gray hair around his temples. He wore eyeglasses and he spent an inordinate amount of time deciding whether he wanted to look over or through them, resulting in him bobbing his head up and down. His wife was Tom's age and a beautiful woman. She had reddish-brown hair and hazel eyes that seemed to burst from her rosy cheeks. Tom always felt shy around her, as if she could read his mind.

"We've been expecting you," Joshua boomed. "I ran into Bynum a couple of hours ago and he said he thought you would make it to my house today. They couldn't have selected a finer man to gather the census. How is it going so far?"

"I started about midday and you are my seventh household, so not too bad. Lucinda, how are you?"

"Fine, Tom. You are just in time. Supper is about half an hour from being ready and we set an extra place for you."

"Thank you, but I couldn't intrude. I have supplies I have brought along."

"Nonsense. I won't take no for an answer. Have you made arrangements for the night?"

"I was planning on making camp down near the springs."

Joshua forcefully inserted himself. "Change those plans! We'll have a room made up for you and you can sleep under roof tonight. I'm sure there will be plenty of nights you have no choice but to sleep out of doors, but tonight you stay with us. Now let's get your census information recorded and put away before we eat, and then we'll have a cigar and whiskey on the porch when it cools off a bit. No arguments, counselor, we insist. I'll have Samuel help you unhitch your mule and put him up for the night."

Tom attempted argument but his heart wasn't in it. Conversation with Joshua was always enjoyable, and it would be good to sleep in a proper bed his first night out, so he surrendered after a halfhearted protest. Joshua and Lucinda had a boy and two girls under five, a boy and a girl under ten, two young female slaves, one young male slave, and one boy-child slave for a total of twelve souls. The recording complete, he packed his papers, washed up, and joined the Roberts for supper. After the meal he and Joshua retreated to the porch as planned and over cigars and whisky discussed the news of the day, the Indian Removal Act and the growing fear in the South of a slave insurrection. The topics had been recounted at every house Tom visited, and Joshua sensed his reluctance to discuss them at length, so he changed the subject.

"Tom, we want you to join the lodge. You've every quality we look for in prospective Masons. I've been after you for years now. What can I do to persuade you to become a Freemason?"

Tom shifted uncomfortably in his seat. He had feared this subject might come up.

"I don't know, Joshua. I'm not the fraternal-order type. My opinions diverge from the mainstream of thought on most contentious subjects. I'd hate to be a disruptive force in your meetings, and I would derive no pleasure in bitin' my tongue."

"You mustn't pay attention to all the anti-Masonic propaganda bein' spread. People with no knowledge of our practices have been making false claims for as long as we've been around. Their biggest problem seems to be with our secrecy. Our ceremonies would appear strange taken out of context, that's why we keep 'em secret. We ain't a religion. Matter of fact, when we're in session discussions of religion or politics are forbidden. Our mission is to make good men better, and marshal those men to make the world a better place. Some of the greatest men in our country were Masons: Washington, Revere, even President Jackson."

"I'm not sure he is the best example for your recruitment, Joshua."

"Now don't be castin' aspersions on our president and my Masonic brother, Tom," Joshua said with half a smile.

"I've already sown discord. Think of the damage I can do in a closed meetin'. I'll consider your gracious invitation. Maybe when I have finished the census, I can look into it more."

"That's all I can ask. I don't think you'd ever regret it."

They talked a while longer on lighter subjects until their cigars were nubs and the whisky glasses empty. It had been a long day and Tom was ready for sleep. Before he dozed off, he thought about his first day, and the full weight of the task at hand struck him. He already missed home and Sarah and the children, and he thought of the days and nights he would be apart from them in the coming months.

CHAPTER 28

Isaiah made love to Ellen that night for the first time since their wedding. As Ellen was traumatized by her rape, and still recovering from childbirth, Isaiah had waited for her to signal her readiness. He had been prepared to wait as long as she needed. When she told him she was ready to be his wife in all ways, he had taken her in his arms and held her for a long time.

They lay side by side, glistening in soft sweat from their exertions and the heat of the cabin on the late-spring night. They looked up into the darkness, each lost in thought. Isaiah thought of Anne, thankful that Ellen could not see his face in the dark, or read his mind. Finally he spoke in a low whisper so as not to wake the girls.

"I know how we can get free."

"What?"

"Mr. Tom has a whole stack of maps. I seen him looking at 'em when he was gettin' ready to leave. I can figure 'em out so we can find our way north."

"You think we can just start walkin' north?"

"No, I been thinkin' on it hard. Mr. Tom gonna be on the road a lot this summer. We lay aside food and tools without nobody missin' 'em, hide 'em away in the woods. Time gets right, we head out."

She leaned on her elbow, peering through the darkness, trying to see if he was serious. "And then what? A colored man and woman with two little children traipsin' through Carolina, just tippy-toein' they way to freedom? We'd get picked up the first day, and then what?"

"I've been a-workin' on my writin'. I think if I could see a pass or somethin' like it, I could make us up one, or even somethin' saying we're free. If'n anybody stops us, we show 'em the paper. We'll travel by night and sleep durin' the day off in the woods. If we leave when Mr. Tom starts one of his trips, nobody'd know we was gone for days. Miss Sarah cain't be leavin' to go tell nobody. We could be full outta Carolina before anybody knows we're gone."

"Isaiah, think about what you're sayin'. Rachael's so little. We can only carry so much food. What we do when we run out? We'll starve out there on the road if the patrollers don't get us first. And what if'n they don't believe yore papers? Best thang they bring us back here; worst thang they sell us south to some ole mean master ain't as nice as Mr. Tom and Miss Sarah. They could split us up again. They could rape me again." Her voice trailed off to an even lower whisper as the thought filled her mind.

"I know it's scary. Don't make up yore mind yet. Let me think on it some more. It's just we may never get another chance like this. I told you I'd find some way for us to be free and I meant it."

"I know you did and I wanna be free too. I believe in all them dreams you shared with me, but they been kind to us here. Mr. Tom works alongside you in the fields, and Miss Sarah don't ask me to do nothin' she don't do herself."

"But we still their slaves. The work we put in all goes to them. You remember Monticello? We all thought we was safe, thought we'd be freed when the president died. Now here we are, all scattered to the wind . . . some of us dead. Who knows where our brothers and sisters and friends are, what they goin' through right this minute. What happens if Mr. Tom goes broke, like President Jefferson did? You think he wouldn't sell us to keep a roof over his own family? Child, it makes my head spin. No, as long as you a slave, yore life in somebody else's hands. Somebody else benefitin' from yore hard work. What happens to our daughters, our grandchildren? They get sold off down the river to some big cotton plantation someday, worked like dogs and then dumped in the clay. No, I will be free and see my children free or I die tryin'. I'd ruther be dead and my family with me than know they ain't nothin' but misery waitin' all the way down the line!"

"Soothe yourself, Isaiah. I know you wanna do right by us, and I'm yore wife, I go wherever you lead. Let's go to sleep now and we'll talk on it more later. Ain't nothin' clear in the dead of night."

CHAPTER 29

June 2, 1830

D AY BROKE WITH thick gray clouds the color of lead rolling in from the southwest, and Tom expected there would be storms before the day was out. He looked at the map of Franklin he had made and realized that if all went according to plan the households he would interview today would include his in-laws and his parents. "It may be a stormy day in more ways than the weather," he told himself. He shared breakfast with the Roberts, thanked them multiple times for their hospitality, and set out.

He covered the first several households at a quicker pace than the day before, trying to establish a routine he hoped to follow in the coming days. The orientation meeting in Morganton those many months ago had predicted the challenge he faced in the interviews. With each house he visited, he expanded his introductory message to include the questions raised in the previous homes. They all wanted assurance that the information they provided would not result in new tax assessments. Many of them asked about how long the government would keep the information, and who would have access to it. Some asked about penalties for noncooperation, assuring him they were going to cooperate fully. A few asked him about the job of collecting the data and how he had gotten the job. Tom tried to incorporate as many of these elements as he could into his introductory speech. What he couldn't avoid without appearing rude were the inevitable conversations about family and county gossip. Everyone wanted to congratulate him on his new baby and offer condolences for Rebecca, if they had not seen him since her death. He felt a small stab of pain at the recollection each time they raised the subject.

By midday he came to the home of Benjamin Brittain, his wife's older brother. Benjamin had fought in the War of 1812 and acquired a significant number of land grants. He had bought and sold parcels at a rapid pace over the past few years and, with the profits from that and the trading post he operated with the Silers, had become one of the wealthiest men in the county. He helped raise Sarah when their father died, which is how she came to be working in the store the day Tom first met her. Tom pulled up to the Brittain house and was met by a Black boy of maybe ten years old, who took Rufus's bridle in hand, holding him steady while Tom dismounted.

The boy told Tom that his master was down in the quarter, but the mistress was in the house. Tom thanked him and climbed the steps to the wide porch. He knocked on the front door and was shown to the parlor by another colored servant. A few minutes later Celia Brittain arrived and confirmed Benjamin was in the quarters.

"We had a bit of trouble today, Tom. One of the darkies back-talked Benjamin, and you know his temper. He give him a good whoopin' and he's talkin' to the rest of 'em now. I sent Alice to fetch him. Let me get you some tea while you wait."

A short while later she reappeared, a tray of tea cups in hand, followed by her husband. Benjamin was rolling down his sleeves and straightening his shirt. Tom noticed a drop of blood staining one sleeve.

"Tom, how good to see you! How's my little sister and your children?"

"All good, Benjamin. Sarah told me to tell you hello."

"That's good to hear. You know I worry about y'all so far out there in the hinterlands. Daddy made me promise I'd watch out for Sarah, and it's hard to fulfill that commitment with her so far away. I've often wondered if you mightn't been able to save poor little Rebecca if you'd lived here in town. If you ever want to rejoin civilization, I could find something for you here."

Tom felt the blood rising under his collar and filling his cheeks. He had promised Sarah he would not get into a war of words with her brother and extend the divide that already separated them. She knew her brother well and knew how condescending he could be to everyone. But he seemed to enjoy goading Tom.

"That's very generous of you, Ben, but we're quite happy on the farm." Tom knew he hated the abbreviated version of his name.

"So, Celia tells me you're here on the census business. I heard you accepted that position. I'd 'a thought that a clerical undertakin'. What enticed you to take the job?"

Tom took another breath before responding. "I view it as quite an opportunity. Far from being a clerical position, I'm deputized as an assistant United States marshal. The pay ain't bad and I get to explore the entire county and meet every citizen. I hope to parlay the results into a future political career."

"Well, I'll be. I had not thought of that angle. How very shrewd of you, Tom. It sounds like your future is bright, a planter in the makin' and a future representative of the people."

"Well, we have time to strategize out there in the wilderness," Tom said. Before Brittain could respond, he continued. "Speakin' of which, I need to record your census information and get back on the road if I'm to stay on schedule."

Celia's adult brother was staying with them, and with the children there were eleven White inhabitants. Brittain provided the information on his slaves, which totaled eleven as well.

"Celia told me you was havin' trouble?"

"It's been addressed. I expect no more trouble." Tom dropped his head and looked at the census sheet. "Do you have some concern with the handlin' of my property? I was not aware that was within the scope of the census taker's duties."

Tom looked back up at him. "No, it's not within my official duties. I possess a couple of slaves myself, and I wonder about the effectiveness of the whip and if it's brandished too quickly by some owners. Not you, of course. I cain't see whippin' my man and getting his best efforts. But I'm sure every situation is unique."

"Assumin' your assets increase over time, I'd like to get your perspective when you got more experience in the matter. In the meantime, I've found the only thing they understand is the lash. They're little more than beasts, and must be trained accordin'ly. I've learned that in many years of real-life experience. Perhaps they didn't cover that in your studies at the university."

"No, you're right. The art of whippin' was not part of the curriculum."

"That may explain your squeamishness."

The two men sat glaring at one another for an uncomfortably long time. Celia, who had been silent witness to the exchange, tried to break the tension by asking Tom if he wanted more tea.

"No, thank you very much, I gotta be goin'," Tom replied and stood, gathering his materials.

"My sister seems to have made a suitable match after all."

"I'll pass along your approval to Sarah. She'll no doubt be pleased. By the way, you got some blood there on your sleeve, Ben. You don't want that to set in."

"So I do. Thank you, Tom."

The Brittains stood on their porch and watched Tom roll away down the road. "He's a smart-ass son of a bitch, ain't he?" Benjamin said, turning to go into the house, not expecting an answer from his wife.

CHAPTER 30

TOM FUMED AS he made his way to the next house, angry more for allowing himself to be drawn into an argument than with Brittain's condescension and sarcasm. To do this job, he would need to be on guard against revealing his opinions, even with people he knew well. He composed himself before reaching the front door and conducted the interview without drama. He hoped the next one would be as uneventful. As if on cue, he heard a rumble of thunder in the distance. He pulled up in front of the big house and sat for a few moments gathering his thoughts.

The elder Thomas Love was a powerful man in western North Carolina and eastern Tennessee. Like his brother Robert, he had acquired large tracts of land in the wake of the Cherokee treaties, often taking grants instead of cash as payment for the surveys in which he had taken part. The two brothers had organized the militia to confront John Sevier and prevented him from forming the state of Franklin when they were still young men. Like his brother, he had served in various positions in the North Carolina government as a representative from Haywood County. No matter what he achieved though, he could never escape his older brother's shadow. Their sibling rivalry had grown more intense with time. He could never tell if Robert was as passionate about the competition, which made it even more maddening. At some point, Thomas gained the sobriquet of "General," though he had never attained that rank in military service. Someone thought it humorous to have the younger brother outrank the

Colonel. Thomas had never referred to himself by the title, but Robert had gotten wind of it, and jokingly used it when introducing him to some colleagues in Raleigh. Thomas had been furious, but Robert had laughed it off, and the nickname stuck.

The rivalry had driven a wedge between the General and Tom from a young age. Robert had always been partial to Young Tom, thrilling him as a child with stories of his adventures in the Revolution and fighting Indians. He had given him a horse when he was ten years old, descended from the famous sire Victor of All. When he was older, Robert had taken him along on the big survey of 1820, and they had spent weeks together exploring the wilderness. Robert had encouraged him to attend the university and had helped him get accepted. He had helped him get his farm and now the census position. The General's jealousy grew in proportion to the attention Robert gave Tom.

His father had been absent for much of Tom's life. Between managing the land he owned in Tennessee and spending time in Raleigh when the General Assembly was in session, the General was away from home more often than not. When he was home, the friction was palpable. The General was not a harsh man and enjoyed a reputation in the community as a kind and generous neighbor. Despite his wealth, he had humble beginnings and never had trouble relating to the yeoman farmers and tradesmen that populated the county. He got along well with his other children, although he believed in strict discipline and was not reluctant to use his leather belt in dispensing familial justice. But it was different with Tom. As the years passed, the General became more and more critical of Tom's every action. Tom responded by avoiding contact with his father, heading off into the mountains when his father would return home from one of his trips. The chasm grew with each passing year. Neither of the men was happy with the estrangement. They cared for each other on many levels, but every effort at rapprochement resulted in one of them saying the wrong thing at the wrong juncture, sending them spinning away from each other in anger.

Tom dismounted from his carriage and Joshua, one of his father's servants, greeted him. He was about the same age as Tom and was his companion on many of his escapes into the woods. Even that had been a source of friction between Tom and his father, as he fumed over Joshua being taken away from his duties. For Joshua, it was the closest thing to freedom he had ever experienced. Wandering through the woods with Tom had been exhilarating and enlightening. Tom spoke of things he learned at school, of ideas and philosophies. He talked of places far away, where people lived very different lives. Joshua most enjoyed staring up into the night sky while Tom pointed out the planets and the constellations, and explained the workings of the heavens. Joshua would ask penetrating questions about the world, how things came to be and how things interconnected; many questions for which Tom had no answers. The thing Joshua hated most about slavery, more than the drudgery, more than the violence, more than the hopelessness, was the fact it denied him an education. He knew he had a good mind, but he despaired knowing it was wasted in mindless menial labor. He carried that load every day, and it was heavier than any the overseer assigned him.

Two babies come into the world. One is born into privilege, nurtured and cared for by doting parents and servants. He is raised up, given an education, made heir to his family's accumulated wealth and connections, his potential for success unlimited, free to pursue his dreams. The other is born in deprivation, suckled at his mother's breast while she labors in fields not her own. He is pushed down, denied rudimentary schooling, inheriting his family's sentence of lifetime servitude and degradation, his prospects bleak, his dreams futile. Why does heaven smile on the one child, and turn its face from the other?

"You took a wife yet, Joshua, started your own family?"

"No sir, still waitin' for the right gal. Someday, maybe. Everybody here's already paired up. I guess I waited too long to make my move."

"Nonsense. You're still a young man."

"What brings you this way, Mr. Tom?"

"I'm takin' the census for the county; going house to house getting a count of all the people that live here."

"That sounds interestin'. You goin' up in the mountains? I hear they's people settlin' up there all the time."

"Yes, I'll be making my way up there this summer and early fall."

"By yourself? You need a good man to accompany you, somebody to make camp and cook and take care of this old mule you got here, and I know just the man!"

Tom laughed. "I'll bet you do. Seems like another lifetime since we went traipsin' through the woods, doesn't it?"

"Yes sir, it shore do. Them's some of my happiest times. You 'member that time we climbed up that jagged old mountain to the bald up on top?"

Tom thought for a moment until the recollection came to him. "Yeah, Andrews Bald. I remember the smell of the balsam firs."

"We got to the top, and there sits a lone Injun. We scared hell out of him. He didn't expect to see nobody up on that old mountaintop. Said he had followed a black panter up there, and when he got to the top, the panter turned into an eagle and flew off."

"He was waitin' on a sign, and I guess we was the sign. I'll never forget the look on his face, though I ain't thought on that in years, Joshua."

"Me neither." Joshua was pensive until a fresh memory emerged. "How 'bout that time we run up on that big bear sow and her cubs up on Cut Cane? I thought we was dead, shore."

"Yeah, we riled her up alright. That was the fastest I ever run. I guess she turned back to her cubs or one of us was in for a maulin'. Good thing I was faster'n you."

"Mr. Tom, I recollect it different. Way I recall it, I heard you hollerin' behind me the whole way to the river."

"Well, we'll just have to agree to disagree, Joshua. I guess only the bear knows the truth."

Joshua laughed. "You see, Mr. Tom, you need me along. Who'll keep you out of trouble up there in the woods, back in them hollers?"

"You make a good point, Joshua. I'll ask my father about it. Where is he, by the way?"

"The General at his Tennessee property. Been gone a good couple'a weeks now. We expectin' him back any day now."

"My momma in the house?"

"Yes sir. Yore mule here need some oats and water?"

"That's Rufus. He never turns down a meal. We'll see about your joinin' me for part of my expedition. You were always good company."

"Thank you, Mr. Tom. I'd enjoy that more'n you know."

Tom bounded up the stairs to the porch, knocked once, and then eased the door open. "Anybody home?" His voice echoed in the big house.

Martha Dillard Love was upstairs when she heard her son's voice, and she came bounding down them like a woman half her age. She embraced him without words for several minutes before releasing him to look at his face. "Thomas Love, how could you stay gone so long? Don't you know how I've missed you? Where are Sarah and the children?"

"They're home and doing fine. I started the census yesterday, so I guess you could say I'm here on official business. I know Uncle Robert told you about it."

"Yeah, he told me about it. You know I'm dyin' to see my new grandson and James and Julia. I ain't getting' any younger."

"I know, Momma. Maybe I can bring 'em up this fall for the market when the crops come in. I know Sarah'd like to get into town and see you as well. Joshua said Daddy's in Tennessee?"

"Yes, I've told him he should sell all that, but land is everything to him, you know as well as me. He's gettin' too old to be on the road this much. He should be back anytime. Will you be stayin' with us? He'd be disappointed if he missed you."

Tom looked at his mother with a wry smile. "I'm sure he would be very upset."

Martha shook her head in dismay. "I don't understand you two. You're so much alike. Why cain't y'all get on?"

"We've been over it so many times, Momma. Nothing I ever done has satisfied him. If I'd hung the moon, he'd say it was crooked."

"He just wants the best for you."

"I think he fears my decisions are somehow a poor reflection on him. He never misses an opportunity to slight my home and farm."

"He owns so much property; you know he would've liked to help you get started. He offered to give you land."

"Yeah, but I would've never heard the end of it. The land I own I bought, and the house I live in, I built with my own two hands. I should think he'd be proud of my independence."

"I'm sure he is, in his own way. You accepted help from your Uncle Robert."

"Yeah, he's helped me, but he's never held it over my head like Daddy would've."

"I cain't tell you how it hurts me to see the two of you at odds."

"I know, and I try to be on my best behavior with him, but you know how he is. We're together five minutes and he is probin' me for weaknesses like we're in a battle."

"I've been married to him for forty-two years. I know how he can be better'n anybody."

"You're an angel to have put up with him."

They spent the next hour catching up on the events of their lives since they had last been together, with updates on all his siblings and their children, and other assorted aunts, uncles, and cousins. Martha Love was the unofficial historian of the Dillard/Love clans and could recite the genealogy back to the old countries, and the more recent comings and goings of the families. Tom listened patiently as she gave him the complete rundown before he finally began to squirm. She recognized he had reached the limits of his endurance and patted his hand.

"Some day when I'm gone you'll think back and wish you had listened to my old stories. I was the same at your age. All young people are the same. What I'd give to have just a few minutes to talk to my momma and daddy again, to ask them about their lives and hear their old stories. Guess I'll have plenty of time to talk to 'em in heaven, Lord willin'."

"I'm sorry, Momma. I enjoy your stories and catchin' up, but this census work is time consumin'. I'm behind already and it's just the second day. When I'm done, I'll bring Sarah and the children and we'll catch up, I promise."

With that he pulled out the census documents, explained them to his mother, and recorded his own parent's information. They now owned thirty-six slaves, including seventeen children under ten years old. He reckoned they had to be one of the largest slaveholders in the county. Martha told him they probably owned over five thousand acres of land as well.

"Father's done well for an orphan boy."

"Yes, he has. He'd love to hear that. Might help bridge the gap between you two."

"Maybe so. I'll keep it in mind."

They chatted a while longer. Martha was disappointed that he would not be staying overnight. When he finally rose to leave, she hugged him tightly, and he kissed her on the forehead. As he walked out the front door, he saw Joshua and remembered their discussion. He asked his mother if

Joshua could assist him in the coming months, and she said she would take it up with his father.

After repacking his documents, he urged Rufus back onto the road, both relieved and saddened that he had missed his father. He thought back to what his mother had said about missing her parents and realized how she had aged since he had seen her last. She would soon be sixty years old. "It's odd the special significance people attach to reaching another decade in life," he thought, but he couldn't deny the impact it seemed to have.

When he turned thirty, a new urgency had overtaken him, a vague feeling that somehow he was behind and needed to catch up, though to what, he couldn't fathom. Had he undertaken this whole census business, taken on responsibility for a family of slaves, all out of some underlying fear that he was behind where he was supposed to be at this stage of his life? What would he be like at forty, fifty, or sixty, like his parents? Would the passing of each decade bring an increased anxiety about his position in this imaginary race he was running against himself? He knew what Sarah would say: "You think too much." He flicked the reins and called out to his mule, "Make haste, Rufus, Sisyphus commands you!"

CHAPTER 31

THE STORM CLOUDS had brought distant thunder and a refreshing breeze, but no rain, for which Tom was grateful. He moved from house to house that afternoon with renewed urgency. His first cousin Dillard Love, the son of his Uncle Robert, owned the third house he visited after his parents. He wasn't sure how he would be greeted, although they had always been friendly to one another. He assumed Robert had told him about recommending Tom for the census job, and he didn't know if there might be some jealousy at play. His fears were unfounded and his cousin greeted him like a brother. Dillard had opened a sawmill and a store and, with all the new construction underway, was doing well. His white frame house had a fresh coat of paint and a well-appointed interior with imported furniture and impressive artwork. Besides the sawmill and store, he owned large tracts of land in both North Carolina and Tennessee. He also owned twenty-four slaves, making him, after Tom's father, the largest slaveholder in the county. All of which Tom thought about in relation to his earlier musings on the road. Maybe he wasn't just racing himself, but the expectations associated with being a member of a powerful family.

He covered several households through the afternoon, all of them small farmers or laborers, with young, growing families. None of them owned slaves. They were all second- or third-generation Americans, Scots-Irish. Among the group he interviewed that afternoon was a cobbler, a saddle maker, and a cooper. Unlike his father's or cousin's homes, they all occupied cabins similar to Tom's, the design ubiquitous throughout the frontier. They were eager to welcome Tom into their homes and were proud to have their names added to the rolls. One wife expressed her displeasure at not having her name recorded along with that of her husband. Tom shared what news he had picked up along the way, and answered questions, many unrelated to the census.

By late afternoon the clouds had broken up and slivers of sunshine peeked in and out as Tom made his way, coming at last to the home of Nimrod Jarrett. Jarrett was a year older than Tom and they had gone to school together as children. He had one of the few licenses to distill and sell liquor in the county. He was warned more than once by Sheriff Bell about selling to the Cherokee. Jarrett was loud and had a strong opinion on every issue of the day. Tom was calculating how to make his exit as he knocked on the door.

"Tom Love! You ain't servin' me papers for somethin', are you?"

"No, Nimrod, no papers this time. You guilty of somethin' I should know about?"

"Like I'd be apt to confess!"

After the required exchange of pleasantries and the reason for Tom's visit, Jarrett took the floor.

"So did ya hear about the Injun legislation Old Hickory got passed last week?"

"Yes, Bynum was tellin' me about it yesterday."

"It's about damn time somebody had some backbone. They ain't no room in this here country for them murderin' savages. Move 'em out west where they can butcher and scalp each other is what I say."

"That'd cut into your business, wouldn't it?"

"Don't believe everything ya hear, Tom. I cain't help it if some of my product gets misdirected to the Nation, can I?" he said with a wink and a nod. "I don't reckon I'll have any problem with sales when they're gone."

"No, whiskey is one of the few products that sells in good times and bad."

"True enough. I think Jackson'll be the president we all thought he'd be and more. Take care of the Injuns and then he can tackle keepin' them black Irish Papists out of the country. If we don't do somethin' to stop 'em, they'll overrun us in our own damn country."

Tom squirmed in his seat. "I don't reckon it'll come to that."

"It will if'n we don't do somethin' to stop it! They come here with nothing but the shirt on their backs and their rosary beads and their blasphemous idolatry and expect us to take care of'em. Which reminds me: I don't see why I should have to pay taxes to support widows and orphans."

"Come now, Nimrod, you don't mean that."

"I do! Don't get me wrong, I feel sorry for'em like any good Christian, and I got no problem with charitable giving and the churches helpin''em out, but I shouldn't be forced through taxation to support nobody. It's un-American!"

Macon County had a social welfare provision for the education of orphans. As wards of the court, girls were required by law to receive eighteen months of schooling for at least three months a year, and when they reached the age of eighteen, they were given a spinning wheel, one bed, and a set of clothes. Boys were taught reading and writing and to figure as far as the single rule of three, and trained in a trade. At eighteen they were given a horse, saddle, and bridle, together worth at least seventy-five dollars, and two suits of homespun clothes with shoes and socks. If trained as blacksmiths, they were given a set of basic smith tools. The costs of their care and education were paid for from the general fund.

"It'd be nice if charity alone provided, but we both know it only goes so far. You don't want orphans livin' in the streets and turnin' to stealin' to feed and clothe themselves, do you?"

"It's all I can do takin' care of my own. The government shouldn't force me to take care of other people's children."

"I wish you knew how you sound, Nimrod."

"I know exactly how I sound. Your own father was an orphan, weren't he? He made his way in the world without the government takin' care of him."

"His older brother, my Uncle Robert, helped take care of him until he could take care of himself. The point is some of these children have nobody."

"Everybody got family sommers. They don't take care of their own because they know the government'll do it for'em."

"Well maybe Jackson'll take care of that too," Tom said, trying to change the subject. Jarrett would not relent.

"Don't mock, Tom. I believe Andrew Jackson was anointed by God to save this country. He's one of us and he speaks for the little man."

"I wasn't mocking, Nimrod. It has been a long day and I just need to get this census information from you and finish up."

"You're welcome to stay here tonight, Tom. We'd be glad to have you. We can talk politics into the night."

Tom struggled to keep his face expressionless. The thought of being cornered by Nimrod Jarrett for a night was stomach turning. "That is very kind of you, Nimrod. I'm gonna stay in Stiles's hotel tonight, but let's get this census business wrapped up."

Jarrett had six family members, including his four children, and six slaves. Tom recorded the information and said his goodbyes as quickly as good manners would allow. He wondered as he climbed up behind Rufus what had transpired in Nimrod Jarrett's life to make him so cantankerous. He thought back to their school days and tried to recollect what kind of boy he had been. His home life did not seem that different from the other children growing up on the frontier. He recalled hearing that his father had been strict and used a leather strap in the administration of discipline, but that wasn't unique in a "spare the rod, spoil the child" society. Nimrod had two brothers, neither of whom was as ornery as him. As he rode along, glad to have the Jarrett place behind him, he remembered little snippets of their schoolyard interactions. Little Nimrod had a nasty habit of breaking in line. Once, Tom had watched as Nimrod bullied a little albino boy, his hair white and skin so fair it was almost translucent. Tom felt a pang of remorse as he remembered watching the boy humiliated by Jarrett but, like the other children, doing nothing to stop it. Some people are just mean by nature, he told himself.

Tom thought of other people he had known since childhood. As he pictured them in his mind, first as children and then as adults, it occurred to him that most people's personalities never changed. They all matured, of course, but the traits they exhibited as children seemed to stay with them for life. Caring, generous children became caring, generous adults. Angry, defiant children became angry, cantankerous adults, and so on. He realized there were exceptions, but he couldn't think of any in his own experience. He turned the mirror around and looked at himself. Had he changed from the child he was?

He remembered a line from one of Wordsworth's poems: "The child is the father of the man." How is it, he wondered, that the years pass and your body grows and changes, but the entity looking out of your eyes never changes? Of course, your opinions change on different subjects, your likes and dislikes may change over time, but all the while, the "you" inside your head is always the same. "Yes," he told himself, "I'm the same boy I have always been." Then he added, "And I'm glad I'm Tom Love and not Nimrod Jarrett."

CHAPTER 32

HE WRAPPED UP the next two households in short order and, as dusk fell, pulled up to Charles Stiles's hotel. There was a livery next door, and he unharnessed Rufus with the help of a teenage boy who identified himself as one of Stiles's sons. He gave the boy two bits to cover lodging and food for his mule, which he rubbed behind the ear, thanking him for another good day's work. He unpacked his bag and census documents from the cart and went into the modest hotel. Besides the hotel and livery, Charles Stiles also owned a grist mill on the river where most of the county took their grain to be rolled into flour or meal. Unlike Nimrod Jarrett, Charles Stiles never met a stranger, and it was hard to find anyone in the county who didn't have a high opinion of him. He knew everyone's name and never failed to greet each of his customers with a warm smile and a friendly hello, which he now conferred on Tom.

"Let me help you with those," he said as he took the bags from Tom. "I been expectin' you! You're the talk of the town. How's it goin' so far?"

"Thank you, Charles. So far, so good, but I'm ready for a hot meal and soft bed if you have either available."

"I got both, and I even reserved the Presidential Suite for you!" he replied, laughing.

"Did I miss a president visiting our fair hamlet?"

"No, but if they come, I'll be ready!" And they both laughed.

"I'd like to get your census information before I wash up for dinner. You'll be the last entry on page one."

"That doesn't sound very prominent, but I'll take what I can get."

They sat at a table in what served as the reception area. Two oil lamps lit the room; the ceiling was streaked a light gray from their smoke. A well-worn rug covered the pine floor, and an inexpensive reproduction of an English garden scene adorned one wall.

"How many children do you have now, Charles?" Tom asked after laying out his papers and dipping his pen in the inkwell.

"Five strappin' lads and three fair lasses, so far. Kizzy and I are blessed, although we had a little girl stillborn last year."

"I'd heard that. I'm sorry, Charles." Tom got the breakdown of the ages of the eight children and posted them in the appropriate columns. "Do you own any slaves?" he asked.

Charles hesitated before answering. "No, Tom, I don't own any people."

"Alright, although I would have thought with all your business interests you would have acquired some Negroes to assist you."

Stiles now stiffened. "When I cain't manage my affairs myself, or with the help of my family, or pay someone for their labor, that'll be a sign for me to scale back my operations."

"I'm sorry, Charles, I have overstepped myself. Please accept my apologies."

"No apology necessary, Tom. What other information you need?"

"That's all. It's pretty simple. Now, if you wouldn't mind showin' me to the Presidential Suite, I'll stow my belongin's and wash up for supper."

"Supper'll be in the dinin' room in about an hour. We got a couple of other gentlemen guests as well. I'll introduce you when you come back down."

He led Tom upstairs to a small bedroom with a feather bed, a small desk, and a side chair. The room smelled of cigar smoke. Charles brought a pitcher of water with a basin, a bar of lilac-scented soap, and a towel. After he left, Tom washed up and then rolled out the finished census sheets. The first sheet listed the heads of households and the counts of the White families. The second sheet contained the tally of slaves and free colored persons. Tom took out his pen and added the columns and rows and then cross-checked them. The total number of souls he had counted in the first two days was 315, of which 125 were slaves, with one free Black child he had counted at the Gray's. The number surprised him, as his father and cousin owned a significant share of the slaves, but the total was higher than he had expected.

For several minutes he sat sucking on the top of the pen as he looked at his handwriting on the sheets, remembering the names and the faces and the houses he had visited the last two days. He pulled out two sets of blank sheets and began copying from the original, trying to improve his script with each entry. He was finishing the second copy when a knock came at the door. Charles was standing there, peeking past Tom at the papers spread around the room drying.

"Supper's ready, if you are, Tom."

"Thank you, Charles. I lost track of time. I'll be right down." He cleaned his pen and stored it, looked at himself in the small mirror that hung over the desk, and headed downstairs.

CHAPTER 33

"Gentlemen, please allow me to introduce Mr. Thomas Love, who is collecting the data for the US Census for our county. Tom, please meet Mr. Franklin Walker of Rutherford County and Mr. Sidney Cook of Philadelphia, Pennsylvania."

"Mr. Cook, you are certainly a long way from home." Tom shook hands with each of the men as they took their seats in the dining room. "Will you be joinin' us, Charles?"

"Thank you, but I already ate. I make it a habit to dine with my wife and children, which leaves me free to attend to my guests' needs, but I'll join you after for some brandy and cigars on the front porch, if that's alright."

His wife, Kizzy, and their daughter Amanda assisted Charles in serving the men their supper of fried chicken, boiled potatoes and collard greens, corn bread with sorghum syrup, and fresh sweet milk.

"Mr. Cook, how do you like our mountain fare? I expect it's different from what you are used to in Philadelphia," Tom asked after the Stileses had served the food and disappeared into the kitchen.

"It looks delicious. I'm famished. I'm gonna watch you to see the proper way to handle the syrup, though."

Tom and Walker looked at one another and smiled. "Well, I like to mix my sorghum with a little butter and then spread it on my corn bread. If you've never had sorghum, it has a unique flavor, which I think you'll like."

"I'll give it a try."

"Are you gentlemen traveling together?" Tom asked.

They looked at one another before Walker responded. "No, we're just meetin' as well."

"What brings you to Macon County?"

As Cook prepared his sorghum, Walker responded. "I come over from Rutherford to buy cattle. There's a man here rumored to have the finest polled Hereford stock in western Carolina. I believe he's a relative of Mr. Stiles, our host. His name is Benjamin Stiles. Perhaps you know him?"

"I do indeed, and the rumors are correct. I bought a bull from him myself a couple of years ago."

"Excellent. I'm meetin' him tomorrow and hope to buy several head, if the price is right. I grow Herefords myself and want to inject some fresh blood into my herd."

"Mr. Cook, what brings you all the way from Philadelphia?"

"I'm looking into purchasing property for my father."

"He's looking to move here?"

"He is. I'm afraid he's in failing health, and his doctor has suggested that mountain air, higher elevations, and less severe winters would be good for him. His lungs bother him, and when winter comes, the smoke from the coal furnaces seems to aggravate his condition."

"Coal furnaces?"

"Yes, we've been excavating stone coal from mines in the western part of the state for some years now, and its use is growing in Philadelphia. It's superior to the coal found in Virginia, and is an excellent fuel for heating, although the smoke can be a problem for people with breathing issues, like my father. So I'm here looking at land with an eye towards building him a home."

"What line of work are you in?"

"I work for my father's company, which distributes coal in Philadelphia."

"That's very interestin'. Mr. Love, tell us about the census," Walker asked. Tom gave them a brief explanation and answered their questions.

After he finished, Cook followed up. "What do you do for a living when you're not conducting the census?"

"I do a bit of legal work, wills and land contracts and such, but I'm a farmer primarily."

"How is the land here in Macon?" asked Walker.

"Bottomland's rich, as you'd expect. The hills are thinner and rocky, which makes it difficult. I wish the soil was less red clay and more topsoil, but you make do."

"Do you enjoy farming, Mr. Love?" Cook questioned.

Tom thought a moment before answering and then nodded. "Yes sir, I do. There's a lot of hard work and a fair amount of risk. You're at the mercy of the elements. But I own a piece of earth, for a while at least. I know every foot of my property, which areas are fertile, and which need work. I know every one of my farm animals and when it comes time to take 'em to feed my family, I try to be gentle. So, yes, I like farmin'. Cain't think of anything I'd rather do."

"Do you own any Negroes, Mr. Love?" Walker asked.

"Yes, I acquired two and their children last year from my uncle." Tom took another bite of greens as he answered.

"I have twenty now in total," Walker said. "What's the feelin' up north, Mr. Cook, regarding our 'peculiar institution,' as Vice President Calhoun describes it?"

"As a guest in your fair land, I'd not want to express any opinion you might find unpleasant. I've encountered differing views on the matter, particularly here in the western portions of the state, and it seems best to tread lightly," Cook replied, wiping his mouth.

"You're right. There are residents of the region who are not slaveholders and who disapprove of the practice," Tom replied.

"They're in the minority and keep their opinions to themselves," Walker interjected.

"Perhaps further east, but here in the mountains I'd say the sentiment is split, and being of Scots-Irish stock, they're not shy about expressin' their views. I've seen relatives come near to drawin' blood over the subject."

"We have something in common, Mr. Love. My family is Scots-Irish as well. My father, although eager to move here, is not supportive of slavery. He's not extreme on the matter, but he's concerned about its effects on society and fears it may cause a rupture in our country."

"How so, Mr. Cook?" Walker asked, his tone sharper.

"As I feared, the very topic has soured the amiable spirit of our meal. Let's find another topic for conversation, shall we?"

"I'm sure Mr. Walker did not intend to sour the mood, but I for one would like to hear more. We're insulated from the sentiments of our fellow countrymen. Surely we can have a civil discourse among gentlemen?"

"I meant no disrespect and concur with Mr. Love. Please, Mr. Cook, speak your mind. You're a guest and we honor hospitality above all."

"I don't dare presume to speak for all the people of the North, any more than you gentlemen can speak for all southerners." He paused and took a drink of milk. "I believe the general feeling is consternation. It's been less than fifty years since we ratified the Constitution. The 'peculiar institution' was a temporary state of affairs, we believed. Some very influential gentlemen assured us the practice was on its last legs. When they abolished the importation of additional Africans, it was supposed to die a slow but certain death."

"I'm not sure who made such a declaration, Mr. Cook," Walker said.

"The entire Virginia delegation, including Washington, Jefferson, and Madison, insinuated that lifelong involuntary servitude would cease to exist in a democratic republic. Yet here we are, less than a generation removed from their efforts, and instead of shriveling, the 'peculiar institution' is expanding, and the number of enslaved people is growing. I've heard estimates of two million slaves in the country. At this pace, what will it be in fifty or a hundred years? We also believed it would be limited to the southern states. Instead, it's expanding westward with the country. Will there at some point be a majority of slave states, and could that majority impose the institution on all states? You've seen the tension over fugitive slaves. How great will be the tension when there are four million or five million or ten million slaves?"

The tone of Cook's voice had never changed, and the question hung in the air for several moments, as Tom and Walker waited to see if the question was rhetorical or if Cook expected an answer. Before they decided the matter, Charles Stiles entered the dining room.

"I hope I'm not interruptin'," he asked as he detected the chill in the room. "If you gentlemen have finished your supper, I thought we'd head out to the porch for the cigars and brandy I promised. It's cooler out there now."

"By all means, Charles, it is gettin' a little warm in here." Tom stood, and they followed their host out the front door. Stiles had placed a silver tray on the little table in front of four rocking chairs, with a bottle of brandy, four snifters, and hand-rolled cigars. The men chose their seats, with Tom on one end, followed by Cook, Walker, and then Stiles. Each man had picked up a cigar as he passed the table, and Stiles poured a generous portion of brandy into each glass and passed them down, keeping the last for himself. It was indeed cooler outside. The twilight was settling in and the first lightning bugs had appeared.

"Gentlemen: our host!" Tom said and raised his glass, followed by the other men. Stiles took a candle he had brought with him, lit his cigar, and passed the light down the row. After each man had lit his cigar, they settled back in their rocking chairs as they puffed their cigars to glow in the fading light.

"I hope everyone enjoyed their meal?" Stiles asked. They all expressed their satisfaction and thanks.

"The conversation was quite stimulatin' as well," Walker said. "We were discussin' the status of our 'peculiar institution' and Mr. Cook was giving us the northern perspective."

"My limited perspective, Mr. Walker."

"None of us were privy to the conversations of the founders, Mr. Cook," Walker said, continuing the conversation as though there had been no break. "I don't know what the northern delegations came away with, but I can tell you the southern states would not have ratified the document without an understanding that the institution was protected. Our culture and economy is based on the fact, upheld by the Word of God, that the Negro race is inferior to the White race and designed by God to serve us. As to future states, why shouldn't the South extend its system into the new territories? You fear a majority of slave-holdin' states imposin' their will on the nonslave states. Might a majority of nonslave states seek to deprive us of what the Almighty has ordained and undermine our entire way of life? And there is only one response to fugitive Negroes. They are the legal property of southern citizens and must be returned to their rightful owners."

"I see I missed quite a conversation over supper." Stiles took another draw from his cigar and blew the smoke out into the gathering darkness.

"I would add," Walker continued, "that we are gentlemen here and honor your opinions. However, there are those in these parts that would greet your position with hostility. As you continue your travels, I would exercise caution."

The four men sat with their cigars glowing in the dusk, as the import of Walker's comment hung over them.

"Thank you for the warning, Mr. Walker. I will indeed exercise caution. That troubles me most. The Constitution guarantees freedom of speech, and assembly, and the press. Yet across the country any discussion of the dangers of the system are being stifled, often with violence. I've read that here in the South it is against the law to publish any opinion critical of slavery or to even use the word *abolition*. Even in free states newspaper publishers are being threatened with violence for addressing the subject. Where does this lead?"

"There are limits to any freedom. You cain't incite people to riot. Anything that could cause unrest among the Negroes and lead to violence is seditious and intolerable."

"So an editorial warning of the dangers of slave insurrection because of the conditions of their servitude is forbidden because it could lead to insur-rection? People who oppose slavery, who disagree with your assertion that it is ordained by God, who are concerned about the conditions of the enslaved, are to lose their own freedom of speech? That a person who is opposed to slavery must not only remain silent, but must cooperate in the capture and re-enslavement of fugitives found in a free state, galls the conscience. It seems to some of us that the nation is enslaved to slavery."

"Are the men working in northern factories and in your coal mines not enslaved economically?" Walker responded.

"Conditions can be difficult, and their options are limited. However, they get paid for their labor, and are free to walk away, which a slave may not do. I've heard that argument but find it unpersuasive. I'll propose a compromise: If the North passes laws to improve the lot of workers in factories and mines, would the South agree to end the practice of slavery?"

"That is not a reasonable compromise, sir. The South has the vast bulk of its capital invested in slaves."

"What if the federal government reimbursed the slave owners for their losses?"

"Southerners contribute a significant amount to the coffers of the federal treasury. We would be paying ourselves and lose our labor as well."

"How about this: Would the South agree to set a date in the future for the emancipation of the slaves and agree that any children born after a specific date would be free when they reach maturity?"

"No sir, I do not believe we could agree to that, for the reasons I have already given."

"Would you agree that families should not be torn apart?"

Walker leaned forward in his chair. "That is for each owner to decide, though I'm sure due consideration is given when possible."

Cook sighed, but Tom thought he was the only one who heard it. "At a minimum, could you agree to establish a commission to monitor the conditions of slaves and to set reasonable guidelines governing their care and treatment?"

"No sir, we would not. Slaves are the property of their owners and their treatment is their private concern. An owner has so much invested he won't help but see to the health of his property of his own accord. He don't need the government over his shoulder."

"I've heard reports of serious abuse from former slaves who made their way north. I have seen, myself, the backs of former slaves scarred from the lash. While you may be a benevolent owner, I'm sure you can see that where there is no oversight, the possibility of abuse exists?"

Walker sputtered and then found his voice. "The men of the South are honorable gentlemen, and I'm sure these are isolated incidents."

"Mr. Walker, in all candor, I don't know how you could make such an assurance, unless you have canvassed the vast region of the South. You raised the treatment of workers in the North. I offer compromises to address the issue, all of which were rejected out of hand. Your position is no doubt shared by your southern brethren: slavery must continue in perpetuity, not only where it exists, but spread to the western territories. It must encompass not only current slaves but all future generations as well, with no provision for emancipation, and there can be no interference by any agency to insure their beneficial treatment. Do I misrepresent your position?"

Walker looked dumbfounded and turned to Tom and Stiles for support. "Gentlemen, as fellow southerners, what is your response to Mr. Cook? I have expressed my sentiments, but perhaps hearing it from you might persuade him to better appreciate our position."

Tom had listened with rapt attention to the argument. Three thoughts kept coming to his mind: Isaiah's lash-scarred back, Ellen birthing Wright's bastard child, and Susan weeping when separated from her aunt.

"Well, I wouldn't presume to persuade Mr. Cook or anybody else on matters of conscience. I've only had servants about a year now. I've tried to treat them with compassion. My concern is for the practicality of the matter. As Mr. Walker said, our economy depends on slave labor. I can see where the founders and the people of the north figured with time it'd fade away. But with each passing generation, we tie more and more of the wealth of the South up in slaves. Without them, the South's economy might collapse. How would we handle millions of freed slaves? I'd be open to some compromises you described, even the idea of having somebody look into their welfare. I know there are some hard men and some cases of mistreatment." Tom's voice faltered, and he feared he sounded weak.

"I believe it was Jefferson who said, 'We have the wolf by the ears, and we can neither hold him, nor safely let him go.' Is that what you're saying, Mr. Love?" Cook said.

"I guess so. My servants were owned by President Jefferson, by the way."

"It's always struck me as remarkable that the author of the Declaration of Independence could pen such a grand expression of freedom and abide slavery in the same genius mind. The idea of holding a wolf by the ears while it grows ever larger and more ferocious is not comforting. I fear at some point we can no longer control it and it will consume us. Have you known many freed Negroes, Mr. Love?"

"No, I don't believe so."

"There is a sizable community of free Negroes in Philadelphia. I've met several of them, and found when given a reasonable opportunity, they're more than capable of being self-sufficient and contributing to society. All they require is access to education or a skill and that we remove the boot of oppression from their necks. If you only see colored people living in the squalor of plantations, you reach the false conclusion that that circumstance represents their highest achievable station. If any of you would care to visit me, I would consider it an honor to introduce you to some of these individuals. I think it would alter your perceptions."

Walker spoke up again. "There ain't nothing you could show me that would change my position on the matter. Mr. Stiles, you've been quiet. What do you think?"

"I'm afraid I'm not as eloquent or educated on the matter as you gentlemen. I just go on my own experiences and those of my family. My granddaddy, Benjamin Stiles, came to this country from England in the 1740s. He told my father about how he and his family were run off their land in the old country. They were poor people, just tenants. Their landlord decided he could make more money raisin' sheep than takin' their rents, so he threw them off the land my granddaddy's family had lived on for generations. Benjamin was still young and unmarried and he decided he'd take his chances in America, so he indentured himself to a plantation in tidewater Virginia to pay for passage. His term was seven years. That must have seemed like a lifetime to a young man. They worked him like a dog. He said he came near to dyin' more than once. They beat him, starved him, made him sleep in a shack with no heat in the dead of winter. Towards the end they tried to provoke him to violence. If he had lashed out, they would've penalized him with more years of indenture, so he just took it. When they finally released him, he owned nothin' but the shirt on his back and a few shillings they gave him for seven years of hard labor.

"His son, my father, John Stiles, fought in the Revolution in the Continental Line. He's got a place up at Sylva in Haywood County, still livin'. Whenever I asked him about the war, he told me he fought for freedom. Ain't nobody in my family ever owned slaves. They didn't believe in it, and neither do I. The only thing that got my granddaddy through indenture must have been the idea that when it was all over, he'd be free to live his life as he wanted. He might not have made it if it had been a life sentence. I don't know how the slaves make it with no hope. For me, I wouldn't want to be owned, so I don't want to own nobody."

"You're too modest, Mr. Stiles. That was quite eloquent." Cook had thought of his father as Charles spoke. The weather might be a balm to his health, but this area was very much still a frontier, and for a man used to living in a city like Philadelphia, it would be a shock. He knew how his father felt about slavery and he imagined him trying to hold his tongue. There were people here in the mountains that you could reason with though, he realized.

Walker thought about voicing further argument, but he realized they had all said their piece and there was no point pushing it further. He had expected Tom and Charles to back him up, but when they had staked out their positions, he realized he was in the minority.

Tom thought of Isaiah and Ellen, of the conversations he had with Sarah, and of the things he had seen. He finished his brandy with one long swig and put the glass back on the tray. "Gentlemen, it's been a pleasure meetin' you and breakin' bread. It's been a long day and another one comin' tomorrow, so I'm going to beg your leave and retire. You've all given me a lot to think about as well. Charles, thank you for the cigars and brandy. They were excellent."

The other men finished their drinks, stubbed out their cigars, and said goodnight as well, the echo of their voices fading into the sounds of the spring evening.

CHAPTER 34

June 4, 1830

THE HOUSE WAS silent as Tom mounted the front porch steps and knocked on the stout wooden door. He had made excellent progress the day before, visiting thirteen households in total. They followed a common pattern, with a patriarch occupying the original homestead and his older children, having started families of their own, living next door on parcels carved out and given to them by their parents. The Buchanans, the Wilsons, and the Morrisons all fell into this category and he had recorded their entries and listened to their stories. They were yeoman farmers, second- or third-generation descendants of Scottish settlers who had taken wagon trains from Philadelphia, where they had landed in the New World, proceeding down the eastern side of the Appalachians until they arrived and settled in North Carolina. They had greeted him with enthusiasm, shared their fresh country cooking and cold well water along with their stories, and bid him farewell as they pointed him to the next house down the road. He was standing now at the door of Jeremiah Green, the patriarch of the sizable Green clan.

"Come in, Thomas," said Polly Green. "I'm afraid you're catchin' us at a bad time. Jeremiah has taken to his bed, which is very unusual for him. I've never seen him in bed with the sun up in all the years I've been his wife." Polly was an old woman with a weathered face and hunched back, with her long, gray hair rolled in a bun atop her head.

"I'm sorry to hear that, Mrs. Green. Is there anything I can do?" He followed her into the simple home.

"I don't think so. The doctor was here earlier and said his heart is weak. All he could recommend was bed rest and a little whisky twice a day. Jeremiah gave up liquor when he was younger than you. Hasn't had a drop in going on forty years. I sent my son George up to James Buchanan's place. They make the best liquor around about, I guess. They've got that still up at the spring in the holler."

"Yes ma'am. I was at the Buchanan place yesterday. He was glad to share his spirits. I told him he needed to get a license or Bynum Bell will be visiting him." Tom smiled as he said this, knowing that Bynum was a frequent customer of the Buchanans.

"Can I give you what you need for the census, or do you have to talk to Jeremiah?"

"I'm sure you can help me. I just need a count of the people in your household and their ages."

"Alright, I can do that. They's one thing you can help me with. Jeremiah told me he wants to make his will in case he don't make it through. Could you make one up fer him?"

"I'd be happy to, if he's able to talk and sign his name."

"He can do both. What do you charge for a will?"

"I believe one dollar should cover it."

"That sounds fair enough."

"We'll need a couple of witnesses. Maybe we could get a couple of neighbors? No one named in his will can witness it."

Mrs. Green called weakly into an adjoining room: "Rebecca, would you come here, please?"

A pretty teenage girl of perhaps fifteen with reddish hair and green eyes came bounding into the room. "Yes, Mamaw?"

"This is Mr. Love. He's here on gov'ment business and is gonna make your papaw's will. Run down to your daddy's place and tell him to round up some of the Wilsons, or Honeycutts, and bring 'em here as soon as he can, alright? How many you need, Thomas?"

"Two's enough."

"Yes ma'am." The girl took off out the front door.

"My granddaughter, she's been staying here helpin' me."

Tom took a seat at the table and Mrs. Green provided the count for the household while they waited. After he put his census documents away, he took out several sheets of plain rag paper he had in his case, and with his pens and inkwell, he followed Mrs. Green into a back bedroom where the old man lay propped up on two pillows. Tom at first thought they were too late until he saw his chest gently rise and fall.

"Jeremiah?" Mrs. Green leaned over her husband and called his name softly, her hand on his shoulder, until he finally stirred. He looked disoriented for a moment, finally looking at Tom as he tried to recognize him. "Jeremiah, this is Tom Love, the General's son. He's here taking the census. He's a lawyer and he'll take your will for you, if you're still a mind. Are you up to it?"

He answered in a raspy voice. "Yes, I'm glad to see you, young man. I don't think I got long, though only the good Lord knows. Polly, help me sit up, will you?"

"Let me." Tom laid his tools on a side table and carefully helped the old man into an upright position. "Are you sure you feel like doin' this, Mr. Green?"

"I don't think I have the luxury of puttin' 'er off. I may not have another chance and I'm guessin' you got other business." He tried to laugh but broke into a ragged cough instead. When he finally had his breath, he looked up at Tom. "How we go about this?"

Tom looked uncomfortable and glanced from Jeremiah to Polly. "Well, it's usual that you dictate the terms of your will to your attorney in private."

"Polly darlin', could you give us some space?"

"Of course. Mr. Love, I'm gonna get Jeremiah here some water, can I get you anything?"

"No ma'am, I'm fine, thank you, though." Polly Green left and closed the door behind her.

Tom arranged his papers and took out his pen and dipped it in the inkwell. "Is Jeremiah Green your full name?"

"Yes. My daddy was Jeremiah Green as well. He was killed by the Indians up on the Cumberland Plateau when I was a young man. I always felt guilty I wasn't there to try to save him and Momma."

"If you had been there, we might not be doing this now."

"True enough. But I never got to say goodbye to 'em. I hope to see them both straightaway on the other side of the River Jordan. That'll be a glad reunion!"

"You must harbor powerful feelings towards the Indians."

"For a while, it filled me with the most violent hatred for them. I killed an Injun one time, but it give me no satisfaction and it didn't bring my folks back. I went through one of their villages up on the Oconaluftee and they lived in dire straits. Then I heard about the massacre of them Indian young'uns at Yahoo Falls back in 'to."

"I've not heard about that incident."

"The settlers and the Injuns over in Tennessee were fighting back and forth for some time. One of the White families got kilt in a raid, and Sevier organized a troop to get vengeance. They heard that some Injun young'uns had been taken to this place called Yahoo Falls for safety. The troop attacked the place and supposedly killed all the Injuns, including the women and children. They said 'nits make lice' to justify what they done. Sevier found out and tried to keep it quiet, but word got out. They's been enough bloodlettin' on both sides. When I found the Lord, I realized I needed to forgive the Injuns, and so I have."

"That's commendable. We're all livin' on Cherokee land, after all."

"Yes, we are."

Tom reorganized his papers to bring their attention back to preparing the will. "I have to ask you, Mr. Green, for the law. Are you of sound mind and body in making this will?"

"I reckon my mind is still clear, but this old body is wore plum out." He coughed again as though to emphasize his statement.

Tom asked the questions he needed to draft the will. This was the only will Green had ever made. He wanted to be laid to rest on the grounds of the new Baptist church down the road, which he had helped build. He had no debts, which he was very proud of. Provisions were made for his wife to have the use of their farm for the rest of her life, and then it was to pass to his oldest son. Ten dollars were to be given to each of his remaining eleven children. He wanted his prized rifle to go to his oldest grandson, his fiddle to one of his daughters, because she was the only one who had taken the time to learn how to play it. When he could think of no other specifics, Tom took his notes and began drafting the document. While he wrote, Jeremiah pondered, before asking, "It ain't much, is it?"

"I think you've much to be proud of. You have property, a handsome farm, a big family gathered around you. What more can a man ask for?"

"Thank you, Tom. That's very kind of you. It's just I was thinkin' about my younger self. I was gonna set the world on fire, do big things, and make a name for myself. I don't know where I got such expectations, but they were real and strongly felt. Here I am at the end of my life and it just feels . . . incomplete."

Tom stopped writing and looked at Jeremiah Green and for a moment saw himself lying there, years down the road. "Mr. Green, I've never met or read about any man who thought he had accomplished everything he should have in his life. Great leaders, generals, philosophers: they all felt they could have done more, or done things differently. We never measure up to the standards we set for ourselves."

"You're a wise young man, Tom. I know your daddy must be proud of you. And you're right. I am proud of what I've done here, and I hate leavin', but I got a mansion in glory, paid for by the blood of Jesus and given to me though I'm undeserving of it. It's just . . ." He faltered, coughed, and then sat pensively for a moment before continuing. "It's just I fear when I'm gone, in a few short years there'll be no trace that I was ever here: nothing but a rock with my name on it, and it'll soon be erased by the rain and the cold and the passin' of time."

"A man once told me you live as long as you're remembered and as long as your blood flows in the veins of your descendants. You'll no doubt have many descendants. Someday down the line someone'll say, 'You've your granddaddy's eyes.' Your last will and testament'll be kept in the county courthouse for who knows how long, and I recorded your name on the census roll. They're small things, I know, but maybe we leave more of a mark on the world than we realize."

There was a soft knock on the door and Polly Green opened it a crack. "Tom, my son is here with Moses Wilson and James Honeycutt, whenever you're ready."

"Thank you, Mrs. Green. You can send 'em in."

The three men crowded into the bedroom and Jeremiah's neighbors awkwardly greeted him. Tom explained what was happening and then placed the will in front of the old man. He read it through and then nodded at Tom, and scrawled his signature on the last page, then leaned his head back against the pillow, his eyes closed. Tom showed the men where to sign their names in witness, then signed it himself and affixed a wax seal to make it official. The men then filed out, leaving Tom and Jeremiah alone again.

"I gotta be going now, Mr. Green. Is there anything else I can do for you before I go?"

"No, Tom. I can die in peace now. Good luck to you, and remember, life is short. Make the most of yours."

"Thank you, sir, I'll do my best."

Polly handed Tom a silver dollar on his way out and thanked him. On his way down the steps, Tom realized he had never prepared his own will.

Jeremiah Green would live another nine years.

CHAPTER 35

June 7, 1830

Tom surveyed the ill-kept grounds as he approached the cabin. Weeds grew in profusion around the buildings and extended into a decrepit garden that desperately needed a hoe. There was no sign of activity, and Tom thought the place might be abandoned. He was nearly finished with the third page of the census, and his plan was to wrap up the sheet today and start for home before it got too late. The porch planks creaked as he crossed them and rapped on the door. After a moment he heard movement inside, so someone was home. The door opened just a few inches and a young woman's face peeked through the crack.

"I don't take no customers until nigh on evenin'. Come back aifter four o'clock. If the horseshoe is hung up, I got another customer, so you'll have to wait yore turn on the porch." With that pronouncement, the door closed again in Tom's face.

He stood perplexed, unsure of what had just happened or what his next move should be. In a flash the answer dawned on him, and he felt the back of his neck grow hot. He shifted his weight from one foot to the other, making the planks creak anew, and knocked again. It opened a little wider this time. The woman was in her midtwenties, he figured, with black hair that hung loose around her shoulders. He thought her eyes were dark brown, but he couldn't tell for sure in the light. She wore a plain calico frock that was just a little tight and accentuated her figure, in particular her ample bosom.

"Are you hard 'a hearin' or an idiot?"

Tom realized he was staring and thought for a second that he must look like an idiot. "I'm sorry. My name is Thomas Love. I'm a deputy US marshal here on government business collectin' information for the census." He wasn't sure if this show of formality made him look any less foolish to the woman.

"You ain't here to have your corn cob shelled?"

"My corn? What?"

"Your flagpole saluted? You ain't here for a roll in the hay?"

"No ma'am, I'm married. I told you, I'm here for the census."

"Married?" She snorted a laugh. "If it worn't fer married men, I'd have no business at all. What's in it for me?"

"I'm sorry, nothin'. It's the law. Everybody's gotta take part."

"Time's money. I don't do nothin' for free. Times is hard."

"Yes, they are, but I'm afraid there's no pay for providing the information."

"Alright, come on in then, I guess." She pushed the door open and turned her back to him, leaving him to follow her into the dimly lit cabin. Tom started to close the door behind him and then changed his mind, leaving it half-open.

As his eyes adjusted to the light, he noticed two small children, a girl of maybe five years old and a boy who looked to be no more than three, standing staring at him, their eyes wide and mouths agape.

"Ya'll go on outside and play while I help this feller." They shuffled past him without breaking their gaze and disappeared outside. The woman pointed to a table and then asked Tom if she could get him anything, which he declined.

"Ma'am, I didn't get your name."

"Patsey—Patsey Barker."

"Thank you. Is it Mrs. Barker?"

"I suppose I'm still married. Ain't seen my husband though in close to a year. I don't know if he's alive or dead. He took off to Georgia to make his fortune pannin' for gold, damn fool. I got a letter last fall tellin' me he was in some place called Dalonahgay and that he would either send for us or come home once he made his fortune. That's the last I heard from his sorry ass."

"I'm sorry. It's just you and the two children?"

"Yeah. Rosa's nigh on six and Nehemiah just barely three."

"Is your husband providin' for you?" Tom regretted the question as soon as it left his mouth.

"No sir, and the county won't help neither cause I ain't a widder legal. I tried to keep the farm goin' but most of the crops rotted in the field last year. Sold the last of the animals except for the milk cow durin' the winter to try and make ends meet. I cain't sell the place cuz it's in my husband's name. I am reduced to entertainin' menfolk to keep food on the table."

"Do you have any family who can help?"

"We moved here from Kentucky in '27. My daddy didn't cotton to me marrying Edward, said he was no count. Seems he was right. I thought my life was gonna be different. Edward said we was gonna travel. I just wanted so bad to get out of that stankin' little cabin I grew up in, get out from under my folks. Now here I sit in my own stankin' little cabin in the middle of the woods without a pot to piss in. I sent Momma a letter askin' her if she'd loan me enough money for me and the kids to come home, but I ain't got no reply. For all I know they done passed on or don't want me to come back. You'd think she'd at least write her own damn daughter back, wouldn't you?" Tom nodded in reply. "I'm in a terrible trap and I cain't see no way clear." She dropped her head and studied the dirt under her fingernails.

"Have you tried the church?"

"Ha! A deacon come round about Christmas time and brought a basket with food and clothes. 'Fore he left he told me he'd like to help more. Told me he'd gimme a dollar for a poke. That's how I got into this line of work. I guess he went off and bragged to his friends cause after that the women in the church won't talk to me but all their menfolk beat a path to my door." She tried to laugh, but it was weak and had no mirth about it.

"How about if we're finished with this census stuff, I give you a poke for a dollar? Help a woman in tough times?" She reached out her hand and gently placed it on his, and raised her face to look at him.

Her touch was like a jolt of electricity. He felt his heart race. His breathing became shallow, and he felt his passion grow, and for a fleeting second the thought of taking this woman flashed through his mind. He looked into her eyes but saw no passion, only deep sadness. He saw they were hazel after all, and he thought of Sarah's eyes. Tom dragged his hand away from hers. "I'm sorry, Mrs. Barker. I have great sympathy for your plight, but I cain't do that."

He remembered the dollar that Polly Green had paid him for the will. He took it from his pocket and put it on the table. "I hope this'll help. I know some people in the county. Let me see if there ain't some sort of help for families in your condition."

"Thank you, Mr. Love. I'm sorry for being so for'ard. I've become hardened with all this on me and forget myself sometimes."

"There's no need to apologize. I cain't imagine being in your straits. I have to be on my way now, but I really hope things turn around for you."

He drove off thinking of Sarah. What would she do if something happened to him? She wouldn't go back to her brother's home. He couldn't see her going to live with his parents. Could she make it on the farm on her own, with three small children? Would she get remarried? Could Patsey Barker get remarried, given what she had done to survive? A woman alone on the frontier was in a dire position. He suddenly felt a new sense of urgency to get the next few interviews completed and be on his way home. He needed to see Sarah.

CHAPTER 36

DESPITE HIS BEST efforts, dusk was gathering as Tom finished the day's work. It was a beautiful late-spring afternoon, and he decided to camp by the river and make his way home in the morning. The roads were too rough to navigate in the dark and damaging the cart or hurting Rufus was not worth the risk, no matter how he wanted to be home. He had slept under a roof every night during his trip, so spending the last night outside held a certain attraction for him. He picked a nice level spot overlooking the river where the water churned white as it passed through giant boulders. There was a little spring that emerged from an outcropping nearby and emptied into the river, its path flanked by Christmas ferns that gave it a primeval aspect. Tom removed Rufus from his harness and gave him oats and let him drink from the spring. He unrolled the oilcloth Isaiah had made to create a lean-to and laid out his bedding underneath. He gathered dry wood for a fire and, after a few minutes with his flint and fire steel, had the tinder burning. From his remaining larder, he prepared a meal and finished eating as the sun set.

The sound of the rushing water surrounded the campsite. Tom sat on a rock in the gloaming and lit a pipe from a stick he took from the fire. He hoped the smoke would deter the mosquitoes that had started to swarm. Several small bats darted back and forth over the river as they attacked the bloodsuckers. He wondered how they maneuvered in the fading light, avoiding each other while snatching up tiny mosquitoes and other insects.

While he was watching them, a large bird flew over and landed in one of the sycamore trees on the far side of the river. He could just make it out in the high limbs, although he couldn't see what it was. A moment later he heard it call out and recognized the plaintive call of a barred owl: "Who cooks for YOU, who cooks for you ALL?" From farther down the river he heard its mate respond, and the owl flew off in that direction.

As he sat smoking his pipe, the full moon rose over the distant peaks. He watched it rise until it cleared the hills and its glow flooded the woods around his camp with an eerie light. Tom sat transfixed, his mind unfocused, not thinking, but absorbing everything around him. The sound of the water merged with the croaking of the frogs and the drone of the crickets into one harmonious hum, and the sound grew, filling Tom's head. The light from the full moon filling the glade took on a life of its own, rippling through the forest in waves. The trees seemed to flutter in the light, as they would in a breeze. He felt as though he were floating above the rock he had been sitting on. A wave of moving light rolled through the forest towards him. He felt his body brace as though preparing to be bowled over, and then the wave washed over him. He was carried away with the wave and for a moment, or an eternity, he was floating free in the ether, connected to everything but touching nothing.

A log in the fire popped and Tom found himself once more on the rock. He took a deep lungful of air and exhaled and wondered if he had been holding his breath. The sound of water and the play of light had triggered something from deep inside him. He sat there for a long time trying to replicate the experience, listening to the river, looking at the moon, relaxing his body and breathing, but nothing came of it. He wasn't crazy, he was reasonably sure. It had seemed real. He wasn't sure what to make of it.

He got up from the rock and stirred the fire. Sparks flew and he followed them into the night sky until they disappeared. Where the sparks died, he saw the stars. The light of the full moon dulled their luster, but they were still there. Tom lay down and gazed up at them, entranced. "So far away," he thought, "and yet I could reach up and touch them." He stretched his arm heavenward as though he could. He remembered being a little boy looking at the stars and wondering if someone out there was looking back at him.

Isaiah looked up at the full moon high overhead and then back at the Loves' cabin. Sarah would be asleep by now. The dogs had been lured to his cabin with pieces of meat, and Ellen's job was to keep them quiet. Trotting to the blacksmith shop, he eased the door open, allowing a shaft of moonlight to penetrate the dark shed. He knew the space like the back of his hand and could have found his way blindfolded. Hidden under a pile of rusty metal in the corner were two weapons he had labored on most of the week. Using scrap metal, he had crafted a short pike with a sharp point and a hacking blade on one side and a long knife that could have been a short sword. He removed them from their hiding place and felt their weight in his hands. They were rough weapons, but they could kill a man.

He stepped out of the shop, closed the door behind him, and looked around to make sure he was unobserved. Carrying the weapons, he made his way to the woods beyond the edge of the farm, slipping through the rows of corn and beans he had cultivated that day. Navigating in the moonlight, he found the rocky outcropping he used as a landmark and then his stash. He had dug a hole the size of a child's grave, buried a box made from scraps of wood left over from his and Ellen's cabins, and cloaked its location with fallen branches and leaves. Inside he had placed materials needed for their escape. There wasn't much so far, just some spare clothes, a cup and bowl, and some candle nubs. The most important gem was a copy of a map he had made from Tom's collection, reproduced on a piece of leather and wrapped inside an oilcloth. Wrapping the weapons inside another oilcloth, he laid them inside the box, then replaced the lid and camouflage. Again he scanned his surroundings to make sure he was unobserved.

Isaiah clambered up the outcropping, and took a seat on a flat boulder. His brow was beaded in sweat, not from heat or exertion but from the danger he knew he was inviting. A slave with weapons was the greatest fear of southern slaveholders, and transgressions were dealt with in brutal fashion. Isaiah had no way of knowing how Tom Love would respond to finding a cache of hidden weapons.

The plan unfolded in his mind. He would gather as many supplies as he could pilfer without discovery over the coming weeks. Tom would be back in a day or two, if he kept the schedule he provided when he left. Isaiah knew there would be a series of such trips over the coming months. Once he had enough provisions laid by, he would time his escape to late summer or early fall, leaving after Tom, and following a different route. He would forge a pass with some excuse for a family of unaccompanied Blacks to be on the road. His handwriting was still rough, and he didn't know if it would fool anyone, despite his practice each night. More troublesome than the style was the content. He wasn't sure what to write, but he had to think of a story that would pass muster if patrollers stopped them.

Once in the mountains, he would head north, using his map. The mountains ran through several states all the way to Pennsylvania. Since childhood, he had heard that if you made it to Pennsylvania, you would be free. He would hide himself and his new family in the vast wilderness as he made his way there, traveling by night and hiding out during the day. The surrounding forest was bathed in silver light, and it occurred to him they should time their escape with the harvest moon, if it coincided with one of Tom's trips. It was a good plan, he decided. Glancing around the site one last time, he climbed down from his perch and hurried back to the cabin.

CHAPTER 37

June 8, 1830

SARAH WAS EXCITED to hear about Tom's exploits and spent the morning after his return plying him for details. As usual, she had to pull the particulars out of him, Tom being parsimonious with the juicy details that made for effective storytelling. Having spent the last week caring for the children and the farm, Sarah was not about to accept parsimony. As they strolled around the farm, he told her about his eating and sleeping arrangements, about the houses he had visited, and the county gossip he had collected. He told her about some of the more interesting people he had met, and all the people who had asked him to say hello to her. She was most interested in hearing about their families and rolled her eyes when she heard about her brother. He told her about writing the will for the dying old man, and his curiosity about the couple with the single free Black child, but he paused before deciding that he would not tell her about the lone woman in the cabin.

"I wish I could go with you," she said, filling the gap. "I'll bet I could get a lot more details."

"Of that I have no doubt, but I only have six months to complete the work," he responded, smiling over at her.

"Women being more efficient, I'm sure I could get it done in five months and get the extra details too." And she stuck her tongue out at him.

"You're right on that point as well."

"It ain't fair men get to do all the excitin' things in life. I know I'm smarter than half of the men I've met."

"Again, no argument. It occurred to me more than once while I was out there how lucky I was to find myself in that dry goods store the day I first saw you. I cain't imagine how different my life would have been without you."

"You're just tryin' to change the subject."

Tom chuckled. "No, I'm serious. It also got me worryin' about what would happen to you and the children if somethin' happened to me. I prepared the will for Jeremiah Green and I realized that here I am a lawyer and I've never drafted my own will. You are smart, but it's hard for a woman alone in the world."

"I know it is, so you have to make sure you don't go nowhere."

"I don't plan on it." He leaned over and kissed her on the cheek. "How were things here while I was away?"

"Everything went fine. Ellen has been a big help and Isaiah has been workin' like this was his own place, although . . ." She hesitated.

"Although?"

"He's just been actin' a little different. Nothing in particular, just kind of distracted. I suppose he's still mournin' his wife. But I can make no complaint about his work. He cleared that section of bottomland you've been lookin' at for two years, hoed the vegetable garden until they's not a weed in sight, and chopped a cord of wood."

"I was gonna get to that bottomland."

"I know you was," she said, and patted his hand. "He's been workin' in the smith shed and the cornfield, and he patched that place on the barn roof."

"I was going to get to that too. What was he doin' in the smith shed?"

"He said he was makin' gardenin' tools."

"Hm. I'm gonna check in with him after dinner. I'll have to commend him on all his labors. I had an interestin' supper conversation with a couple of fellers at Stiles'. Man from up north was critical of our 'peculiar institution.' Gave me a lot to think about."

"Like what?"

"I don't know. Just tryin' to see into the future, how this all plays out. Seems like the country is more divided than I ever seen it. Everybody just keeps takin' harder and harder lines. I expected somebody from up north to have strong feelin's about it, but they's a lot of people right here in Macon dead set against it as well. Eventually the pot's going to come to a boil."

"Sarah tells me you've been quite busy while I was away."

"No shortage of work needin' doin' around a farm."

"That's for sure. Everything looks real good. I couldn't be doing this census if it weren't for your work." Tom hesitated before finishing his thought, reluctant. "I appreciate it."

Isaiah was feeding the hogs, and as he finished emptying the slop bucket into the trough, he stopped and looked at Tom. "Thank you, sir. Don't believe nobody ever said that before."

"How are you and Ellen doin'? Do you need anything?"

"We doing tolerable well. Gittin' used to married life, and each other. Havin' my Susan has been a balm. I thank you again for bringin' her to me."

"You're welcome. I only wish I could have brought your Anne back as well."

Isaiah merely nodded in response. "As far as needin' anything, I could use a new hat." He took his off and looked at it as he spoke. The crown was sweat stained half the way up and the front brim was a rusty color from the untold number of times he had removed or adjusted it with hands covered with red clay. The brim had a tear that he had tried to mend with needle and thread, and there was a hole in the top that couldn't be properly repaired.

"I can see that. There's a man in town, Christopher Setzer, that sells hats. I could use a new one myself. I'll get us both one on my next trip."

"When is your next trip, Mr. Tom?"

"I'm lookin' to leave Monday week. Why don't you show me what you've got done while I was away, and let's talk about what needs doin' comin' up. Sarah tells me you've been busy in the smithy?"

Isaiah didn't breathe for a second and struggled to remain nonchalant. Tom's tone was relaxed and there was no hint of accusation. He had expected that his activity might raise questions, and he had prepared a response. Now he just needed to breathe and answer. "I sharpened up the axe, hoes, and shovels and made some crowbars we can use on the fences and such. I always enjoyed smithin'. My uncle run the smith at Monticello and he used to let me help him durin' the winter when things was slow. They's somethin' about makin' things out of cold iron with nothin' but fire and your muscle."

"That there is. Well, let's look things over. How's the baby, by the way?"

They spent the rest of the afternoon walking the farm discussing the priorities Tom identified. They were both concerned about the dearth of rain. There had been several days when clouds had gathered but passed with little more than a sprinkle. The crops were still healthy, but summer was around the corner, and a sustained drought would be devastating. Isaiah described an idea he had to get water from the river to the fields of corn and wheat in the bottoms, using wooden sluices and a small waterwheel. They discussed the materials needed and the time frames involved, and laid out a plan to start on it. Not for the first time, Tom was impressed with the way Isaiah's mind worked and his ability to distill a problem to its essential elements. He thought as well of the discussion with the three men on the boardinghouse porch.

CHAPTER 38

July 1, 1830

TOM SET UP camp, ate an early supper, and reclined against a boulder, intent on reading a few stanzas of Lord Byron's *Childe Harold's Pilgrimage* in the afternoon light. He had read the book in school, but had not opened it since. Looking for something to take with him, he had scanned his bookshelf on his way out the door and the book of poetry caught his eye. It seemed appropriate given his progress on what he now considered his own pilgrimage. He was halfway through his third week of travels and was ahead of schedule. The ninth page of households was complete, and according to his tally he had counted seventeen hundred people. Canvassing the northern section of the county near the Oconaluftee River, he had picked a little cove to make camp. Rufus was attacking a bag of oats when he raised his head, perked up his ears, and looked around before focusing on Tom, who looked up from his book to meet the mule's gaze.

Tom realized the dell was quiet. The birds had stopped singing, the crickets that supplied their usual steady chorus were silent, and the katydids that had been sawing in the afternoon heat had ceased as well. Tom sat motionless for several seconds, as he and Rufus both cocked their heads in unison, listening. He reached for his gun, leaning against the gray trunk of a giant tulip poplar. Whatever had caused nature to go silent might be a threat.

The still air began to buzz in soft vibration and the boulder he leaned against magnified it. The sound followed a moment later. It started like the scratching of someone playing a washboard and gradually intensified to a high-pitched vibrato like the single note of a dulcimer endlessly repeated. Rufus strained against the rope and started twitching his hind legs as the sound grew in intensity. Tom jumped to his feet and soothed the mule as his panic rose. The noise was coming from all around them and echoed throughout the glade, amplifying the effect. Tom stood with his mouth open in awe, amazed at the volume. He kept thinking it would hit a crescendo and then dissipate, but it had reached what seemed to be a constant drone that showed no sign of diminishing. He put a hand over his left ear, which had always been sensitive to loud noises, as he continued to comfort Rufus.

Then he noticed the hillside in front of him. The forest floor sparkled in the bright afternoon sunlight and rippled like a lake on a windy day. "What the hell!?" he said out loud, although he could barely hear his own voice above the din. He checked Rufus's tether to make sure it was tight and then started walking up the hill. He had not gone far before he realized the ground was covered in writhing, flapping insects. Some began to rise from the ground into the trees, their wings shimmering in flight. Although there was very little breeze, the effect of countless insects wafting through the trees created an effect like the wind blowing through the woods. They were everywhere and the source of the deafening whine. He saw them all around his feet and reached down and grabbed one.

The creature was about an inch long, with a black body and large, bright-red eyes with a single black dot in the center. The bulging eyes sat atop a flat, chinless face. Their wings were translucent, with orange veins fanning through them, and the outer rims were orange as well, as were the legs. They looked like a strange mixture of a cricket, a grasshopper, and katydid. Tom stood puzzling over the creature, examining it as the chorus continued unabated.

"It's a cicada!"

Tom jumped and spun around to see an Indian man standing a few feet behind him. He stood holding the squirming bug in his hand, staring as though he were seeing a ghost. It was the man he saw standing by the river on the road to Franklin, the first day taking the census. He recognized the colorful turban and vest and the deerskin pants and moccasins. A bird tattoo was prominent on his right arm, above gleaming copper bands.

"I'm sorry I scared you," the man yelled, even though he was only a few feet away. "There was no way to announce my coming. The song of the cicada is overwhelming." He extended his hand and Tom dropped the cicada, wiped his hand on his britches, and shook it, introducing himself.

"I am Ka-lows-kih. It means *locust* in English, and I go by Jim Locust. But you can call me Jim."

"Pleased to meet you, Jim. I thought these were locusts." he said as he waved his arm at the swarm of insects surrounding them. The two men stood a foot apart now as they struggled to make themselves heard.

"Some of your people call them seventeen-year locusts. My people call them *lolo*, but I knew a White man who told me they are cicadas, not locusts. They live underground for seventeen years and then emerge to find a mate and start the process over again. They'll only live a short while in this phase, just long enough to mate. The females'll lay their eggs in the trees. After they hatch, they fall to the ground and burrow, where they spend most of their lives."

"How'd you come to be here now, Jim?"

"My grandfather sent me. Our people have a story that the lolo brought the beans when the world was created, and so we celebrate their return. This is a sacred place. They say more emerge here than anywhere. To be here when they come forth, to hear their song, to see their red eyes and orange wings flashing in the sun, is to be blessed by the Great Spirit, or so my grandfather believes. I came here for him. He has been marking the years until their return, but he's too old for the journey. I made it my pilgrimage. I been makin' my way here for some time, stoppin' to visit places that are special to my people. Are you here to see the cicada too?"

"I had no idea this would happen. I've heard tell of seventeen-year locusts, but I thought it was a old wives' tale. This just seemed like a nice place to make camp. I'm countin' all the people who live in this county for the government."

"Do you count the Cherokee as well?"

"Only those who pay taxes to the government."

"Those who own land apart from the Nation, you mean?"

"Yeah, I suppose that's the way of it."

"So we don't matter enough to the White people to even count," Jim said, shaking his head.

"Your family lives in the villages?"

"My father is Oos-ko-tih, but he has taken the White name John Panter and owns a farm on land outside the Nation near Valleytown. He follows the Christian religion. My grandfather, Cos-kel-lo-kih, won't speak to him."

"What does your grandfather's name mean?"

"A hog bit him when he was a boy, and the name means *hog bite*. I went to live with him to learn the old ways when I was free. My father told me it was up to me if I wanted to live as our ancestors lived or if I wanted to follow the White man's ways. I spent the first part of my life on my father's farm, going to the missionaries' school, where I learned to read and write English."

"You decided to follow the old ways, it seems."

"I haven't decided, but being here now, hearing the lolo, makes me think the ancient ones know some things worth knowing and saving."

Tom nodded, and they studied one another before turning to watch and listen as the cicadas played out their last days on earth in a riotous chorus. The sun reflected off their gossamer wings, and the sound of their desperate mating calls echoed through the forest. It was one of the most amazing things Tom had ever witnessed. As he stood there listening and watching, he thought about how similar it was to his experiences at the falls last year and by the river a few weeks back.

"You're welcome to share my camp tonight," Tom said.

"Thank you, if you don't mind the company."

"It would be my pleasure."

"My pack's back up the trail a ways. I'll get it and be back in a while."

They shook hands again and Tom watched the Indian walk away, the hawk feathers lifting behind him, lighter almost than the air. Tom walked back to camp and resumed his place at the boulder. He found where he had left off with Lord Byron, but decided to just listen to the cicadas. They made concentrating on poetry difficult anyway. He remembered the mission Beverly Daniel had given him, and thought about how it might affect Jim Locust. He was camped here on land the Cherokee considered sacred. They knew when and where the cicadas would erupt over a seventeen-year span. What else did they know about the land they had lived on for generations, information that might forever elude the White settlers pouring in? Things lost forever when they were forced off the land and made to travel west?

And how would the Cherokee adapt to a land with which they had no relationship, no history?

After a while Jim came walking down the trail towards him. He was a handsome young man who carried himself with a proud bearing. He had a pack slung over his shoulder and carried his rifle in one hand and a dead rabbit in the other.

"I brought supper. I couldn't come into your camp empty handed."

Tom didn't tell him he had already eaten. "Thank you kindly."

Jim laid his things to one side, took a seat on a rock, and started skinning the rabbit. Tom took out the small cook pot he had just cleaned up earlier and brought it to the creek, filling it halfway up with water. He added some dried vegetables and hung the pot from the chain on a metal tripod over the fire. Jim began dropping in parts of the rabbit as he cleaned it.

"That is an ingenious setup you have there."

"My servant Isaiah came up with it. He's very inventive. He made the wagon I use as well," Tom said, nodding to the cart.

"I noticed that on the day you drove by the river."

Tom grinned. "I get a lot of looks on the road. But it works well. I don't think I could've gotten this far up the road with a regular wagon."

"My people never made use of carts with wheels. It would have made things so much easier. White people make many more things than the Cherokee. We're at a disadvantage in trading."

"Even the Whites in Carolina are at a disadvantage. We import most of our manufactured goods from England or the northern states."

"It is good to be self-reliant. Before the White people came, the Cherokee traded with the other tribes, but we depended on no one else. It was only when we saw the goods of the White people that we found we were missing things. Our people were content without them until they knew they existed. Now we spend our time tryin' in vain to gain them and are less happy."

"I've met many people over the past few weeks. They're by most measures prosperous, but they're unhappy cause they have less than their neighbors. Human nature I reckon. Your English is very good, by the way."

"The missionaries at school taught us. They're from the north. They were strict and wouldn't allow us to speak Cherokee. At night my friends and I would speak Cherokee in secret so we wouldn't lose our ability to talk to our own people."

"That must've been difficult."

"Yes, but now I speak two languages. I think it'll be important for the Cherokee, if we're to live alongside the White people."

"You said the teachers were missionaries. Are you a Christian?"

Jim dropped the rest of the rabbit meat into the cook pot, scraped the bones and entrails into the skin, and walked off into the woods to dispose of them, leaving Tom's question hanging in the air with the din of the cicadas. When he returned, he took his seat on the rock again.

"About the age of twelve, the missionaries pressured me to confess my belief in Jesus so I wouldn't go to hell. I didn't want to abandon the beliefs of my people, but I didn't want to go to hell either. After a while I said the words they wanted to hear and they baptized me in the Little Tennessee. That river is sacred to our people, so I told myself I was honoring both faiths."

"I have found rivers to be very spiritual places myself."

"As I grew older, I questioned what I was bein' taught. The missionaries would become angry whenever I spoke about it. They said the Cherokee beliefs were superstitious myths that we must abandon. But I kept thinkin' of my grandfather and my grandmother. They're humble people and good. Some things they believe are myths, I know, but so are things the missionaries taught us. How is a talking snake and magic forbidden fruit any less of a myth than Uktena the horned serpent? How is a bush that talks and burns without being burnt up different from the buzzard flapping his wings to prepare the earth for plants and animals? How is an evil being like Satan different from Nun'Yunu'Wi? By the time I left school I was skeptical of both religions. I feel like a man lost between two worlds sometimes. It's only in the mountains, in the woods, by the rivers, that things seem true."

Tom nodded and smiled. "Can I read you something, Jim?"

"Of course. I hope I haven't offended you."

"Quite the opposite. I've met a fellow traveler. I was reading poetry by a man named George Gordon when you came up. This one is about a young man on a pilgrimage tryin' to find his place in the world."

Tom stood up and retrieved the book, opening it to stanzas of the third canto, and began reading, speaking in a loud voice above the cicadas:

> But soon he knew himself the most unfit
> Of men to herd with Man; with whom he held
> Little in common; untaught to submit
> His thoughts to others, though his soul was quelled,
> In youth by his own thoughts; still uncompelled,
> He would not yield dominion of his mind
> To spirits against whom his own rebelled;
> Proud though in desolation; which could find
> A life within itself, to breathe without mankind.
> Where rose the mountains, there to him were friends;
> Where rolled the ocean, thereon was his home;
> Where a blue sky, and glowing clime, extends,
> He had the passion and the power to roam;
> The desert, forest, cavern, breaker's foam,
> Were unto him companionship; they spake
> A mutual language, clearer than the tome
> Of his land's tongue, which he would oft forsake
> For nature's pages glassed by sunbeams on the lake.

Tom closed the book and sat down. "A year and a half ago, my oldest daughter died. I was grievin' and I reached a point where I wasn't sure I wanted to keep livin'. I went into the woods to find an answer. After a time, I found myself at Cullasaja Falls, one of my little girl's favorite places. I found peace there. Like you, I feel trapped between worlds myself sometimes."

"Waterfalls, rivers, and springs all have great meaning for my people. Cullasaja is one of the most sacred. People go there to purify themselves in its waters. Water is life. Nothing lives without it. What you read was beautiful. I'd like to hear more of it."

"Let's eat our supper and then we can read before the light fails us. When we part, I would like you to take the book and read all of it."

"I couldn't take your book. You have a strong attachment to it, it seems."

"I do, and that's why I want you to have it. There are so many people, but I have met only a handful I consider kindred spirits. We're both on a pilgrimage. That we crossed paths here must have some meaning, I think."

"I feel the same way. Our people believe when you receive a gift, you must give one in return or offend the spirits. I would like you to have this." He removed a copper armband and handed it to Tom.

"That's too much."

"No, it's very fair. I'll think of you every time I read the book and you think of me when you wear the band."

They ate the stew and afterwards Tom read as he had promised until it was too dark to see the words. They talked about the poem and its message for some time until the conversation faltered and there was a long silence.

"Jim, there is something I gotta tell you."

"What is it?"

"I fear there are very hard times ahead for the Cherokee."

"Harder than we have already endured?"

"I fear so. President Jackson is determined to move all the Indian tribes to the West, and he's passed new laws to make it so."

"We heard that, but our leaders believe he is just usin' it to force us to surrender more land. I hate that son of a bitch. Our people fought with him against the Creeks at Horseshoe Bend, and he has repaid us with blood and tears."

"He wants all the land for White settlers. The governor of Georgia is pressing him hard to force the Cherokee and Creek out of that state, and Carolina and Tennessee are following suit."

"What more can we do? We gave up so much of our land already. We made a Cherokee alphabet like the English have, and have our own newspaper. We've got a government and courts like the Whites. Many have adopted the Christian religion and the English language. Some even own slaves like the White people."

"Many settlers still bear the Cherokee ill feelings because of past battles. Some Indians killed women and children and took scalps and desecrated the dead. Those wounds haven't healed."

"It's true warriors became mad with battle rage. But the Whites killed our women and children too, and some took scalps and mutilated our dead.

If we don't fight back the Whites take our land, and if we fight back the Whites say, 'The Indians are savages and must be removed.' What would you do if someone came to take your land, your home? What if the people from Georgia came to Carolina and said, 'We want this land, you must take your family and move to an unknown place'? Would you not resist?" Jim's voice quivered with anger.

"I'm sorry to have angered you so. I consider you my friend, as I have said, and just wanted to warn you, so you could tell your people."

"What good to tell them if there is nothing to be done?"

"I wish I knew. It may be necessary to dissolve the Nation and completely adopt our ways."

"If we do that, are we still Cherokee? I remember a saying the missionaries taught us: 'What does it profit a man to gain the world and lose his soul?' You must be an important person in the White community, if they ask you to make the count of this entire region. Couldn't you tell them we've made peace and want only to live on our remaining land with our families and our traditions?"

"I'm not an important person by any means. But I know some important people, and I'll carry that message to them."

They talked for a while longer about less contentious issues before agreeing to turn in for the night, although they both lay awake for a long time before sleep overtook them. They woke the next morning with the sun and shared a simple breakfast. When the time came to part, the cicada's song still echoed through the forest, although with less fervor than the day before.

CHAPTER 39

July 4, 1830

THE BABIES WERE down for a nap, James was reading a book, and Susan and Julia were playing with dolls on the porch. Sarah and Ellen sat down for the first time all day and each released a tired sigh.

"So much for the day of rest," Sarah said as she began stringing the beans that sat in a pile on the table. She stopped and looked away. "What day is it?"

"Sunday, Miss Sarah."

"No, what day of the month?" She paused again. "I believe it's the Fourth of July! How on earth did I lose track of the days?"

"Independence Day," Ellen replied, and tilted her head, as she did when she was deep in thought.

"What is it, Ellen?"

"I was just thinkin' back on Independence Day at Monticello. Seems like it was a bigger day than Easter or Christmas. President Jefferson set a big store by Independence Day. We all got the day off from workin'. They was a big picnic and fiddle music and people come from all over to pay respects to the president. At night they'd set off fireworks. That was the most amazin' thing I ever see'd. You ever seen fireworks, Miss Sarah?"

"No, I cain't say as I have. That must'a been somethin' to see. Maybe they'll have fireworks in Franklin when it gets a little bigger."

"Yes ma'am."

"Do you miss Monticello?"

"My people more than the place, my momma mostly. I been real blue since the baby was born . . . just cain't seem to shake it. I keep wonderin' where my momma is and if she alright, and what she'd say about little Rachael."

Sarah put the beans down and rubbed her temples. "I know how you feel. Ever since I lost my Rebecca, I been down. My momma died when I was just a young'un. I kin barely remember her now. Many's the time I wondered what she'd be like with the kids. Rebecca was most like her, I think," she said, before changing the subject. "How are things 'tween you and Isaiah?"

"He a sweet, kind man, and patient and understandin'. He treats Rachael like his own daughter. But he ain't over losin' Anne. He loved her so much. I remember seein' them together at Monticello. He light up at the sight of her. I's afraid he sees her when he's lookin' at me."

"I know it's been hard on him. He's been very patient with little Susan. How's she doin'?"

"She's fine. Young'uns are quicker to heal than grown folk. She loves heppin' with little Rachael."

"We ain't gonna let Independence Day pass unnoticed. I say we have a picnic and our own little parade. Let's get these beans on."

That afternoon they had a picnic and a parade on the Love farm. They ate in the shade of the big oak tree, serenaded by the buzz of summer insects. They held a barnyard parade featuring a horse, a mule, and three goats, led by the children while Isaiah played Tom's fiddle and they all sang "Yankee Doodle" at the top of their voices, over and over until everyone but Julia tired of it. When evening came, they paraded around with candles that passed for fireworks. It wasn't Monticello on the Fourth, but they all enjoyed themselves.

"I wish Tom was here," Sarah told them afterwards, chuckling. "I hope he was somewhere to enjoy the day. It's always been special to him."

It was just past noon when Tom pulled up to the next house. It was a sizable cabin, well made, with a generous porch and an oversized front door was made of solid oak. He had debated doing any census work today, it being both Sunday and Independence Day, but he had been too far away to make it home the day before, and he didn't want to waste an entire day. He had spent a leisurely morning eating and breaking camp, allowing people time to attend church and get home before he knocked on their door. A middle-aged Black woman greeted him and escorted him to the living room.

A few minutes later the woman returned, leading an elderly man into the room. He relied on a walking stick with a silver handle for balance. He still had a head full of white hair, and his face was brown and wrinkled from obvious years in the sun. His back had a slight stoop, but otherwise he held his head high as he made his way across the room. Tom jumped to his feet and greeted him. The man introduced himself as William Fortune and Tom explained his purpose.

"Ten years have gone so fast. They make you work on the Lord's Day?"

Tom flushed with embarrassment. "No sir, and I'm sorry to bother you on Sunday. It's a big county, and I hated to lose a whole day. I won't keep you long, I promise."

"I meant no criticism, young man, just a curious, crotchety old man. We're glad for the company. Betsy, come meet young Mr. Love!"

Betsy Fortune entered the room, a short, plump little lady with ruddy cheeks and a big smile, wearing an apron and one of those muffin-top caps ladies wore in the previous century. She greeted Tom and then they all took a seat.

"So, Mr. Fortune, how old are you and Mrs. Fortune?"

"I was born in 1756, making me seventy-four, I reckon. Betsy here is a spring chicken. She was born in '57. She'll be seventy-three the first of September."

"Does anyone live with you here, besides your servant?" Tom asked as he was filling out the form.

"No, just the three of us, although Clarinda is more family to us than servant."

In the next room, Clarinda overheard the comment, rolled her eyes, and shook her head. She was ten years old when she was ripped from her mother's arms and given to Betsy as a wedding present. She never saw her family again.

"How old is Clarinda?"

"She must be about fifty-four."

"You were alive during the Revolution. Happy Independence Day by the way."

"And to you as well. I fought in the war."

"It's an honor to be sittin' here with a Revolutionary War veteran on Independence Day. Where did you serve?"

"I fought with three different outfits. I was born in Albemarle County, Virginia. Right after the declaration was issued, I volunteered with Captain James's Virginia company. I served a few months with them and they furloughed me when the damn British burned our house down." Betsy looked at him with disapproval. "I rejoined a while later with Colonel Lindsay's Virginia Regiment and ended with General Washington at Jamestown in '81."

"Did you meet General Washington?" Tom asked, his eyes wide.

"Never face to face, but I saw him many times in the camps. Great man."

"Those must have been hard times."

"I remember being hungry most of the time. Hunger is something you never get used to. We slept out in the open in all kinds of weather. I remember waking up one night with snow on my blanket and my teeth chatterin'; couldn't get 'em to stop to save my life. But we endured somehow. My poor brother Benjamin didn't make it, though. He died at Valley Forge in April '78."

"I'm sorry. We owe you all a great debt. What do you remember most about the war?"

"Not as much as I used to, but some things still stand out. The first time I stood in the line and watched a British squad approach us in them scarlet uniforms with their drums rollin' and their flags flappin' in the wind and their bayonets glimmerin' in the sun, I almost shat myself. It was a scary sight. We fired off a volley before they were within range and then hightailed it for the trees. They kept their line and come on at us, but we had the better ground and some cover, and they could see we had the advantage. They got off a volley at us and we returned fire, woundin' a few of 'em, before they retreated. That was my first taste of battle. Somethin' you never forget, I guess."

"I cain't imagine what that must have been like. Was it like that every time you went into battle?"

"The terror never stops, but you learn to handle it different. After you see your comrades cut down in line beside you, when you hold one of your friends in your arms as he cries out for his momma, takes his last breath, something else takes over. Rage becomes more powerful than fear. You couldn't charge an enemy line unless you was mad as all hell, although the word *mad* don't hardly do it justice. It gives you power you never knew you had. The other way I handled it was to tell myself I was already dead. Whenever a bullet struck the man standin' right next to me, I thought, 'Why him and not me'? A man in the British line had drew a bead on someone in our line, and he picked the man beside me instead of me. So every time I figured it'd be my turn. But my number never came up, so I sit here in my dotage tellin' old war stories on Independence Day, while noble comrades rest in unmarked graves. I'll see 'em again soon, Lord willin'."

"Albemarle County, that's Charlottesville, right? You ever meet President Jefferson?"

"Fore he was president. I went with my daddy to his plantation to buy nails. Monticello was still under construction. I remember his red hair. He wasn't famous yet, so he was just another planter to me. We knew the Madisons as well."

"I cain't believe I'm sittin' in the parlor of a man who was neighbors with Jefferson and Madison and fought under Washington, and on the Fourth of July to boot!"

"I'm just an old farmer, but I was fortunate enough to be on the world's stage at a very auspicious time and place."

"That's quite the understatement. I've taken up more of your time than I planned, but I cain't tell you how much I've enjoyed this time with you. Thank you both for your hospitality."

"We enjoyed the company."

Tom drove off down the road with a big grin on his face, eager to get home and tell Sarah how he had spent his Independence Day.

Chapter 40

July 27, 1830

THE MERCILESS MIDDAY sun beat down on Tom and Rufus as red dust swirled around the cart, kicked up by the plodding mule. The sky was cloudless and the listless leaves hung from parched trees in the shimmering heat. Tom couldn't remember the last time it had rained, but he knew it had not been in July. His last trip home left him worried, and setting out on the road again had been more difficult than usual. He and Isaiah spent most of the time he had been there working on the waterwheel at the river and carrying buckets of water up the hill to the vegetable garden. The wheel had been difficult and time consuming to build and, when complete, provided far less water to the crops than they had hoped. But it was more than his neighbors were getting. At every house Tom visited, the first topic of conversation was the drought. Every farmer wore a worried brow as the prospect of a failed crop loomed. They all scanned the skies, searching in vain for the cloud that would bring relief.

As he ventured farther from Franklin, the distance between homesteads grew. Most of his days now were spent on the road, perched in the uncomfortable seat of the cart, baking in the summer sun, interrupted only by the brief interviews of the worried homesteaders. The novelty of the first few weeks had given way to something like drudgery as the miles piled up in the heat. He was growing tired of hearing himself deliver his introductory speech, and the hospitality of his neighbors seemed to reflect his nettled disposition. The heat and the drought were sapping everyone's patience.

As the miles and hours passed, he spent the time thinking about the patterns that had formed in the data he collected. The inhabitants of Macon County had followed similar routes to the frontier. Their parents or grandparents had arrived in Philadelphia from Europe and made their way down the Great Wagon Road. Groups of families had arrived in the New World and migrated together in wagon trains headed south. They were all linked by marriage, sometimes with multiple brothers of one family marrying sisters of other families, such as his father and uncles: the Love brothers marrying the Dillard sisters. In some respects it reflected the clan system their ancestors had adhered to for centuries in the old countries.

A majority had acquired their property through land grants dispensed by the state for their services in the Revolution or the War of 1812. Grants were issued both for military service, including hiring a substitute, and for contributing to the war effort by supplying horses or supplies. The original grantees would then transfer sections to their children, or will it to them when they passed. Tom had been to valleys occupied by clans of related families, ruled by a handful of aging patriarchs. Some followed the ancient tradition of primogeniture, leaving their entire estate to their oldest son, while others divided their lands between their offspring, leaving to future generations the quandary of ever-shrinking farms.

There was a great deal of unanimity among the inhabitants of the county for most topics, but he had found a stark chasm with the slavery issue. Most families owned no slaves, and some became quite vocal when Tom asked them about it. The divide was more pronounced than in the eastern sections of the state he had visited. It was rare and even dangerous for citizens in Raleigh, for instance, to voice even mild dissent regarding slavery. There were many reports of mobs trashing newspaper offices or riding people out of town on rails for comments viewed as critical, let alone abolitionist. But the citizens of the western mountains were often outspoken in their contempt. Tom had taken to asking if there were any other inhabitants of the household instead of asking if there were any slaves to avoid the acrimony prominent in some responses.

His ruminations ended as he came to a fork in the road. He pulled Rufus under the shade of a towering chestnut tree, took off his hat, wiped his brow with his kerchief, and consulted his map. The left fork was new, built by Thomas Welch's road jury last year. It would take him west across a ford of Burningtown Creek and right up to the boundary line of the Cherokee Nation. The right fork continued north to the Tennessee turnpike road that led to Knoxville. He took the left fork, hoping to gain some elevation and respite from the heat. He could bathe in Burningtown Creek and let Rufus get some water.

After fording the drought-diminished creek, now barely a trickle, the road narrowed to a track just wide enough for his cart and climbed through a magnificent stand of ancient beech trees. The towering mottled trunks were white in the midday sun and stretched away in both directions. There was little undergrowth beneath the giants, and Tom enjoyed the view as he rode along. The path became more and more serpentine, as the builders had bypassed the largest trees and rock outcroppings, and grew rougher. The canopy provided welcome shade, and the temperature moderated somewhat, which benefited Rufus, laboring with the steady climb. The beeches gave way to hemlocks, making the road feel more constricted. Tom had expected to pass homesteads by now, but he rode along with no sign of human activity for almost an hour.

He reached the crest of the ridge and came to a stop to let Rufus catch his breath. He climbed down to stretch his legs and gazed out at what he believed was Burningtown Bald across the valley. The view from here was incredible and the mountains off to the west lived up to their name, appearing blue in the afternoon haze. As he scanned the lands below him, he saw a wisp of smoke and reckoned it to be a homestead. He gave Rufus a handful of oats and some water and started down the ridge. He passed several areas of cut timber, which had left the ground open, and shrubs and weeds now grew. The road flattened out and followed a creek bed, now dry. Rufus stopped without warning and lifted his head, his ears at attention. A man in brown homespun pants and a shirt the color of red clay, wearing a black felt hat with a wide brim, stepped from behind a tree. He had a thick black beard stained with tobacco juice. He leveled a musket at Tom and blocked the road.

"That thar's far 'nuff, mister."

Tom raised his hands to show he was unarmed. "Afternoon, sir. I'm a deputy United States marshal here to gather the census."

The man considered him for a minute without lowering his gun. "Yore trespaissin' on my property."

"This's a public road if my map's right. I'm required by law to visit every homestead in the county and count every person. I can show you the paperwork with my authority if you'll lower your gun, Mr. . . . ?"

"Mashburn, Jeremiah Mashburn. Yore papers don't mean nothin' to me. I cain't read nor write, and I ain't a-takin' part in yore operation, and I speak fer my neighbors in the holler. You kin jus' turn yore lil cart around and head 'er back the way you come."

"Mr. Mashburn, it's a hot day and I've made a long ride up the ridge here. The law requires you to cooperate with me. It'll only take a few minutes of y'all's time. I just need the names and a count of the people livin' on the place. As soon as I get that, I'll be on my way and you can go back to your business."

"And I done told you we do not WISH to cooperate. This here's a free country and we've a right to be let alone. My guess is this is about the government wantin' to raise some kind of tax or steal our claim. We done paid our grant and fill't out the papers in Franklin last year. This here's my land and I've a right to say who comes and goes on it, and my patience is wearin' thin."

Tom struggled to not lose his temper, which he knew would only inflame the situation. He could feel his face reddening and the sweat running down his back. He took a deep breath and lowered his voice. "Mr. Mashburn, I'm your neighbor as well, got a place near Sugartown Creek. I've been all over these mountains since I was a boy. We've never met, but I understand your position. I can only give you my word that my takin' the census has nothin' to do with taxes or your property at all. If I turn around now, I'll just have to come back with Sheriff Bell and he's gonna want to bring men with him. At that point, you'll have broke the law and he'll have to arrest you. You're not gonna want that, and it might lead to someone gettin' hurt or killed. Ain't there someone in the holler who can read the paperwork?"

"You're a long way from the sheriff or anybody else. It might be to my benefit to end this process right here, if it's as you say."

"Now you're gettin' into some dangerous territory there, Mr. Mashburn. Threatenin' an officer of the law in the conduct of government business is a felony. I left Sheriff Bynum at the fork of the road on the other side of

Burningtown Creek. He had business at a place on the turnpike. He knew I was headed up this way. We're to meet up before dark back at the fork. If I don't show up, he's gonna come lookin' for me." Tom let the lie hang in the air for effect. "Why are you makin' this so goddam hard? You hidin' somethin' down there?"

Mashburn hesitated before answering. "I got nothin' to hide. You say yore a marshal. We have had some trouble here. Maybe it's best we have some help with it." He stepped out of the middle of the road, lowered his weapon, and used it to wave Tom by.

"I'll be right behind you. My place is up on the right."

"Move on, Rufus," Tom said, and the cart started down the road. Despite the heat, the hair stood up on the back of Tom's neck and his heart raced as he half expected to be shot in the back before he got to the cabin. He wished he had told someone where he was going. If Mashburn did him harm, no one would ever know what happened to him. He imagined Sarah waiting on the porch for her husband, who would never return. He put it out of his mind and thought of options. His unloaded pistol was under the seat, but pulling an unloaded gun on someone was a desperate last resort. He would have to use his wits and talk his way out of this fix. That was his best bet.

The cabin came into sight as he rounded a bend in the road. It was of typical construction for the area and wasn't that different from Tom's place. It sat in a clearing with little shade, and Tom figured it must be an oven inside. They had cleared a field behind the cabin and corn was shoulder high, though yellowing from the drought. The barn stood off to one side, along with the outhouse, far enough away to keep the smell at a respectable distance.

Then Tom saw the body. He reined Rufus to a stop and tried to process what he was seeing. Just inside the barn alley, against a stall door, a man—or maybe a youth, given his slight frame—was spread-eagled, his arms tied around the door to keep him upright. He wore only deerskin pants. His naked back was lashed, and the blood had coagulated in dark stripes. Flies hovered in a dark swarm around him, so dense it took Tom a moment to discern his dark black hair.

"What in God's name?" he said.

"We caught him and another Injun stealin' our hawgs. James Pearson shot the other 'un dead when he raised his weapon. This one tried to run, but we caught him. I whooped him, give him thirty lashes, but we don't know what to do with him now. If we turn him loose and he goes back to the Nation, he's liable to brang a war party down on us. But we didn't think we had the 'thority to kill him outright neither. Yore a marshal, what's the law say?"

"He's still alive?" Tom asked in a shocked voice, as the man appeared dead to him.

"He was this mornin'. Lemme check."

Mashburn walked over to the Indian, grabbed him by the hair and pulled his head back to look in his face. "Well, I reckon that settles that. I guess the heat got to him."

"You killed a man over a hog?"

"I didn't kill him tentional. The penalty for stealin' hawgs is thirty lashes. That's the sentence I carried out."

"The sentence is carried out by the court after he's convicted, and prisoners ain't left hangin' on a stall door in the July heat after the punishment neither."

"We caught 'em red handed. The other 'un drew up his weapon."

"What weapon?"

"He had a tomahawk. Pearson reacted on his instincts. That was self-defense, pure and simple."

"How old were they?"

"How do I know? Old enough to steal swine. They got what they had a-comin'. You ever been in a fight with Injuns?"

"No, I ain't."

"Well, I have. They're savages. I lost an uncle in the risin' up on the Cumberland. Took his scalp and cut off his manhood. I didn't intend for that 'un to die, like I said. We a long way from the sheriff out here. We gotta defend what's ours. I needed that hawg to keep my family fed through the winter. I don't know if we're gonna have a harvest if this damn drought don't break. It's a bad situation all round. I wish none of it happened, but what's done is done."

Tom dropped his head and looked at the ground. He could tell Bynum what had happened, but he knew nothing would come of it. Public sentiment and the risk of a Cherokee response would ensure that. "Get him down from there. We can at least give him a proper burial. Where'd you bury the other one?"

"Out there on the edge o' the woods where the ground ain't so hard." He pointed to a spot between the field and the woods. Tom saw the fresh dirt of the first grave.

"Get your shovel. You got somethin' to wrap him up in?"

"Nothin' I can spare."

Tom took his blanket from the cart and threw it at the man in disgust.

The dust flew and stuck to their sweat-covered faces and arms as they took turns digging. They laid the Indian boy's body in the ground and covered it with the soil his ancestors had trod for thousands of years. They didn't know his name and Tom had no words to say, so they walked away in silence. He washed his hands and face in the water that trickled from the spring near the house. He thought of Jim Locust, standing by the river, crowned by his colored turban, thought of their conversation as the cicadas' song filled the air, and wondered what would become of the Cherokee.

Only Pearson and Mashburn had carried out the death sentences on the Indians, but to Tom the entire valley seemed covered in blood. As he interviewed the other inhabitants, though, they were no different from the other families he had met over the spring and summer. He gathered their names and numbers as quickly as he could and made his way back over the ridge, reaching Burningtown Creek as the sun set. Clouds appeared over the mountains and the sunset was a brilliant display of orange, red, silver, and gray. Tom camped by the water and that night it rained. "The rain falls on the just and the unjust," he thought, as the rain beat down and spilled over the oilcloth.

CHAPTER 41

ISAIAH LISTENED, GRATEFUL for the sound of rain falling on the cabin roof. He was tired of carrying water and grappling with the waterwheel that had never worked quite as he imagined. Maybe the rainfall signaled the end of the drought.

The light from the lantern flickered and sent shadows dancing along the walls. Susan sat in his lap with *The Swiss Family Robinson* open in front of her, sounding out the words she recognized, having her father pronounce the more difficult ones. Isaiah was proud of her progress and smiled as she made her way down the page. Ellen had just put Rachael down and stopped to listen, standing beside them, her hand on Isaiah's shoulder. Susan came to the end of a chapter and Isaiah closed the book, signaling the end of the lesson.

"You reckon you could teach me?" Ellen asked as Susan slid from her father's lap.

Isaiah looked up at her and put his hand on hers. "Of course! Sorry I ain't offered you afore now."

"I was kinda shamed to ask. I weren't never round no readin' back home. You 'member how it was, body get whooped, caught with a book. I figgered it'd be too hard or maybe I's too old to learn it, but I been listenin' to you and Susan and thought maybe I could try it."

"I'd love to teach you, Ellen."

"You think I could learn to read the Bible?"

"Readin's readin'. You just gotta learn the letters and then use 'em to build the words and so on. Only difference is they talk funny in the Bible, leastways the parts I read."

"I went with Momma to hear the White preacher that come round after President Jefferson died. Momma shore enjoyed that. I can still see her settin' there listenin'. She's the one taught me to sing them ole songs. She'd be tickled to know her gal learn't to read the book." She smiled at the thought. "I hope she's sommers she can hear some preachin' and sangin'."

"Me too."

CHAPTER 42

August 12, 1830

Tom turned Rufus onto the Savannah Creek road northeast of Franklin, looking for a place to make camp for the night. The sight of a man standing by his horse on the side of the road studying a map brought him to a stop. The man wore a dusty black suit with a gray shirt that had once been white, buttoned to the neck, and a black hat half a size too small. Tom hailed him. "Evenin'."

"Good evenin' to you, sir! Could I trouble you for some information?"

"How can I be of help?"

"I'm looking for the Dillard Love store. I think my map's off, as it says I'm standin' in front of it." They both laughed, as there were no structures of any kind within sight of the crossroads.

"Dillard Love's my cousin. His store's off the state road 'tween Franklin and Waynesville, near Bryson. This road'll lead you to that road, where you'll bear right."

"How far?"

"Ten or twelve miles."

"I'm supposed to meet some folks there today."

"Cain't make it 'fore sundown, and I wouldn't recommend tryin' the road in the dark. Storms we had a couple of weeks back washed some places and I fear it'd be hazardous goin'. I'm fixin' to camp for the night. You're welcome to share a fire."

The man looked perplexed, and he glanced at his map again as if it would yield different results, shaking his head when it did not. "If you reckon it won't put you out, I'd gladly share your camp."

"I'd welcome the company. My mule Rufus here is companionable only to a point, and I believe he's tired of hearin' me talk. They's a pasture just ahead that lies next to the creek. I know the owner and he won't begrudge us makin' camp there."

The man introduced himself as Francis Robison and shook Tom's hand.

They made their way to a little hayfield that had been cut and gathered. Tom unharnessed Rufus and let him pick the tender new grass while Francis unsaddled his horse and turned him loose as well. Tom unpacked the food and cooking utensils from the cart while Francis gathered wood for the fire from the nearby woods. Evening was almost upon them before they could sit down and eat.

"What takes you to Dillard's store, Francis?"

"Meetin' a group of parishioners to travel to the camp meetin' revival north of Waynesville next week. I hope they'll not be too concerned when I don't arrive."

"I heard they was to be a camp meetin' up that way. Methodists, right?"

"That's right. Should be a good time. There'll be a week of preachin', singin', prayer, and personal testimony. I'm the new circuit rider for the Western District, so it'll be an excellent opportunity to meet folks. I'm still learnin' my way around."

"How long you been at it?"

"This is my first circuit. I tutored a couple of years under Brother Bill Matthews back in Gastonia. The bishop must've thought I was ready to venture out on my own, cause here I am."

"I've heard circuit ridin' is a hard venture. Have you found it so?"

"It's hard bein' on the road all the time. My hind parts are calloused up from the hours in the saddle. Winter's hardest, of course. Most folks are glad to see me comin'. Many open their homes to me, or at least their barns. They're glad to have somebody to do weddin's, baptize their youngun's, or say a few words over the dearly departed, even if sometimes they been in the ground fer a spell. Lord knows the field is ripe for the harvest of lost souls. There is much wickedness afoot I fear."

Tom nodded, thinking about what he had witnessed over on Burning-town Creek. "You find folks receptive to your message?"

"Brother Bill told me the secret is to reach the woman of the house. If they get converted, everybody follows suit, which is odd, cause Saint Paul said to focus on the master of the house, and if he's converted, the whole household'll follow."

"That was his error. Everybody knows who the real master of the house is." They both chuckled.

"What's yore business, Tom, that you're out on the road in your cart?" Tom gave him his usual spiel.

"We're on a similar mission then! Yore a-countin' souls for the government and I'm tryin' to add to the count of souls listed in the Lamb's Book of Life. I am reminded of the census that was taken when the Savior was born."

"Here's the thing I don't understand about that story. The point of a census is to get a count of the people living in an area. Why would Rome decree everybody return to their ancestral home to git counted? My ancestors come from Virginia and Scotland. If everybody had to set off to the place their grandfather or great grandfather lived, how would we know who lived in Carolina? It doesn't make sense."

"I get lots of questions about the faith. I cain't answer most, and have'ta call on the Lord. John Wesley taught that we must defend every doctrine with reason. He went to Oxford, you know," Francis said with visible pride. "Any conflict 'tween the scriptures and our understandin', is cause our rea-sonin' is imperfect."

"Well, I've never claimed my reasonin' was perfect."

"My formal education is limited. My mother died givin' birth to my baby sister, and my daddy turned to whiskey for comfort. If it weren't for the charity of kind neighbors, we'd a wound up in the gutter with Daddy. They saw to our needs and a little education and shared the Gospel with us. Their kindness and charity is the reason I chose this path."

"I'm sorry for your struggles, Francis." Tom imagined the travails of an orphan on the frontier, and thinking how different his life had been. "You ever hear of Thomas Paine?" he asked.

"The feller that wrote *Common Sense* during the Revolution?"

"That's him. Somethin' of a hero of mine. He wrote a book called *The Age of Reason*. Made the point that religion is based on personal revelation. Somebody says they had an experience or were told things by angels or the spirit, and we should believe 'em."

"I cain't say I heard voices, but I had a conversion experience. It was like a great weight was lifted off me, and I could breathe free for the first time in my life. I'll never forget it."

"You're certain of your experience, and we can talk about it, but what do we make of stories from centuries ago, from people we don't know and cain't question?"

"If you're talkin' about the Gospels, we gotta trust that God inspired their writings."

"Don't we have to use reason too? When Jesus was born, men didn't know that the sun is a star and that the earth goes around it, instead of the other way round, or that all the stars are suns like ours. So they have the story about a star coming and hangin' over Bethlehem. That couldn't a been."

"Why not? Ain't nothin' impossible for God."

"The closest star to us is the sun. You cain't find no particular place on earth by the sun or the moon. A star close enough to stand over a town would burn the earth to a crisp. Over in Revelations, it says one third of the stars will fall on the earth, but even one star couldn't fall on the earth."

Francis sat for a long time, mulling over what Tom had said. "I hear what you're sayin', but just because they didn't know what we know don't change the truth of the gospel."

"If the fellers that wrote the book get such basic things wrong, what do we make of it? It's hard to read about talkin' snakes and nine-hundred-year-old men and not wonder how much is made up."

"A doubting Thomas?"

Tom laughed softly. "I reckon so. It's my nature. Tom Paine said, 'My mind is my own church.' I reckon that's a pretty good motto."

"'Woe to those who are wise in their own eyes and prudent in their own sight.'"

"What about everybody who never heard the Gospels, who live their lives as best they can? Are they to suffer eternal punishment for the sin of ignorance?"

"That's why we must spread the Gospel to every corner of the world! Are you saved Tom?"

"I reckon I been saved many times: the first time I looked out over the wide world from the top of the Smokies, first time I heard Mozart played at school, first time I looked in my wife Sarah's eyes, and when I saw my children born. No doubt I may be saved a few more times before my days are done. I been lost, too. My little girl died last winter and it was so dark I 'bout couldn't see my way out. But I cain't un-know what I know. Would you have me condemned for followin' the truth as I see it?"

"I'm sorry for yore loss Tom, truly. I ain't no judge. The ways of the Lord are mysterious to man. He's perfect and righteous, and his ways'll be made clear in time."

"True religion should be clear to all of us, without prophets or saints, just by studyin' creation."

"I don't see anybody followin' such a religion."

"No, you're right. It's hard to compete with religions that been around awhile and promise eternal bliss if you submit and eternal damnation if you don't. To my way of thinkin', true religion has to answer the question, Why are we here, what's the purpose of all this?"

"To give glory to God."

"I don't know what that means. If God is everywhere, he must be everything. The universe is an awful big place." He looked up at the star-filled sky. "Everywhere you look might be filled with things livin' and dyin', and all part of God. The question is, why? What if the whole point is just the livin' and dyin'? If God is everywhere and everything, he's experiencin' everything, the joy and the pain, the thrill and the sorrow, all of it. Maybe he's growin' and learnin'."

Francis sat staring at Tom for a long time. "How does it all end, then?"

"I have no idea, and nobody else does either."

"God knows everything."

"He knows everything that's happenin' and has ever happened, but he cain't know what ain't happened. What'd be the point to all this if the future is set and God already knows the entire story? If you knew how the rest of your life was gonna play out to the last detail, what'd keep you goin'? If the point is experience, I have to believe the thrill of surprise is the most important part, for us and God. If not, why go through all of this?"

"What do you think happens when we die?"

"I'm here now, if only for a heartbeat in the great scheme of things. There's a beautiful world filled with excitement and adventure and people and places I love. I've experienced great joy and great sadness. I'm thankful for this life. When it comes my time to go, I hope I'll die as I've lived, and somehow my story is remembered, if only by my family and friends. They say you live as long as you're remembered. Maybe that's so."

"Don't you want to see your little girl again?"

Tom turned to stare at Francis, trying to decide if the question should anger him. He took a deep breath and paused a long time before he answered in a soft, even tone. "I see her every single day, Francis, and I expect I will until I draw my last breath. In my dreams we're together, sittin' by the falls, lookin' for four-leaf clovers and readin' poetry . . ." He trailed off. "I'm human, and I would like nothin' better than to believe we're all reunited with the ones we love. That don't change how I understand things and my place in the world."

"Do your loved ones feel the same way as you?"

"To be honest, you're the first person I have ever shared it with. I don't do much preachin'. Most people don't wanna hear anything that challenges their beliefs. After he wrote *The Age of Reason*, Tom Paine was shunned by his friends and only a handful of folks showed up for his funeral, after all he done for the country. 'Cast not thy pearls before swine,' eh?"

"They's too much uncertainty in your view. People want assurance, blessed assurance. People I've met ain't very philosophical. They lead difficult lives, strugglin' to survive, beset by calamity, and are terrified of dyin'. They want to know there's a God in heaven who watches out for 'em, listens to their prayers, even if he don't always choose to answer 'em. They want to know that this ain't all there is. I'd hate to be a slave who don't believe they's a heaven on the other side of this life. Most folk wanna believe when they die they'll go to a better place, where they'll reunite with the ones they've loved and lost. They want to be saved, and they want the evil folk that stalk their world punished. I'm afraid your philosophy offers 'em none of them assurances."

"I know all that too well. It's comfortin' for a doctor to tell a dyin' man that he's gonna get better, but that don't make it true."

The fire had died down and darkness had descended. The moon had not yet risen, and the vault of space was an inky black background for the blaze of stars and the bright swath of the Milky Way. A meteor flashed across the sky, prompting a grunt from both of them.

"When I was a little boy, I imagined the sky was a dark blanket spread over the world and that they was little pinholes in it that let the solid bright light behind it shine through," Francis said. "I guess a shooting star wouldn't fit that view."

"Probably not, but I like the image. When I was little, I wondered if they was other people like me sittin' out there on some other world, lookin' my way and wonderin' the same thing. I still do sometimes."

Another meteor came flashing across, and many more after that, some of them dim and brief, some bright with a long arc. A few ended their existence in a spectacular flash.

"I remember readin' about this," Francis said. "Every year this time there's lots of shootin' stars. The Papists call 'em the tears of Saint Lawrence, cause it happens at his birthday."

"Whatever they are, they're beautiful."

CHAPTER 43

Isaiah sat in the rocking chair on his porch and watched the shooting stars and wondered. He strained his ears to see if they made any sound, but he could hear nothing over the steady clamor of the crickets. Ellen and the children were asleep inside, and he had the world to himself to think. It was a pleasant night for August, and it made him think of autumn. His box, buried out in the edge of the woods, was full of just about everything he could think of for their escape. He had tools, clothes, maps, and weapons. As the time for their departure got closer, he would stock food in the cache.

He had found a pack of letters sent to Tom over the years and had pored over them, evaluating their content, style, and handwriting. His own script was still rough, but he had made considerable progress. Still, without a sample pass or order to work from, he didn't know how to create something to satisfy a patroller if they were confronted on the road. He was constrained as well by the lack of paper. Tom had a packet of clean sheets, but he dared to take only a few lest it raise suspicions. He had used an old newspaper to practice his penmanship, writing in the margins and across the print. The same constraints governed the quill and ink he had "borrowed." He didn't know what he would say if Sarah caught him rummaging through Tom's desk. Reading the news and the letters, and writing himself, he came to appreciate more than ever the power of the written word, and understood why the owners were so adamant to prevent their slaves from acquiring the skill.

The biggest issue facing Isaiah was getting Ellen comfortable with the plan. The more time she spent with Sarah, the closer they became, and they were spending a lot of time together. With Tom away and Isaiah taking care of the farm and planning the escape, Ellen and Sarah shared large parts of the day. He would see them sitting and talking as they worked, shelling peas or spinning yarn. In the garden or the fields they were never far apart and passed the time and the hard work talking. Every time he broached the subject of their escape, Ellen seemed less enthusiastic. She would raise the same objections and fears, and after hearing his responses, she would just shake her head and go back to whatever task she had been working on.

He understood her reluctance. Other than the trauma of losing Anne, the past year had been remarkable for him. His work didn't benefit a wealthy planter. Everything he did went to feed, clothe, and shelter the people he shared the farm with, including his new family. But he knew what Ellen couldn't admit. This interlude would disappear. The Loves would become more successful and buy more slaves. They would hire overseers to run their property, and the lash would reappear. Or the Loves would face hard times and need to sell one or all of them to make ends meet. They could be separated again. Ellen wanted to believe this situation was permanent, and Isaiah knew it could disappear as fast as the flash of one of the shooting stars.

The rocking chair was creaking now, as Isaiah weighed the impact of the news Ellen had shared tonight. She was with child again, his child. Buoyed by the thought of another child, he worried about the cruel world it would have to navigate. What would this mean for his plans of escape? Looking east across the dark ribbon of the river, he waited for the next meteor to streak across the sky.

CHAPTER 44

T HE LAST SEVERAL days Tom had spent at home, working with Isaiah in the mornings and traveling around to his closer neighbors to gather the census data on those afternoons when the heat made working in the fields difficult. Today they were harvesting the second cutting of hay from the upper pastures. They stood together in the growing heat, swinging their two-handed scythes in unison, laying the sweet green grass down in little semicircles to dry in the sun, before ricking it later in the week. After finishing a section, Tom stopped to remove his hat and wipe his brow, and Isaiah followed suit.

"This is a fine edge you've put on the blades, Isaiah. They're going through the grass like a hot knife through butter."

"Thank you, Mr. Tom. Cain't cut hay with a dull blade."

"I like how you have curved the handle too. Puts the blade at just the right angle without havin' to break your back. How'd you do that?"

"Trick my daddy taught me. I cut a couple of nice, thick hickory saplings, put 'em in a steam box I made, and then stretched 'em against some metal pegs till they dried. Then I soaked 'em in some linseed oil. Reckon our grandkids'll be usin' these handles when you and me long gone, Mr. Tom."

As they stood leaning on the scythes, they saw a Black man coming up the hill towards them. "Who can that be?" Isaiah asked.

"That's Joshua." Tom raised his hand and Joshua returned the wave as he approached.

Tom introduced the two men, who shook hands and assessed one another. "I didn't know whether to expect you, Joshua."

"Miss Martha got yore letter and asked Old Mr. Tom about me comin' out with you when he was in town. Old Mr. Tom weren't too keen on the idea, but Miss Martha wore him down. He gimme a pass to come down to your place."

Isaiah's eyes narrowed.

"My daddy's back home?"

"He was, but he left today fer Raleigh on political business. We started together at first light." He looked around at the hay. "I thought with that dry spell we had everything was gonna die out. What can I do?"

Tom handed his scythe to Joshua. "I'm gonna visit our new neighbor Mr. McDowell and get his census information this afternoon. Help Isaiah finish up this field. Isaiah, if ya'll finish early, see if they's anything Joshua can help you with."

"Apples are the future, Tom."

The new cabin stood on a cleared slope that ran away down to Sugartown Creek. It belonged to Silas McDowell, who had this year moved from Asheville to this property, not far from Tom's place. Tom had been on the road when his neighbors had helped Silas with the roof and barn raising, and this was his first chance to meet his new neighbor.

"I've done a lot of research, and I have no doubt that this country has the perfect conditions to produce outstanding varieties of apples. Plant 'em on the eastern-facing slopes to get the morning sun and to mitigate the effects of the afternoon sun in the summer and the cold western winter winds, and I assure you the yields will be impressive. The Cherokee cultivated some very interesting native varieties, but they propagated only through seed, being unfamiliar with the benefits of grafting."

"I got a few trees left on my property by the Cherokee. My servant grew up at Monticello, and he's been graftin' some of ours."

"I've read of the innovative agricultural techniques employed by President Jefferson. I should like to talk to your man if I may. I attended Newton Academy, which your uncle founded."

"I was a few years behind you. You had quite a reputation."

"All good I hope?"

"An academic of the highest regard. You spent a lot of time up in the mountains catalogin' different plants and animals, right?"

"Flora mostly. There are plants found there I believe exist nowhere else on earth. I was also very interested in the geology, and I've published some of my findings."

"I'd like to read 'em."

"We'll get you some copies before you leave. Come back this fall and I'll give you an apple sapling to plant when it gets cool. The thing about planting apple trees, or most any fruit tree, it requires faith in the future. It'll be several years of prunin' and nurturin' before it ever yields significant fruit. Many people don't have the patience."

"A virtue in very short supply."

"I might ask a favor of you, if you'd be so disposed?"

"What can I do for you?"

"I plan on running for clerk of the court in the fall election. I don't yet know my opponents, and being new to the area, I don't have many contacts. The next time you go into Franklin, I wonder if I might accompany you and gain some introductions among the community leaders."

"I'd be happy to, and would welcome the opportunity to spend the ride there and back pickin' your brain. I look forward to having a neighbor with common interests."

CHAPTER 45

JOSHUA AND ISAIAH sat on the rocks surrounding the springhouse and drank from the cool, clear water. The shade of the gigantic oak trees was as welcome as the water after their time in the hayfield. It had been over a year since Isaiah had talked with another Black man and he relished the company as much as the shade and cool water.

"So you know'ed Mr. Tom a long time?" Isaiah asked after slaking his thirst.

"Since we was young'uns. I ain't see'd him much these last few years. He don't come round too often. Him and his daddy don't get along. He always treated me fair enough. How things round here?"

"Tolerable well. You saw him workin' out in the field. Don't put on as many airs as most White folk. I'm still a slave, though. How're things at yore place?"

"Old General Tom, he comes and goes. Most of the time he's a son of a bitch. Has a fitful temper. Don't mind havin' his foremen use the lash if things ain't to his likin'. The only good thing is, he's gone most of the time. He owns land here and over in Tennessee and splits his time 'tween 'em and then runs off to Raleigh on political business ever so often. Rumor is he got a woman in both places, but I ain't never see'd it when I traveled with him. I'd gladly trade places with you."

"What makes 'em so different?"

"Hard to say; they been sideways since Young Tom was a boy. He couldn't never do nothin' to please the old man. Young Tom do everything he could to stay away from him; spent days at a time up in the hills. They let me go to keep an eye on him. When he weren't traipsin' through the woods, he had his head in a book. He couldn't wait to go away to school. Asked his old man if I could go with him, but he said no. Don't reckon he ever asked him for another thing, and Old Tom rich as Solomon. I'm surprised he let me come down here."

"They let you travel by yo'self?" Isaiah asked.

"Ever' now and then. Give me passes to show the paterrollers if I get stopped. Everybody knows the Loves in these parts. They own half the damn county. Send me into town now and then to fetch supplies. Not like I could run off. Between the paterrollers and the Injuns and the bears, Black man wouldn't make it far."

"You ever know'ed anybody to get away?"

"A couple fellers I know tried; they was caught and drug back. Fitful whoopin's and then made to wear them damn manacles."

"What does the pass say?"

"How should I know? Says I can be out, I guess."

"Can I see it?"

Joshua pulled the piece of folded paper from his shirt pocket and handed it to Isaiah, who unfolded it and studied the content.

Joshua watched him with surprise. "You kin read?"

"Tolerable well."

"Does Mr. Tom know?"

"Yeah, even gimme a book for Christmas. Don't let on I told, he's mighty skittish 'bout it."

Joshua sat stunned for a few moments before continuing. "I don't doubt it. The White folk in a tizzy about colored people readin' and writin'. Some free man wrote a book down on slavery and they's all fit to be tied. I heard Old Tom and the missus talkin' 'bout it. Where'd you learn?"

"On President Jefferson's plantation in Virginia. Old man Jefferson had children by his housemaid so they was treated half-White. They let 'em learn to read, and they passed it along to a man named Peter and he taught me, in secret."

"How'd you come to be in Carolina?"

Isaiah told him his story as Joshua shook his head.

"I'm sorry, brother. Sounds like you done had a hard time. You best keep that readin' under yore hat, though. Anybody find out you and Mr. Tom might both go down."

"I know it." Isaiah had memorized the wording and the format of the pass. It was far simpler than he had imagined, just a note really, and he had no doubt he could create one that looked more official. He took one more look and handed the pass back to Joshua, thanking him. He thought for a moment about sharing his plans, but decided against it. Joshua seemed too close to Tom, and he could see no benefit in taking the risk.

CHAPTER 46

August 26, 1830

AT THE LAST minute, Tom had changed his plans. He decided to take Isaiah along on the next leg of the mission and leave Joshua to tend the farm. Sarah planted the idea in his mind, suggesting it as something of a reward for Isaiah's efforts over the past months. Joshua was disappointed, but the time away from Old Tom's and the change of scenery was respite enough for him.

Tom and Isaiah stopped at Wallace Gap to let Rufus and Isaiah's mule catch their breath after the steady climb. The midmorning sun was up behind them and they had been on the road since first light, stopping to record the handful of households they passed along the way.

"Turn downhill from here," Tom said after they had admired the view in silence for a short while. "That's the headwaters of the Nantahala over there." He pointed to the little creek visible among the trees. "It flows west and then northwest into Cherokee territory towards Valleytown."

"What does *Nantahala* mean?"

"I been told it means *land of the noon-day sun.* It cuts through a gorge and the only time you get sunlight down in there is midday. There's a handful of new farmsteads in the hollers down yonder, and Marshal Daniel wanted me to check on things in the Cherokee lands. We'll follow the river trail, turn north towards Wayah and then back towards Franklin. It should take us the better part of a week."

An hour later they came to a cluster of new cabins lined up along the widening creek in a piece of bottomland that must have been cleared long before by the Cherokee. Several children were playing near the creek when they spotted Tom and Isaiah approaching. They stood for a moment gawking and then the tallest of them turned and started running towards the fields behind the cabins, followed by the rest of the group, hollering at the top of their lungs. A group of adults were working in the field, their heads just visible among the tassels at the tops of the cornstalks, and they turned from their work to see what prompted the commotion. One of the men started walking through the rows of corn towards them. He was tall, with weathered coppery skin and short black hair covered by a gray felt hat, which he removed and raised in greeting as he approached. Tom responded in kind.

Tom introduced himself and explained his mission. The man identified himself as Buckner Guye and told Tom that he and his family had moved into the valley the previous year.

"Are you Indian, Mr. Guye?" Tom asked as he unrolled his census form on the table inside the cabin he was invited into, and where they were joined by Guye's brother, one of his sons, and his wife.

"Half-Indian, Mr. Love."

"I see." Tom began recording his name, listing the numbers of the household on the following sheet under the labels "Free Colored Persons" as they had instructed him back in Morganton. "Cherokee?"

"No sir, we's part of the Catawba people, on my mother's side. We was livin' on the reservation, on the side of the Catawba River called Turkey Head, when the tribal leaders leased the land to South Carolina. They give us some of the money from the first year's rent and sent us on our way. My daddy's people sided with the Americans in the war with the Redcoats so we could git a land grant here. Weren't a fair trade, though. This land ain't near as good as what we left on the Catawba, too damn rocky and hilly."

"It can be hard. I live east of here on Sugartown Creek. I've heard of the Catawba people."

"Ain't many left. The smallpox nigh wiped us out."

"How're you gettin' on with the Cherokee?"

"Could be worse, I reckon. Some of 'em hoped us with the barn raisin' last year, and my brother's oldest gal married one of 'em." He nodded at his brother across the room, who grunted and nodded in response. "I was a little worried at first. I know how it feels to see your land took by somebody else."

"Did the Catawba and Cherokee get along before?"

"I only got old stories to go on, but it seems the old ones fought over boundaries off and on. We thought supportin' the Americans would've bought us more, but as my mother used to say to my father, 'White men got short memories.'"

"Sounds like somethin' my wife would say about all men." Tom chortled, but no one else joined.

They made small talk for a while longer, and then Tom visited the rest of the cabins, recording the separate households, followed by the curious children between each stop. The children stood watching as Tom and Isaiah rode away down the wide trail into the woods.

CHAPTER 47

THE SOUND OF the river echoed through the gorge, growing in volume as Tom and Isaiah followed the ancient track along its banks. Their timing was perfect, though he had not planned it that way, and the midday sun illuminated the canyon. The steep banks leading down to the river were draped in mountain laurel, their glossy leaves shining against gnarled branches. Dark boulders, covered in moss and pocked with ferns where enough dirt had accumulated to support them, littered the riverbed and the banks, many of them as big as a cabin. Water churned and foamed around and over them, the sun reflecting off the drops as they sprayed into the air, countless cataracts and falls adding to the din. It had been years since he had beheld the majesty of the roaring Nantahala. He stopped and took it all in, remembering the opening lines from his favorite poem, and marveled at how reciting it in his mind could still make his pulse quicken after all these years, and how perfect it was for this moment.

> Five years have passed; five summers, with the length
> Of five long winters! And again I hear these waters
> Rolling from their mountain springs with a soft inland
>   murmur.
> Once again do I behold these steep and lofty cliffs,
> That on a wild secluded scene impress thoughts of more
>   deep seclusion;

And connect the landscape with the quiet of the sky . . .
These beauteous forms,
Through a long absence, have not been to me
As is a landscape to a blind man's eye:
But oft, in lonely rooms, and 'mid the din
Of towns and cities, I have owed to them
In hours of weariness, sensations sweet,
Felt in the blood, and felt along the heart;
And passing even into my purer mind,
With tranquil restoration

"Never see'd nothin' like it." Isaiah sat marveling at the scene.

"I cain't think of many places I ever seen that are more beautiful. How long have these waters rushed through here, and with what force, to have created this? Our lives are just the blink of an eye in comparison." He paused for a long while before continuing. "I always planned to bring Rebecca here. She loved the wild places."

"I'm sorry you lost her."

"She was smart as a whip and had the sweetest disposition."

"I'm sure, Mr. Tom. She's sittin' by a river in glory that puts this to shame, waitin' for her momma and daddy to join her."

Tom started to speak and then paused, thinking back on his conversation with the circuit preacher. "I'm sure she is, Isaiah."

CHAPTER 48

THEY TOPPED THE last ridgeline hungry and tired and looked out over a tranquil valley, *Konehete* in the Cherokee language, meaning *the long valley place*. It stretched away to the southwest in the afternoon sun, the ribbon of the river sparkling. This was the breadbasket of the Cherokee Nation and field after field of corn, beans, pumpkin, squash, and okra spread across the fertile plain that nestled between the ridge Tom and Isaiah stood on and the procession of ridges that stepped up to the peaks west. Below them, close upon the banks of the Valley River, lay the village known to the Whites as Valleytown. From Tom and Isaiah's elevation, the Cherokee looked like ants milling about among the fields and lodges with little curls of smoke emanating from their cook fires. In an open field near the center of the village, a group of men were playing ball, though from the distance they couldn't tell which version of the sport it was. They stood admiring the panorama below, letting the mules catch their wind, before setting off down the hill.

As they approached the village they were greeted by a pack of a dozen dogs of various sizes, barking and yelping, running up to them in groups of two or three, before retreating with their tails between their legs. A similar number of children who had been playing near the river soon joined the dogs, adding their shouts to the dogs' chorus, creating a cacophony announcing their entry. Tom looked at Isaiah and shrugged his shoulders, and they continued their slow march into the village. A group of men emerged from behind a row of lodges, shouting at the dogs and children and waving them away, till they stood in a rough line blocking further progress. They were tall and strong and covered in sweat and dust, and Tom assumed they must have been playing ball. He raised his hand in greeting and after some hesitation one of the Cherokee, who appeared to be the oldest of the group, raised his hand in response. Before Tom could speak, he heard his name called and saw another man coming up behind the group, pushing his way through.

"Tom, hello!" Then he spoke to the other men in Cherokee.

"Jim Locust! It's good to see you again, my friend!" The two men stepped towards one another and grasped each other's forearms in the Cherokee form of handshake. "This is Isaiah."

The two men nodded to one another and Jim introduced each of the Cherokee men, first with their Cherokee name and then the English: Ato-hi—Woods, Kanuna—Bullfrog, Waya—Wolf, and Wohali—Eagle, the man who had raised his hand to Tom. Tom shook each of their hands in the Cherokee manner as Jim introduced them. Isaiah stood back, watching, unsure of his place in this ritual. Tom failed to notice his apprehension.

With the introductions complete, Jim informed them they had come at a very opportune time, as the village was celebrating the feast of the first fruits, the biggest festival of the Cherokee calendar. Tom recalled reading about the festival in William Bartram's *Travels*, and Jim gave him a summary of the week's activities. They had spent the last few days cleaning out their lodges and disposing of all their old clothing and other items, including any old foodstuffs, burning them in a communal bonfire, followed by dancing and games. They then fasted for three days, drinking only water and eating small amounts of honey. The first fruits of the harvest were being prepared for the feast tonight, which Tom and Isaiah were welcome to attend as honored guests.

Jim led them through the village, pointing out things and introducing Tom to the leaders and the guests from other villages there for the cele-bration. There were hundreds of Cherokee gathered, and everywhere they went, the people were talking and laughing, stopping only to look up as Tom and Isaiah passed. Seeing them accompanied by Jim put them at ease and they would just nod and go back to their banter. The men stopped for a while to watch the ball game as the onlookers cheered and jeered the players. Tom had seen a game before, but this one was played with special fervor and blood was being spilled in profusion. Two of the players stood with their hands on their knees after a vicious collision, trying to gather their senses. An older man stepped up to Jim and spoke to him, looking and pointing at Tom.

"He wants to know if ya'll want to join the game."

Tom looked at Isaiah, who looked back at him as you might look at someone whose sanity you questioned, then shook his head. "We are honored by the invitation, Jim, but we wouldn't want to deprive someone else of their spot. Please extend our thanks," Tom said with a wry smile. Jim translated to the man, and they both snickered.

They watched for a good half hour, questioning Jim about the strategy of the game and commenting on the best players. Jim told them this was a friendly match and that all the players knew each other well.

"You should see the games between villages. Broken limbs and skulls are common. It's safer than our doin' battle, though."

They continued their tour and passed a lodge with two women sitting outside, their faces streaked with soot and tears, swaying and singing in low voices.

"They're in mourning," Jim explained. "Their sons went huntin' together about a month ago. They ain't been heard from since, and we're afraid they were taken prisoner or killed. We've searched for weeks, but found no sign. They've vanished without a trace."

Tom froze, trying to keep his emotions from showing. "How old?"

"Sparrow's fourteen, Possum thirteen. Their fathers are still out lookin' for 'em. They're good boys. I think the worst part for the mothers is not knowin'. Come, I want you to meet my grandfather."

Tom replayed the image of a boy's limp body hanging from a stall door: the blood crusted on his back, flies swarming, the black hair hanging loose on his shoulders. Had it been Sparrow or Possum? Now they were both lying in unmarked graves up on Burningtown Creek and their mothers were singing dirges, wondering what had become of their sons. It had been horrific when it was two nameless bodies. Now that he knew their names and stood in their village and saw their friends playing where they should be, it was a punch in the gut. He should have put a musket ball in Mashburn's ugly head that day, he thought.

"You alright, Mr. Tom?" Isaiah asked. "You look like you see'd a ghost."

"I just need some water. The heat, I guess." He sat down on a log outside the closest cabin while Jim went to get water. Should he tell them what he knew? He weighed the options in his spinning mind. It would not bring the boys back, but it would give the parents and the village closure. But it might start an uprising that could cost many more people their lives, both White and Cherokee. They might kill him and Isaiah in their rage. He regretted not going to Sheriff Bell when it happened. The judgment seemed sound at the time, but now it just seemed cowardly, and he felt like a coward. How could he sit with these people and share their food, carrying this secret. Then he remembered why he was here. Beverly Daniel had asked him to assess the Cherokee's position, determine what kind of resistance they would offer, and last but not least, size up the choicest pieces of land.

Looking down the valley towards the Blue Ridge he saw rows of corn, their golden tassels shimmering and swaying in the August sun. Children splashed and played in the Valley River. Women laughed and talked as they prepared the evening feast. The lodges were well built and clean after the annual ablutions for the festival. Cheers erupted from the ball field. All of this would disappear in the coming days. How long did they have? Jackson would never relent and the tide of White settlers would never abate. They had passed the law, and it was only a matter of time. When the regular army came marching through the same pass he and Joshua had just come through, this village and the entire valley would be defenseless against muskets and cavalry and cannon. They would mow the Cherokee down like the hay he and Isaiah cut back on his farm. If he told them about the boys, it might only hasten that reckoning. The army might look for any excuse to put their plans in place, and an uprising, with settlers killed and farms burned, would be the perfect opportunity. Acknowledging this didn't make it any easier to swallow.

They found Jim's grandfather in his cabin, an ancient man with weathered, creased skin the color of tanned leather. He wore a beautiful purple-and-gold turban, very like the one that Jim had worn when Tom first met him. Jim made the introductions and translated for them, as Hog Bite spoke no English. He welcomed Tom to the village and asked him about his mission. He wanted to hear what he thought of the cicada eruption and expressed great sadness that he could not witness it himself. They talked about farming and hunting and fishing. He asked about Tom's farm and remembered hunting there as a boy and trapping fish in the great weir on the river. Finally, he asked the question Tom had dreaded.

"He wants to know if it's true the Great White Chief means to take all the Cherokee land," Jim said.

Tom took a deep breath before answering. "I'm sorry to say it is so. Not all Whites agree, but they passed the law."

"Our leaders at New Echota are going to Washington to ask Jackson to turn from this wickedness and honor the many treaties the Cherokee have signed. Chief John Ross himself is going to lead the negotiations," Jim said for himself.

"I hope they're successful. I think the governor of Georgia has poisoned the president's mind towards the Cherokee. Perhaps Ross can change his mind, or his heart."

"Chief Ross is a powerful man. My grandson tells me you are a powerful man and have agreed to speak for us as well?" Jim again interpreted.

"As I told your grandson, I'm not a powerful man, but I know some people who have power, and when I go to them in the fall with the census, I'll pass along what we have spoken of. In the meantime, the Cherokee here in Carolina should take no actions that might undermine the negotiations."

"That is wise counsel. We have done everything they have asked us to do. I am a Christian now and follow Jesus Christ, the son of the Great Spirit, as the missionaries teach." Jim translated, but then added his own comment. "My grandfather mixes the old beliefs with the Christian beliefs."

"We're all just makin' it up as we go along," Tom replied.

They smoked tobacco together from a pipe Hog Bite produced and continued talking until the sun was going down and the cry went through the village that the feast was ready. Tom helped Jim get his grandfather up and accompanied him to the place of honor at the head table. They all ate their fill and then turned to dancing and singing, which went on late into the evening. Jim explained the rituals to Tom and Isaiah and interpreted the songs.

At one point, Tom noticed Jim and Isaiah involved in some deep conversation, though he couldn't hear what they were talking about above the din and the steady beat of the drums. He saw Jim put his hand on Isaiah's shoulder, removing it when he saw Tom was watching.

The village retired when the moon was well up. They invited Tom to sleep crammed into Hog Bite's cabin, an honor he didn't feel he could decline. Before long, the snoring reached a level Tom feared would raise the roof. Even though he was bone tired and stuffed full of food, sleep would not come. He couldn't get the fate of the two boys, or their grieving mothers, out of his mind.

CHAPTER 49

September 1, 1830

THEY DEPARTED VALLEYTOWN as they had entered, paraded out by a chorus of yelping dogs and shouting children. They headed back into the mountains, following the Franklin Road, to return to the business of gathering census numbers. By midday they had crossed the Nation boundary line and found themselves back in Macon County. The number of farms increased as they made their way east. As the shadows stretched across the valley, they came to a cabin tucked into a glade beside a creek, flanked by rows of cornstalks stripped of their ears. A wisp of smoke curled from the chimney. Outside the cabin stood two wagons, loaded to overflowing with household items and farm utensils. A tall, thin man wearing a red plaid shirt and coarse woolen pants emerged from the barn carrying a pair of shovels.

"Tom Love, as I live and breathe!"

"Hello, Sam. It's been a long time. Looks like you're goin' sommers."

"Headed west, friend, leavin' at first light. Hop down from that contraption. You're just in time for supper."

Tom climbed from the cart and the two men embraced. They made their way towards the cabin with Sam Griffin's arm draped over Tom's shoulder, leaving Isaiah to unharness Rufus. A pretty woman wearing an apron with flour handprints on it met them at the cabin door. She threw her arms around Tom as well.

"Tom Love, you always seem to catch me lookin' my worst," she said after releasing him and running her hands across the sides of her hair to tame her auburn locks.

"Julie, your worst puts all the other women in this county to shame. You're pretty as ever. I still cain't understand what this scarecrow here did to woo you."

"It was my vast fortune, obviously," Sam said, sweeping his arm to incorporate the humble farm.

"Hope you don't mind eatin' what I've pulled together from what ain't packed."

"We're so hungry, we'd eat old leather if it's seasoned up right and covered in sawmill gravy."

"That just happens to be the menu." Sam laughed.

Tom and Sam had been friends since childhood and had gone to the same one-room schoolhouse. They had worked on the road juries together and spent untold hours fishing and hunting in the mountains. It had been close to two years since they had all been together, time slipping by as they raised their families and worked their farms. Sam and Julie had two young boys and a little girl just walking.

"Yore man's welcome to join us as well, Tom," Sam said as Julie set two more places at the table.

"Thank you. That's Isaiah. I brought him along to help with the census."

"I heard you was in charge of that. Do you mean to count us, what with us leavin' and all?"

"It's based on where you were livin' the first of June, so yep, you'll show up in Macon County."

"I wonder where we'll be ten years from now when they do it again."

"I cain't believe you're leavin', Sam."

"We'll catch up after supper and I'll fill you in."

They ate a meal of fried streak o' lean with redeye gravy and big cat's head biscuits, with roasted corn on the cob, string beans, and fried okra battered in cornmeal. They sopped their biscuits in sorghum syrup and fresh butter for dessert. There was more than enough for everyone, even with the two unexpected guests. After they finished, Sam led Tom to the back porch to smoke pipes, while Julie cleaned up and packed the dishware into the last niche in one of the wagons. Isaiah volunteered to help her.

"So what on earth could pry you out of these mountains, Sam?" Tom asked as they settled onto the porch steps, the rocking chairs having already been packed.

"Well, it were a hard decision, I can tell you that. It's just got too damn hard and I cain't see no way clear. I got nigh on a hundred acres on paper, but they ain't no more'n ten or twelve on any kind of flat ground. The rest is so hilly and rocky, it's all I can do to put food on the table, much less have any left over to git ahead. If that drought hadn't broke when it did, we'd a been up agin it shore. I done cut and sold all the timber 'cept for the last stand of chestnuts. Seems like all the game's been hunted out. I ain't see'd an elk or buffalo in I don't know when, and the whitetails are few and far between. I'm tired of feedin' my family' squirrel an' possum an' poke salad, Tom! Julie deserves more to life than livin' hand to mouth. Momma died this past spring, and me and my brothers sold the old place and split the proceeds. I sold this place to the Ammons, so I got a little gold in my pocket for the first time in my life. Julie's brother left for Texas couple years back. He says the land is good out there and they's lots of it, so . . . we're bound for Texas."

"I thought the Mexicans put a stop to any more Americans immigratin'?"

"We heard that too, but Julie's brother told us if we couldn't get a grant, he'd sell us a piece of his land at a good price. He says it's so big out there another American or two won't be noticed. He got a sizable tract before the Mexicans got squeamish."

"It's a long way to Texas."

"That it is, but I got a cousin in Arkansas said we could winter over with them and head out after."

"I hate to see ya'll go, but I understand. Maybe things will be better for you out there. It's too bad we ain't seen more of each other these past few years, but I thought of you often and it'll make life a little harder knowin' you're so far away."

"Don't go gittin' sentimental on me, Tom. It's hard enough leavin'. These mountains are all I've ever know'd. I love every knob and holler. I'll miss the waterfalls and the cricks and the smell of the balsam stands. I'll miss the dogwoods and mountain laurel when they bloom, and the whip-poor-wills and the scrooch owls. It's mostly flat land in East Texas. That'll be good for farmin', but I think I'll feel nekked without the mountains wrapped around me like a quilt. In a world where everything's always changin', they stay the same."

"'One generation passeth away, and another generation cometh: but the earth abideth forever.'"

"I don't believe I ever heard you quote scripture, Tom. As I recall, you favored Jefferson and Paine. Did you get religion on me?"

Tom chuckled. "Let's just say it's hard to beat some passages for their poetry."

"I never pictured you a slave owner, Tom, after them stories you told about yore daddy."

"Just kinda happened. It was my Uncle Robert's idea, that and this census business. I was goin' through a tough time after we lost Rebecca and I just found myself goin' along with it."

"What does Sarah think about it?"

"She went along with it for me, though she wasn't happy. I think she's enjoyed the help from the woman though, and Isaiah, he's a hard worker. The farm's never been in better shape." He told Sam Isaiah's story.

"How do you get him to work?"

"We've stood eye to eye a couple of times, but other than when he tried to run off and find his people, we ain't had a problem. Big planters got overseers to manage their people, but I don't know how these small farmers do it, when it's just you and him working side by side, day after day. Knowin' what I know now, I ain't sure I'd do it again."

"Gits too bad you can always sell 'em, I guess."

"I don't believe Sarah'd lemme do that, given what's happened to 'em."

"Cut 'em loose then?"

"The state's made it nigh on impossible. They just passed new laws to discourage it. In order to free 'em, you gotta file a petition with the court, post notices and a thousand-dollar bond. Assumin' no one objects and the court grants it, they got ninety days to leave the state or the bond is forfeit and they can be held and fined five hundred dollars. If they can't pay the fine, they're hired out for up to ten years."

"Jesus. I had no idea."

"That ain't the half of it. They cain't play cards, cain't have slaves in their houses, hell, they cain't even preach the Gospel to other colored folks."

"You knew all this before you signed on?"

"Some of it, but the laws about settin' 'em free was just passed this year, and I took 'em on last spring. I told Sarah that Washington and Jefferson and that bunch owned slaves to justify it. Takin' the census I've seen a lot of things, though. Some people treat their slaves worse than dogs."

"What're you gonna do?"

"Hell if I know."

Isaiah had come around the side of the cabin after helping Julie and stopped as he heard the men talking. Standing in the shadows, he digested the conversation, his mind racing. He hadn't heard all of it, but he heard enough. He eased back around the cabin and rolled out his blanket under the cart, pretending to be asleep when Tom came around later.

The next morning Tom and Sam said their farewells and parted, going in opposite directions. Sam Griffin died at Goliad, Texas, in 1836, executed with the members of Colonel James Fannin's militia in the Texas Revolution.

CHAPTER 50

September 11, 1830

Tom and Joshua finished their breakfast and prepared to break camp. They were half a day's ride from his father's farm, and Tom expected to gather the count of the few remaining families on their way before leaving Joshua at his parents'. Joshua had accompanied him on his route the last few days, and Tom could sense that he was not excited about returning. As they sat drinking the last of their coffee, Joshua looked at his cup and spoke.

"I enjoyed this time with you, Mr. Tom."

"I'm glad, Joshua. You been good company and great help. I appreciate your takin' care of the farm while me and Isaiah went into the Nation. I know it disappointed you not goin'."

"It's all good, Mr. Tom. I like your farm. It got me a wonderin'." He hesitated before proceeding. "I was wonderin' if you might think about buyin' me from your daddy. You know I'm a good worker and I'd be good help."

Tom stared into his coffee cup before looking up. "I'm not sure my father would part with you, Joshua."

"Yes sir, I do know, but Missus Love might talk him into it. You know he cain't deny her nothin'. I don't mean to talk out of turn, sir, but the older Mr. Thomas gits . . . well, he ain't as patient as he used to be and his temper gets the best of him now and then." Joshua didn't tell Tom about the blows and the whippings that had become common when the old man was home.

Tom studied Joshua for a moment. "There was a time when father was patient? I must'a missed that period of his life." They both paused. "I'll talk to 'em when we get home, Joshua, see what I can do."

"Thank you, Mr. Tom. Isaiah and Ellen seem like fine folk. 'Tween the bunch of us, we'd have yore farm hummin' in no time!" Joshua said, before realizing the insinuation. "Course, it in fine shape now. Just we could really make it somethin', workin' together."

"I'm sure we could, Joshua. You don't have to sell me on the idea. If I talk you up too much though, I won't be able to afford you!" Tom replied, and they both laughed.

They arrived at the farm after noon, and once again, his father was away. Tom wondered if he was ever there. He spoke to his mother about Joshua's request, and she agreed it would take some doing to get the old man to part with a valuable slave like Joshua. She agreed to make the effort before kissing Tom on the cheek and begging him again to bring her grandchildren to see her, reminding him she was not getting any younger.

Isaiah looked at the documents spread before him. He had forged three passes, allowing him to be out running errands for different people. The names were pulled from the census reports Tom had stored in his office, and he only used slave owners. He had worked for hours at a time in his cabin practicing his penmanship, and as he looked at the finished products, he was proud of the results. No one should suspect that they were forgeries. The last document granted him and his family full emancipation from Thomas Love. He was uncertain about the wording and feared it lacked legal language that would make it appear legitimate, but he had affixed a seal he made in wax at the bottom of the page, and to his untrained eye, it looked authentic enough.

His supply box was full, and he figured there was enough food to last the family two weeks. They would have to find more food on the way. It would be nice to have some money, but he could see no way to come by it. He had taken things around the farm he reckoned no one would miss, but the only thing he intended to steal was himself and his family. He compared the maps he had copied to Tom's originals, and was satisfied with their accuracy. The moon was full, but he couldn't risk leaving if Tom might return, and they expected him any day. He would have to wait for Tom's next trip, which he assumed would be in a fortnight, if he kept to his routine. But he still had to persuade Ellen. She was terrified of being picked up on the road, and her pregnancy had served to increase her trepidation. Isaiah figured that was the only thing standing between them and their escape. He replaced the documents in their hiding place, blew out the candle, and went to bed, although sleep would again be slow to come as he turned the details of his escape over in his mind.

CHAPTER 51

September 13, 1830

SARAH, ELLEN, AND the children were sitting on the front porch seeking relief from the late-summer heat when Tom arrived home in the gathering dusk. James and Julia bounded down the steps to greet their father, James hugging him around the waist and Julia his leg. Sarah stood with little Jesse under one arm and hugged Tom with her free arm, kissing him on the cheek when he reached the top step.

After Tom finished his supper, he and Sarah took a walk down towards the river while Ellen cleaned up the dishes and watched the children. As they walked along, Sarah laid out the argument she had been rehearsing in her head for several days. She wanted Tom to free Isaiah and Ellen and their children, and provide them with a few acres to call their own. Tom listened and didn't speak until she had finished. Then he explained the list of laws dealing with manumission passed by the legislature. When he finished, Sarah looked at him with a cocked head and furrowed brow.

"They'd have to leave the state?" she asked.

"Yep, that's the law."

"How they supposed to move to another place, knowin' nobody, no friends or help?"

"I reckon they wanna make it hard as they can to free 'em and don't want no free coloreds hangin' round where they can stir up the slaves. If you wanna free 'em though, they'll have to leave."

Sarah stood looking off across the river at the swaying cattails in the soft light of the setting sun. "It's just been nice havin' Ellen to talk to, another woman. I thought if we freed them they could set up house nearby. We could give 'em a little plot of land, maybe. Don't seem right them bein' forced to move off sommers. I'd miss havin' her to talk to is all, and she's a good help. Didn't know how much I missed talkin' to another woman."

"Don't know what we'd a done if it hadn't been for Isaiah all this time. I thought it enough to not be a harsh master, but I reckon that's what we all tell ourselves. I've stood on people's porches we know and looked out at hovels they got for their people that ain't much better'n pig sties. Seen 'em strung up and whooped for little things, with me standin' there watchin'. And you and me seen for ourselves families split up and girls like Ellen . . ." He paused without finishing, as he saw Sarah grimace. "And I swear every one of them men would claim they are Christian masters."

"But you ain't been like that."

"No, but I was talkin' to somebody a while back who said somethin' that made me think hard. He told me people looked at somebody like me and my ownin' slaves made it respectable. Remember when I first told you about Uncle Robert's plan? I rattled off all the respectable people who owned slaves and that if they did it, it must be alright."

"I remember."

"After what I seen, I cain't believe that no more. We tell ourselves we're honorable owners, that we ain't like the bad ones, but that's a lie, cause even if we treat 'em well, we still own 'em, them and their children and grandchildren. That's got to be more painful for some than a whippin'. I realized it would be for me. You said sometimes good men do bad things, remember? You were right. Until I saw other men that ain't much different from me, I was blind. If it hadn't been for this whole thing, Isaiah and Ellen and the whole census business, I might have never seen it for what it is."

"What are you going to do?"

"I'm going to take Isaiah with me when I go back out. There's a free colored family living down on Brasstown Creek I'd like him to talk to. They may be the only free colored family in the county. Would you be okay, just you and Ellen here for a few days? We'll have most of the crops in."

"We'll be fine."

CHAPTER 52

September 20, 1830

THE MEN SPENT the last days of summer bringing in the harvest, working from sunup until sundown every day except Sunday. The women worked just as hard, preparing the produce that would feed them through another winter for storage and organizing the surplus to sell at the market in Franklin.

It had stunned Isaiah when Tom told him on Sunday night that he would accompany him for the next round of census collection. He had tried to convince him he should stay on the farm to care for the women and children, but Tom was adamant. As he lay next to Ellen, staring up into the darkness, he saw his chances of his taking his family to freedom slipping away. If his plans were delayed another two or three weeks, he would risk having them in the mountains with winter setting in. He might not even have another window of opportunity, as Tom told him he was nearing completion of the census.

September 25, 1830

They pulled into the Anderson farmstead just after noon, scattering chickens and children as they arrived. Isaiah looked at the children and then at Tom as he hopped down from the cart.

"I thought it'd be helpful for you to meet the Andersons. They're the only free colored family in these parts."

As Isaiah dismounted, an elderly Black man with a gray beard and stooped back appeared from the front door, followed by a younger man, whom Tom assumed was his son.

"Mr. Anderson?" Tom called to him.

"Yes sir, William Anderson, but everyone calls me Will."

"We're here collectin' the census. How are you today?"

"I'm tolerable well. Rheumatism strikes me when the weather starts changin', but I get along. This is my youngest son, Henry. I'm sorry you just missed dinner, but I can have my wife rustle you somethin' up."

Tom introduced Isaiah. "Thank you, but we ate back up the road. We won't take up much of your time, just need to get a count of you and your family members."

"I'm relieved. I was afeared you was here about them new laws they passed 'bout free colored people got to leave the state."

Tom reassured him about their visit.

"I been a free man since 1783, when I got out of the army. My ole master sent me to the war in his place to fight with the Americans, me and my daddy both. They give us our freedom after, and land grants to boot. We been afeared somebody'd try to use this new law to take our land and run us off."

"I can see where you'd be concerned. If the legislature passes a new law, they shouldn't be able to enforce it against people who were livin' under the old laws. I'm a lawyer on the side, and I'd be happy to take your case if it comes to it."

"That's generous of you, sir, although currency is scarce these days. What would you charge for your services?"

"If it comes to it, we can work out somethin' reasonable. I'd consider it an honor to represent a Revolutionary War veteran. Where'd you serve?"

"Our master, Mr. John Anderson, substituted us when Cornwallis come through. We fought at Guilford Courthouse under General Greene, and then to Yorktown and afterwards until '83. My daddy lost his leg at Yorktown."

"I've had the pleasure of meeting several veterans gathering the census. We owe you all a tremendous debt."

"Thank you, sir. I'm not sure the folks up in Raleigh appreciate our service."

"We'll make sure they do. Can we go in and get your numbers down?"

"Come in. Do we need Henry and Isaiah here?"

"No, we can take care of it."

"Henry, show Isaiah around and get their mules some water, would you, son?"

"Yessir. Come on, Isaiah."

Tom and Will Anderson disappeared into the cabin, while Isaiah and Henry went to the well to draw water.

"You're the first free colored people I met," Isaiah said.

"All thanks to my daddy and granddaddy."

"How is it for ya'll?"

"We get on alright. It's hard sometimes. We grow enough to feed our families. Daddy had six children. All but me and my oldest brother moved up north. We live on land Daddy got for his service. He thought about all of us leaving, but the Whites won't give us half what the land's worth. He got my other brothers and sisters north, cause he was afraid they'd be kidnapped and sold into slavery."

"He sounds like a wise man. It must have been hard though, to send his children off."

"He cried like a baby every time one left."

"Does he ever hear from 'em?"

"They write him letters from time to time."

"He can read?"

Henry looked over his shoulder as though someone might overhear. "You got to be careful. Yeah, we can read, but I don't know what they would do to us if they found out."

"I can read too. I think the White folk fear us readin' more than anything."

"They know what we might find out. They want to keep us ignorant of the world. We're closed off from everything here, though. The White folk that live next to us is mean and keep watch all the time. Hard always lookin' over your shoulder."

Isaiah could only nod to express his understanding of their plight.

"We try to sell our surplus, but if you undercut the White folk's prices, they raise hell, and if you price it too high, you cain't sell it. It's hard to get the coin to buy what we cain't make. But whatever we make, we keep. It's ours. However hard it is though, it's better'n bein' a slave." He realized what he had said. "I'm sorry, brother."

"You just speakin' the truth."

"Is your master a hard man?"

"No, he ain't too bad. But we still somebody's property. I don't intend to live the rest of my life that way, though. Somethin' gonna break."

"I wish you luck, friend."

Tom emerged from the cabin, rolling up his census sheet. "Isaiah, you ready?"

"Yes sir." He shook hands with Henry and mounted his mule, following Tom as he made his way back up to the road.

CHAPTER 53

THEY MADE CAMP beside Brasstown Creek and built a good fire against the cool evening. After they had eaten and cleaned up, Isaiah sat on a rock, interlocking his fingers and studying them before he spoke to Tom without looking up.

"Mr. Tom, was they a reason you wanted me to meet them folk today?"

"Yeah, there was. I been doing a lot of soul searchin' these past few months as I've traveled about. I seen a lot of things that bother me." He paused and poked the fire with a long stick, sending up a swirl of sparks. "You ever think about the chain of events that lead you to where you are?"

Isaiah looked up from his hands and into Tom's eyes. "I reckon I spent most of my life figurin' on that."

"Me too, now that you mention it. When I was in school I had a religion class and we discussed whether we have free will or whether everything is predestined."

"How did you come down on it?"

"I don't know that I've made up my mind yet." Tom chuckled to himself at the irony. "We're the result of all the decisions our parents made before we were born, and the decisions their parents made, and all the random events that brought them together in the first place. If I hadn't been on a survey trip with my uncle, I might have never met Sarah. And I think about the decision I made when my uncle offered to send you and Ellen to me so I could gather the census."

"Difference is, Mr. Tom, most all the decisions in my life been made by other people. 'Bout the only real decision I ever got to make for myself was choosin' Anne to love."

"I understand. But now you gonna have to make a decision. Me and Sarah been talkin' and we want to offer you and Ellen your freedom. But it comes at a steep price. The law says if I give you your freedom, you gotta leave the state. You'd have to go north to one of the free states. I've never been there myself. I don't know what dangers and obstacles you'd face gettin' there or what kind of reception you'd get. My idea was to let you run a blacksmith shop for a few months while I file the paperwork with the court. We'd split everything you make and you could take the money and the tools when you leave so you'd have a way to make a livin' when you get where you're goin'."

Isaiah looked from Tom into the fire and studied the flames as they danced above the glowing coals, his heart and mind racing. "You said a decision was required. What's my other choice?"

"You can stay and work on my farm. Legally you'd still be my servant, but I'd section off some land for you to farm on your own. Maybe the law'll change in the future, and if it does and I can free you without you havin' to leave, I'd apply all the labor you give me between now and then towards the land. But the law may never change."

"So the decision is freedom with danger and uncertainty or slavery with security in the short run and uncertainty down the road?"

"I guess that sums it up pretty well. So think on it and let me know what you decide."

"Meaning no disrespect, Mr. Tom, but I don't need to think on it. I thought I'd be freed when President Jefferson died, and people decided otherwise. I know it'll be hard and dangerous choosin' freedom. As long as I'm a Black man livin' in a White man's world, life's gonna be hard. But it'd be worth almost any risk to live free. I've dreamt it my whole life. I'll take your offer with a full and thankful heart."

"If anyone can make it, you can. You know near as much about farmin' as anyone I've met. You can build and fix things. And you can read and write. We'll start plannin' when we get back home, and I'll find out what paperwork I have to file. Hopefully by spring you'll be where you decide to be."

CHAPTER 54

October 28, 1830

THE STACK OF census sheets were rolled out on the table in front of Tom. There were sixty-two, half of which recorded the heads of households and White inhabitants and half the corresponding sheets that contained the tally of slave and free colored inhabitants. There were 811 homesteads listed, and Tom had visited all of them over the course of the summer and fall. He had finished his mission with a little over a month to spare. He could boast that he knew Macon County better than any other man alive. There wasn't a road, lane, path, or trail that he hadn't traversed. He had been in Franklin's finest homes and the humblest of cabins, slept in boardinghouses, guest rooms, barns, sheds, and, more often than not, under the starlit skies. Most of the people he met were small farmers and businessmen, living out their lives as best they could under difficult circumstances, without much complaint, thankful for their homes and families.

The total population according to his reckoning was 5,332 souls. There were 2,487 White males and 2,333 White females. There were 458 slaves owned by fifty or so families, and the largest slave owner was Tom's father with thirty-six. Fifty-four people on the rolls were "free people of color," which included certain Indians, Blacks, and mulattoes. Tom had gone over the rolls with Sheriff Bell and the county registrar, John Dobson, and he was confident that he had accounted for every household in the county. The law required that he post a copy in the courthouse for public review and he wanted to have it up before the election in November. After that, he would carry his copies to Morganton to turn them in with the other western North Carolina enumerators before the December deadline, and meet with Beverly Daniel, completing his obligations.

The next several days were spent making three copies of each page until his writing hand was cramped and stained with ink. As he copied each name, their faces would appear to him, and he would remember some piece of their story. For many of them, this might be the closest they would ever get to a permanent record they were here, in this place and time. Their names might be recorded in a family Bible, in the deed book in the courthouse, on their wills, and on a slab of etched stone to mark their final resting place. This entry on a federal census roll, their names on a single line, with numbers representing their family members, and their slaves, would be a lasting record of where they were in 1830.

"Where are we on the list?" Sarah asked. She had tiptoed up behind Tom, placing her hands on his shoulders and kissing the top of his head.

"Right here on page forty-three." He flipped the pages to show her where his name was listed.

"I would have thought you might have listed us first or last?"

"No, I kept everyone together by where they are located. Someone looking at them later will at least know who neighbors were."

"That makes sense. I still don't think it's fair that they list only the men. Obviously men came up with the plan."

"Well, it's a list of heads of households, so where women are the head, they're listed." He showed her some entries where that was the case. He shared the final tallies with her as well.

"It's hard to believe there are over five thousand people living in the county already. It's growin' fast, ain't it?"

"Seems like it. Pretty soon you won't be able to throw a rock without hittin' somebody."

"I'm just glad it's almost finished. I've missed you, bein' gone so much."

"And I've missed home, although it has been an adventure, and I've learned a lot about myself. Maybe I'll do it again next time."

"Wonder what things'll be like in ten years?"

"We'll see, if the fates allow. If they go by as quickly as the last ten, it'll be here before we know it."

CHAPTER 55

THE FOUR MEN sat in the dining room of the Catawba Hotel in Morganton. Beverly Daniel, John Phillips, Robert Love, and Tom finished their dinner and waited for the waiter to clear the table. Tom had spent most of the meal regaling the older men with tales of his adventures over the summer and fall. He told them of having guns drawn on him, of being propositioned by lonely women on more than one occasion, and of finding respondents in various stages of undress. He was amazed at the number of whisky stills he had encountered and assured them there was a wide range of quality produced, as he could personally attest. The older men laughed as they lit their cigars.

"You'll be interested to know that Washington sent word this week that the deadline for filing has been pushed back. I guess some other states have had problems," Beverly Daniel said.

"I'm glad I didn't know that. I think my wife would have killed me if this had gone on much longer."

"I'm interested to hear what you found over in the Nation. How are our friends the Cherokee?" Beverly stared at Tom.

Tom shifted in his seat and took a breath before responding. "Well, sir, they're uneasy, as you might expect. I spent some time in Valleytown and they're afraid of this new legislation. Their chiefs are tellin' 'em not to worry. John Ross and the Ridges are pressin' their claims and have said they'll go all the way to the Supreme Court. Their brethren are being pressed hard down in Georgia, so they're treadin' lightly. They're buildin' cabins and clearin' land to replace what they've lost. The fields were standin' tall with corn and beans and sorghum. They wanted me to take back the message that they are followin' White ways. Many have converted to Christianity. They've got a newspaper out now called the *Phoenix*, which they're proud of, that's printed in English and the new Cherokee alphabet that Sequoyah developed. They've got a constitution and courts set up down at New Echota in Georgia. I don't see that they pose much of a threat to anybody if they're left alone. They are keeping their noses clean for sure. We should just leave 'em be, that's my view."

Daniel and the Colonel looked at each other. Robert spoke first. "There'll be no dissuading Jackson, I'm afraid. The act has passed and there's no turnin' back."

"What if Marshall and the Supreme Court rule against them?"

"Jackson don't give a damn about the Supreme Court. He knows where his bread is buttered. Last time I looked, the court didn't have an army," Daniel responded and took another draw from his cigar. "You think the valley is the best farmland?"

Tom tried not to show how the turn of the conversation had deflated him. He knew this would be the outcome of his report, but he felt dirty and complicit. The faces of the Cherokee men flashed before him, asking for his help, and then the women as they mourned their lost boys. But he gave the answer he knew the men were looking for. "Yes sir, it's a broad, open valley with rich soil and good water." He reluctantly added details about the numbers of Cherokee living in the valley, their condition, and their concerns about the new legislation. He described the quality of the farmland and the variety of crops the Indians were cultivating. When he was finished, he turned his palms upwards to show there was nothing else he could add. He realized it was a symbol of surrender.

Daniel and Robert Love again exchanged glances. "Do you think they'll put up much resistance when the time comes?"

"It's hard to say, but they're not in a position to resist any significant show of strength. Bows and hand axes ain't much use against muskets and cannon. My guess is most of 'em will go quietly. A few of the most determined will disappear into the mountains to hide out. There's not much sustenance there though, so it will be hard on 'em when winter sets in."

"Excellent information, Tom. Robert, you were right to recommend your nephew here." Daniel produced a bottle of whiskey and poured a liberal shot in each of their glasses. "Gentlemen, this is my last bottle of Bowmore. I saved it for this occasion. Here's to the very successful conclusion of the 1830 census in North Carolina. Tom, you are to be commended for your efforts." They all raised their glasses and drank. The whisky seemed to burn more than usual to Tom.

November 26, 1830

Tom collected his pay from John Phillips the next morning and, in turn, paid his uncle what he owed for Isaiah and Ellen. He had drawn up a bill of sale, which he had him sign, knowing he would need it as part of the package he would have to file to start the emancipation proceeding. John Phillips and Beverly Daniels witnessed it to make it legal. Tom had debated whether to tell his uncle about his plans, but something made him decide against it. He knew his uncle would try to talk him out of it. At a minimum, he would get angry, and Tom didn't want to part from him on bad terms. He also knew his uncle was the most powerful man in western North Carolina, and if he threw his weight against the proceedings, he could thwart his plans. Robert told him he was very proud of him, and Tom thanked him for his confidence and everything he had done. The two embraced and said their farewells under the cold gray November sky.

CHAPTER 56

December 20, 1830

THE WAGON WAS full. Tom and Isaiah had loaded it with food, old clothing, a few old toys, and firewood. Isaiah made sure everything was secured as Tom and Sarah said their goodbyes.

"This is good of you, Tom," Sarah told him as she adjusted his coat collar against the chilly wind.

"It ain't much, but it may get 'em through the worst of the winter and at least brighten their Christmas a little."

Tom had gotten around to telling Sarah about Patsey Barker, the woman whose husband had run off to Georgia looking for gold, leaving his wife and two children to fend for themselves. He had decided the woman's recent vocation to make ends meet was not a detail he needed to share. The thought of the family left to their own devices with winter looming had gnawed at him, and so he had proposed to gather some necessities and deliver them to the family before the holiday. Sarah concurred, and they had spent the last few days pulling together what they could to help.

"Bring the axes, Isaiah. We'll cut some more wood there. You know how they'll go through a cord." He turned to Sarah. "We'll be back before supper tomorrow." He kissed her on the forehead and hugged her. Ellen came out of the house, her belly large with child, and kissed Isaiah goodbye as well. The women stood and waved as the men drove the wagon down the path.

The skies had cleared and a softer wind blew in from the southwest as Tom and Isaiah pulled their wagon in front of the cabin in the late afternoon. Nothing seemed to have changed from the time Tom had first visited months ago. Off to one side of the clearing, a swarm of flies hovered around what appeared to be a couple of squirrel skins and entrails. A rusty axe stood at a forty-five-degree angle, the head buried in a log.

"Start unloading the wood, Isaiah. Stack it over there against the crib. That should keep it dry. I'll check with the woman about the food and clothes."

Isaiah nodded his assent and pulled the wagon around the cabin closer to the crib after Tom jumped down. Glancing around, Tom surveyed the condition of the farm as he made his way to the door, thinking they might also offer to make some repairs before they left. He stepped up onto the porch and was reaching to knock when the door flew open. Standing in the doorway was Amos Wright with a musket leveled at Tom's gut.

"Well, I'll be goddamned if it ain't high-and-mighty Mr. Tom Love!" Another man stood behind him, with a short-cropped brown beard, squinting against the afternoon sun. Tom raised his hands to chest level. "Barker, this is the feller I told you about that got me fired, whipped, and run out of the county."

"What brings you to my place, mister?" the man behind Wright snarled. "You mean to git a poke from my wife?"

"I brought supplies to tide this family through the winter, since, if you're her husband, you abandoned them."

"Who the hell you to judge me? I been workin' like a dog to make a way for them. Don't you come on my place judgin' me!"

"See what I mean? Him and his folk think they're better'n everybody else. Well, Mr. Love, you gonna regret stickin' your nose in somebody else's business this time!" Wright shoved the musket into Tom's gut, almost making him fall backwards down the steps.

"Don't hurt him!" Patsey Barker appeared in the doorway as the two men crossed the porch. "George, he was one of the few people to hope us."

"I'll bet he helped, helped git your dress off. Git back in the house and stay out of this!"

Isaiah appeared from around the corner of the cabin carrying his axe, responding to the shouting. Wright and Barker turned to look at him, and in that instant, Tom grabbed the musket barrel. In the scuffle for control of the gun it discharged, the ball hitting Tom in the upper abdomen just a few inches below his sternum. The force of the shot drove him backwards, and he stumbled before falling on his back, his hands grasping the wound.

Without hesitating, Isaiah charged. Reaching Wright first, he swung the axe with his full weight, driving it into the man's chest. Before Isaiah could wrench the weapon free, Barker tackled him, and the two men rolled in the dust, swinging at one another before Isaiah gained leverage and rolled Barker onto his back. Straddling him, he pummeled the man's face with his fists. Barker stopped struggling, but Isaiah didn't quit until he felt the woman pulling him off the unconscious man. He scrambled to his feet and surveyed the carnage. Patsey Barker crouched over her husband wailing. Two small children had appeared and ran to their mother's side, screaming and crying as well. Wright lay flat on his back with his eyes open, the axe lodged in his chest at the same forty-five-degree angle as the rusty axe in the log.

He ran to Tom's side and saw his hands spread over his stomach, covered in blood. Tom's face was white as a sheet and his eyes jerked back and forth as he tried to focus.

"You gotta get me home, Isaiah," he said in a hoarse whisper.

"I don't think you can travel, Mr. Tom."

"I have to see Sarah. I cain't die without seein' her one more time."

"You ain't gonna die, but we gotta git you to a doctor right now."

"No, get me home, Isaiah. Please."

Isaiah stood up, his mind racing. He decided that the first thing he should do is dress the wound, so he ran into the cabin and grabbed the sheet off the bed, ripping it as he ran back out. Leaning over Tom, he moved his hands away and tore his shirt open, revealing the bleeding wound. He took a strip of the sheet, folded it, and pressed it against the hole, putting Tom's hand on it to hold it in place. Rolling Tom on his side, Isaiah saw that his back was sticky with blood, confirming that the ball had exited, although he was not sure whether to be relieved. Pulling Tom's coat and shirt up, he took another strip of sheet and pressed it against the exit wound before rolling Tom on his back again. He wrapped the rest of the shredded sheet around Tom, tying it on the side to hold the bandages in place, each movement soliciting a fresh moan.

He ran behind the cabin and in a moment was back with the wagon, throwing the supplies they had brought onto the ground. When it was empty, he ran back inside, grabbed the pitiful excuse for a mattress off the bed and threw it in the wagon. Lifting Tom, he wrestled him onto it. From one of the baskets they had brought, he retrieved a blanket and spread it over Tom. Patsey Barker was still huddled over her husband, and Isaiah went to her.

"He ain't gonna die, but Mr. Tom might. I need you to git in the back of the wagon and tend to him till we get him home. The kids can ride up front with me."

Patsey shook her head and bent over her husband again.

"I ain't askin'," he said, and he grabbed her arm and pulled her to her feet, dragging her to the back of the wagon. He pushed her up into the bed and when she resisted, he pulled her face towards his. "If this man dies, it's gonna go hard on you. You need to pull yo'self together and nurse him like yore life depended on it." He then lifted the two wailing children onto the seat, as their mother tried to quiet them. He ran into the cabin one last time and returned with two oil lamps, anticipating he would need them when night fell. With that, he grabbed the reins and snapped them to start the mules. The sharp movement elicited a new moan from the back of the wagon, and Isaiah tried to calculate how much speed he could make without causing Tom further trauma. The wagon disappeared down the path, leaving the two men lying in the blood-soaked dust.

They stopped at the first house they came to after turning onto the Franklin Road, the Samuel Reynolds farm. Dusk had descended on the shortest day of the year and lantern light was visible in the farmhouse windows as Isaiah banged on the door. It creaked open, revealing Reynolds holding his musket against the unknown threat. Isaiah described the situation and asked for water and clean cloth for fresh bandages. After consulting with Samuel, they decided Patsey and the children would stay there. Jacob, his oldest son, would take over for Patsey and tend to Tom as they made their way home. Samuel would ride north to Franklin to fetch a doctor and alert Sheriff Bell to the violence that had shattered the day. Isaiah lit a lantern and set out down the dark road, praying that Tom would make it.

CHAPTER 57

December 21, 1830

ISAIAH LOST ALL track of time as he strained to see beyond the few feet of bouncing light the lantern provided. Every bump elicited fresh moans from the back of the wagon, followed by periods of quiet, which he feared the worst. The best he could manage was a trot from the mules, and the slow progress was nerve-racking. There was just the faintest glow to the east to show that dawn was approaching when he found the turnoff to the Love farm.

"We're almost home, Mr. Tom."

The only response from the rear of the wagon was another low moan, but Isaiah was relieved to know he was still alive.

Sarah watched Rebecca playing with little Jesse out by the springhouse. They were sitting in the clover that grew in the shade of the red maple.

"Don't let the 'skeeters eat him up, 'Becca."

"I won't, Momma."

Sarah sat bolt upright in the bed at the pounding of the door. She knew it was still night, but she had no idea what time it was. The pounding grew more intense, and as she jumped from the bed, she recognized Isaiah's deep voice. The children were now awake and Jesse was squalling, soon joined by Julia. James had jumped from his bed and was beside Sarah as she pulled her coat from the peg on the wall and wrapped it around herself. With her heart in her throat, she pulled the door open to see Isaiah standing with Tom in his arms, his head on Isaiah's shoulder, his eyes closed. His face was white in the light cast by Jacob Reynolds's lantern.

"Oh my God! What has happened!" Sarah cried. "Tom! Tom!" she called as she reached out to touch him.

"Where can I lay him, Miss Sarah? He's hurt bad."

The beds were upstairs and Sarah knew Isaiah would have a hard time getting him up the narrow staircase. "James, take Jacob upstairs and pull the mattress off my bed and bring it down here. Quick!"

The two disappeared up the staircase, leaving the lantern with Sarah, who held it aloft, trying to ascertain the nature of Tom's injury. Ellen appeared behind Isaiah. "Ellen, can you build up the fire and get some water boiling?"

The boys reappeared, dragging the mattress behind them. Sarah pointed to where she wanted it placed on the floor and held the lantern while Isaiah struggled to lower Tom onto the mattress. Tom's head lolled to one side, but he opened his eyes and in a hoarse whisper called Sarah's name. She was beside him in an instant, wiping his forehead and pushing his hair back from his eyes. She remembered laying on the mattress months ago when delivering Jesse. Tom had promised her they would grow old together.

"I'm here, Tom. I'm here." She looked down to see the blood-soaked bandage on his stomach and gasped. She looked at Isaiah with her mouth open and tears flowed down her cheeks.

"They shot him point blank. The ball went clean through and come out his back. I bandaged him up as best I could. He's lost a lot of blood. We rode through the night to git back home. He wouldn't have it no other way. Mr. Reynolds is on his way to Franklin to fetch the doctor and the sheriff."

Sarah tried to comprehend what Isaiah was telling her. "Shot? By who?" she stammered.

"That man Wright what brought me and Ellen here." Ellen looked up from her efforts at the mention of Wright's name. Isaiah saw the look of shock on both women's faces.

"He ain't gonna hurt nobody else," he said through clenched teeth. "He was at the cabin when we got there, inside. Mr. Tom went to the door, and I started unloading the wagon. I heard some yellin' and come runnin' with the axe in my hand. He was pointin' the gun at Mr. Tom and it went off and Mr. Tom fell back'ards. I hit Wright with the axe, kilt him, but it was too late. I wanted to take Mr. Tom to a doctor in Franklin, but he wouldn't go no place but here."

"Thank you, Isaiah, for gettin' him home."

Sarah began cutting Tom's bloodstained clothes off and removing the soaked bandages. She cleaned the wounds as best she could and dressed them again. The bleeding had subsided. During their ministrations, Tom floated in and out of consciousness. Sarah was not sure if he knew where he was, but she spoke to him in soft tones, reassuring him. Isaiah knelt by them until the sun had come up. His eyes were red, and Sarah couldn't tell if it was exhaustion or he had been crying. He was sore from the fight and bone tired from the wild ride through the winter night. She told Ellen to feed him and put him to bed.

Just after noon Sarah heard horses outside and directed James to get the door. It was Doc Andrews and Sheriff Bell. While the doctor examined Tom, Bell told Sarah what he knew, based on his brief interview of Patsey Barker at the Reynolds place. Her husband had returned from the goldfields of Georgia a few weeks before. He had met up with Wright, an old friend of his, buying liquor at a trading post in the Nation, and invited him back to the cabin the day before. They heard Tom arrive and discussed roughing him up, but she didn't think they planned to shoot him. Her story matched what Isaiah had told Sarah, and he was satisfied that he had the facts.

The doctor finished his examination and commended Sarah on her care for the wounds, but he was worried about the internal damage to his organs.

"Is he gonna make it?" Sarah asked, apprehension clear from her face.

After a long pause, the doctor responded, shaking his head. "It's in God's hands."

CHAPTER 58

December 23, 1830

FOR TWO DAYS Tom floated in and out of consciousness, lost in a gray netherworld occupied by ghosts and phantasms, voices he didn't recognize unconnected to bodies floating around him. Some apparitions that assailed him in the dark hours he did know. He saw the Indian boy, his back bloody and flies swarming him, but he wasn't dead. He was walking through a cornfield, knocking over the stalks as he stumbled, searching for something. Then Tom heard the dirge of the mothers, and he realized the boy was trying to find them in the corn. Wright appeared, his face contorted in a savage grin, and he was pushing Tom, harder and harder, poked in the gut until he couldn't breathe. He saw his father, looking down at him from a horse, shaking his head, and then turning the horse to ride away down the road. Tom called after him but no sound came from his throat but a harsh crackle that sounded like a crow. He felt himself floating away, the world below getting small and spinning like a whirlpool. Then Sarah would appear, her eyes locked on his eyes, her hand in his hand, her voice soothing him, the faint scent of lilac wafting over him, and he would feel himself drawn back to earth.

On the afternoon of the second day, he regained consciousness. He knew he was at home, could see the landscape painting on the wall, and his beloved books. He tried to move, but the pain struck like a knife and took his breath, almost sending him back to the shadowlands. Sarah heard him and was by his side in a flash.

"What happened?" he whispered.

"They shot you, Tom. That bastard Wright shot you in the belly at the Barker place. But you're home now and I've got you. Your momma and daddy's here. They're with the children outside."

Tom took a moment to digest the information. "How did I get here?"

"Isaiah brought you home. He drove through the night to get you here."

"What happened to Wright?"

"Isaiah took care of him too. He'll cause no more pain in this world. The other feller has disappeared."

Tom closed his eyes for a minute, absorbing what he had been told. When he reopened them, Sarah asked if he could drink some broth and he thought he could. The act of trying to raise his head was too painful though, and she was afraid he would choke drinking on his back. She called out and Isaiah helped her prop him up on some pillows.

As he lay there, it occurred to him he might not survive this, and then the thought gripped him: What would happen to Sarah and the children? He remembered he had never written his will.

"Sarah, you've gotta get Joshua Roberts here."

"Why, Tom?"

"He needs to draft my will."

"Tom, don't talk so. You're gonna get well. You're gonna beat this. Don't even think otherwise. I can't bear the thought!"

"Sarah, please. It'll be alright. I'll fight with my last ounce of strength. But we gotta do this."

CHAPTER 59

December 24, 1830

T OM HAD RALLIED. He took nourishment from warm chicken broth. Some of his color had returned and there was no sign of fresh bleeding. Joshua Roberts arrived at noon and expressed his sympathies for Tom's condition. Tom told him he wanted to dictate his last will and testament. Roberts organized his papers and began the interview. Tom remembered interviewing Jeremiah Green, the old man on his deathbed, and wondered if he was still alive. He recited the preambles as Roberts recorded them. He wanted to be buried next to Rebecca. He left everything to Sarah, except his rifle, which he left to James.

"What about your servants, any special arrangements?"

The question stunned Tom. He had made a promise to Isaiah. There had not been time to start any of the proceedings. He had assumed he had plenty of time. "We always assume we have plenty of time," he thought. State law made special provision for slaves emancipated through last wills and testaments, but he didn't know if the new laws changed that.

Then he thought of Sarah and the children. How could she manage the farm by herself with three young children? He remembered the widows he had encountered during the census. They had to rely on the charity of family and neighbors. The image of Sarah, haggard and poor, knocking on a door for a handout with three little children presented itself in his mind. He thought of the commitment he had made to Isaiah, his promise to see him freed, but it only took him an instant to decide. Sarah would need Isaiah and Ellen to run the farm, to survive.

"They go to Sarah as well."

Roberts finished the will, and witnessed by two of his neighbors, Tom scrawled his signature. Roberts set his seal, and it was finished. He gave the document to Sarah for safekeeping. The men said their farewells, wishing Tom a full recovery and mumbling, "Merry Christmas," and shuffled out, escorted by Sarah. Tom laid his head back and closed his eyes, releasing a sigh, thankful that was finished.

He lay like that a moment and then opened his eyes and turned his head. Standing in the corner, leaning against the little bookshelf, he saw Isaiah. He had been there the entire time, unnoticed, and Tom knew he had heard. They locked eyes, but neither man said a word. Tom was the one to break eye contact, turning his head and closing his eyes. Isaiah, gripping his hat, glanced down, shook his head, and walked out of the cabin.

December 25, 1830

It was a somber Christmas on the Love farm. Dark clouds and chill winds reflected the pall that covered the cabin. Sarah awoke to find Tom burning with fever and lapsing in and out of consciousness. When she checked his bandages, there was a terrible odor and fresh discharges that were rust colored. Throughout the day he alternated between burning up and freezing, and Sarah responded by piling on quilts or applying cool, damp cloths. He couldn't keep anything down and was growing visibly weaker. By nightfall his eyes appeared yellowish and he began rambling incoherently.

CHAPTER 60

December 26, 1830

HE WAS WALKING through the woods down an old Cherokee trail. It was spring, he knew. The dogwoods were in bloom, their creamy white petals standing out in pockets in the forest. The maples and the chestnuts, the poplars and the sweetgums were just budding out. Here and there a native azalea was in bloom, golden flowers on some, crimson on others. The sun was bright in a clear blue sky, and he felt the softest breeze on his face. He figured it must be about planting time. But for now, he was just following the path through the woods he loved so much. He heard a noise, a soft hum at first, growing as he walked along, and he recognized it as water flowing. He must be near the river.

Soon he was trotting along the path, feeling strong, his lungs pumping the fresh mountain air in and out, the sound of the water growing in his ears. He emerged from the forest into a clearing, and he knew where he was. He was standing at the foot of Cullasaja Falls. The water cascaded down the rocks, the drops reflecting the sun, a prism formed by the spray, the colors soft and diffuse. Then he saw her: Rebecca, sitting on a rock halfway up the cataracts, wearing her favorite blue dress, a bunch of wildflowers in her hand. She looked down and saw her father and smiled; the dimples forming in her cheeks the way he loved.

Sarah was by his side when he drew his last breath. The last word he ever spoke was "Rebecca."

They buried him the next day, beside his daughter as he had requested.

CHAPTER 61

December 30, 1830

"Miss Sarah, I wonder if I might talk to you a spell."

"Certainly, Isaiah."

"I know you still grievin'. We all are. What happened to Mr. Tom is a terrible tragedy. I cain't tell you how sorry I am."

"Thank you, Isaiah, and thank you for gettin' him home. Least he could pass here under his own roof with his family beside him."

Isaiah nodded his head and fumbled with his hat, unsure how to proceed. "A while back, Mr. Tom told me he was gonna give Ellen and me and the children our freedom. Did he say anything to you about that?"

"Yes, Isaiah. We talked about it. I'm sorry all this happened before he could fix it." She paused, and an uncertain future yawned before her. "Anyways, it's on me now and I intend to see it through. I'll have to talk to somebody who can help me with it, a lawyer I reckon, or Tom's family, but I'll see to it. Just give me some time."

"Yes ma'am, thank you, Miss Sarah. That means a lot to me. In the meantime, I'll be all the help I can here."

CHAPTER 62

THE FIVE MEN sat around the table in General Thomas Love's dining room while the fire roared. It was the middle of the afternoon, and Joshua served them all whisky in the good glasses. The General commanded the gaze of the other men. Bynum Bell sat across from him, and Nimrod Jarrett, John Alman, and Benjamin Brittain filled the other slots. Jarrett had the floor.

"Look, nobody's disputin' that it was a tragedy, and that man Wright got what was comin' to him, but a Negro has killed a White man and seriously injured another, justified or not. If a wild animal tastes human blood, you gotta put it down or it'll attack again. Slave knows he can kill a White man, ain't no tellin' where it leads."

"You sayin' we ought to hang him? What was he supposed to do with Wright shootin' Tom?" Bell replied.

"What if the other slaves see that one of them killed a White man and there ain't no repercussions?" John Alman volunteered.

"My sister's out there with him alone. What's stopping him from escapin', or worse?" Benjamin Brittain said, glowering from one face to the other.

"It was my son; I'll take care of it. I'll have him brought here for the time bein' and then I'll sell him south. He'll be out of the county and that should satisfy your concerns."

"What about Sarah? Will she go along with it? She'll need help with the farm," Bell pointed out.

"I'll take a crew down from time to time to help and send a boy down to take care of the chores. She took Tom's loss hard. She ain't of a mind to make a decision like this," Love replied. "I'm meeting a man from Raleigh here tomorrow. I'll head down there the day after. It'll wait until then."

Joshua refilled their glasses and then disappeared into the kitchen. He found Martha Love giving instructions to the cook for supper.

"Missus Love, we gettin' low on oil for the lamps. Could you give me a pass to go into town and get some?"

A few minutes later Joshua was headed out of town. As soon as he passed the last house, he urged the horse into a gallop and headed for the Love farm. He didn't know how he would account for his absence when he returned, and fully expected that he would receive a beating at a minimum. He had already decided it was worth the price.

Joshua rode into the farmyard with the horse lathered from the ride. Isaiah was chopping wood and looked up in surprise at Joshua's arrival. Sarah stepped out of the cabin at the sound of the horse's hooves, wondering what fresh problem was at hand. Joshua had intended to give Isaiah the information in private but realized he didn't have the time or an excuse, so he stood in front of the cabin and told them about the conversation he had overheard and the plan the men had adopted to make Isaiah disappear.

Isaiah stood stunned. For the second time in his life, the death of his owner threatened to turn his world upside down. Both of them had promised him freedom. Both had died without fulfilling that promise, their obligations and concerns overshadowing any commitments they had made to him, a slave. First, he was sold south and separated from Anne and Susan. Now he was to be sold farther south and separated from Ellen and his children. Rage welled up within him.

Sarah was no less angry. These men were going to decide her life without as much as a discussion. Still raw from Tom's death, she was angry that her husband had died trying to help someone else, killed by a mad dog. Now, her wishes were not even considered by men who had shown no interest in her well-being to that point. She looked up at Isaiah. "You have to go."

"Go where?"

"North, to freedom, just like you and Tom planned."

"But he was gonna get a court order, do it legal so I could take my family and leave like a man . . . have a chance to make it. I'll be hunted this way, and if they catch me, they's no tellin' what'll become of me. How can I run with Ellen and the children? She ain't far from deliverin' and it the middle of winter."

Sarah paused, biting her lip in thought. "You're right. Ellen and the children'll have to stay here with me. You can make it on your own. When you get clear, when you're free in the north, you can send for 'em."

"I cain't leave my family!"

"Isaiah, I'm sorry it's this way, but we got no choice. If they come for you, I won't be able to stop 'em. They'll haul you off and they'll be nothing we can do. At least this way you got a fightin' chance. But we gotta hurry. If we had a paper sayin' you was free. I got Tom's seal. It'll look official. If you're stopped, that might get you through."

"I got papers, made 'em up myself."

Sarah looked at him, questions forming in her mind.

"She's right, Isaiah," Joshua said. "This is the only chance you got. If you leave quick, you kin git up in the mountains with a two-day jump on 'em afore they even know you gone. Miss Sarah can tell 'em some story about where you went to buy you some more time. Travel at night. Hide out in the day."

"You'll need supplies, maps, other things. Decide now, Isaiah."

He stood looking at them and he knew they were right. This was his only hope. He thought about his secret cache hidden in the woods and his earlier escape plan. "I got some supplies laid by already. If I can git some of Mr. Tom's cold-weather clothes, coats and the like, that'd be helpful. Can I take the cart I built for Mr. Tom for the census, and old Rufus?"

"Yes, of course. I think he'd want it that way."

"How can I say goodbye to Ellen and the gals? How can I leave 'em? You'll take care of 'em for me, Miss Sarah until I can send for 'em?"

"Of course, Isaiah. Joshua, you better get back before they miss you and suspect somethin'."

"Yes ma'am."

"I cain't thank you enough, Joshua," Isaiah said and embraced him.

Two hours later, as the winter dusk descended, Isaiah and his family stood beside the odd-looking cart and said goodbye, with Sarah and the Love children watching. Cold tears ran down all their cheeks as they embraced one last time, not knowing when or if they would ever see each other again. Susan, never fully recovered from losing her mother, held onto him, refusing to let go until he pried her away and kissed her on the cheek and forehead. He mounted the cart and pulled away down the path into the gathering darkness, pausing just a moment to look at the mounds of red clay that marked the final resting places of Thomas Love and his daughter, before he disappeared into the mountains.

The half moon stood overhead in the cold, clear sky. Combined with the stars and the ghostly ribbon of the Milky Way, it made the crossroads visible to Isaiah as he approached them. He brought Rufus to a halt and watched as their breath hung in the pale light. Their trip to this point had been silent and fast. Isaiah had all but memorized his maps by this point, having pored over them for months, and he knew this was his first decision point.

Straight ahead lay the road to Franklin. He might get through the town before dawn, but the risk of being observed was too great. The only real choice was to turn left and follow the trail along the Nantahala River, the path he and Tom had taken last fall. It would be treacherous going in the dark, the canopy of evergreens blocking the limited light, but there was little chance of him being spotted at night, and there would be an abundance of places to hide out during the day. What worried him was that it would mean going through the Cherokee Nation.

His hands were numb with cold, as the thin leather gloves provided little in the way of warmth, and his face stung every time the breeze freshened. He sat there for a time, thinking about his life and all the events that led him to this crossroads, alone in the middle of a winter night. He thought of his father and his mother and his beloved Anne. He thought of Ellen and the children. Leaving them behind had been the hardest thing he had ever done. He realized he would never be free until they were with him once again, and they would never be with him unless he made it north. He would make it through whatever danger lay ahead, for them. He pulled his collar up, took the reins, and pulled Rufus onto the dark track. "Giddyap ole boy, we got a long road ahead."

CHAPTER 63

April 19, 1831

SARAH AND ELLEN walked behind the plow as it turned up the loose soil, their bonnets providing some relief from the sun, already hot for this early in the spring. Sarah dropped the kernels of seed corn, and Ellen came behind her, dropping the beans alongside them. James followed with the hoe, raking the dirt back into the furrow to cover the seeds. A young slave named Alonzo, on loan from her father-in-law, guided the mule and plow. His efforts were appreciated, even though his furrows were crooked. When they reached the end of the row, they all stopped to stretch their aching backs.

As Sarah stood resting, drinking spring water from a gourd, she saw a wagon pulled by two fine horses driving up the road towards them with two men on the seat. She handed the gourd to James and went to meet them.

"Good mornin', gentlemen. Can I help you?"

"Good day, madam. Do we have the pleasure of addressing Mrs. Love?"

"That's me."

"My name is Jeffery Lovell, and this is Mr. Anthony Sheffield." They both bowed.

"What can I help you fellers with?"

"We're members of a religious organization called the Society of Friends. We traveled here from a community in Pennsylvania on a mission of mercy, if you will. A few months ago we made the acquaintance of a Negro man I believe you know, a Mr. Isaiah Paine?"

"Isaiah! He's alive?" Sarah gasped.

"Yes ma'am. He has survived quite an ordeal. He managed to make his way from your farm here, according to his account, all the way to Pennsylvania, where our community took him in. The story of his life was quite moving. His travails touched our congregation and they agreed to assist him. They took a collection to provide for our travels here and to provide funds for the, shall we say, 'acquisition,' of his wife and family, if you would be so agreeable. Mr. Paine assured us you would be. I have a letter here for you from him." From his waistcoat he produced the letter, which she eagerly opened.

> *Dear Miss Sarah,*
>
> *By some miracle I find myself in the free state of Pennsylvania. I was helped by a Indian man name of Jim Locust, who was friends with Mister Tom. He knew a missionary man that had helped school him who has pity on slaves. With their help I made my way along the mountain ridges north. I avoided capture several times by the skin of my teeth. Now I been welcomed by a group of kind Christian people who have give me shelter and work and more important, agreed to help reunite me with my family. I am trusting that your feelings towards me and my family have not changed and that you didn't suffer no harm from helping me. I pray that you and your family, and my darling Ellen and children are safe and healthy. If you are still willing, will you allow the good people bearing this letter to pay you for the freedom of Ellen and the children? I shall repay them when I have put aside the money. You was always a kind and generous mistress to me and my family. I never received no better treatment in all my years. I hope God will bless you for the kindness you have shown me.*
>
> *Very truly yours,*
>
> *Isaiah Paine*

Sarah wiped her eye with her sleeve and refolded the letter. "This is wonderful news! Ellen and Susan'll be so glad to know he's safe and that they'll be with him agin. It was awful kind of you folks to help him."

The two men looked at one another. "That is very good to hear, ma'am. We weren't sure how we would be received, and we're not sure how to proceed. As we said, our congregation, though not wealthy, provided us with funds to secure Isaiah's family. We're just uncertain how you folks handle this . . . process. Please pardon our clumsiness."

"I couldn't sleep if I took yore money. My husband promised Isaiah and his family he'd free 'em before he died. I wouldn't tarnish his memory by sellin' them. I'd ask you to give the money to Isaiah and his family to help 'em."

The two men looked at one another and smiled.

"Isaiah told us you would say something to that effect. However, knowing your circumstances, he was determined that you not be left in financial straits through your generosity. He made us promise not to leave without making sure you accept it. You wouldn't make us break our promise, would you?"

Sarah hesitated before replying. "No, I wouldn't do that."

Ellen wept tears of joy when Sarah broke the news to her. She was overwhelmed by the news that Isaiah was alive and free, and that she and the children were to be freed and reunited with him. She was frightened at the idea of joining two strangers to leave the safest place she had ever known. Sarah reassured her, despite her own mixed emotions. They packed up the family's few belongings and loaded them into the wagon.

"Miss Sarah, I don't know what to say. I feel bad leavin' you here by yo'self."

"I'll be fine. God'll make a way."

"I thank you for the kindness you showed me. Ain't see'd much in my time on this earth. Don't know how I'da made it when the chillun' come, if'n you hadn't been there."

"I'm sorry for what happened to you, Ellen, but I have enjoyed yore company, and I'm thankful I got to know you. Now git on outta here 'fore I change my mind."

The two women embraced, both of them wiping tears away, before Ellen climbed in, joining Susan, Rachael, and a little baby boy named Isaiah.

Sarah watched the wagon disappear down the road into the woods, and she thought of the day Tom had pulled away, promising to be home for supper the next day. She thought of the night Isaiah had set off down that road into the darkness, and how in her heart she had never expected him to survive. Now Ellen and her children were leaving down that same road to be reunited with him. The weight of an uncertain future bore down on her like a stone. She remembered the conversation with Isaiah when Tom had gone for Anne and Susan. Her life had seemed hard when Tom was alive. With him gone, it now seemed unbearable. She had never felt so alone in her life. She turned from the road that had taken so many people she cared about away and saw the two little rock tombstones on the hill, and went to talk to Tom and Rebecca.

AFTERWORD

A FTER SEVERAL YEARS of legal challenges, in 1838 the administration of President Martin Van Buren authorized militia led by General Winfield Scott to round up the remaining Cherokee and relocate them to lands in the west, the infamous Trail of Tears. Approximately twenty thousand Cherokee and two thousand of their slaves were relocated from the Southeast. Estimates of the number who died on the Trail of Tears range from two thousand to eight thousand.

One band of four hundred Cherokee from the Oconaluftee area, who lived on land owned by William Holland Thomas, a White man, was allowed to remain. Another band from the Nantahala area, numbering about two hundred, was allowed to remain for helping capture the old prophet Tsali's family. They stayed in the Qualla Boundary area, and together the two groups became known as the Eastern Band of Cherokee.

Slavery would continue to roil the southern Appalachians for years to come, with frequent conflicts between proslavery and antislavery groups. When the Civil War erupted in 1861, counties, towns, and individual families split over the issue. Many young men from the mountains fought for the Union, often facing friends and family across the battlefield. Lurid tales of bushwhackers roving the mountains assaulting families on the opposite side of the conflict were passed down in family lore. More than 620,000 Americans died in the Civil War.

Thomas Love was an actual person. In fact, there were two of them. Both "General" Thomas Love, Sr., and "Colonel" Robert Love had sons named Thomas Love. Thomas Love conducted the Macon County 1830 census. The principal character of this story, however, is a hybrid of those two men and is fictional, as are his wife, Sarah, and their children. Many of the characters in this story, such as Robert Love, Thomas Love, Sr., and Beverly Daniel, are historical figures and aspects of their stories are true. Other aspects are fictionalized. Many characters are taken from the actual census roll; however their stories as recorded here are fictional.

Isaiah, Anne, Susan, and Ellen were enslaved African Americans owned by Thomas Jefferson. Their names are recorded in Thomas Jefferson's Farm Book, and their ages as recorded by President Jefferson match their ages in the story. The "roll of Negroes," part of the Jefferson Farm Book, can be found in the Monticello Plantation Database. The fates of most of the enslaved people of Monticello and the other Jefferson plantations, following his death, have been lost to history.

The versions of the poems appearing in the story, which are now in the public domain, are collected in David Perkins's *English Romantic Writers*.

BIBLIOGRAPHY

Bartram, William. *The Travels of William Bartram*. Pantianos Classics, 2016. First published in 1791 by James & Johnson (Philadelphia).

Brazier, Robert H. B. *A New Map of the State of North Carolina*. 1833. 86 × 211 cm. Fayetteville, NC: Published under the patronage of the legislature by John Mac Rae; Philadelphia: H. S. Tanner. https://lccn.loc.gov/2006459002.

Brodie, Fawn M. *Thomas Jefferson: An Intimate History*. New York: W. W. Norton, 1974.

Dunaway, Stewart. *Macon County, N.C. Road Records: Volume 1, 1829–1840*. Morrisville, NC: Lulu Press, 2011.

Jacobs, Harriet. *Incidents in the Life of a Slave Girl written by Herself*. New York: Barnes and Noble Classics, 2005. First published in 1861 by Thayer and Eldridge (Boston).

Lane, Lunsford, and African American Pamphlet Collection. *The narrative of Lunsford Lane, formerly of Raleigh, N. C., embracing an account of his early life, the redemption by purchase of himself and family from slavery, and his banishment from the place of his birth for the crime of wearing a colored skin*. 3rd ed. Boston: Hewes and Watson's Print, 1845. PDF. https://www.loc.gov/item/03027371.

Paine, Thomas. *Common Sense and Other Writings.* New York: Barnes and Noble Books, 2005.

Perkins, David. *English Romantic Writers.* New York: Harcourt Brace Jovanovich, 1967.

Sedgwick, John. *Blood Moon: An American Epic of War and Splendor in the Cherokee Nation.* New York: Simon and Schuster, 2018.

US Bureau of the Census. *Population Schedules of the Fifth Census of the United States, 1830, North Carolina.* Microform, Series: M19; Roll: 123. https://archive.org/details/populationsc18300123unit/page/n47/mode/2up.

CPSIA information can be obtained
at www.ICGtesting.com
Printed in the USA
LVHW091048250621
691133LV00015B/426/J